THE REDEEMED

THE ROADHOUSE CHRONICLES BOOK 2

MATTHEW S. COX

DIVISION ZERO PRESS

The Redeemed
Roadhouse Chronicles Book 2
© 2016 Matthew S. Cox
All rights reserved

ISBN (ebook): 978-1-949174-48-9

ISBN (print): 978-1-949174-49-6

CONTENTS

END OF THE RAINBOW

Content with his third pass over the ledger, Kevin closed the black and white marbled cover, securing it with a rubber band. He leaned both hands on the dusty counter covered in beat-up linoleum and shot a glance to the right, down a short concourse lined with long-dead shops. Outside, four islands' worth of ancient gas pumps stood covered with weeds and windblown detritus. Whoever had owned the rest stop prior to the war had bothered to convert only four filling stations to electric. That left twenty gasoline pumps rotting in place, with who-knows-what kind of mess lurking in subterranean tanks. Pre-war fuel might've been viable for six to eight months... Every time he felt a spark of motivation to clean it up, the idea of what fifty-year-old gasoline sludge would be like changed his mind. Not that many functioning cars remained on the roads these days. Having the ability to charge every operational vehicle left in the world all at once—throwing even more money at Amarillo—could wait. The six-port board in front of the building would do for now.

Of course, if he did revamp the old gas pumps to charging stations, he'd have the highest-capacity roadhouse within two hundred miles, though he'd have to buy more plugs, cables, patch panels, and probably more batteries as well. Far too much money to spend on *maybe* having more than six people needing to charge their rides up at once. He sighed and shifted his gaze to the room before him.

On the left, a space formerly used as a seating area for fast food counters held freestanding tables as well as the original booths along the window. Around the seating area, spaces which once housed a tiny donut station, McDonalds, KFC, map shop, bookstore, and a store that sold random crap like keychains and tee shirts, had been modified into large 'premium rooms' for guests to spend the night.

Right of the counter, a handful of tables continued into the walkway that used to run past a huge coffee shop. With the help of Tris and Paul, he'd converted the café that took up half the building and separated it into individual chambers. Where once motorists lined up for overpriced java, an opening led to a C-shaped passage with twelve tiny rooms for the economy-minded traveler.

The narrow hallway left of his counter led to restrooms; the men's, they'd converted to the store where he sold weapons, clothes, and other supplies people offloaded here, as well as anything the Code let him take from the corpses of any poor bastard killed on the premises. Fortunately, that had only happened once in the six months since he'd opened the doors.

A grin formed as he traced his fingers down the notebook cover. The Code didn't bother to set any guidelines for how much he could take out of drivers' pay, but he'd been doing it long enough to know that anyone who went over ten percent wound up with an empty room and a ledger full of untaken work. Wayne rode the limit—ten on the nose—though Hagerman sat isolated enough from other roadhouses that no one did much more than gripe about it. People in that area with cargo to move didn't enjoy a lot of choice. If they had the ability to reach another 'house, they could transport the shit themselves. This section of Interstate 80, about twenty minutes west of the ruins of Rawlins, Wyoming, didn't have quite the same cushion of nothingness around it, so Kevin opted for six percent.

Granted, he got about five times the traffic as Wayne's place, so it worked out.

Kevin stretched, folded his arms, and surveyed the dining area, quiet in a lull of moist chewing and the scratching of forks on metal plates. Four regulars and seven passersby joined in the mutual headspace where nothing else existed but for the food in front of them.

Kaz, a hulking tanned guy in road-worn leathers, reminded him of the irritable scimitar-wielding giant from an old movie he'd watched as a kid. Fortunately, the man's temperament was far more amenable to civilization than some insane warlord's henchman. He kept to himself at the corner table, near the door to one of the premium rooms.

Past a family of five—man, woman, and three kids six-ish or younger, Athena occupied a table next to another newcomer. The girl liked white. Liked white in the way some men liked steak and blowjobs. White pants, white shirt, white car. Heck, she'd even tried to paint her sidearm. The young blonde might've been eighteen if she were lucky, and reminded Kevin of himself at that age. *At least she's keeping her eye on the room.*

Despite her focus on eating, the scrape of her voice picked at the inside of Kevin's skull. From the look on the face of the dark-skinned behemoth at the table with her, someone he hadn't seen before, that man had about reached the point of being done with her too. Of course, few men would object to a pretty blonde helping herself to share a table with them, but after fifteen minutes of that one's nonstop mouth...

A scattering of dust-covered men lined the booths along the front windows. Brief conversation while dropping off their food suggested they traveled west, looking for a larger settlement to join. Only two were armed.

Laughter, deep and raspy, burst forth from the table nearest the counter. Fitch, perhaps one of the most regular of regulars, thumped himself in the chest to dislodge whatever bit of food his sudden mirth got stuck in his throat. A sheen of sweat beaded across his dark brown forehead. His partner, Neeley, a skinny, wiry blond about Athena's age, leaned over the table with a yellow grin. The man looked he'd been on the wrong end of lung cancer for a few years, but maybe he merely lost the genetic lottery. Most of the joke they shared eluded Kevin, though it had something to do with the younger man being hot in a dingy tank top and fatigue pants while Fitch kept his heavy black leather coat on.

Kevin smiled. *Armor. He knows how it is.*

Kaz stood with a grunt and carried his empty plate up to the counter. "Damn sight better 'n last time. That little woman of yours finally teach ya how ta cook?"

"Heh. I wouldn't let *her* hear you say that." Kevin winked. "Besides, she can't cook either. Been a couple weeks for you, right? Got a new employee."

"No shit." Kaz leaned an elbow on the counter. "She cute?"

Kevin laughed. "I'm not sure my cook's interested in sex for coins, but I can ask." He glanced over his shoulder at the hole in the tile-covered wall connecting the kitchen to the main room. "Hey Sang?"

A grey-haired man with pronounced wrinkles and a mild stoop leaned out of a cloud of steam. "Yeah?"

Kaz coughed and stood upright.

"He says your food's good. Wants another portion of chips." Kevin grinned at the dirty look he got from Kaz, but he wasn't missing a chance for a 'hard sell' on an extra order of fries.

"You got an old man cookin'?'" asked Kaz in a voice a notch above a whisper.

"Sure why not. He's good at it." Kevin shrugged.

"Man, you need to get a workin' girl or two in here." Kaz glanced around. "Used ta be this place in Glimmer—"

"Yeah." Kevin smirked. "I heard about that. Word I got is Petersen didn't much care for slavery."

Kaz cringed. "Aw, shit. Serious? Thought they was just into kink."

Kevin propped himself up on the counter, arms wide. "Nah. Those women from Cloud9 didn't wanna be there. Them chains weren't dec'rative."

"Shit." Kaz shook his head at the floor, exhaling hard. "The world can be a fucked up place. Any idea how that went down?"

"A bit." Kevin chuckled. "Bad things happen when stupid people run their mouths to the wrong little woman. So... Lookin' for work?"

"You know it." Kaz grinned. "Pocket gettin' thin."

"Well." Kevin flipped open his notebook and leafed to a page of current parcels. "Since you're lookin' to scratch that itch... Glimmertown's still got plenty of prostitutes; like fleas on a dog. I got a box of rec drugs headed out that way. Your cut's 100 coins. Job's prepaid, so you'll need to come back here to cash out. Course, lose it and you're on the hook for 1250."

"What kinda shit?" Kaz huddled closer, lowering his voice again. "Tell me there ain't no salt in that box."

"Nope. Some Psilo, Lucy, and a whole bunch of weed."

"Awright." Kaz stood straight as the old Korean reappeared in the window and set down a hubcap full of round-sliced French fries dusted in orange and black powder. "I'll do it."

Kevin smiled at Sang and moved the hubcap plate to the counter in front of Kaz. "Two."

Kaz begrudgingly handed over a pair of dimes and picked up the plate. "Your ass is lucky them shits is good. I'll take the run. Haven't been to Glimmer in a while. Any rush on it?"

"Only rush is wanting to get valuable cargo out of your car as fast as possible." Kevin laughed.

"Right." Kaz raised the plate as if in toast before returning to his table. "Gimme ten minutes."

Fitch sidled up to the counter a little to Kevin's right as soon as Kaz cleared. He had a bit more salt in his salt-and-pepper afro than last time, though smile wrinkles around his eyes inferred a good mood. "Kev."

"Fitch." Kevin raised his hand and they clasped forearms. "How'd it go up in Spearfish?"

Neeley propped himself against the counter at Kevin's left. His Adam's apple and nose got into a fight to see which one protruded more. "Ran into some Night Riders near the spur offa Route 16."

Kevin cringed, thinking of giant black SUVs laughing off his bullets. "Shit."

"Wasn't as bad as it sounds," said Fitch. "No up-armored trucks this time… bunch of land-boat cars. Nothing the .50 couldn't handle. They weren't 'spectin' no pickup truck to move like my Banshee."

Neeley chuckled.

"Six active wheels." Kevin bit his lip. "Not sure I'd gamble on that much power consumption. Might strand yourself out there. I'm curious how you did that."

"Hah." Fitch flashed a blinding white smile. Grey-black beard stubble shimmered on his cheeks. Teeth that clean on a man half way to forty seemed somehow wrong. "Ain't nobody but me gettin' within ten feet of the Banshee's innards."

Neeley pouted.

"Well, or Neeley." Fitch laughed. "I will tell you the rear two ain't 'lectric. Got a separate drive train with an ethanol-eater for when we need to haul ass."

Kevin worked out some rough design schematics in his head. "The dead weight worth it when you're not using it?"

Neeley and Fitch exchanged a glance.

"Considerin' we here now?" Fitch clucked his tongue. "I'd say yes. Them Riders don't take slaves."

"Well, if you ditch and run, they supposedly don't bother with you, less you shot at them." Kevin shrugged.

"A chance I am not wont to take." Fitch raised a finger. "Besides. Ain't nobody layin' their grubby mitts on the Banshee long as I'm 'live."

"Got anything good?" asked Neeley.

Kevin perused his list of pending runs. "Got one almost made for you guys. Shipment headed to a settlement in Deer Lodge, up on I-90... used ta be Idaho? Two-thousand rounds of 9mm."

Fitch let out a long whistle.

"Jesus crapping Christ," said Neeley.

"It's involved, but the pay's good." Kevin pointed at the page. "Need to head to Ween's place and pick it up. People at Deer Lodge'll give you four grand in coins. Three K of that goes back to Ween. Sixty to the 'house, and 940 is your cut."

"And if something takes a shit, we're into you for the lot." Fitch rubbed a hand over his face, accompanied by the hiss of beard stubble scraping callous.

"Been sitting on this one for you guys." Kevin smiled. "Banshee's got the best odds of pullin' it off. It's an open run, but I won't call it in to the network so no one's aware of it. Course, that also means you gotta get to Ween's fast before someone else does."

Neeley frowned.

Kevin raised his hands as if in surrender. "Hey, I could call it in, but then word'll get out two thousand bullets got wheels. If you want that heat, say the word."

"Naw." Fitch gestured at a row of bottles behind Kevin. "Gimme a finger of somethin' smooth and we'll head on out. Ween still in the same place?"

Kevin whirled about, grabbed a bottle of random brown liquor, and poured a little in a tumbler glass. "Four."

Fitch dropped three pennies and a quarter, and shot the drink back in one gulp. Judging from the wince and eye-twitch, it didn't hit him as smooth as he'd hoped. Kevin held up the bottle, but Fitch waved him off. "Naw. God damn man, what is that shit?"

Kevin shrugged. "No idea. No label." He sniffed it. "Could be Scotch. Could be sour mash."

"Could be engine de-greaser." Fitch coughed. "Awright. We're on."

Athena draped herself over the counter as the two men headed for the door out. "Hey there, Kev-O." She winked. "Got anything worth my time?"

He leaned on his knuckles and shifted his weight to one leg. "Could use someone ta run a bit west, head down 789 to the Carver place. Almost out of sausage... and whatever other meat they've got what looks decent."

"Food?" Athena rolled her sapphire eyes. "Seriously? You're sending me for food? I'm not a kid."

He let his gaze roam up and down her body. She had an inch or two of height on Tris, and a curvier, more athletic shape, not to mention bigger breasts… but something about her face made her look 'too young.' Perhaps her wide-eyed eagerness. Perhaps that sense of 'immortality' that plagues the brain of someone not yet into their twenties. White, long-sleeved shirt, mostly open over a bra, white-grey camo fatigue pants, and sneakers… no armor. "I know a guy who can hook you up with some protection." He gestured at her chest. "Not a lot 'tween you and bullets."

"Gee, thanks, *Dad.*" Athena sighed. "Armor's only gonna slow me down. I like being able to move. Besides, I'm too fast for any of those old men."

Kevin chuckled, eyeing the little white Honda outside up on fat mudder tires and a fourteen-inch body lift. "That thing is gonna roll over like Wayne's mother the minute you take a turn goin' faster than fifteen. You'll turtle it belly up and get ripped to pieces." *Most marauders wouldn't kill her. Hmm. With Glimmertown out of the slave trade, wonder where they'd sell her?*

"Stop looking at me like I'm twelve." Athena folded her arms. "You don't have to protect me. I'm a fuckin' *driver*, Kev-O. I can handle myself. You got somethin' better than god damned grocery shopping?"

"I can put you in to run 400 phials of Void Salt to Glimmertown."

The room went dead silent in an instant.

"Now you're talkin'." Athena slapped the counter.

"Now I'm being a smartass." Kevin laughed, then leaned up on tiptoe to raise his voice to the room. "Ain't no Salt anywhere within fifty miles of this place. Repeat: that was a joke."

A din returned over the course of a minute, though two of the 'travelers' shot him long, worried stares.

Athena crossed her arms. "What's your problem with me anyway? You think women are weak or something?"

Kevin glanced up at a soft *thump* in the ceiling. "Maybe I did when I was your age, but my eyes have been opened." He sighed at her and lowered his voice. "It ain't you bein' a girl. You come off like some hotheaded kid that's gonna get herself hurt. I ain't gonna send you into no shitstorm 'til you're at least not goin' to be stupid about it." He pulled his shirt aside to show off a few bullet scars. "Took me a few years and a few close calls not to be 'too good' to need armor."

"Yeah, yeah… You're just an old man now." Athena's tone came off halfway between serious and playful. "I'll think about your food run. What's the payout?"

"Twenty."

She threw a wave at him. "That's not even worth moving my car."

"Call it a test to see if you can finish something." *Damn, now I sound like Wayne too.* "Promise you a little more exciting of a run if you can handle a few cucumbers."

She glared.

"Oi, can I watch?" yelled Neeley.

Kevin pinched the bridge of his nose. "You know what I mean. Vegetables. And get some damn armor."

Athena tapped her foot, pursed her lips, and cocked her jaw to the side. "So you'll give me a run worth my time if I fetch your groceries?"

"I'll toss you a job with a little more risk, yeah. What sort of gear you got on that little wind up car?"

She scowled. "One M2 Browning where the passenger seat should be, fixed forward. Usually, I make the pirates shoot each other by driving circles around them. Don't need to be drowning in weapons when you know how to drive."

"Is that so?" He smirked before leaning up on his toes to appraise the little Honda again. "Well, I suppose you're high enough off the ground that mounted guns'll go under the cabin. 'Course that thing's a rollover waiting to happen."

"You said that already. I've got a roll cage."

He chuckled. *Damn she sounds like I did ten years ago.* Kevin grabbed a handful of coins from the lockbox under the counter and dropped fifty in a cloth pouch. "Mr. Carver's got my order ready. Pick up whatever other meat he's got with the change."

Athena took the pouch with a frown. "You know this is beneath me."

"Perhaps. But you're here. I need this done, and your car is fast."

She took two steps backward, pointing at him with the hand holding the pouch. "Okay, fine... but you're gonna give me a real job when I get back."

He nodded. "Yep." *Dammit Tris. You're rubbing off on me.*

⟶ ⟶ ⟵ ⟵

WORRY SETTLED IN THE PIT OF TRIS' GUT; WHENEVER SHE LIFTED HER HEAD out of the electronics cabinet and looked to the west, she half-expected to see a flotilla of Enclave hovercraft leading a giant plume of dust. She sat back on her boot heels and dabbed sweat away from her eyes with her forearm. Kneeling among the solar panels on the roof, she wondered how much longer it would be before Nathan found a way to ignore the Council of Four. She glanced at a wet spot on the sleeve of her sky blue jumpsuit, and past it to her dirt-smeared hands.

A faint sizzle of electricity emanated from the components. The occasional whiff of ozone floated by in the dry air. Dense clusters of sagebrush littered the brown to the east of the roadhouse, but to the left, flat nothingness. She gathered her hair out of her eyes and turned south, gazing at the distant hint of mountains. Perhaps desolation could shield her from the Enclave… or at least Nathan's petulant wrath. It's not as if she had anything of value. Anyone Nathan had told his plan to probably shared a great laugh about her having *The Cure* in her headware. Not the actual cure to the virus responsible for the Infected, but music he'd put in as a cruel joke—and awful pun. She growled. Shooting Neon in the head to free those enslaved women had been a spur of the moment thing she felt neither guilt nor joy over. She daydreamed about killing Nathan slow, then bit her lower lip. Even an asshole like him… she was not that person.

Tris clapped dust from her hands and reached into the space beneath solar panel 5C: fifth unit in from the right side along the third row back from the front. Ten thousand of Kevin's hard-earned coins had won him forty solar panels and the right to call this place a Roadhouse. Also, it prevented the military force in Amarillo from putting a bounty on his head for 'copyright infringement.'

A third of the array had gone down between last night and this morning. They woke up to find a swath of the status panel in the office lit up red. The panels were wired in series, so a broken connection in 5C killed everything forward and right of it, knocking out an entire corner of the grid. Kevin commented about 'Christmas Lights,' but whatever that meant escaped her. Corrosion crumbled away from the contact point under her fingertips. Everything inside the relay box looked forty years old and covered in enough silt to prove it. If the panels hadn't still had their factory plastic film when they arrived, she'd have thought them salvage.

Tris double-checked the panel's switch was off before taking a wire brush from her toolbox and attacking the primary contacts. Her entire body shook with the effort of sawing the brush back and forth. Green-brown crud flaked off and carried away on the wind.

The front door clattered open and banged closed a few seconds later. Two men discussed a run up to Deer Lodge. Minutes later, a heavy car door creaked; she recognized Fitch and Neeley's voices.

"Aww damn," she muttered.

She hopped up and ran to the edge of the roof, trying to wave to them before they pulled out. Neeley, behind the wheel, caught sight of her and waved. Fitch nodded as dirt sprayed forward from four of their pickup truck's six tires. They reversed around in a turn before taking off to the west. Tris watched for a moment, thinking that the ribbon of paving they followed had been meant for eastbound traffic. She found it hard to grasp how, before the war, driving the wrong way could prove fatal.

Had there ever been so many cars that they couldn't dodge each other?

Tris loped back to the open panel on the south-facing side of solar panel 5C, her already worry-sick gut burdened by a sense of somber loss for the entirety of civilization. This place... this 'Wyoming' as Kevin had called it, looked as empty as though no one lived here even before the war. Miles in all directions of brown dotted with green, the occasional rickety structure, signpost, or long-abandoned truck visible in the distance.

She grumbled and resumed scrubbing the contact point. A few minutes later, it shined, and she reattached the wires, which fastened with spring-loaded connectors. Push in, quarter turn clockwise, and they caught on little nubs.

"Just an overdue cleaning," she said to no one in particular.

Tris flipped the orange plastic cutoff switch to the upright position. A few tiny LEDs winked on inside the cabinet. Dull metallic *clonks* came from the panels ahead and right of her. The third one in at the second row made a loud buzzing noise and belched black smoke before a loud *bang* went off inside it.

"Shit."

She sprinted around the row to 3B, fanning at the inky cloud, and turned the panel off. Her throat filled with the flavor of burned silicon and rubber. After opening the cabinet, she waved the smoke away some more. The inky black cloud eventually thinned enough to reveal a molten connector. Fortunately, the wire itself was intact—merely the insulation around it had caught fire. This unit also had so much dirt and corrosion, it appeared to have been in service for decades. Since the wire remained too hot to touch, she took her time collecting her toolbox and repositioned herself in front of the smoking panel array.

Curiosity got the better of her and she pulled apart the inner workings of 2B. It, too, had a buildup of gunk on the wires and a quarter-inch deep layer of dark grey dust inside.

Tris sighed. "Dammit. He hooked these all up and didn't think this much dirt was strange?"

She puffed away some of the dust and tried to dispel a cloud that tasted much worse than burning insulation. After spitting a few times, she glared at it, searching for any clues to explain why solar panels still sealed in plastic had so much crap. Letters molded in the metal cabinet read: Manf: APR 08 2018 LOT 1852.

"Damn. These things *are* old." Anger flared up in her chest and warmed her cheeks. "Bastards scammed him… Amarillo sold him prewar junk." Rage faded to dread. "Ugh. I gotta check them all so we don't burn the entire place to the ground."

She cleaned the contacts in 2B, reseated the wires, and put a fingertip on the switch.

"Please don't blow up. I promise I'll clean you all." Tris flicked the switch, and the faint vibrating thrum of active electronics surrounded her. She let off a sigh of relief a second before her stomach growled. "Okay, guys. I need some lunch. I'll be back right after I eat. Please don't die on me."

I'm talking to solar panels. She wiped sweat from her forehead again. *Maybe I've been in the sun too long.* After tossing the wire brush back in the toolbox, she stood and made her way toward the roof access hatch. A flash of pink caught her eye by the last panel of the rearmost row, 10D. A yellow-yarn-haired rag doll in a pink dress lay bent in half by where the panel array's leg bolted down. She picked up the twelve-inch tall toy and locked eyes with it.

"What are you doing up here?" She looked to the south. "Dammit, Zoe. I told you not to go on the roof." *Next time we visit Ned, I gotta bring this… and I'ma yell at her for ignoring me.* She eyed the edge. Falling from a one-story building probably wouldn't have killed the girl, but had the girl been hurt, Tris would've felt horrible.

She clutched the doll to her chest and approached the rusty metal flap over the ladder down into the building. Another glance off to the west showed no sign of approaching Enclave threats… or anything else beyond the endless open terrain. Could it be that Nathan's fear of exile or punishment outweighed his obsessive-compulsive need to 'tie up a loose end?'

Tris fussed with the ragdoll's hair. *Will I ever be able to stop worrying?* She half-smiled at the goofy face on the toy. The place had been too damn quiet without Zoe and her brother around. Kevin seemed happy to settle in, and despite her initial doubts, he'd shown zero signs of regret at 'not being out there' anymore. As much as she loathed feeling useless in terms of ending the threat of the Virus, Kevin had a point. How much could she accomplish alone? She pictured the imposing black and steel gates of the aboveground portion of the Enclave complex, the mounted weapons, the armored guards... even if she could raise an army out here, one of their troopers could wipe out dozens before going down. While her hardware might be on par with theirs, they had more training, more experience, and better gear. One of her—perhaps two if Zara could be talked into helping—wouldn't tip the scales.

Tears of frustration gathered at the corner of her eyes. Kevin constantly reminded her that not being able to cure the Virus hadn't been her fault. It's not like she'd had the real cure and lost it... she never had it to begin with. She didn't mess up. Nathan was an asshole.

Tris chuckled. *Maybe I should let go. I guess it's nice enough here. Could I be happy?* She squeezed the doll and let her thoughts drift to the echoing memory of a child's giggle while playing. *If we're going to settle down, might as well commit to the whole settling down thing.*

"Maybe..." She traced her fingers over her stomach, thinking about Zoe giggling, trying to forget what it felt like to be strapped down on a medical table for 'routine tests.' "If they didn't take them all."

A LOUD, SQUAWKING *BEEP* FROM THE BACK ROOM GOT KEVIN RUNNING. He ducked into the office across the hall from the kitchen and grinned at a plywood board full of forty green lights. Relief spread over him. Not having to replace a dozen panels felt like finding a bag of 1,500 coins.

"Tris, you are amazing," he muttered at the ceiling.

He pivoted on his boot heel and wandered into the kitchen. The air still held the essence of greasy meat and fried potatoes. Sang reclined on his bed, a thin foldaway mattress pad scavenged from an old sofa bed, reading. The old man hadn't had much to his name beyond a suitcase of old books when he arrived. Since he'd been here, Kevin had quietly dropped word with drivers he'd expected to see again to keep an eye out for books. A couple spare coins here and there was a small price to pay to brighten the day of a man who was happy to work for room and board.

"Hey boss." Sang looked up, smiling. "Someone order?"

"Not yet. I'm sending Athena down to Carver's to pick up more supplies."

"Ahh, good. Good." Sang nodded. "We are running low on sausage and potatoes."

Kevin glanced at the giant silver fridge they'd salvaged from the former burger place. The solar array on the roof had more to offer than charging vehicles. "Yep. It's ordered. Since we've been doing okay this month, I'm picking up some extra meat."

"Oh? What?"

"No idea." Kevin smiled. "Whatever Carver's got available. We'll find out when Athena gets back."

"Sounds—"

Wham. A heavy *thud* reverberated in the walls.

"Try it, asshole!" shouted Athena.

A deep male voice roared in response.

Sang nodded to the left. "Better get out there."

"Shit." Kevin pushed away from the doorjamb and ran to the front room.

The huge dark-skinned man Athena had been sitting with stood by a flipped-over table, hand poised over a pistol on his belt. He had his back to Kevin, gold sewn-on lettering spelled 'Rook' between his shoulders above a crude rendition of a castle tower in silver permanent marker. Athena hovered a few steps away in a chin-forward lean, a nascent grin still on her face. Despite the top of her head barely being even with his pectorals, she showed no sign of fear. One finger teased around the handle of a 1911 on her belt.

"Come on, Rook. You think I'm all talk? Pull that thing out and I'll show you what a 'little girl' can do."

Rook snarled. His cheeks reddened and his eyes bulged. Perhaps the mental capacity to understand firearms had left him; he seemed about to strangle her.

"What are you waitin' for, old man?" Athena glided a step to her left, adding a sultry bat of her eyelashes. "Don't keep a girl waiting all day. I could use the coins from selling your shit."

"Hey," yelled Kevin, pointing. "You kill him in here, his shit belongs to the house. You know the Code."

Athena's expression soured. "That's horseshit, you damn thief. He runs his mouth into a gunfight, the shit's mine."

"Runs *my* mouth?" Rook grabbed a fistful of his hair and pulled. "Argh. You irritating little bitch. You got a lot of nerve. I oughta—"

"She's faster than she looks," said Kevin. "Just walk away."

"You're not taking my shit." Athena glared at Kevin. "That's bull."

"One…" Kevin walked to the end of the counter. "It's the same in every roadhouse from the West Coast to the Mississippi. Someone gets dead in a 'house, all their crap belongs to the 'house. Ain't about gettin' crap, it's about not shooting the shit out of the place." He waved his arm as if to indicate the room. "This is supposed to be a place of respite. Preserve the sanctity of the Roadhouse Network and all."

Rook drew his leg back, eyeing a chair, but decided against it. He stormed up to the counter. "Whiskey double, and a room."

"Luxury room or cot-in-a-closet?" asked Kevin.

"Small room's fine," muttered Rook.

"Nine." Kevin kept half an eye on Athena while pouring some JD in a tumbler. He set it on the counter next to nine coins, a mix of nickels and pennies. After collecting the money, he fished a key out of a steel bin next to the cash box. "Room five."

"Thanks." Rook fired off a dire glare at the grinning blonde, and tromped past Kevin toward the small rooms.

Once he'd gone out of sight into the narrow corridor, Athena rolled up on the counter. "So…" she twirled a strand of hair around her finger, smiling. "You should give me that bigger job now. You obviously think I can handle myself."

Kevin dropped the coins one by one into the box, not looking up at her. "If he'd wanted to throw down, he'd have shot you when you decided to give me the evil stare. You broke eye contact. Half a second is all it would've taken… assuming he didn't miss."

She narrowed her eyes.

"And at about ten feet… he wouldn't have missed." As the last coin fell into the cash box with a *clink*, he shifted his eyes up to regard her. "You may think you're hot shit, but you're just a seventeen-year-old with more balls than brains. You're basically me at that age—with tits."

Athena fidgeted and rested one hand on the edge of the counter. "Nice try, but I'm nineteen." She showed off a strange metal holster that looked like her gun might fall out of it if she jumped. "Got a quickdraw rig. I'd have had him easy."

"Except for the part where you broke eye contact. You kill anyone yet?"

"Yeah… of course."

Kevin chuckled. "Outside of a car? I don't mean lighting someone up with that .50 of yours. You ever look into a person's eyes after you put a round through their heart, see the realization in their last two seconds of life spread across their face that they're dead."

"It's not gonna work, pops. You're not gonna scare me into going home and being a 'good little girl.'" She threw herself onto a barstool and slapped the countertop. "Gimme a beer."

"Not what I'm trying to do." He filled a mason jar with some of Wayne's homebrew. "Two."

Athena fished out a pair of quarters and set them on the Formica. "So, what are you trying to do then?"

"I'm tryin' not to have to carry your dumb dead ass out back and bury you." He set the beer down and scooped the coins into his hand. "All I'm sayin' is, don't take stupid chances, and don't look for fights where you don't gotta have 'em. You run the road long enough, you'll get more than you ever wanted."

Athena rolled her eyes and took a sip. "I dunno how you can do it… just sit here." She leaned back, closed her eyes, and smiled. "I can't imagine being stuck in one place doing the same damn thing every day. I'm gonna be driving 'til I'm too old to walk."

She really is just like I was.

Kevin glanced over his shoulder at a metallic *thud* from the back hallway. His expectation of seeing Tris soon after the roof hatch closed proved correct. She glided over and leaned against him. After a quick kiss, he looked at Athena again. "If it's what'll make you happy, go for it. Just remember, stupid equals dead." His voice became Wayne's in the back of his mind. "There's a fine goddamn line between confidence and foolishness, and fools don't live long."

"Sure thing, gramps." Athena winked. "Hey Tris."

"Hey." Tris leaned up and kissed him again on the lips. "There's a problem."

Kevin shot a look at a ragdoll in her hand. *Oh shit. She wants a kid.* "What kind of problem?"

Tris stuck the doll on the shelf behind the counter, under the panel full of room keys. "The electronics on the roof are almost sixty years old. All of it was manufactured before the war."

"That's bullshit." Kevin glared at the ceiling. "They're brand new... even had the plastic film on the solar plates."

"They're stamped." Tris set her hands on her hips. "I'm not lying."

"No... not callin' bullshit on you... That Amarillo gave me salvage."

Tris wiped her sooty hands off on a rag. "I don't think any of it was used... probably sat around in a warehouse. I'm going to have to clean everything. It might not be a big deal that the stuff's so old, but if we don't deal with it now, it's going to be a mess."

Visions of roadhouse-in-flames danced across his mind. "Shit. Yeah."

"Relax. I'll get started on it after lunch, but it'll take me a few days to go over them all." She locked lips for a third time, wrists crossed behind his neck.

After a few minutes, the *snap* of a coin touching the counter made him look. Athena smirked at him.

"What's that?" He gestured at the dime.

"Figured if I'm getting a show I should pay for it." She winked at Tris, who threw the cleaning rag at her.

"Sang?" called Tris.

"Yes, boss?"

"Can you please whip me up some lunch?"

"What you want?"

"Whatever we have the most of." Tris let out a breath, turning to Kevin. "How's the stock?"

"Low, but Athena's about to run to Carver for us." Kevin grinned.

The teen drained the three-quarter full beer without coming up for air. "Yeah, yeah. I'm goin'."

Tris collected a tray with a burger on it from Sang via the hole in the wall to the kitchen, then flopped on a folding chair behind the counter, using her lap for a table.

"So other than our solar array being dangerously old, what else was wrong with it?" asked Kevin.

Tris finished chewing her first bite. "Corrosion on the contacts. Broke the circuit. I'm gonna be up there a while."

"I'll go with you." He smiled, but looked away as a man, woman, and three kids all stood at once. After a bit of murmuring amongst themselves, the man walked over.

"Nah. There's only one wire brush and you gotta watch the shop." Tris winked and took another bite.

"Afternoon," said Kevin.

"Howdy." The man directed a suspicious squint at Tris for a few seconds before making eye contact with Kevin. "How much ya askin' fer one o' them big rooms a night?"

"Ten."

The man nodded and fished out an assortment of coins. Soon, the family disappeared through a door into what had, prior to August of 2021, been a cookie and cupcake shop.

"There's only one bed in there," said Tris around her hamburger. "Do we have any extra blankets?"

Kevin leaned forward and kissed her atop the head. "You are so beautiful."

She smirked, waving a round slice of fried potato at him. "Are you trying to be stingy and not come off as an ass?"

"Nope." He sighed with a hint of a smile. "All that you worry about, and you're still so sweet to people."

She suppressed a laugh and tossed the fry into her mouth.

"So… you want a baby huh?"

Tris gasped and started choking.

He patted her back until she coughed up a mangled wad of potato and took a few raspy breaths. Tears streaming down her cheeks, she gave him a startled look. "Where'd that come from?"

"Oh, you had a certain look in your eye when you came in with that doll."

"Zoe was on the roof." Tris scowled. "I told that girl not to play up there. What if she falls?"

Kevin leaned back, stretching. "Maybe she'd learn to listen then."

"Do you miss it?" asked Tris.

"Miss what?" He leaned his butt against the shelf behind the counter.

She waved her half-burger around. "The road… the adrenaline… traveling."

His lips curled into a contemplative frown. Wayne had joked about that… *Soon as you find yourself lookin' out at everyone else livin' the life while you're sittin' still, you'll wish you'da had fun with all that money.* Kevin smiled. "Not really. Not as much as Wayne was sure I would. Guess I outgrew it."

She finished her lunch in silence, set the tray aside, and stood. After a long, lingering stare, she kissed him again. "So, what are you thinking about?"

He licked his lip. "I think I'm gonna have a burger."

She jabbed him in the side, grinning. "Ass."

He laughed and brushed her hair off her face. "I'm thinking how glad I am those idiots carried you into Wayne's."

She jabbed him in the ribs again.

"Ow. What was that for?" He rubbed the spot.

"For leaving me tied up so long." She stuck her tongue out at him, and laughed. "Okay, I'm gonna go get started on the panel guts."

"Careful. Don't fall." He winked.

She gave him a raspberry and disappeared down the hall past the kitchen. Kevin shifted. He caught sight of the yellow-haired ragdoll and gritted his teeth. Driving other people's crap from settlement to settlement had its scary moments, but the idea of having a kid of his own… now *that* was frightening.

2

BARREN

Rumbling in the ground drew Kevin's attention to the door, and the shadow of an enormous olive-drab semi-truck. The glimpse hinted at tires as tall as a man, and a ladder on the side next to painted-over US Army markings. Liquor bottles on the shelf behind him clinked together as the titan passed close to the front door and proceeded around in a wide, circular turn before nosing up to the westernmost charging spot.

He looked up at the ceiling. "Damn, I hope the system can handle the pull from that monster."

A *click* from the panel announced someone had plugged in a moment later, in time with the indicator light going yellow. Another click preceded the adjacent bay showing a plug as well. Soon after, two dark-haired men in their later twenties entered, followed by a pair of pale tween girls who appeared to be identical twins. Three women and an older teenaged boy with an infant in his arms brought up the rear. Everyone except for the infant carried a weapon. Assault rifles on the adults, both of the girls had handguns in thigh holsters, and the first man through the door also carried a blade akin to a medieval broadsword in a leather harness on his back. All wore green camouflage combat fatigues, though the twins had mismatched flip-flops instead of combat boots. The mood among them seemed friendly, if guarded.

"Afternoon," said Kevin. "Can't say I've ever seen one of those things before."

The man flashed an annoyed smile. "Usually we don't need to come in to charge. Got our own panels on the trailer, but damn pirates did a number on 'em. Headin' to Amarillo to get some replacements once we finish this run."

With a shoulder pat, the somewhat younger man behind him walked off toward the tables, leading the rest of the small army to the biggest round table in the middle of the room. The teen bearing the infant sat near a red-haired woman two-ish years his senior, and both tended to the baby. The twins headed for the bathroom, accompanied by the oldest of the women. Kevin assumed mother since they all had the same shade of chestnut-brown hair.

Kevin shook his head. "Ugh. I don't think Amarillo will sell panels to a rig." *Besides they might be older than shit.* "Hear there's a settlement 'round ol' Fernley, if ya keep goin' west on 80. Guy there name 'o Wilkins."

"Didn't Amarillo put out a contract on him a few years ago?" asked the second man. His uniform shirt bore the name 'Stubblefield,' though odds were, it had been scavenged.

"Yeah, they did." Kevin indicated the charging panel control with a thumb over the shoulder. "Six coins for the juice. 'Course no one took them up on it. Wilkins and his people don't set up fake roadhouses. They help settlements. Made too many friends for anyone to mess with him."

"Hmm." The first man, 'Henderson' according to his shirt, rubbed his chin. He set six coins on the counter. "What's available food wise?"

Kevin collected the money and flipped both switches; the lights pulsed in a slow blink, still amber. "Burgers, fries, think there's some sausage left too… and soup. Need rooms?"

Henderson nodded at the wall. "Nah. Got bunks in the trailer. Thanks though. Food for eight then. Mix it up."

"You got it." Kevin headed out from behind the counter to collect a handful of dirty plates before walking into the back.

Tris appeared from a doorway at the end of the hall and met him halfway to the kitchen. "Saw that truck come in. Need help down here?"

He leaned over, arms full of dishes, and kissed her on the cheek. "You're amazing. Sure. I'll help Sang cook, watch the counter?"

"'Kay." She brushed past him and disappeared into the main room.

Kevin elbowed the kitchen door aside. He dumped the plates and forks into a basin sink before giving Sang an apologetic look. "Big order. Eight people."

"Wow... small army." Sang set down his book and rolled off his bed to his feet.

"Yeah. They've even got the camo." Kevin opened the spigot to rinse his hands, but jumped back as the pipe spat and hissed. "Gah!"

"Give it a sec. Pump's been struggling... or the well's drying out." Sang wiped his hands on a towel. "What they order?"

"Assortment... burgers, fries, soup. Figured I'd help."

Snapping in the hallway announced the approach of small flip-flops. Both twins peered into the kitchen, curious until their mother tugged at them. Sang waved; the girls smiled and walked off, back to the front room.

Sang resumed cooking, whistling to himself. The water caught up a second later, allowing Kevin to wash his hands. Soon, he tended a number of patties on a grill, not quite able to tell if they were beef, venison, or dust-hopper. The old man leaned over to sprinkle them with seasonings every so often while spending most of his time on the fries, soup, and a steak big enough for two people to share. He'd arrived with a large footlocker full of all sorts of jars containing spices, herbs, and powders; with any luck, his stash would last a few years.

"Hope your girl drive fast." Sang gestured at the fridge. "We running low."

Kevin chuckled. "Yeah, that little windup toy of hers is fast."

"You doing well here." Sang grinned. "I am happy to have found this place."

He's gettin' kinda old. "Heh. It's good to have you. Your fries are already a legend along this stretch of 80." Kevin rested his weight on the spatula hand, leaning on the front edge of the grill. "Not that I'm trying to get rid of you or anything, but if you have any family you want to get back to, say the word. Pretty sure my car still works."

Sang bowed. "Much kind of you, but there is no one." A glimmer of sorrow fled from the elder's eyes.

"I'm sorry." Kevin slid the spatula under a burger and flipped it, dodging grease spatter. With the mind-numbing sizzle of meat flooding his senses, he stared at the wires connecting the heating element up to the ceiling, and to the solar-charged battery. How much of his dream hung on the aging hardware. Without the panels, no cooking, no charging... wouldn't be much of a roadhouse.

For a little while, the two men stood without speaking amid the scratch of a spatula or the scrape of a soup ladle.

"Marsing," said Sang.

"Hmm?" Kevin glanced over. "What?"

"I can feel the wonder on you." Sang teased the ladle around in the soup. "I lived in a settlement called Marsing, a few hundred miles north and west of here with my son, Jae-Yong."

Kevin looked away from the grim expression on the old man's face, and nudged a burger back and forth across a small sea of grease. "Sorry."

Sang let his head droop, nodded, and stood straight again. "Thank you. He was nineteen."

Tris appeared at the door, mouth open as if to speak, but the mood in the air struck her mute.

"He go with some of his friends on scavenging trip to Boise. Six of them leave, four came home." Despite the topic, the elder spoke with a calm resignation and no increase in gloom upon his features.

Kevin sighed as he scooped finished burgers from the grill onto a waiting group of buns. He winced, realizing he'd forgotten to ask Athena to see if Carver had any flour for sale. "I... damn. Sorry. Didn't mean to bring up bad memories."

Sang nodded without looking at him. "I understand. It is good to unburden oneself of such things. Jae-Yong did return, but he had haunted eyes." The ladle scuffed against the pot; the rhythm of a slow stir competed with the noise of bubbles.

Kevin glanced over at the old man's face amid a cloud of fragrant steam. He didn't want to ask if the boy had killed himself out of guilt.

"Two days passed. Jae-Yong remained in his bed. He did not want to see anyone."

"Depressed?" asked Kevin.

Tris crept in, standing at his side.

"No. On the second day, he showed me a mark on his arm where he had been bitten. Infected."

Tris gasped. Kevin cringed.

"I am a weak man." Sang stopped stirring, staring into the still-whirling mass of brown liquid, beans, and potatoes. "I could not bring myself to kill my own boy. Many died when he lost his sanity. I was exiled."

"Oh, no," whispered Tris. She stared at the floor.

Sang inhaled, held it, and let the air out his nose. Several seconds of silence passed before he lifted his head with a faint smile. "I had intended to wait until Jae-Yong was no longer Jae-Yong, but the change came on him while I slept. I still do not understand how I was not his first victim."

Kevin clapped him on the shoulder and squeezed. "There was still enough of him in there. I don't know that I could do any different in that position."

Sang nodded. "Thank you."

He ladled soup into bowls without another word. Whatever question Tris had entered with remained lost. She hovered at Kevin's side with the posture of a child expecting punishment until he handed her a pizza-platter turned serving tray full of burgers. She carried it out into the hall, followed by Kevin with another tray bearing soup bowls and the giant steak.

"Hey…" He caught up to her. "Enough of that look. It's not your fault. You might've come from the Enclave, but you're not *part* of it."

She sniffled. "I know. It's just that… I could've done something to stop—"

"No, you couldn't have." He grumbled. "You did not screw anything up. They sent you out as a living weapon."

Tris spun to face him, nearly causing two burgers to slide off the tray. "But… I have to do something."

"You? Why? Because you're from there? Are you a geneticist? A doctor?" He slouched. "Look, I don't mean to be an asshole… but really. What do you think you're supposed to do?"

She grumbled and resumed walking toward the front room. "I dunno. It just feels like I *should* be doing something. If I'm not feeling guilty over not stopping the Virus, I'm feeling worried that the Enclave is going to show up and try to kill me."

"Easier for them now that we're stationary."

"No." She whined at him. "I'm not complaining about this place… you're so happy here. *I'm* happy here… I just…"

"Feel guilty. Yeah." He followed her over to the round table and set the platter down. "Here ya go. Some burgers, soup… and Sang threw in a steak. Probably venison."

The twins eyed the steak.

"Thanks," said Henderson. "What do we owe you?"

Kevin considered a bulk discount, but remembered they wouldn't be renting rooms. Their clothing and gear appeared to be in good repair. He added up what the portions would've cost one at a time. Five coins for the steak, three each for burgers and fries, two per soup bowl. "Meh, call it an even thirty."

Henderson accepted the price without flinching, and handed over coins. "Smells good."

"Let me know if you need anything." Kevin carried the handful of coins to the counter and fiddled with the lockbox to get the combination open.

Tris leaned on him. "I'm about a third of the way done with the panels. Some were worse than others."

"Hope that rig doesn't blow anything out." He threaded an arm around behind her back. "They've got it hooked up by two leads."

"Probably two independent battery clusters. Something that size might have tandem drive trains or one's a backup." She rested her head against him. "I do feel safe here, but I'm not sure I deserve it."

"You had nothing to do with anything the Enclave did." He kissed her atop the head. "Where's all this guilt coming from?"

Tris sighed. "I don't know. It's like I used to know and forgot. Sometimes when it's quiet, I feel like... I dunno, you ever walk into a room and forget why you went there? I get that feeling a couple times a week." She fidgeted. "What if they made me forget something?"

Kevin raised an eyebrow. "They can do that? That's only a little unnerving."

"Well... I got months of 'training' in a couple weeks." She tapped her sneaker tip on the floor and wobbled her foot side to side. "I've never seen anything about erasing memories."

"Simulations aren't the same as just putting information into your head. You learned things the usual way, just faster."

"I guess." She twisted around to peer out the door. "I'm surprised you haven't gone climbing all over that truck to see how it works."

He grinned. "Oh, I've been tempted... but it'd be rude."

The door swung open with a clatter of the dead hydraulic assist. A large man with shoulders bulky to the point he appeared not to have a neck stumped in, followed by a skinny man in black leather who resembled a skeleton in a man-suit. Kevin's back muscles stiffened. These two constantly flirted with the edge of civility. Whenever they stopped by, someone always got hurt. Pedro Trujillo, aka 'Bull,' and his backup driver, Ajay Samed, who had tried to call himself 'Reaper,' but got tired of the way people made a joke out of it, him being so skinny and all.

"That was quick," said Kevin. He leaned on the counter. "Run into much trouble?"

"Couple of Topekans felt all sorta charitable." Bull grinned a disaster of teeth at him. "Got a trunk full o' salvage."

Ajay's laugh slid in and out his nose, hissing past a clenched jaw.

"They still using those flimsy ass buggies?" Kevin flipped open his notebook, turned to the taken jobs page, and found the entry where he'd sent the pair to Rossville, Kansas with two footlockers' worth of tee shirts. "That was a collection run."

"Yep. Was." Bull gave him a long, measuring stare before unhooking an orange-and-black hip satchel from his belt and dropping it on the counter. The clink of coins mixed with the rustle of nylon. Before Kevin could grab it, the man dropped his paw of a hand on top of it. "Interesting little arrangement you guys have. Ever wonder why people don't just keep the money? We're the ones gettin' shot at."

Kevin shifted his weight back onto his left leg, and surreptitiously flicked the snap open on his holstered .45. Tris reacted to the change in his body language and took a step left, hand on the Beretta at her hip. "You both know I did my time behind the wheel. Roadhouse makes it possible for you boys to operate. Not like Reaper's gonna dry hump the car to charge the batteries."

Ajay's grin ran off to a scowl. Bull glanced off to the side for a second, failing to hide a smile.

Kevin counted the coins out of the hip pouch and sectioned sixty-five out of the five hundred. He pushed sixty to Bull, tossed five in his cash box, and put the remainder back in the hip pouch for the merchant to pick up. He handed it over to Tris. "Put that in the safe, hon."

Bull's smile flattened. "What if I say I think you should give us all sixty-five?"

Kevin offered an appraising frown. "Then I'd say you're forgetting the Code. You're gettin' twelve percent on a milk run. Most operators'd leave you forty."

"Yeah. You right about that." Bull brushed his leather jacket aside to expose a pair of .44 revolvers. "Maybe it's time for a change, and I'm thinkin' that change looks like sixty five coins."

Kevin raised an eyebrow. "You've got a strange sense of humor. If I didn't know you, I'd think you'd just threatened me in my own roadhouse. Of course, I know you're just messin' around. That ain't how the Code works."

"You hear 'bout Spring Grove?" Bull flicked his thumb around the hammer of his still-holstered weapon. "Someone shot up a 'house in South Dakota, and ain't no one do nothin' about it."

Ajay flashed an opportunistic grin. "Yeah, man. Maybe they don't know who did it. Maybe they don't care."

The group from the big rig shifted in their seats; everyone but the teenaged boy holding the infant pulled weapons into their laps.

"I call the runt," whispered one of the tweens.

Her sister nodded and eyed Bull.

"Sounds like a load of BS to me," said Kevin. "Five thousand coin bounty's a heavy weight to carry. If someone 'hit' Spring Grove, it'd be all over the airwaves. How many people drive a bright red Tahoe with black bull heads on the doors?"

"Those are supposed to be bull *heads*?" asked Tris, eyebrow cocked. "I thought they were cow spots."

Ajay's eyes shifted back and forth between Bull and Kevin.

Bull hovered his hand over his pistol, fingertips barely touching rubber. "What if I think that's all a load of crap?"

Kevin hardened his stare. "Then I'd think I'm about to collect a stupidity tax of sixty-five coins, plus have a bunch of shit to sell."

Bull's moustache twitched.

"Bullet'll be coming out the back of your skull before the tip of your barrel clears leather." Kevin leaned his head to the left until his neck popped, and did it again to the right. "Shame to spoil a good working relationship like that."

Bull met his stare for a moment, glanced at Tris, eyed the people at the big, round table, and relaxed. "Heh. Just fuckin' wit' yas." He grinned and dropped ten coins on the counter. "Beer and burger each and a bunk."

Tris cocked an eyebrow. "You boys sharin' a bed or does the little guy get the floor?"

Ajay glared at her.

"You know what I mean." Bull grumbled. "Two rooms."

Kevin swept the coins into his hand. He could squeeze twelve out for the order, but didn't feel like cleaning up after a gunfight. He banged on the wall twice and yelled through the hole. "Sang, need a pair of burgers."

"No problem, Boss," shouted Sang.

After filling a pair of mason jar glasses, he set them on the counter and indicated the seating area with a nod. "Pick a table. Food'll be out soon."

The group in camo relaxed somewhat, though they continued to watch Bull as he headed for a table in the back corner and sat facing the door in. Ajay leered at the youngest of the adult women among them, a girl of perhaps seventeen or so with straight black hair. The twins leaned against their mother, edging away from where the two men sat.

"What was that?" Tris pressed up to Kevin. "You trying to start a fight over five coins?"

He didn't take his eyes off Bull or Ajay, not the way 'Stubblefield' stared at them. Whatever his real name was, the man looked like he could be the twins' father or older brother. "Shit. Somethin's gonna go down. And it ain't the coins. It's the Code."

She jabbed him in the side. "The Code isn't gonna help you if you get shot."

He broke his stare at Bull and tapped one finger on the tip of Tris' nose. "They were just testing me. Not even Bull's got the balls to risk bringin' Amarillo down on him."

"Yeah, but you'd still be dead." Her gaze fell to the floor.

"Everyone knows there's cameras. He'd have to kill everyone in here and burn the whole place down, and hope that the black box melts. This guy Holloway killed the man who'd been runnin' the Hagerman Roadhouse before Wayne got it. Poor bastard couldn't show his face anywhere near a road or settlement. Bounty eventually got up to eleven grand. Site inspector carried his severed head around for a couple years as proof too."

She squeezed her fingers through his shirt on both sides, pulling him against her. "I don't care about the cameras. I want you alive, not avenged."

Scuffing boots made him look up at 'Stubblefield,' who approached the counter. "What's the deal with those two? Wasn't expecting them to go for that badass act."

Kevin glanced to his right, over the counter at the man in camo. "Just a pair of drivers in from the road. And it ain't an act." He patted Tris on the shoulder. "She would'a killed him 'fore his gun left his hip."

"Heh. No doubt." The man gave Tris a head-to-toe glance. "Where'd you find one of those?"

Her smile flattened. "I'm not an android."

"No shit... Mind?" He reached as if to give her bicep a squeeze.

Tris lifted her arm an inch.

"Hmm." He let go after a few seconds. "You're right."

Kevin blinked. "You can tell that easy?"

"Sure." Stubblefield smiled. "Arm's too spindly and soft. Damn odd how much she looks like one though."

"How do you know that?" asked Tris.

"We're from Fort Missoula. Spend the winter inside, summer caravanning. They had a pair of those Persephone units in shipping cartons like big ass dolls. Larry got it in his head an extra pair of hands wouldn't be a bad idea, though f'ya ask me, he'd been fixated on how, uhh, 'anatomically correct' they looked. Anyway, thing wakes up and goes on a rampage. Headed straight out; killed anyone who got in its way like we'd 'captured' it or something. Needless to say, we demoed the other one."

Tris gulped. "I'm a person."

"And she's anatomically correct," said Kevin.

Tris punched him in the side, but grinned.

A ripple of gunfire erupted from the seating area. Kevin startled and whipped his head around to find Ajay lying dead on the floor and Bull sliding lifeless from a bench seat into a heap under the table. His huge Ruger .44 slipped out of his fingers and hit the tiles with a *clatter*. Henderson and two of the women held smoking M-16s. The twins had pulled their Glocks, but didn't seem to have fired. The teenage boy lay on the floor, shielding the infant.

"I was expecting something like that." Kevin grumbled.

"What the fuck happened?" asked Tris.

"Don't care." Kevin glanced at the hole in the wall. "Sang, never mind those burgers."

Tris gawked at Stubblefield.

"No problem, Boss," yelled Sang.

3

THE DOOR'S ALWAYS OPEN

With a heavy grunt, Kevin rolled Bull's underwear-clad body into a grave about three hundred yards north of the roadhouse. He entertained a moment of grim humor that Bee would've taken the underpants as well. Some things just were *not* worth two coins.

It'd take another damn nuke to get rid of those stains.

Stubblefield and Henderson helped dig, cutting the task down from 'all night and into tomorrow' to 'the rest of the night.' According to Henderson, 'don't sleep' was *not* the correct thing to say back to a woman after her family refused to sell her. The whole thing sounded like Ajay's mouth wrote a check Bull's reflexes couldn't cash. Kevin wondered if Bull had been in on it or if the skinny idiot set off that bomb as a surprise. Not much point wondering about it now.

"Well, Bull… sooner or later, you were gonna wind up on the wrong side of the argument." Kevin took a moment to catch his breath before reaching for the shovel again.

The men helped, tossing dirt over the bodies.

"'Preciate the help."

"No problem," said Henderson. "Least we can do."

"And thanks for havin' your girl check our panels. Didn't look the type." Stubblefield chuckled.

"What type?" asked Kevin.

"You know… smart." Stubblefield shrugged. "She's cute. Didn't expect her to be a tech too."

Henderson chuckled. "Don't mind him. He's been hit in the head too many times."

"No problem." Kevin laughed, but it rang hollow. Not that he objected to the man's apparent belief that pretty equated to dumb, but a firing squad had gone off in his roadhouse. That's what it had been. Really, when he ran it back and forth under the rolling pin of his mind, 'firing squad' was the only way to call it. Five automatic rifles opened up on Bull and Ajay over a threat that might not have been anything more than a toothless attempt to salvage a bruised ego. Any one of those bullets might've caught someone off a chance ricochet. It could be Tris lying at the bottom of a hole in the ground. Any day might see bullets flying around the room; at least on the road, he *expected* danger at every turn. The roadhouse offered the lie of safety. *I gotta trust in the Code.* "She okay?"

"Yeah. Nothin' we haven't seen before. Jaime's tough." Henderson patted down dirt. "That shifty bastard threatened her and she wasn't gonna risk it."

Henderson shook his head. "She ain't takin' shit from no one since she had a baby."

Kevin exhaled, sputtering his lips. "Dumb bastard. Girl's got a rifle in her lap and he runs his mouth."

Stubblefield snickered. "Darwin at work."

"Huh?" asked Kevin.

"Oh… survival of the fittest. The dumb weed themselves out." Stubblefield swung the shovel up and rested it over his shoulder. "That should about do it then."

Kevin looked around, surprised at how dark it had gotten. "Yeah. Time to pack it in."

He led the way across the desert to the back door, past a pair of dumpsters, and through a cinder block-walled corridor running behind the stores-turned-private rooms. An offshoot led to the main area, emerging between the counter and the bathroom hallway. The men went to their table while Kevin stowed the tools in a closet. By the time he reached the counter, the group had left. Lights in the side windows of the giant semi cab implied they'd retired to their bunks.

Tris' butt protruded out from under the table where Bull died, shimmying back and forth in time with the scratch of a brush on the floor. At the clonk of Kevin's boot heels on the ceramic tiles, she sat back and looked up at him. "This is my least favorite part of this, you know."

"You're *still* cleaning up blood?" He grabbed a rag and got down on one knee to help.

She harrumphed. "I spent a few hours on top of their trailer, remember. Couldn't do anything for the two shattered panels. I doubt Amarillo could either. That rig's got gallium arsenide multi-junction units; don't see that anywhere but old satellites and military bases. I did manage to get them back up to seventy-two percent. Half their array went down due to a slug that hit the fuse cluster. Skimmed the underside and embedded in the roof. Didn't look damaged from the outside, but a line diagnostic led me right to it."

Kevin wiped traces of Bull from the facing seat. "I won't even pretend I know what you said."

"Amy gave us a couple bottles of wine to thank me for the repairs. They can probably get home now without needing to stop again."

He cringed. "How old is it?"

"They make it themselves at the fort. Plum wine?" She shrugged.

Kevin rubbed his gut, imagining the kind of shits that would give him. "S'pose someone will buy it." He stared at her, watching her hair wave about as she scrubbed the floor. Gratitude that she'd not taken a bullet left him speechless.

"Added thirty seven rounds of .44 to the shop. Two .44 Ruger revolvers, five sets of jeans, three pairs of boots, two jackets..." Tris scrunched up her face in thought. "Found a .308 rifle in the truck, about ninety rounds for it... didn't count yet. Couple knives. What're you gonna do with their ride?"

"Put the word on the radio. Someone'll buy it. Could get four grand for it if I pushed, but I'll say two just to get rid of it."

"Alternating clusters."

"What?" Kevin, stretched forward to dab blood from the wall, glanced at her.

"They've got two batteries. One charges while they drive from the other."

"Ah."

She gave the seat another once-over. "At least they shot him in the chest. No brain matter."

"You are such a romantic."

"I know." She hugged him. "You're sweaty."

"Shower?" He grinned.

"Nah." She hooked a finger under his shirt collar and tugged him into a kiss. "Bath."

———※——※——※—·—※——※——

DREAMS OF DRIVING ALONG AN ENDLESS DESERT ROAD CAME AND WENT. A world rendered in washed-out sepia tones reassured him sitting behind the wheel again—and not the past six months running his own roadhouse—belonged to the realm of imagination. Kevin awoke on his back with Tris face down on his chest, head tucked under his chin. She'd switched up the old wives' tale and fell asleep within seconds of their finishing. The hot bath of hours ago had soothed the soreness from grave digging; he'd almost passed out in the water. After almost an hour of sex, half of which happened in the tub, he couldn't tell if he was too tired or too worried to sleep.

Nerves had been Tris' thing over the past few months. Virus, Enclave, Nathan, random drunken idiots with guns. She didn't have the same kind of faith in the Code. She hadn't grown up around it, seen it work, seen the fear in men's eyes when they realized they'd breached it. Some things, a person just *didn't* do: steal or damage a car parked at a roadhouse, steal from a roadhouse, attack the proprietor of a roadhouse, get smashed on moonshine and drive a pickup truck through a roadhouse...

He slipped his hand up to the curve where her ass sloped down into her lower back. Worrying about someone like Bull giving Tris a hard time never much occurred to him. She could handle just about anything the Wildlands threw at her... if she saw it coming. A stray bullet was another story.

The yellowing drop ceiling didn't have any answers lurking in its tiny, black holes. Somewhere around the time he'd turned fifteen, he'd got it in his head he'd be happy forever as a driver. Adventure, glory, shooting 'bad guys,' and going anywhere/doing whatever he wanted. At twenty... four—or somewhere around that age—a bullet changed his mind, both about spending the rest of his life on the road as well as thinking of armor as 'too heavy.' The spot twinged, but he didn't feel like moving Tris' breast away to scratch himself. He'd frequented Wayne's ever since he'd been about seventeen and on his own, and now he'd become Wayne—or at least a bad imitation thereof.

He glanced at the wall by the door. *I can't remember if Wayne locked up at night. No, of course not... he's got Bee. Androids don't sleep.* His sigh fluttered her snowy hair. *Maybe I should hire a night guy.* Their bedroom occupied what had been a small management office on the second story, right above the dining area. His door had a lock. The store full of gear had a lock; all the bedrooms downstairs had locks, and Sang usually locked himself in the kitchen at night. At worst, someone might steal his chairs.

For some time he lay still, eyes closed but wide awake. Even the gentle motion of her breathing failed to offer the solace necessary to pass out.

What am I worrying about?

A *creak* and *jangle* emanated from the hall outside.

Crap. He suppressed a cringe at the scrape of the front door on the tiles. Kevin rolled to his left, easing Tris onto her back and covering her with the blanket as he slipped out into the chilly night air. "Yeah, yeah..." He mumbled and hurried into his pants, shirt, and boots.

The door rattled again.

"Fuck's sake, I'm coming," he muttered. He got three steps to the door before he reversed to grab his .45 and stuffed it in the back of his belt.

Ten feet of hallway led to a cramped stairway. Kevin descended and squinted at dim room where a male figure in a long duster coat leaned against the door. The man pushed the door open and pulled it back against himself in a continuous motion, like a teenager trying to fan shit fumes out of a bathroom. Scraggly black hair hung down from a brown cowboy hat. With each pull or shove at the door, he let off a soft grunt. He leaned so far to the side, his grip on the door might've been the only thing keeping him from collapsing.

A good distance out in the desert, the wavering beams of headlamps illuminated the scrub. Whoever he was, he'd parked a quarter mile or more away.

"Hey, buddy. You awright?"

"Ngh," said the man. "I..."

"You shot?" Kevin approached, left hand raised, right creeping around behind his back for the gun.

"Ngh!" The man snapped his head up, tossing hair away from his face. Bulging bloodshot eyes locked onto Kevin. Dark bloody slime seeped over his teeth and dribbled down his chin.

"Fuck!" shouted Kevin.

He yanked the .45 and brought it around; the Infected pounced at him, too fast for a human to move. The gun went off before his back hit the chilly floor, a useless bullet out the window into the night sky. Hard red tile met Kevin's skull with a dizzying jolt. He swung his left arm up in an elbow strike, more to get something in front of the thing's chest before it got close enough to bite.

"Ngh!" roared the Infected, gaping mouth leaking bloody saliva onto Kevin's shirt.

Panic shot a bolt of adrenaline down his limbs. He worked his arm around into a grip on the man's throat and forced him to the left, rolling onto his side. The Infected grabbed his wrist, squeezing.

Kevin let off a wail and bashed him in the temple with the handle of the .45, trying to get the creature to let go before the bones in his arm splintered. The fiend didn't care much about the blow to the head; however, the hit distracted him into biting the gun instead of Kevin. He thought about firing, but the angle sucked—he'd only put a hole in the man's cheek and spray Infected blood all over the room. He jerked on his arm, crushing a tooth, pivoting the gun to put the barrel in line with brain stem.

The Infected's eyes flared wider. With a desperate groan, he seized two fistfuls of Kevin's shirt and hurled him to the side like a bowling ball into the arrangement of tables and chairs. He tucked fetal, guarding his head with his arms as he careened through dozens of steel legs.

When he stopped sliding, Kevin rolled onto his hands and knees and realized his right hand no longer had a gun in it. He looked up at the Infected crawling toward him. The once-man spat the .45 to the side, ignoring, or too far gone to comprehend its purpose as a weapon.

"Kevin!" yelled Tris.

"Infected!" shouted Kevin.

The man rushed forward. Kevin grabbed a table, pulling it down as a shield a second before the fiend slammed face-first into it. Fingers came around the edges, trying to grab him. Failing that, it tried to crush him. The creature's superhuman strength shoved him across the floor until his back met the side of a booth seat. Behind him, Fitch and Neeley's snoring reverberated in the private room.

For fuck's sake. "Fitch!" Kevin thumped the door with his elbow twice.

Pressure pinning him to the wall ceased. Kevin didn't have time to take a breath of relief before the Infected grabbed the edge of the table and yanked it to the side. For a second, with nothing between him and the

Virus other than a torn shirt, time froze. Kevin shook off the paralysis of phobic panic and, emitting a keening howl, raised his legs to plant his boots in the thing's chest as it leapt for him.

He shoved with both legs, launching the once-man over two tables. Kevin scrambled to his feet and pounded on the door behind him.

Tris ran naked into the room, katana in hand. "Kevin!"

The Infected leapt to its feet again and whirled at the nearer-sounding voice. It managed one loping step before her arms blurred into motion. Two swings in the span of one second severed its head and left the blade impaled to the hilt in its chest. Tris held the thrashing corpse steady with a two-handed grip on the sword until it ceased moving and fell limp to the rear.

A spray of dark blood painted her otherwise paper-white body. She held her arms slightly up, as if she'd stepped in something foul. "Where did he come from?"

Kevin couldn't quite grasp the nuances of language yet, and gestured at the door with a 'meep' sound.

Sang hurried into the room carrying a shotgun. He glanced at Kevin, then Tris, and shook his head. "You two too rough. Wake up in middle of the night." He blinked at her. "Too much blood. You hurt him."

Tris pointed the katana at the dead man. "Infected."

Sang paled. "Oh, no."

"It's fine." She glanced down at herself. "I'm immune. Ugh, this is disgusting. At least I don't have to burn my clothes this time."

The door opened behind Kevin. The question Neeley almost asked stalled when he looked up and caught sight of Tris. A dumbstruck smile spread over his face.

"You two fuckers sleep too hard." Kevin rasped.

"Sorry. What'd we miss?" Neeley kept staring at Tris.

"Infected." Kevin stood and blocked the small man's view. "It's over. Go back to sleep."

Tris speared the severed head with the sword and headed for the door. "I'll clean this up."

"Is that a risk?" asked Sang, gesturing at the mess.

"Yeah." She grumbled. "At least he was kind enough to move all the tables out of the way first."

Kevin's legs, back, and butt throbbed. "That was me." He smiled. "Figured I'd clear a nice spot out for a fight."

She gave him a worried look. "How bad?"

"Just bruises." He rubbed his leg, though his effort failed to conceal his shaking hands from her.

Tris took a step toward him, but hesitated. "Uhh."

"Hug later. I'm fine. You're covered in death sentence, hon."

"Right. Can I get a couple pails of warm water, Sang?"

"Sure thing, Boss." Sang rushed back to the kitchen.

"Uhh, we'll be in here." Neeley shut the door.

Kevin leaned against a table, allowing his body to tremble out the last bits of adrenaline. Tris went outside with the impaled head, and returned a few minutes later to collect the body. Thankfully, she didn't use the katana to carry it out. This, of course, left a large trail of blood from the puddle where the man fell to the door. Kevin didn't want to move even an inch closer to it. Screams filled his memory; the couple who'd taken him in as a boy searching for him after some Infected got into their little settlement.

Shaking, he bowed his head over his crossed arms and waited.

⁕⁕⁕⁕⁕⁕⁕⁕

TRIS HAULED THE DEAD MAN OUT TO THE HIGHWAY AND SET THE BODY ON the pavement next to the head. She sliced off a large portion of his shirt where it remained clear of blood, and wiped herself down before cleaning the blade. Cheeks burning from embarrassment, she walked with deliberate purpose back to the building and padded to the kitchen. Sang glanced up at the creak of the door, and hurriedly looked away.

"Little while longer, Boss. Water's still cooking." He gestured at two metal buckets on electric burners.

"'Kay."

She backed out and headed for the smaller outbuilding behind the main roadhouse Kevin had set up as a garage. The Challenger lived there most of the time, though sometimes when a 'gambler' had an issue, he'd move it to work on someone else's ride. Tris smiled at the indignation in his voice when he called a driver who couldn't fix their own car a gambler. As if the very concept of a driver not bothering to learn how to fix their ride had insulted him, or he considered it the pinnacle of idiocy.

After snagging a small canister of ethanol, a glow plug tester, and a glow plug, she headed back out to the body. A gentle night breeze passed over her bare skin; the ethanol sloshed in time with her steps. Cold dirt and the occasional sharp rock underfoot kept her hustling. Once she made it to the highway, Tris poured fuel around the corpse, eyeing the road in both directions. *Please don't let anyone drive by and catch me out here naked.* Satisfied the body had a liberal soaking of fuel, she poured a short trail off to a safe distance. After socketing the glow plug in the tester, she held it to the liquid and pushed the button. The trail erupted in blue flame, which raced back along the length of the trickle. In seconds, a bonfire raged on the highway.

Tris held the katana in the flames for a little while, perhaps longer than necessary to ensure any latent virus particles died. Despite the horribleness of a burning corpse, she stood close to the fire to ward off the chill of the night out in the vast open nothingness. Glancing at a sliver of reflection in the blade, she swallowed the dread that immunity might be another Enclave lie. She tilted the sword, moving the reflection down off her face to her blood-smeared chest. Something in the back of her mind welled up out of nowhere, bringing the assurance she had nothing to fear.

She leaned the point of the sword in the dirt and eyed the stars. *Where'd that come from? Ugh why am I just standing here? Anyone looking at me would think I'm doing some kind of tribal ritual.* Leaving the man to burn, she jogged back to the safety of the roadhouse. Kevin had passed out at a table with his head down. The want to cling to him battled with the worry the sticky residue all over her could kill him. She grumbled and sighed at the huge puddle of blood. Killing Infected was a pain in the ass when you had to clean up after it.

"Damn." She sighed at herself, certain her cheeks had as much color as they could possibly get. Maybe everyone mistook her for an android because of her unusual skin tone? At least, unusual for out here. Most people in the Enclave had skin as white as copier paper. "Fuck it. I'd have to burn anything I wear."

The storeroom upstairs contained a bundle of old curtains, likely removed during renovations not long before war broke out. The material flaked when she moved it, but offered the best (and most disposable) option to sop up the mess with.

An hour or so later, she dropped an armload of bloody cloth on top of the man's ashes, added more ethanol, and lit another fire. Sang carried the buckets out and poured one after the other over her while she stood on the road, wiping herself down with her empty hands. Despite the heat in the water, within a minute, her teeth chattered from the nighttime wind.

He'd been thoughtful enough to bring a blanket, which she eagerly wrapped herself in.

Back inside, she dribbled ethanol around the tile floor where the blood stained it, and lit it with the glow plug. A few of the tiles cracked from the heat, but at least she felt confident the virus was gone. With that done, she jostled Kevin to his feet, and carried him back to bed.

4

SPOILS

Kevin shot upright, fast enough to fling Tris aside. He stared at the pile of old cubicle wall panels stacked a few feet beyond the end of the bed. The vision of Infected Tris from his nightmare faded away. He drew his legs up and rested his forehead on his knees. A soft, warm hand slid across his back.

She leaned against his side. "Hey… you okay?"

He nodded, despite breathing hard. "Yeah. Freaky dream." The scent of eggs and sausage got him to look up. "Last night… that really happened?"

"It did. I cleaned it up. Burned it out. It's gone."

"How…" He slid his legs off the mattress, feet on the floor, and rested his elbows on his knees. "What the fuck is an Infected doing here? We're out in the middle of nowhere. They're not supposed to be this far away from population centers."

Tris shivered and drew the blanket tighter around herself. "Remind me not to go out into the desert at night while naked and wet again. I'm *still* freezing."

"Mmm." He raked his fingers up through his hair.

"There's a van off in the scrub a little ways north of the road. Door was still open. He either had a ride or was still driving when the Virus destroyed his mental faculties."

"I had a gun in his mouth." Kevin's head snapped up. *Fuck. Where's my Dad's .45?* "Where—"

She pointed at the desk by the door. "I got it. It's okay." She embraced him from behind and kissed his cheek.

Relief came over him. He guided her by a finger on the jaw into another, longer kiss. "One minute, he seemed to know what a gun was, the next he didn't."

"He couldn't have been sick too long then." She got out of bed, stretched, and reached for her jeans. "That's actually a good thing. Most of the viral mass would've been in the CNS instead of the bloodstream. The first eight hours after the loss of higher brain function sees the lowest contagiousness in the blood..."

"So he wasn't dangerous?" He palmed her ass, giving it a squeeze before she covered it.

"Oh, he was... just not *as* dangerous. Probably would've required getting five or six drops on your tongue instead of one."

He froze with terror.

"Shit, I'm sorry." She buttoned her jeans and stooped over to hug him. "I shouldn't have said that. You're phobic."

"Anyone with any common sense is phobic." He forced himself to stand and get dressed. "Whatever Sang's doing down there smells amazing."

"Yeah." She wriggled in to a blue flannel shirt.

"Thanks." He pulled her in to another squeeze. "For saving my ass yet again."

She grinned. "Your shot woke me up."

"Shit. Window." He stepped into his boots, and grumbled all the way down to the main room. Nobody made windows anymore. He'd have to scavenge one from some other rest stop, leave a gaping hole, or do something. *Tarp it is...*

Athena perched at a table by an empty plate, a permanent scowl of impatience directed at the counter. As soon as their eyes met, she smiled. He gave her a 'need a few minutes' wave, and leaned his head through the hole to the kitchen.

"Morning."

Sang waved without looking back. "You hungry, Boss?"

"Yep. That wonderful smell dragged my lazy ass out of bed."

"Food order got here. Everything look good," said Sang.

Athena approached the counter and leaned on her folded arms. "Okay, so I got your groceries. Can I have a real job now, Dad?"

Kevin chuckled. "Okay, but I'm going to ask you to run back to Carver's on the way. I forgot to order flour."

She sighed.

He waved her off. "Real job on the way." Sixteen pages deep in the marble notebook, he poked his finger into a half-filled out line. "You know where Ween lives?"

"Oh for..." She grumbled. "That crazy old bastard on Heron Lake? That's fuckin' New Mexico."

"You said you wanted a real job, right? One out of three *real* jobs is going to send you to Ween. Better get used to him."

Athena tapped her fingers on the counter.

"Well, I understand if you can't handle the run. That little car of yours doesn't have much room to sleep in. Drivin' between 'houses will add a day to the trip."

"I can handle it," yelled Athena. "Fine. What is it?"

"Standard Ween run. You'll need to go to Spring Creek Nevada, which isn't too far offa Route 80 west of here. You'll be meeting a guy name 'o Geers... Daniel, I think. Anyway, he'll give you 'leven hundred coins. Go to Ween, pick up his order of bullets. Give Ween 900 coins. Drive the ammo back to Spring Creek, then come here. Twenty coins come back to me, hundred n' eighty are yours."

Athena's ice blue eyes shifted left and right. Annoyance, disappointment, anger flitted by in sequence. "That's a lot of damn running around. Don't you have any bounties or stuff sitting in the back for delivery?"

"I thought you wanted a 'real' job?" Kevin grinned. "What exactly did you think you were getting into anyway? All this life is, is driving O.P.S. around. Marauders can almost smell a load of ammo, or a sack of a thousand coins. Bet you'll get your wish on that one." He gestured at the hallway to the right of the counter. "I got a Kevlar-panel jacket in your size."

"Gimme a job moving Opie S then." She folded her arms.

"Heh." He grinned. "I'm trying to. It means Other People's Stuff. So, deal?"

"I don't need armor. It'll just slow me down." She put her hands on her hips. "Okay fine. I'll take the run. What did you want from Carver's?"

"Flour. Twenty pounds if he's got it. Whatever he's got otherwise."

"Okay. Whatever. What's it pay?"

Kevin gave her a long stare. "That jacket. If you'll wear it."

Athena's mouth hung open. "God dammit! I already have a father. I don't need another one."

Fitch and Neeley, seated at a table near the room they'd slept in, both laughed. Neeley leaned back a little farther to stare at her ass.

"Well…" Kevin smiled. "Okay, so I might feel a little guilty if you got yourself killed doing a job I gave you." He pointed at her. "Before you scream at me that you're not a child… that 'untouchable' thing of yours says you are."

Tris glided in from the back with two plates. She set them on the counter and sat on the metal folding chair next to Kevin.

"Yeah, yeah. I know. You took six slugs before you 'wised up.'" She rolled her eyes. "How much would you sell that jacket for?"

"Forty…"

She fidgeted. "So you're willing to pay me forty coins to pick up some damn flour?"

"Only if you keep and wear it." He winked. "It won't make people think you're a coward. Might even trick them into believing you're competent."

Athena gave him the finger while shaking her head along with an eye roll. "Fine. Whatever. You gonna pack me a lunch too, Dad?"

"Two coins." He winked.

Tris turned away; she shuddered as if laughing in silence.

"Asshole," muttered Athena.

Kevin grinned.

FAR ENOUGH AWAY THAT THE ROADHOUSE SHRANK TO THE SIZE OF A matchbox, Kevin found a dusty grey van wedged into the ruins of an old post fence. Judging by the lack of damage to the bumper, he figured the thing had been barely rolling forward when it hit. The tires, fortunately e-motors, had dug themselves in a few inches. He guessed the Infected hadn't quite lost *all* of his mind at that point, and got confused at why the van stopped going forward. After accelerating didn't work, he'd abandoned it and gone wandering… likely attracted to the lights across the road.

Above the passenger side front corner, a boxy .50 caliber machinegun sat on an armored ring with a gearbox on either side, hinting at a powered swivel mount with some manner of targeting optics.

Careful not to touch anything, he peered in the open driver door. The seat had no sign of blood or body fluids, and Tris had spent some forty odd minutes after Athena left reassuring him that the Virus was not transmissible via air. Not even sweat could do it.

"Saliva or blood," he muttered.

Upon noting the van's console lit up, he climbed in. An eight-inch screen in the center of the dash painted the interior light blue. Over the passenger seat dangled a military flight helmet. Bolts in the roof gave away the position of the gun, and a drum full of ammo hung from above a little behind the passenger's headrest. Half the windshield and the entire passenger-side door window had armored plates instead of glass. A single joystick sprouted from the armrest with a trigger-style button. The interior of the helmet glowed soft green. Unable to contain his curiosity, Kevin slipped into the seat and pulled the helmet on.

Rather than a visor, it had prewar 3D gaming goggles rigged to the optics on the turret. After flicking an 'arm' switch above the glovebox, the turret moved wherever he turned his head.

"Whoa." He hesitated at trying the trigger, not wanting to waste .50 ammo if the thing wound up working. "Bad idea not to test a weapon... Oh, fuck it. Not like I'm about to ride off to war. Who was this guy that he had this kind of hardware...?" *Okay, for a van I can sell for like six grand, I'll deal with an Infected waking me up in the middle of the night.* He pointed at the clouds. "That's not a request for round two."

As soon as he flicked the arming switch to the off position, the turret centered itself and drooped. He let the helmet bob back up on its wires and shifted to the driver's chair. On the center display panel, white lines traced out a GPS navigation map—of Kentucky—along with a notification of 'failed to acquire satellite.'

"Yeah, no shit."

Six white buttons lined the black frame on either side of the screen, and it took him only ten seconds to get into the vehicle diagnostics and control system. The charge meter showed a mere eighteen percent, likely from it having been on all night. After resetting the security code to 2957, he pulled the door closed, backed away from the fence, and drove due south toward home.

The noise coming from the back end as the van bounced over the desert gave him daydreams of a trunk full of coins. After parking in the leftmost space, he leapt out of the seat and headed for the back to investigate the wonderful jingling he'd heard. A single olive-drab footlocker sat against the left wall, tied to padded rails with a few turns of clothesline cord.

Though the box bore a hasp for a padlock, it hadn't been secured. His greedy anticipation collapsed to icy disappointment when he lifted the lid and found spent brass instead of coins. He drummed his fingers on the thin wood.

"Hmm. Ween might want this… gotta be a couple thousand in here." A few sweeps of his fingers revealed a mix of 9mm, .45, .44, and some 5.56 brass. He frowned and let the lid slap down. "Shit. This might be an active run." As deflating as it was to lose salvage rights to a roadhouse 'job-in-progress,' the Code didn't compromise.

He returned to the driver's seat. After a search of cup holders, center console storage compartment, sun visor flaps, and glove box failed to turn up any notes or maps about a job, he shifted his attention to the display screen. A few button presses paged through the computer to the system logs. The last time the van had been hooked up to a charging station bore a timestamp with latitude/longitude coordinates that lined up with Interstate 80 close to Hastings Nebraska, likely a roadhouse.

Kevin tapped the screen. "Hmm. So this guy probably picked up the brass there… but was he sick when he left?"

According to the computer, the van had been there three days ago. Kevin rummaged more, finding some old soda bottles, useless paper trash, a couple DVDs, but nothing of any real value beyond the footlocker full of brass. Likely Tris had already gathered anything salable. No paper maps lurked anywhere he could find.

"The guy's either got a damn good memory or he's an idiot." He grumbled, got out, and walked around the van three times before he found the charging plug behind a folding front license plate. "You're lucky she burned your ass. I'd shoot you again for hiding the damn thing."

He unwound the cable and plugged in. Infected or not, he now had *two* extra vehicles. Bull's Tahoe had no mounted weapons, but it was red. Some idiot would pay extra for that. The van, more to the point the 'neato factor' of the turret, was definitely worth keeping. Of course, keeping it would require driving it. The nine-year-old in him wanted to light something up with the optically aimed turret, but his adult brain reminded him that targets tended to fire back.

Nah. I'm done gettin' shot at.

Kevin shoved the door closed, keyed in the security code using rubber buttons under the handle, and strolled inside with a big grin on his face.

Tris stood at the counter, fanning a metal tray full of recently-boiled mason jar glasses. Her face, half her chest, and her shoulders had been blackened as though a smoke bomb went off three inches in front of her nose. He paused, eyebrow raised.

She glanced up at him; a smile broke the black across her cheeks. "Hey."

"What…" He crossed the room to the counter and slipped through the gap on the left. "Happened?"

"Well pump was faltering."

"And…"

She brushed some char from her shirt. "And, we need a new one."

"Blew up?"

"No, I decided to go crazy with black eye shadow… all over my face."

"What the hell is eye shadow?" He grabbed two glasses out of the basin, indifferent to their heat, and set them on an overhead shelf. "Oh, did you notice if that guy last night got bit?"

"Cosmetics… and sorry. I didn't really bother strip-searching him. Was kinda in a hurry."

Kevin set another pair of glasses overhead. "Yeah. Van got a full charge about three days ago, east of here. Got a feeling that guy lost his shit at our doorstep. Hit a fence post and kept trying to drive."

Tris picked up a glass, but hot-potatoed it between her hands. "Damn how can you touch these?"

Kevin snagged the glass from her and put it on the shelf. "You take on an Infected with a sword, but you're whimpering about a warm glass?"

She exaggerated a pout. "I'm delicate." Sad face lasted all of three seconds before she laughed. Humor survived another ten or so, and she sighed. "As far as I know, a bunch of things can affect how long someone lasts before the Virus leaves them mindless. Exposure type and severity, overall health, body mass, how good their immune system is… There are some individuals naturally resistant who take much longer to get sick. I remember someone mentioning the viral structure was similar to something a large portion of the population had vaccinations for. Chicken pox? Smallpox? Polio? One of those…"

"Well, our friend was definitely not resistant." He put the last of the glasses up top and shook water out of the basin.

"Resistant isn't immune. It just takes them longer to die." She leaned on the counter, firing a morose stare at the floor. "Only the Enclave has a true vaccine for it."

"So you're saying you have no idea how long he might've been 'ticking' before he went feral?"

She shrugged. "Was he bitten once? Twice? Six times? Maybe he shot one at close range and got a mouthful of blood. Did he receive a direct dose of Virus somehow shooting himself up with a tainted needle?" Her eyes widened. "What if the Enclave is sending live agent out into the world again?"

He chucked the basin through the hole in the wall to the kitchen and leaned his hip against the counter. "You think they're gonna come this far east to infect one person? Didn't Doc Andrews say something about sabotaging it from the inside?"

"Yeah, but it's not like the Enclave would say 'oh no, they ruined it… suppose we should stop.'" She folded her arms and grumbled. "They want to kill everyone they think is genetically compromised, and that's pretty much everyone who wasn't born inside the Enclave. That's why I had to… Why it's so important that…" Tears swelled from her eyes.

He wrapped his arms around her and let her sniffle into his shoulder. "What'll it take for you to let go of that guilt? There's nothing you could've done."

"Then why do I keep feeling like I let everyone down." She clung to him.

"You didn't. You wanted so bad for that data in your head to be real… Maybe you're not guilty as much as pissed."

She fumed. "If I ever see Nathan… Oh, I got ash all over your shirt." She swatted at his flannel.

He caught her hands, grinning. "S'okay. Go clean up if you want, I got it here."

She smiled and headed off toward the bathroom. With the room empty, Kevin ducked into the office and flopped on an old canvas-topped stool by the radio unit he'd gotten from Amarillo. He grabbed the CB-style mic and squeezed the talk button.

"Heads up. This is number 42, Rawlins, Wyoming. Had a DOA roll in last night with a trunk full'a spent brass. Grey van. Last charge near Hastings, Nebraska. Anyone got brains on that cargo?"

Kevin let off the button and listened to the hiss.

"*Nein,*" said Gertrude a few seconds later.

"Ain't mine." Beth's voice made him shiver at the memory of the grandmother hitting on him.

"Whazzat?" asked a croaky older man, followed by a series of laughs.

"Might be goin' ta Ween," said Clive, who ran a roadhouse in northwestern Colorado. Something about the voice made Kevin remember the smell of clove pipe tobacco.

Kevin hit the button again. "Looked like he was headin' westbound."

"DOA?" asked Nash. His 'house was somewhere in eastern Nevada or western New Mexico. "Someone killed a driver at a roadhouse?"

A series of grumbles and doubts came by one after the next. Kevin eyed the black plastic grille over the speaker, noting the unusual absence of Wayne or Bee chiming in.

"Don't know the run was official. Tryin' to figure that out." Kevin let off the button to take a breath. "Weren't no attack far as I can tell. No one killed him *here*. He got himself infected. Was nothin' in his head when he came through my door."

A waterfall of curses preceded a loud old man yelling, "Whazzat?"

"Go back to sleep, 'Zat," said Beth.

More chuckling.

"So no one got anything on a footlocker full of empty brass?" Kevin leaned as far as the curly wire tethering the mic to the radio would allow, enough to peer into the main room and confirm it remained empty. He pushed off the doorjamb to stand upright again. "Wayne?"

Silence.

"Wayne, come back?" He flicked the talk button for a few seconds. "Bee?"

"Prob'ly shittin'," said Harold, a gravelly, but deep voice.

"Who's in Hastings again?" asked Earl.

"No one who wants to stay alive." Gertrude grumbled for a second. "Place is full of them things."

"The 'house isn't *in* Hastings. It's nearby," said Clive.

"Shit if I know." Harold clucked his tongue.

Tris walked in, having traded her flannel and jeans for a blue mechanic's jumpsuit. "What are they arguing about this time?"

He set the mic on the desk and grasped her shoulders, smiling. "I was trying to figure out if there was an active run on that box of spent ammo before I took it as salvage."

"Oh. Some 'code' thing?"

"Yeah." He glanced down, chuckling. "Not quite as bad as opening an unofficial 'house or shooting at the guy runnin' it, but interferin' with a driver on an official run is pretty bad." He grinned. "Wish the pirates and raiders cared about the Code."

"Then driving wouldn't be as *exciting*." She smirked.

A few of the voices on the radio attempted to get a response from 'a roadhouse near Hastings,' but no one chimed in to claim it. Kevin stared at the silver-black box.

"What's wrong?" asked Tris.

He shifted to the side, left arm sliding down her back, and pulled her close. "They're not answering…"

"That shouldn't put such a look of worry on your face."

"Neither is Wayne." He tapped his boot. "Wayne's always fast on the radio to tell everyone how wrong they are about whatever."

She started to laugh, but stifled it at the worried glower he fired into the radio box. "Gonna check it out?"

Kevin's eyes flared; his legs locked stiff. "If that Infected came from a 'house near Hastings…"

"Hire someone to go to Hastings?" She rubbed his back.

"I can't send someone there." He wiped at his mouth. "Might as well shoot them myself. No idea what they're gonna find."

She joined him in staring at the radio for a little while. The voices eventually fell silent, still with no one claiming to be at any roadhouse near Hastings… and still no sign of Wayne. She narrowed her eyes. "I'll do it."

"What?" He turned to face her. "No…"

"You've got an idea something's happened there… you think it's possibly full of Infected. Doing nothing isn't much different than sending someone to the place. It's a *Roadhouse*, dammit… *Someone* will eventually stop there." She hurried to where he'd put a map up on the wall. "It's on 80, right?"

"Yeah." He followed, put a hand on her shoulder, and pulled her away from the map. "Look, Tris… I don't…"

"Think I can handle it?" She frowned.

"No… it's not that I'm just worried—"

"That I'm weak and helpless."

"No." He sighed. "I don't want to lose you."

"We can't both go. Between this being your place and—"

"*Our* place." He brushed fingertips over her cheek.

She smiled, eyes half closed. "Our place… and your *thing* about Infected, it should be me. Do you want to just stay quiet and have someone walk into a pack of Infected with no warning?"

"We don't even know that's what happened."

"Exactly the reason we should check it out." Her deep blue eyes glimmered with urgency. "You know me. I can handle a couple infected."

He approached the map at her side, pointing at Hastings. "The 'house isn't *in* the city. Likely along the highway like ours."

"Right. I can make it there in a couple hours if the road's clear enough to fly. I'll be back for a late dinner."

He eyed the doorway to the hall. Sang could watch the place. He could go with her. Infected. If one got her, it wouldn't be much different from a human bite. One drop of blood in the eye and he'd be as good as dead. Her idea to go there. She'd feel as guilty as if she'd shot him herself. Heck, she'd probably wind up shooting him if he turned.

"Please be careful."

Tris nodded. "I will."

"You haven't done any combat driving."

"Nope. I'll just run. The Challenger can outrun most things on flat, straight road." She winked. "You're welcome by the way."

Infected... He gnawed on his lip. "Give me a minute. I'll ask Sang to watch the place while we're out."

Tris grabbed his arm. "Kevin... there might be Infected."

"Yeah. That's what I'm expecting."

"I don't want to lose you either." She clasped his face in both hands and kissed him on the lips. They stared into each other's eyes for a while. "I'll be okay."

"At least let me drive you there." He grinned and winked.

5

ROAD TRIP

T ris opened the padlock securing the metal rolling door to the ground. After pulling it free, she flung the door up, exposing the nose end of the Challenger and releasing a cloud of air filled with the smell of rubber and ozone. At a scuff of boot on blacktop behind her, she twisted around to look. Kevin strode out the roadhouse's back door, sliding into his red armored jacket. Heat shimmer along the ground blurred his boots. A half grin spread over his face as he leaned back to peer at the door over sunglasses.

She stood on tiptoe, arms over her head, fingertips clinging to the underside of the door, and watched him walk. Her gaze lingered on where his jeans wrapped tight about his thighs. *If I didn't know him, I wouldn't believe he's worried.* She let her arms drop and walked into the garage. *Does he miss the road?* She opened the panel by the right front fender and threaded the belt of 7.62 in the fixed-forward M-60 machine gun.

Kevin stopped at the door and inhaled a deep breath through his nose. A mixture of excitement and contentment flashed in his hazel eyes. He moved to the opposite fender and loaded the gun on that side, though he didn't bother looking at what his hands did. The whole time, he kept staring at her.

Tris bit her lower lip. *He doesn't want us to be apart.* She grinned. As much as she wanted to run back inside and spend the rest of the day in his arms, every hour they waited could kill someone. She unplugged the charging cable and let the spring-loaded spool in the wall reel it in.

"You got the rear guns?" asked Kevin.

"Yeah." She scurried around to the back as he hopped into the driver's seat and hit the button to pop the trunk. After loading a drum mag in the M-16 on the passenger side and racking it, she stuffed a huge, curved magazine into the AK-47 opposite it and flicked switches to arm the electric firing circuits. "Weapons hot."

She backed out and slammed the trunk. He drove the car forward, stopping with the rear bumper a few paces from the garage. After pulling the garage door closed, Tris ran around to hop in at his side.

"Don't feel like I'm forcing you to do this."

"I don't." He squeezed her hand. "Wouldn't be right for me to sit there while you run off into the Wildlands. Besides, we've been inside for six months."

"But you love having your own roadhouse." She eased herself back in the seat as he accelerated out onto the highway. A rusting tricycle in the grass along the side of the access ramp between rest stop and interstate put a lump in her throat. Had it been forgotten there by some family on vacation long before the world ended, or...? Her mind filled with the image of a toddler riding it while a mushroom cloud rose in the distance, their frantic parents running to collect them. She covered her eyes. "Ugh."

"What?"

She looked up. Road shot by fast enough to make her guts clench up. "Dark thoughts. Nothing about this. Just being maudlin about the war. Someone left a toy on our lawn."

"Nothing landed all that close here. Whoever it belonged to probably didn't die as a direct result of the war. No one shot Cheyenne Mountain."

"Wasn't that a major installation?"

He shrugged. "I guess. But maybe all those damn movies made it seem indestructible, so they didn't bother trying."

"They?"

"Whoever launched the nukes."

She blinked. "You don't know?"

He leaned toward her, peering over the tops of his sunglasses. "I'm not the one who went to school."

"They never mentioned it." She leaned over to check the dash, and sucked air through her teeth at the speedometer showing 174. "This thing's been sitting for a while... is it a good idea to push it so hard right away?"

"It hasn't been completely idle the whole time. I've been going to Carver's Farm once a week or so. And you did a beautiful job on the drive system... still got a bunch of throttle to give her."

Tris sat up to check out the road ahead. Miles of endless brown flanked a ribbon of dingy grey paving. "Don't hit anything."

"80's pretty clean. Probably sees the most traffic of any road left in the world."

She raised an eyebrow. "How do you know that? You think the whole planet got destroyed? What about all those countries that didn't have anything worth taking?"

"Countries?" He glanced at her for a second before dodging a patch of broken paving that snuck up on him.

"Yeah... El Salvador, Nicaragua, all those places in Africa. At least tell me you've heard of Mexico?"

"That's Mexico, not country."

Tris sighed. "The third world. I guess they're the first world now. If fallout didn't get them."

Kevin blinked at her. "There's more than one?"

She let her head *thud* back against the seat. "This is going to be a long conversation."

"We got a few hours." He put a hand on her leg, squeezing her knee.

———※———※———※———※———※———

AT A TOUCH PAST ONE IN THE AFTERNOON, THREE HOURS AND CHANGE after leaving, Tris decided to abandon talking about her theory that so-called 'third world' countries may have escaped a nuclear war intact and probably continued to live much as they had before the war. Too many stories had convinced Kevin that giant ash clouds wiped out everything save for the few hundred people in this immediate area. What 'some old man in a roadhouse ten years ago' told him had leeched deep enough into his brain that her 'book learning' couldn't dislodge it.

Then again, she didn't much trust the Enclave teachers either... not after what Nathan did.

Interstate 80 had narrowed to only two lanes in either direction... two pin-straight lanes, horizon-to-horizon, separated by about twenty or so feet of waist-high grass. Distant trees dotted the landscape far away to the left and right, beyond endless fields of shifting green. Tris scanned the left side of the road since Kevin felt confident this particular 'house sat on the westbound northern lane. That had been one of the peculiar things he'd mentioned. Despite any semblance of law being gone for more than fifty years, for whatever reason, Drivers tended to respect I-80 for that. It had evolved that someone coming at you the wrong way was assumed to be a marauder or pirate, or simply an idiot worthy of soaking up some bullets.

"There." She pointed ahead at where a patch of crimson stuck out of the wavering tall grass. "I think I see a Roadhouse sign."

He hit the brake hard enough that she leaned forward. As soon as he got the car under fifty, he glided left and cut across the forest of wild grass between lanes. They rode the wrong lane for about twenty seconds before he veered into the exit lane for a rest stop. Her chest tightened up as two parked cars and a small pickup truck came into view, two with doors open. A long, bloody smear led from the driver's side door of the nearest car to a notch in the building over which hung a sign reading, 'restrooms.'

Pale brown-beige bricks at the corner bore several crimson handprints. The front bay window had been shot out and the red neon letters spelling out Roadhouse in a semi-cursive script sputtered and buzzed, the 'adh' in the middle dark.

Kevin wrung his hands on the wheel. "Well, that doesn't look good, does it?"

"Stop here," whispered Tris. She pulled the Beretta off her hip and opened her door.

"Can't be much more than ten at the most." Kevin pushed his door open as well and got out, leaving all the switches on.

She looked over the roof at him, eyebrows furrowed. "Please be careful."

He reached into the car and pulled out the Enclave rifle he'd kept from the 'deal' they'd interrupted. "Oh, I'm all about careful."

Tris slung her katana over her shoulder before easing the door closed. She advanced around the front bumper. "Stay back. Pick them off."

"If I hadn't seen you take out four guys in two seconds, I'd feel like a chicken." He shouldered the rifle, taking aim.

Tris grasped the Beretta in both hands. "The guys in the lab wear sealed suits because they're smart, not because they're chickens. You've already come *to* the place believing there are Infected here. That means a lot." Her heart swelled. "Okay. Going in."

She crept along the access lane for about thirty yards until it met the parking lot. With the building still a good fifty yards away, she glanced back at Kevin. He'd climbed up onto the Challenger's hood, flat on his stomach behind the rifle. He raised his hand for a second to wave. She returned it and faced forward again. The structure resembled a huge rectangle with a notch cut deep into the middle of the front under an overhang, where vending machines and bathrooms lurked. The left half contained the main room, bar and tables, while the wall to the right of the vending machine alcove had fourteen small doors like a motel.

Loose pebbles crunched under her shoes as she edged to the approximate halfway point in the lot. When she aimed the Beretta at the door, her combat headware gave her an estimated range of 28.4 yards in floating numbers hovering to the right of the gun.

"Hello?" yelled Tris. "Is there anyone still alive in there?"

A slam came from inside. Something glass broke on the second floor. A long, gurgly moan emanated from among the vending machines. Metal, perhaps a tire iron, clanged on pavement, though the way it echoed offered little clue as to which side of the building would erupt with Infected.

She raised the Beretta and took a step back. *Shit. Here they come.*

Motion in the window caught her eye first. Her cybernetic implants kicked in, slowing time to a near standstill. A pink-haired woman in armor made from old truck tires wobbled into view, her vacant eyes a clear sign of infection.

Tris whirled and aimed; as soon as the virtual crosshair centered on the woman's forehead, she fired. A coppery dot spiraled off into the distance. She adjusted her aim a few millimeters down and snapped off a second slug before the first made contact. Her bullet burrowed into the skull, and after what felt like two seconds, the back of the woman's head exploded. The second slug entered the face a finger's width left of the nostril.

One man jumped down from the roof, clawing at the pavement like an overexcited dog scrambling to start running without traction. Tris shot into his right collarbone, an angle she figured would put the slug into the heart. She spun away from him before he finished going limp, popping off one shot each at a pair of leather-jacket-wearing men shambling out from the bathroom corridor. Both had blood smeared over their faces, as though they'd been ears-deep in a pile of roadkill.

The *crack* of a rifle from behind went off. Within a second or two to her perception, a pointed slug sailed past Tris on the left at the speed of a fastball and put a ragged hole in the pink-haired woman's chest.

Better late than never. She smiled. Time resumed normal flow once her headware no longer detected threats. After a few quick steps toward the door, another Infected whipped around the far corner by the motel rooms, arms (and penis) swinging. A mangled woman, also nude, dragged herself along the ground behind him. Judging from the location of bite marks on the man, the woman had succumbed to the infection at a rather inconvenient moment.

Her neuronal booster activated again, like a pause button on reality; she shot the man once in the face and once in the chest. She aimed at the woman's head and fired twice. Eager not to have that image in her mind, Tris averted her gaze before the bullets struck.

An instant after the world resumed moving, Kevin fired. She didn't look at the *splat*, guessing that the man's head had burst open. A quick sprint brought her to the door. The *crack* of another rifle shot startled her, as did the subsequent fleshy *thump* overhead. Tris sidestepped to the right as a body in truck-tire armor fell from the roof and landed dead on his back. Arms rigid, she pointed the Beretta at a half-torn-off afro and exposed brain until her heart resumed beating.

"Roof's clear," yelled Kevin.

Bang. Tris pumped a bullet into the dead man's chest at the unexpected voice. She glanced to her left back at the car, a few stands of white hair floating across her view. Again, he held up one hand to wave.

"Damn. I didn't see him coming," she muttered while backing up to check the roof for more stragglers. Seeing none, she risked going inside. "Hello? Is anyone alive in here?"

Five bodies lay on the ground. The reek of whiskey, corpses, shit, and rotting food hung in the air. She suppressed the urge to gag and stepped around a puddle laced with shattered glass. Blood spattered a large mirror behind the bar counter, and thin trails of sunlight streamed in from bullet holes in the back wall and ceiling. A steady, repetitive clicking emanated from the control panel for the charging terminals. From the sound of it, the system detected full charges on multiple ports and tried to trip the circuit breaker, but it didn't work.

Fearing an explosion or fire, she rushed over and jumped the bar. A mocha-skinned woman about her age lay dead in a heap, the victim of a shotgun to the chest. Tris pulled four plastic switches down to power off the charge ports, startled by having to push with actual effort to make them flip. Three of them sparked. *Damn these are stiff... bet that woman needed a rubber mallet to work these breakers.*

She turned away from the no-longer-clicking panel and glanced over the room. The position of bodies on the ground plus all the bullet holes in the wall suggested a firefight where everyone shot at everyone. Her gaze followed bloody shuffle marks from a back hallway, into the room, and out the door. *An infected ran in and they all lost their minds trying to kill it.*

Tris eased herself back over the bar and checked the bodies for signs of Virus. The first man, somewhat pudgy and potbellied, lay on his side near the chair he'd slid out of. A few inches of shotgun poked out from under him. A human bite mark had opened a hole the size of a golf ball in his cheek, and the top of his head was blown out, suggesting a bullet to the skull from behind.

Odds were high Virus existed in the man's system, though he'd been killed before it could work. As much as her brain kept telling her the Infected were alive and not 'undead,' reassuring her he couldn't get back up, too many drivers swapping stories at night kept her on edge. *No weapon as effective as psychology.* She shivered.

Two skinny men lay three tables beyond the heavyset guy, each with a revolver drawn. One had claw gouges on his right forearm and his nose had been chomped off. Dark blood covered his face and upper chest, though it appeared to have come from outside—and matched splatter on the table. She pictured the other dead man shooting an Infected about to bite him, and the gore falling. Perhaps paranoia kicked in at all the viral blood going into a screaming mouth, as he'd not even made it out of the chair alive.

The second skinny man had at least thirteen bullet wounds in the chest and stomach, though no other corpse seemed the likely culprit. Number and spacing suggested automatic fire rather than someone unloading precision shots over and over again. Tris stepped past him to another woman in a green Kevlar vest slumped forward over a table. A dark 1911 .45 pistol lay a few inches from her crossed arms. The way her head rested upon them suggested she'd been crying when she'd died, though the odd greyish tinge to her otherwise dark brown skin eliminated any hope the woman had survived.

Tris put a hand on the woman's shoulder and pulled. The lifeless body sagged back over the seat, milky eyes staring at nothing. The only wound visible on her, a long ten-inch scratch down her right forearm dripped blood.

Oh shi—

The woman sprang from the chair, emitting an inhuman roar. Two fists slammed into Tris' chest, throwing her off her feet. Somewhere between the Infected's ridiculous strength hitting her and her back smacking into the wall twenty feet away, she lost the Beretta.

Unable to breathe in or out, Tris scrabbled at the floor, seeing stars.

The dark woman wobbled on her feet, staring at Tris as if the mere act of standing up had confused her. She canted her head to the side like a confused dog. A low, reverberating wheeze-growl slid out of her nostrils. Glowing spots dancing in her vision, Tris gasped. Pain surrounded her like a too-tight corset.

Fuck... ribs. Tris locked eyes with the Infected, huffing air in rapid, tiny breaths that didn't move her chest much. However long it would take the nanites to stitch broken ribs wouldn't be fast enough.

She eyed a boxy submachine gun on the floor six feet away from the entrance, which likely went sliding under a padded bench seat when its former owner died. Grunting, Tris let gravity pull her over to the right and dragged herself toward the weapon. Burning pain as though a dozen little monkeys savaged her sides with penknives made her scream.

The wall above her burst into a shower of splinters a split second before the report of a rifle shot echoed outside. The Infected let off a wheeze and staggered back, a single neat hole in the Kevlar vest the only evidence of a hit. The woman regarded the injury with confusion before a second shot gouged the vest low on her left side, failing to penetrate.

Tris walked on her elbows, trying to get within grabbing range of the submachine gun. A sudden enraged grunt from the Infected gave her a burst of adrenaline, chasing away pain and pushing her the last foot and a half forward. Her hand made contact with the grip at the same instant a painful, crushing grip seized her left calf.

Another rifle shot preceded a sharp *thwap* from the Kevlar. The woman lunged downward, mouth opening, pulling Tris back by the leg, her other hand going for the head. Somewhere outside, Kevin shouted and the rapid scuff of boots on pavement followed.

Tris howled from the agony in her chest as she pushed at the floor to roll over. The Infected overpowered her easily. Even without being hurt, her neural amplifiers only gave her strength in the upper six percent of human capability—certainly not superhuman. Her palms slid on the bloody floorboards. Every muscle in her back locked and tensed as teeth drew closer to the side of her neck.

Panic came and went. Hot tears streamed down her face. She stopped trying to push up and let her body fall flat, face down. Reaching up behind her head with the Mac-10, she squeezed the trigger and hoped it had ammo.

The weapon fired.

She cringed at the rain of brass on the back of her head and screamed when a hot casing rolled under the neck of her shirt. The Infected released its grip and fell backward. She let off the trigger and forced herself over onto her back. The spray of .45 slugs had shredded the woman's left shin, shattering the bone and making her fall over. Stiff arms flailed as if trying to grab the air for a handhold.

Kevin rushed in the door, almost tripping over Tris' feet. He skidded to a halt, aimed, and ripped a long burst of about fifteen rounds into the woman's Kevlar vest. She went still with a long, heavy sigh, blood burbling up out of her mouth.

"Tris!" He took a knee at her side.

"I'm..." She coughed. "Ow. Shit."

"Saw you go flying through the scope, but the sunlight messed with the Nightvision... had to guess."

"You hit her twice." Tris gritted her teeth and let the mac-10 clatter to the floor. "Careful in here... blood everywhere."

Kevin hovered over her, looking around for wounds. "What happened?"

She recounted getting slammed in the chest hard enough to fly into the wall. "Broke some ribs... feels like all of them. I wanna lie down, but I shouldn't put pressure on them. Help me up?"

Kevin grasped her hands and eased her upright, causing an intense flare of agony in her torso that almost made her piss herself. Teeth clenched, she stifled a scream. He held on, trying to move as little as possible, his eyes wide with worry.

"Tris..."

She bit her lip and shook her head, fighting to weather the blinding pain. "Just... need a minute."

In the subsequent silence, the soft squealing of knitting bones crept up into her skull. A maddening tickle replaced burning. He held her gingerly, until the pins-and-needles feeling subsided to soreness.

"It's done." She tested a deep breath. It hurt, but not to the point she refused to breathe.

"How long is this blood going to stay infectious?" Kevin glanced around. "Are we going to have to burn this place to the ground?"

"How charitable do you feel?" She grumbled. "It's warm, so probably twenty-seven weeks if we leave it alone. If by some miracle they have bleach, I can clean it." *Fuck, what am I thinking? No one out here has made bleach for fifty years... it'd be useless.* "Wait, no... moonshine?"

He chuckled. "Seems almost disrespectful to burn down a roadhouse, even if it is full of Virus."

Tris pulled him outside. "I'll see what I can do." She unbuttoned her jeans and stooped to pull open the Velcro on her shoes.

"Uhh, what are you doing?"

She peered up at him. "I like this outfit. Don't want to have to burn it. Either I strip to clean, and ride home in my own clothes, or I clean and ride home naked."

Kevin gestured at the building. "Might be clothes in the store."

"Wouldn't that be stealing from the Roadhouse?" She shot him a coy wink. "I thought that was against the Code."

"At the moment, this is an empty building. Owner's dead, and uhh, check your legs." He pointed.

Tris squirmed around and looked down. The backs of both her legs looked like she'd been standing a few feet away from an exploding blood balloon. "Shit." She pinched the bridge of her nose, remembering going crazy with the mac-10 over her shoulder. "Oh well. How's the shirt?" She held her arms out to the sides and did a slow turn.

"Spatter on the back."

Tris hung her head. Waist-long strands of snow-white hair glided to the left in the breeze.

"I'm going to enjoy the ride home." Kevin winked.

"Now I have to disinfect myself too." She scowled. "At least I won't have to pay three coins a minute for water while I shower."

He laughed.

Grumbling, she headed into the building. After retrieving her Beretta from the floor, she walked past the counter into a short hallway. On the left, two steel grey doors with round windows led to a huge kitchen, doors farther down on the right led to a bathroom and the office.

Tris stopped at the office, finding it empty and filled with the scent of smoldering electronics. The worst thing in there appeared to be dust, so she eased herself to sit on the edge of the shredded leather chair (careful not to let any blood touch it) and checked over the security system. She tapped one foot while trying to breathe some semblance of life into the digital video recorder. No matter what she pushed, the hardware remained dead. From the amount of clutter piled on top of it, it had been useless for a long time.

"Dammit." She grasped the radio. "Hey, this thing working?"

After a moment, a familiar voice replied with "Who is this?"

She'd heard him before when Kevin used the radio, but couldn't put a name to him. "Uhh, just a traveler. Stopped at the roadhouse near Hastings Nebraska."

"What's going on there?" asked an older-sounding woman. "No one been hearin' from Sierra for 'couple days now."

Tris bowed her head. "Is Sierra a youngish woman with coffee skin and short hair?"

"Yeah," said the man.

She exhaled. "I'm sorry if you knew her. She's... gone. Everyone here's dead."

About nine different voices gasped back over the radio.

"Son of a fucking bitch," croaked a gravelly voice. "Someone's gonna burn hard."

"Infected." Tris cleared her throat. "Before you ask what happened... I can't tell. The recorders are dead. Looks like the equipment's been dead for months. I... honestly it looks like it never worked."

"Infected?" asked a young woman. "That's..."

"Fuckin' a right." The new male voice grumbled something inaudible. "You sound young, girl. Best get your ass outta there."

Tris smiled. "I'm okay." She rubbed her bruised and tender ribs. "Mostly."

"You gonna get turned," yelled the older woman. Beth?

"Not something I need to worry about." She flicked at the mic. She didn't want to say her name over the radio in case Nathan happened to somehow have a way to listen in. "I'm here with Kevin. Shepherd lost a sheep and wants to kill it."

"Oh, hey there, girl," said Beth. "Got ya loud and clear. How bad is it?"

Tris described the scene. "I'm gonna burn the bodies. Put out the word this place should be left alone for a week or two. I'll get started cleaning this shit up, assuming there's some 'shine around to neutralize the virus."

Numerous voices replied with various forms of assent.

She hung the mic on the hook mounted to the desk and headed back to the restaurant room.

Beretta up, she headed through to a hallway in the rear that passed another pair of bathrooms. After a ninety-degree right, she found two more corpses slumped against the wall, a pair of slender women in super-short skirts and halter-tops, both with thin scarves wound about their necks in what had been an effort to hide bite marks. One looked in her fifties, the other less than half that.

I can guess what these two did here... Only reason anyone would bother with cosmetics.

A few steps past them, she found gold. Or at least the store. As good as gold.

She tried the knob; locked. After removing her tools from the heel of her left shoe, she made short work of the deadbolt and repacked them.

Inside, shelves held shirts, pants, skirts, several pairs of boots as well as sneakers, four handguns, a couple knives, a box of road flares... and four steamer trunks' worth of who-knows-what.

"Wow. I hope he doesn't want to keep all this shit; it's not gonna fit in the car."

She grabbed a hideous orange tee shirt, which would cover her to mid-thigh, and a pair of holey sweat pants. Either of which she'd have no trouble burning on general principle, even without Infected blood all over them. Behind the bar out front, she found several gallon jugs of clear liquid, which turned out to be moonshine strong enough to wilt her hair from opening the cap. A board mounted to the wall had twenty-three keys hanging out of twenty-four hooks. Room 24's was missing. She grabbed the key for Room 1 and ran across the parking lot to the first motel door. The small space did have what she'd hoped for, a shower. She left the hideous clothes on the bed for later, and returned to the restaurant.

A storeroom behind the counter area had a couple of brooms as well as a mop and bucket. She dragged the bucket to the bar and dumped in two gallons of moonshine before poking her head out the front door. "Hey."

Kevin, who'd been facing the road, whirled around. "Hey." He smiled the kind of smile that said he'd been afraid she wouldn't come back out. "Done?"

She frowned. "Not yet. That dumpster over there will be perfect for getting rid of the bodies. Any of those cars run ethanol? I'm gonna use up most of the 'shine on the blood inside."

"I'll check." He slung the rifle over his shoulder and headed toward the cars.

One by one, Tris carried or dragged corpses to the dumpster. In the middle of the parking lot, she relieved them of useful objects (weapons, ammo, etc.), but didn't bother taking any of their clothing. The funny looks Kevin shot her while watching her wrangle three-hundred pound men off the ground made her laugh. *You'd think he'd be used to this by now.* After shoving the pudgy one who'd likely killed Sierra with the shotgun over the rim of the dumpster, she stared at her hands. *I wonder how long the enhancements will last?* The idea of being 'super-granny' got another laugh out of her, which in turn caused Kevin to look worried.

"You're enjoying that way too much."

"Random unrelated thought." She winked before a somber realization came on. Normal Enclave citizens didn't get wired up; they reserved enhancements like she had for the security forces... and apparently self-guided resistance-murdering bombs. *Nathan really is insane, spending so much to amp me up only to kill me. Guess he wanted me to believe.*

He walked over with a fifteen-gallon metal can. "Found some eth on the GTO."

"Nice. Just the two prostitutes left and we can light it."

Kevin set his hands on his hips and looked down at the can of ethanol. "Poor bastards."

Tris hurried back inside and carried the dead women one after the next to the dumpster. With the last of the bodies piled in, Kevin emptied the entire can of ethanol over them and set it off with a barbeque grill electric lighter.

"Where'd that come from?" asked Tris.

"The GTO had a bunch of camping supplies in the trunk." He pocketed the lighter. "No idea how much battery it's got left, but it's mine now."

They both backed away from the dumpster as greasy black smoke spilled forth. She frowned again at how bloody she'd gotten and took a step away from him.

"Gonna clean up and shower."

He nodded. "I'll, uhh, keep watching." He hefted the rifle and resumed a position by the door.

Tris spent the better part of the next hour swishing the mop around over bloodstains. She hoped the eye-wateringly potent moonshine would kill most of the Virus. With any luck, people wouldn't show up here for at least a few days, and any viruses that escaped her mop would go inert. With the cleaning done, she walked outside.

"Inside should be relatively safe. You want me to loot the store?"

He slung the rifle over his shoulder and jogged up to her. "If you think I'm okay to walk through there, I'll grab what I can."

"Don't lick the bloodstains. Otherwise, you should be fine." She winked.

He shuddered. "Right. I'll try to resist the temptation."

She ran to Room 1. Once inside, she stripped and stuffed her shirt and jeans in the sink before dousing them with moonshine. Leaving them to soak, she hopped in the shower. After a normal wash, she poured moonshine over her head and down her back, clamping her eyes closed as tight as she could. A little burn seeped in, forcing her to stick her face in the water stream earlier than she'd have liked, but soon, she felt confident her body carried no trace of viral danger.

After giving her shoes a once-over with a moonshine-soaked rag, she put on the awful orange shirt and sweatpants. She'd have preferred to wear *them* to do the cleaning and toss them in with the burning bodies, but with her other clothes tainted, she had to suffer. The idea of being stuck in the car naked with Kevin for four hours excited her as much as it embarrassed her. *Of course if I did that, we'd run into someone... or he'd watch me instead of the road.*

She drained the sink, ran hot water and soap over her bloodied clothing, and rinsed them before wringing them out as best she could. On the stoop, she glanced left at the row of pale blue doors, and felt stupid. "Shit. One key was gone."

In the time she'd showered, Kevin had moved the Challenger up close to the front door. The trunk sat open, as did the driver side door. From the looks of it, he'd been stuffing things in wherever he could. She stood motionless until he emerged with an armload of jeans and cowboy boots.

"Hey..." Tris approached. "What about these cars?"

Kevin glanced at her and overacted being blinded by her orange shirt. She returned a playful frown. His chuckle died to a somber glance toward the steady column of black smoke rising from the dumpster. "I suppose they're salvage now, but there's only two of us."

"That white GTO is nice."

"Ethanol eater." Kevin grumbled. "On second thought, it would be hard to sell it. Not too many 'houses have eth. Tends to be a do-it-yourselfer's car."

The other vehicles, all smaller and mismatched from parts of various makes and models, were about the same level of *meh*. One green thing, mostly VW Beetle, didn't even look like it would survive the ride back to Rawlins.

"Oh well." She put her damp clothes on the floor by the passenger seat. "One of the room keys was off the board. I'm gonna check it. Might be something salvageable in there."

"Who had the room?" asked Kevin.

She nudged the Challenger's passenger door closed and enjoyed a long breath of moonshine-fume free air. "No idea. None of the dead people had the key."

He glanced at the motel half of the building. "Be careful. Could be someone there."

"An Infected would've come running, and a person would've come to see what all the shooting was."

Kevin stared at her. "Please."

She pulled the Beretta out of her holster, feeling silly for wearing a gun belt with sweat pants. "Okay."

Tris advanced along the little sidewalk wrapping around the building, holding her breath in a futile effort to weather the stench of burning flesh and ethanol still wafting from the dumpster. The metal *boomed* and *clanked* from the heat within. She made a quick pass over the vending machine area and public bathrooms, finding little of interest. At the start of the motel half, she skipped Room 1 and peered in the window of the next space. Clumps of green weeds forced their way up from cracks in the wraparound sidewalk, and the occasional tarnished shell casing, condom wrapper, or crushed syringe littered the ground.

One by one, she checked windows, confirming the rooms empty until she reached #12 at the end. She hesitated after rounding the corner, spotting a small pickup parked all the way down the row by the door to #24. Matte charcoal grey, it bore the same Roadhouse logo on the door as hung over the restaurant entrance. A canvas tarp held down by bungees covered the bed, which looked empty from a distance. Plates of steel armor reinforced the cabin, and it had a plow-like mechanism on the front covered in spikes. The slope seemed intended to cause obstacles (people dumb enough not to be in a vehicle) to bounce away rather than push snow.

Tris disregarded rooms thirteen to twenty-three, and headed in a brisk jog to the last one. The door abutted the jamb without closing all the way. She aimed at the knob.

"Hello? Is someone in there?"

After waiting a minute in silence, she nudged the door open with her foot, Beretta raised. A wash of corpse-rot brought on a gag reflex so fast she found herself swooning to the side against the beige brick wall before her brain could process the smell. After dry heaving a couple of times, she sucked in a breath and held it.

Amid a quaint little bedroom with powder blue walls and curtains, a shirtless man in black jeans and cowboy boots lay on the bed, arms out to his sides. Purple blotched his skin, darkest around prominent bite marks on his neck, shoulder, and left forearm. His lips curled in a rictus grin, indifferent to a cluster of flies buzzing about his face, crawling in and out of his nostrils and climbing over his teeth. A thick handlebar moustache came alive with insects, and his gut swelled in protest of his still-cinched belt. Five or six tiny bullet holes, as though he'd been stabbed with a pencil, dotted his chest.

Tris covered her mouth and swallowed vomit. The air hung so think with stench, the flavor of corpse settled on her tongue.

Near her on the left, a thick leather jacket draped over the back of a chair. Decorative red lettering covered it from shoulder to shoulder with word 'Roadhouse' over the illustration of a building with a few cars in front of it. Beneath the picture, block letters read, 'Amarillo – 2061.'

A belt with two empty holsters sat rolled up on the cushion. Past the chair on the floor, a skimpy white dress covered a pair of high heels and two flip-flops. A scattering of small-caliber brass littered the carpet at the foot of the bed, likely belonging to a little chrome handgun dropped near the bathroom doorway. Tris put a hand on her neck, thinking of the prostitutes and their scarves.

"Stupid bitches didn't tell anyone..." *No surprise there. That would've gotten them shot.*

She hovered at the foot of the bed, staring into rotten cloudy eyes. *He's the source. Shit. I just cleaned myself up.* The body looked as though it had been rotting in place for a few days. She wanted to carry him out on the mattress, but it would never fit through the doorway without upending it. Needing an escape from the stink, she hurried outside with one arm braced over her mouth, coughing into the crook of her elbow. After two gulps of clean air, she let go and fell to her knees, vomiting bile.

Kevin jogged around the corner, rifle poised. His 'combat ready' posture changed to one of concern, and he sprinted to her side.

"I'm okay... just, disgusting."

He leaned up and away, peering at the doorway. "Oh, fuck."

She sat back on her heels, coughed, and wiped her mouth. "I never saw someone so into the whole Roadhouse thing that they had a jacket made. What's Amarillo 2061 mean?"

"That's the year the first one opened. Only site inspectors wear those jackets…" Some of the color in his cheeks faded.

"Site inspector?"

He advanced to the door, regarded the jacket, and staggered back with a hand over his face. "Dammit. Yeah. He was a site inspector. Amarillo sends them out every now and then to check up on places. Mostly, they're trying to sell more shit, but they can post bounties or assess fees. If you really piss 'em off, they can even revoke a franchise. Lot of 'em act power-drunk."

"I think he's"—Tris coughed and gagged a little more—"the source of the Virus here… came in sick but not insane. Probably turned while the whores were in his room, bit them. They panicked, tried to hide it and wound up taking out the whole place."

He sighed. "That's not good."

She smirked at him.

"No, I mean… he could've come from anywhere. Site inspectors drive all over the place."

Tris tapped her foot. "Maybe he tried to take a shortcut through a big city?"

He nodded. "Yeah… probably. He still infectious?"

"Highly. Of course, you'd have to get body fluids in your eyes, mouth, or an open wound… it's not aerosolized."

"What?"

She grumbled. "Can't breathe it."

"Oh."

"Guess I'm taking another shower." She handed the Beretta over and reached to take her shirt off.

"Wait. What are you going to do?"

"Drag him outside and light him on fire… then the mattress."

He pointed at the room. "If you drag him, you'll need to rip up the rug. Use the window."

She glanced at the large window, long devoid of glass and covered with a cage of welded rebar. "Good idea."

After unscrewing the bars from the window, she stripped, piling her clothes and shoes well out of the way of contamination. Tris stomped inside and cleared a table plus two chairs out of the way. Holding her breath, she pushed the bed against the wall by the window and ran around to the outside. This side of the building had the sun for most of the day, making the sidewalk feel like she walked on Sang's grill. Kevin hung back a good ways, keeping an eye out for people.

She gathered the bedding and pulled, dragging the body toward the window until gravity took over. Tris jumped away shrieking as the corpse lurched toward her. His back remained adhered to the sheets while the rest of him slid downward, rolling out of the skin like an ill-fitting suit tearing open. He hit the sidewalk on his chest with an echoing splat, arms flailing limp. On impact, his distended belly ruptured with a torrent of purple-black ooze spraying from the navel. A similar stream fountained out of his mouth and nostrils.

The next thing Tris knew, she slouched on the ground with a lap full of vomit. Kevin, about twenty feet away, also hunched over a puddle of puke on the paving. A massive swarm of flies migrated out of the room and surrounded the body, buzzing and whirling about. They landed for a second or two at a time before erupting in a cloud and resettling.

She tried to say 'fuck this, burn it here,' but only managed to get a tendril of bile out of her mouth while gagging. The touch of liquid hitting her breast made her look down, and the sight of dark reddish-brown flecks from the splatter all over her triggered another wave of dry heaving. The stench in the air defied comprehension; every attempt to breathe made her want to throw up again.

Tris crawled away in a random direction until the air no longer tasted like death.

"Tris..."

"F-fuck... this place." She shivered. "I'm done. Charity over."

He reached to take her hand, but she waved him off. "Don't. I don't want you getting sick. Put my stuff in Room 1. I'll be able to stand in a few minutes."

"Okay." Kevin walked off.

She fought the urge to wipe her face, and sprawled there breathing for a little while. Eventually, she got up, held her breath, and dragged the mattress outside to the lot. Dark ooze had stained through to the box spring, which she also removed. After quite a bit of mental preparation, she gingerly grasped the body's wrist. Her fingers squished into the decaying skin, compressing slimy muscle with the consistency of mucus. She dragged the remains onto the mattress pile, a safe distance from the wall for burning, and staggered off into a heap where she dry heaved more.

Kevin returned with another jug of moonshine. He didn't wait for her to move, and doused the soon-to-be-pyre liberally. Still unable to talk, she flung her arm around in a disorganized wave at the bloody mess on the sidewalk. He took the hint and poured moonshine all over it, rinsing the bloody sluice into the blacktop.

Evidently trusting brick and sidewalk not to transmit fire to the building, he lit the puddle. Blue flames spread over the ground, bedding, and corpse with a soft *whoosh*. She stared transfixed at the fire, unable to look away from the body. Not until cold wet met her hands did she notice he stood over her, pouring yet more moonshine on her.

Tris held her hands (the bloodiest part of her) out for a rinse, then stood and let him cover her front and back with the eye-watering liquid. Not wanting to be anywhere near open flame while soaked with homemade moonshine, she ran for Room 1 and the safety of a second tepid shower. Compared to the freeze of evaporating alcohol all over her, the lukewarm shower wrapped her in comfort.

Soon, wet but dressed, she met Kevin by the Challenger, which he'd finished stuffing full of gear from this roadhouse's store. The place had been light on weapons, though it had more clothes than she'd seen in one place before.

"After dealing with this, I'm going to raid the stash." She pointed at the trunk. "Saw a couple things there I liked."

Kevin raised his hands as if in surrender. "Keep it all if you want. You fuckin' earned it. Jesus. I'm going to remember that stink for the rest of my life."

She leaned on him. "Yeah."

He cradled her ribs. "You okay?"

"Hungry, but… yeah." When he looked at the door, she shook her head. "No. I don't trust anything in there. I can wait 'til we get home."

"Want me to grab one of those cars?"

He surveyed the line for a moment. "Nah. Ain't that desperate for coins anymore… besides, Amarillo will reclaim that truck. Couldn't sell it if I wanted to."

She gave him a quick kiss. "Sounds good. Let's get the hell out of here."

"I hear that." He slapped her on the butt and fast-walked to the Challenger.

6

SINKING FEELING

Kevin backed the Challenger into his garage a few minutes past three in the morning. Tris curled up asleep next to him, having been out for at least the past two hours. Unloading could wait until after they'd slept. He rolled the car backward until the tires hit the wheel stops, and shut it down. Yawning, he got out and safed all four mounted guns before putting the ammo in a locked cabinet and plugging in the charging cable.

He carried Tris across the parking lot to the main building, and inside up the stairs to their room. About twenty seconds after he set her on the bed, Sang appeared in the doorway with a sawed-off shotgun.

"Oh. Mr. Kevin." He lowered the weapon and bowed. "I hear someone walk in."

He offered a weary smile. "Thanks for watchin' the place."

"You are welcome." Sang smiled and backed out, closing the door.

Kevin pulled Tris' shoes off before stripping himself, and climbed into bed next to her.

SUNLIGHT ON THE SIDE OF HIS FACE DRAGGED HIM OUT OF SLEEP, ALONE IN bed. He groaned and sat up, scratching his head for a few minutes. A sniffle from the hallway got him moving. After grabbing his jeans, he ambled out the door, hooked a right, and leaned into the 'employee bathroom' at the end of the upstairs hallway.

Tris sat on the toilet, pants around her ankles, elbows on her knees with her face in her hands. She either wept in silence, or had recently stopped crying.

"Hey…"

She looked up, red around the eyes. "Hey." Sniffle.

"What's wrong?" He walked over and put a hand on her shoulder.

She put a hand on top of his. "Nightmare. I was like eight or nine again… the day they took me away from my dad. Only they didn't put me with that creepy couple who acted like my father never existed… I wound up getting dragged out into the desert and left tied to a pole. I barely got loose before Infected came out of nowhere… lots of running and I got cornered. That's when I woke up."

He squeezed her shoulder. "Ouch. When I was a kid, I used to have dreams kinda like that… getting chased by Infected. Only, I always run across the grasslands outside the settlement where I lived as a kid. In the dream, I wake up and everyone around me is Infected. Like to say I shot them all, but… nah. I ran like a little girl."

She poked him. "Not all little girls are the scream-and-run type."

Kevin chuckled. She smiled at him for a moment before standing into a kiss, not bothering to pull her sweat pants up. Kissing and pawing at each other, they made their way back to the bed. She walked out of the sweats, leaving them in the hall. All the pent up energy he'd devoted to worrying about her burst in a waterfall of passion. A good half hour of lovemaking culminated with him on his back, Tris riding cowgirl, until she collapsed as out of breath as he felt.

After a long while of lying in each other's arms, he got up and dressed. She followed suit, and trailed after him downstairs to the front room.

Fitch and Neeley, having returned from their run, occupied one of the tables in the back. At Kevin's entrance, they both began a slow clap. Three other men, each at their own tables, joined in. Tris' cheeks turned pink as Kevin rendered a stageman's bow.

"You want food, right?" yelled Sang. "You work up good appetite."

"Yep." Kevin smiled.

Her stomach growled. "Oh yeah. Extra toast for me."

She sat on her old office chair behind the counter while Kevin leaned on it. Fitch scratched at a grey streak along the left side of his afro and stood. He approached with a hesitant look, not quite making eye contact.

"What went wrong?" asked Kevin.

"Oh, run was fine." He dropped a pouch of coins between them. "No trouble with it."

Kevin dumped the coins out, counted them, and took his six percent. He put his part in the box, the seller's part back in the pouch, and pushed Fitch's share back to him. "So what's with the mug? You look like you're about to tell me something I don't wanna hear."

Neeley fidgeted a bolt around his grease-stained fingers, staring at the table where he remained a good fifteen feet from the counter. The sinewy, scrawny man also seemed afraid to make eye contact.

Sang set two plates in the hole between front room and kitchen, smiled at Kevin, and returned to his cot.

Kevin put the plate with double toast in front of Tris, then leaned over his scrambled eggs and sausage. "Okay, out with it."

Fitch picked at his shirt. The man had to be getting close to forty, and had Kevin by two inches in height, but gave off a feeling like a kid about to get yelled at. "Uhh, we stopped in Hagerman."

Kevin froze.

Tris glanced at him, worry in her eyes. "Wayne hasn't said anything on the radio in a while."

"Was a fucking horror show in Hastings." Kevin prodded eggs with his fork. "Infected."

Fitch's eyebrows climbed, though he brightened up. "No signs of anything like that. Place just looked abandoned. Maybe he's doing a run himself?"

"What for?" asked Kevin. Hunger overwhelmed worry and he shoveled a huge forkful into his mouth. "He's... mmm..." He chewed more and swallowed. "He's set. Gets all the coin he needs from the 'house."

"Dunno, man." Neeley stood and wandered up to the counter, hands in the pockets of his grey workman's pants. "Bee ain't even there. Don't feel like Wayne ta leave the place empty."

"No... No it doesn't." Kevin squinted at the door. *Road trip time.* He looked around the room. His Roadhouse. His dream... Any time he left the property, he might come back to ruins at worst or an idiot with a gun at best. Everything he'd ever wanted was right here. Wayne could take care of himself. Wayne taught him everything he knew about the road. The thought that the old man had been 'kinda-sorta' a father figure brought on guilt. Fitch was right. Wayne wouldn't just up and leave. "I'm gonna check it out."

Fitch and Neeley nodded in unison. "Sounds like a good idea."

"When are we leaving?" asked Tris.

Kevin put a hand on the back of her head and pulled her cheek to his chest. "You wanna stay here and watch the place? This'll be a couple days out."

"Sang?" She looked up at him.

"Yeah?" asked Sang.

"Damn he's got good ears." Kevin chuckled. "Nothing, man. Just talking about takin' another road trip."

"Ah. Okay," yelled the cook.

Kevin let go of her so she could keep devouring her food. "We just left him alone for a day… it's a lot to manage this place alone."

"What… the 'little woman' stays home where it's safe?" Her smile took much of the accusation out of her tone.

"No… That's not it at all. Though, I like the sound of you staying safe."

She knocked a playful punch into his shoulder. "Want me barefoot in the kitchen too?"

"Huh?" Kevin looked at her. "What's barefoot have to do with being in the kitchen?"

"Oh." She held up a bit of sausage on her fork. "Right. You didn't study history."

Confused, he continued to stare at her until it became clear no more detailed explanation was coming. "You guys interested in running down to Ween's? Got a big ol' box of brass. At an eyeball, probably three or four hundred coins' worth. Need someone to run it down there and see if the old coot's willing to buy."

Fitch scratched at his beard stubble. "You know I could watch the place for you. Neeley could handle a run like that solo. Say twenty percent of the take on the brass?"

Neeley nodded.

"Never knew you wanted a 'house, Fitch." Kevin chuckled.

"Well…" A deep, bass laugh bounced off the walls. "Been an idea, but I ain't never had the patience to save up no ten grand."

"The building near Hastings is open." Tris winked.

"Infected?" Fitch held up one finger. "In the immortal words of Socrates: fuck that."

Tris furrowed her eyebrows. "I don't think he said that."

Neeley snorted, laughing.

Kevin held an appraising glance on Fitch while pondering the idea. Of all the drivers who'd come through on a regular basis, he was the most pragmatic. Easily one of the oldest. Neeley had a habit of being a little skittish, but the two worked well together. Perhaps the younger man's energy is what kept Fitch from 'settling in' with his own 'house. Both respected the Code, so it struck him as unlikely he'd risk getting on the wrong side of Amarillo by ripping Kevin off. "Alright."

Fitch offered a handshake, which Kevin accepted. "Done. Anything particular I should keep an eye out for?"

Kevin gestured at the corridor right of the counter. "If someone wants supplies, charge whatever you think's reasonable. Got a truck, SUV, I'm lookin' to offload as well. If anyone's interested, tell 'em 3500 coins, but I'd let it go for two. Don't commit to anything 'til I come back. Jobs can wait a couple days. Oh, Athena might show up before I do." He flipped open the marble notebook and pointed the entry for the run she'd taken.

"Got it." Fitch patted the counter twice. "Go on and put yer coinbox somewhere secure. I 'preciate the trust, but don't want it on me if somethin' funky happens."

Kevin smiled. "That's the change box, not my vault... but if it makes you feel better, I can lock it up."

"Never get too far away from what you ain't willin' ta lose." Fitch winked.

Kevin smiled at Tris. "That's a good philosophy."

Her cheeks tinged with a little blush.

"When you two headin' out?" asked Fitch.

"Where's that brass?" Neeley perked up and looked around behind the counter.

Kevin penned in an entry to the ledger regarding the shipment of empty brass to Ween, wrote '300-400 coins' in the value box, and added 'Neeley' as the driver. "Be right out with it."

"I'll get started on unloading that stuff from Hastings." Tris set the empty plate in the kitchen hole as she got up.

"'Kay. I'll be there as soon as I get Neeley on his way." Kevin gave Fitch a nod and jogged to the back storeroom by the office where he'd put the footlocker.

7

NO ROAD LEADS HOME

Enough time had passed since Kevin laid eyes on Hagerman, New Mexico, that it felt strange to see the place. The quiet streets, dust clouds, and tumbleweeds looked like something out of a fond dream, a peek at a time that no longer existed. All the time he'd spent here, daydreaming about saving up enough money to buy a Roadhouse of his own, yet it felt somehow wrong to be there again. Like he desecrated an old, sacred memory.

A couple of News hung out among their bikes in front of the Bobcat market.

Tris still had the same look on her face she'd had leaving Nederland earlier that morning. Considering the trip's midway point roughly landed nearby, and Tris insisted, they'd spent the night with Bill and Ann. Zoe had been thrilled to see them again, and happier still to get her doll back. Cody, her brother, was more subdued, but given how their exodus from Chicago had gone… Kevin would've been worried had the kid not been affected by it somehow. Zoe's mild whine that she hadn't gotten to shoot any raiders lately unnerved him, as did the reason she hadn't being no raiders had attacked—not that she'd been deemed too little. Her father didn't seem to have a problem with a nine-year-old helping to defend the town.

Kevin wrung his hands on the steering wheel. *Guess he figures being shot is better than being taken by bandits.*

"What's got that look on you?" Tris sat up and peered out at the passing city. "I don't see anything out there."

"Just thinking about Zoe. Aside from you, I'm not used to people being that happy to see me."

"Well, you did bring her brother and father back alive." Tris smiled. "And I know you hate that they let her carry a gun."

"It makes her a target. Anyone with a weapon, even a kid, will get shot at." He turned onto the road leading to Wayne's Roadhouse. The sight of his former haunt chilled him. Not a single car sat out front and no lights were on.

"You make it sound like she's charging into battle." Tris smiled. "I think it's cute that she aims for legs so she doesn't kill anyone."

Kevin glanced at her. "You've got a pretty strange idea of cute."

The car came to a halt in his beloved space, the same parking spot he'd gotten into fights over. He hopped out, walking on autopilot around to the charging panel to plug in. Tris stood with her arms crossed, waiting. Once he'd connected, he started for the door.

"No rifle?" asked Tris.

He looked back at her. "I..." He glanced at the building. "Never even thought of walking in here as even close to dangerous."

"Has it ever been this quiet?" she asked.

"No." He pulled his armored jacket away from the .45 on his hip and crept up onto the porch.

"Hope I don't break the railing again."

"I'll laugh later." Kevin pushed the door aside and entered the old, familiar room. A trace of gunpowder hung in the air, though weak enough not to make him worry right away. "Wayne?" He approached the counter. "Bee?"

Tris, Beretta drawn, cut left and went around behind the counter. "Couple of .45 brass on the floor back here." She leaned down and reached for something. A *click* preceded a weak electric hum. "Turned on the port to charge. Panel's green."

He nodded and swiveled to check the back corner, around the table where he'd killed the bandits who'd abducted her. His memory of the indignant look she'd given him when he'd refused to untie her almost pushed a smile out from under the heavy blanket of worry. He spun at the scrape of a curtain sliding on a rod in time to catch Tris ducking into the back office past a hanging wall of camouflage cloth. *I'm too jumpy.* Kevin let out a mental sigh, and headed for the corridor by the bathrooms.

Wayne's old beat-up brown armor, a Kevlar vest married to a duster coat, remained untouched in its display case between the bathroom doors. Someone had added arms and a smile to the sharpie-markered penis on the men's room door. The throat-scalding awfulness in the air proved Bee still refused to go in there and clean it.

"Wayne?" yelled Kevin. "Bee?" He pushed open both bathroom doors, but found no one other than the fuzzy black mass growing out of the toilet. "Something's wrong."

A short burst of automatic gunfire came from behind him, followed an instant later by a sharp yelp of surprise from Tris. He pivoted on his heel and sprinted into the main room, finding no trace of her or anything else.

"Tris?" he yelled.

"Downstairs!" Her shout sounded equally strong below the floor as it did from behind the camouflage curtain.

Hearing her alive got his heart beating again. He ran through the curtain into the back room, almost wiping out on a bunched up throw rug. Inches from flying face first into an open rectangular hatch about the size of a normal doorway, he caught himself on the side of a desk. Tris curled up in a ball on the floor at the bottom of a handmade wooden stairway, covered in a light dusting of splinters. The steps had blood all over them, continuing in a trail past Tris into the underground space. A matching bloody drag trail continued deeper into the room past the hole in the floor, to a door that opened to the outside along the left side of the building.

"Shit," he muttered before raising his voice. "Wayne's got auto-turrets down there."

Tris looked up at him. "I noticed."

He hadn't seen inside the back room of Wayne's except for once when he'd been seventeen and too ballsy to care going in here might get him shot. As best he could remember, the place hadn't changed at all. The concealed stairs, however, caught him off guard. He'd known Wayne had a basement, but had no idea where the access was. He'd expected something sneakier than a trap door under a rug from Wayne.

Tris sat up and ran her fingers through her hair. She looked up at him, her face drawn with worry. "I think Wayne's in there..."

Kevin eased himself down the stairs, took her hand, and pulled her upright into an embrace. "What happened?"

"I don't know. Didn't get much of a look before my neuralware kicked in and I had to duck. If I wasn't boosted, I'd have been dead. He's behind the turrets. I think he's hiding from something."

The stairwell led down to a small room about the size of a prison cell with a corridor to the right at the corner. Cinder block walls covered in moisture and moss flavored the air with dirt. A scattering of shell casings littered the ground, most of which appeared to be 9mm. He started toward the corridor, but Tris yanked him back at the same instant he noticed the bullet-gouged wood support column at the corner.

"Don't poke your head out there or it'll get shot off."

"Is Wayne alive?"

Tris offered only a helpless look.

Dammit, Wayne... what the hell? "Did you see enough to get an idea how to shut it off?"

"Aside from shooting them?" She stooped to pick her Beretta up.

"What if we kill the master circuit breaker?"

Tris raised her arms and let them flap against her sides. "If I designed turrets like that, I'd make damn sure they had battery backups. Killing the power is the *first* thing anyone would try."

Kevin leaned up to the corner but didn't go past it. "Wayne?"

Tris came up behind him. "I'll shoot them out. If he's hurt, we can't waste time."

"Don't get shot."

She smiled. "Now that I'm ready for it, I'm good."

"If I have to choose between you or Wayne, there's no choice. You don't have to do this."

Tris sniffled. "I love you, too. I'm not... too worried."

He shrugged off his armored jacket and held it up, open. "Just in case."

She put it on, looking smaller for wearing it. "When I hit the ground, drag me back."

Kevin took a knee by the corner.

After a psych-up breath, she blurred sideways into a leap. The Beretta burped like an automatic weapon, a blinding/deafening flash, and she landed on her side. Dust exploded from the wall behind her at the corner. Kevin grabbed her ankles and yanked her away from the corner while flinching from a cloud of cinder block bits and dirt spraying around them.

"Damn!" shouted Tris. She sat up clutching her right arm. Blood oozed between her fingers.

Sputtering servo noises and the buzz of electronics came from the deeper portion of the basement. One .45 slug stuck to the jacket over her hip. He peeled her hand up enough to look at a fray of Kevlar fibers sticking up from the red leather sleeve. A matching hole on the back of her arm was cleaner, as though a drill bit had made a perfect circle.

"Five-five-six," said Kevin. "It hit the armor segment and glanced."

She sucked air between her teeth. "I don't think it hit bone. It'll heal. Oh, damn this burns."

"Maybe a tracer?" He brushed the jacket off her shoulder and eased her arm free. A clean through-and-through wound in her bicep had already shrunk to a pin dot; the bruising around the spot looked worse than the actual penetration.

She winced at it for a second before biting his shoulder and grumbling. "Ugh, the small wounds always sting the most."

"I need me some nanites." He kissed her on top of the head.

Laughing, Tris got to her feet

Kevin took a small satchel from a nail on the underside of the stairway and waved it at the corner. When nothing shot at him, he risked looking.

Beyond a ten-foot section of irregular cinder block-walled corridor, a larger room had filled with silicon smoke. Flickering orange light kept time with the *bzzt* noises, giving away the position of one turret. Two boot-covered feet appeared in the haze on the ground near the far wall, another twelve or thirteen yards farther in.

Kevin crept around the corner, advancing with his .45 out. At the edge of the room, he waved a hand about to clear smoke. Four sentry-gun style turrets lay in disarray around metal shelving, one on fire, two knocked over, and one smashed open and sparking. Wayne slumped against the back wall, shotgun still in his hands across his lap. His vacant expression, open mouth, and three bullet wounds in his upper abdomen said more than Kevin wanted to hear.

"Wayne…" He slumped against the shelves on his left. "You were such an asshole sometimes."

He sniffled.

Tris' hand slid over his back and gripped his shoulder. He didn't want to look at her, not with tears gathering in his eyes. As much of a prick as the man had been sometimes, Wayne was the closest thing to a father figure he really knew. Aside from one blurry memory of a semi-truck cab from twenty-three years ago, he couldn't remember his real dad.

"Aw, dammit, Wayne." Kevin lowered his head. "What happened?"

8

OUT OF WARRANTY

T ris backed up, deciding to give him some room to grieve. She kept her mouth shut. Though the man had been mostly civil to her after Harrisburg, he'd been fully ready to leave her tied hand and foot… and probably wouldn't have stopped anyone from abducting her had Kevin not stepped in. If not for the apparent effect the death had on Kevin, she couldn't have cared less about Wayne eating bullets. One less opportunistic bastard in the world.

"I'm, uhh… gonna." Kevin gestured at the corridor. "You know."

"Want help?"

He shook his head before stooping to move Wayne's shotgun off to the side, leaning it against the wall. Tris crossed her arms and ducked behind the shelf on the right, giving him room to lift and carry Wayne's body out of the basement.

Once the sound of his passage up the stairs faded, she looked around. The shelves held a lot of MREs, as well as some large ten-gallon drums of homemade beer, magnesium flares, a couple coils of nylon rope, one pack of bright fluorescent orange tent spikes, and a pair of old Coleman lanterns that probably didn't work.

Blood spray on the walls in the narrow corridor suggested someone (or some people) had followed/chased Wayne down here, and found out the hard way about the turrets. The absence of shell casings and blood (other than the puddle under where Wayne had been) in here convinced her whoever attacked him hadn't made it past the hail of bullets. The old man likely had a transponder on him somewhere marking him friendly, but it didn't matter much as the turrets couldn't kill anything but time now.

She snagged one of the MREs and headed upstairs to the office. Wayne had thrown a grey tarp over the security console, though whether he'd meant it as a dust cover, concealment, or a 'this crap is worthless' statement, she couldn't tell. Tris flopped in a wheeled chair with grey cloth cushions and put her feet up on the plyboard desk before opening the MRE.

"Hmm. Turkey and gravy." She tore the main entrée packet open and sucked on some of the sludge inside. It didn't taste bad, a bit like the cat food she'd eaten two days after first leaving the Enclave.

While taking small 'sips' of food, she tapped at the keyboard connected to the security system and got a password prompt. She looked around for papers or anything where he might've scribbled the password, but didn't find anything by the time she eaten all the mush from the entrée packet.

Well that's kind of stupid. This whole thing is to tell Amarillo who to go after if something happens... password makes no sense. She scratched at her lips with the empty foil. *Course, the attacker could wipe the data if they left it wide open... there's gotta be a master password.*

She tossed the packet on the desk and typed 'Amarillo,' which didn't work. She tried 'amarillo2061,' but that didn't work either. Tris stared at the command menu pondering the idiocy of having their master password emblazoned on the back of their agents' jackets. She tried a few variations of mixing the words 'Amarillo' and 'roadhouse' with 2061, as well as '1234' and 'password,' 'roadhousemasterpassword,' 'letmein,' and a few other random phrases.

Frustrated, she typed in 'fuckyou' and stabbed the enter key with her middle finger.

It worked.

Tris pressed a hand to her face, moaned, and peered one eye between her fingers at the command menu. "Ugh. Guess we're dealing with adolescent boys."

Hitting 1 for status, she got five small boxes showing the view out of individual digital cameras arranged throughout the building. Three on the main room from various angles, one in the corridor by the bathrooms, and one in the corridor by the bedrooms. All five showed a green dot and 'recording.'

Option 2 from the menu led to the logs. A stream of filenames in green-on-black appeared. For a few seconds, they struck her as random strings of letters and numbers until her brain caught up and she recognized year, month, day, time mashed together. She tapped the screen for the most recent file and waited. Ten seconds later, she felt like an idiot since this old terminal had no touch screen. A few key taps highlighted the line and opened the file, which gave her white snow in a box.

The next file had more white snow, and so on.

"Shit."

Tris spent the next hour or so gnawing on the empty MRE packet while diving into all the diagnostic modules. Everything she ran came back indicating all systems functional. Eventually, she CTRL+ALT+DEL'ed the machine and sifted down the processes list, hunting for anything unusual. She killed a process titled 'CCOS64.exe,' which broke into the base operating system beneath the 'overlay OS' of the camera control software. With full access to the computer, she soon found some configuration files. Hundreds of lines of 'plain English' setting parameters scrolled by. A long string of # marks caught her eye and she slowed the scroll enough to read.

From the look of it, someone had commented out the paths to the diagnostic executables and replaced them with 'allsgood.exe.' Tris smirked. She opened a command window and ran 'allsgood.exe,' which produced an output display that appeared to be the diagnostics module providing a perfect passing report on every component.

A scowl deepened across her face as she got into a robo-clicking frenzy on the keyboard, down arrow, delete, down arrow, delete, over and over again to remove the # marks from the config file. She added one—to cancel out the redirect to the fake result generator. With the de-edited file saved, she reopened the user-level software and ran the diagnostics.

This time, it showed failures in all of the flash memory storage modules. The cameras were recording, but the system attempted to write the video data on silicon shit. She grumbled. *No way Wayne hacked the system.* Within minutes, she had the case open and examined the individual flash drives hidden under a thick layer of dust. The newest one had a manufacture date of September 2017, several years before the war.

They might have worked initially, but burned out after too many overwrites.

"Shit." She dropped the drive in the case and leaned back in the chair with a hand on her forehead. "All this tech is ancient. Of course... what else would it be, not like they're still making stuff." Tris bit her lip. *I thought Amarillo was a big tech center.* Her mind filled with a fleeting memory of driving down a street past four and five story squarish buildings topped with armored soldiers. Neon lights, lots of people out and about almost as if the war had never happened... a big Roadhouse-themed office where once had been a car dealership. A guy with a pea-green bowtie. "That man was *so* cheesy."

The entire experience *did* feel like a scam at first. She'd been truly surprised when the flatbed truck showed up at Rawlins with their solar panels, cameras, wiring, and charging hardware a week later. A specter of doubt resurfaced. She tapped her fingers on the desk while thinking, then hunted around for anything else of use.

To the left of the terminal, on an adjacent desk (this one metal and an *actual* desk as opposed to plyboard on top of cinder blocks), she found Wayne's ledger. A few minutes of looking it over, she realized old, benevolent Wayne had been skimming coins out of the accounts he held in trust for his frequent drivers. Nothing too noticeable, somewhere between three to six coins per transaction. She flipped to Kevin's pages, and read over the history of his account growing from 108 coins over a series of hundreds of deposits until he'd reached the 9918 he had when they met.

She opened the job logbook beside it and compared the payouts for each run Kevin had done to the amount he put in trust. After factoring out an overestimate of six coins for food and charge each day he stopped in, she found a missing 1247 coins over the years it took him to save up. Another driver, someone with less money than Kevin had collected, showed a similar pattern but that man had been cheated out of 800 some odd coins in only nine months. *Guess he liked Kevin.*

A large safe, tall enough to hold rifles, caught her eye in the back corner. Amateur safe cracking killed about a half hour with little success. With nothing else to do in here, she headed down another cramped hallway to the store. Whoever had attacked Wayne didn't bother robbing the place, something she thought odd, especially considering the padlock wasn't secured.

"Hmm. Guess old Wayne had some enemies."

After helping herself to the bag of 9mm bullets, she headed to the kitchen.

"No sense wasting food."

9

TARNISHED DREAM

K evin carried Wayne's body down the hall past the bathrooms. He paused for a few seconds by the display case, contemplating taking the old armor out and putting it on him, but decided to leave it as a memoriam. About forty paces behind the roadhouse, he set Wayne down and returned to the building in search of a shovel. A while of rummaging and cursing later, he headed back outside with a smallish spade from the maintenance closet where Bee kept cleaning supplies.

He grumbled, dreading the thought of having to dig a grave with it… but he couldn't find anything better and he couldn't leave Wayne sitting out for the vultures or whatever else might wander along. By the time he got about a foot and a half deep with a grave-sized outline, he stopped to remove his jacket and shirt and take a few breaths. He kept working for another hour or so before squinting skyward, sweat running into his eyes. The horizon in all directions blurred with a day that had to be past ninety.

Feeling a dry tickle in his throat, he gathered his armored jacket (too valuable to leave unattended) as well as his shirt, and headed inside. He left them on a table and helped himself to two large cups of water before filling a jug. Tris busied herself with the computer in the office, typing away furiously. Still not quite ready to talk to anyone, he took his water jug and returned to the gravesite.

"Sorry it's takin' so long, Wayne. You got a shitty shovel." Kevin sipped more water and set the jug down by the old man's boots. "Tris is pullin' up your security system. I'll get 'em for ya. This just got personal."

An hour or two of miserable digging later, a silhouette caught his eye. A figure appeared in the north, approaching the roadhouse from behind. Kevin stood straight, shielding his eyes with a hand to get a better look. The indistinct outline took on a feminine shape, soon followed by the line of a large shovel over one shoulder. Her teetering gait became obvious, and he knew at once who (rather what) was coming.

"Bee!" yelled Kevin.

The android stopped for a second, adjusted facing toward him, and speed-tottered over. She had on a fuchsia bikini top and black miniskirt with combat boots. A few scuffmarks on her abdomen betrayed the artificiality of her skin, assuming the seams around her mouth and eyes didn't. "Kevin... Oh, it is positive to see you." Her head pivoted downward with a whirr. "You have located Wayne." She simulated a noise somewhere between weeping and a microwave on high. "I am sorry."

Kevin crossed his hands on the spade handle. "What the fuck happened?"

Bee looked up at him and blinked with a *click*. "Nine men in similar apparel entered in a group. They took tables and ordered food. They showed coin, but after they ate, they refused to pay. Wayne experienced heightened levels of emotional distress at the situation. He increased the volume of his voice by thirty two point nine decibels and repeated his request for payment."

Imagining Wayne's reaction to a bunch of idiots trying to stiff him tightened a lump in his throat.

"The men did not display elevated levels of stress indicators when Wayne pointed out they were in violation of the Code. One man experienced a rhythmic, intermittent exhalation with an opened glottis and vocal cord vibration."

"What did you just say, Bee? Was that even English?"

The android tilted her head. "Oh. My apologies. You may be more familiar with the colloquial term 'laughter.'"

He snarled. "Son of a bitch."

"I am unaware of the man's parentage." Bee blinked again. "Wayne produced a firearm as did the nine men. They exchanged shots. Wayne inflicted fatal injuries on two of them before retreating to a position of tactical advantage. I believe he attempted to increase his odds of survival by leading the men into the defense system in the basement while I moved to obtain a superior firearm. The remaining attackers were unaware of the turrets. Five of the nine men left. I interrupted the life processes of one on the porch with a shotgun. Two appeared to have moderate injuries requiring ambulatory assistance from their companions. I have completed cleaning the main room and burying the four dead men, a process which took me fifty-three hours nineteen minutes and eleven seconds."

Kevin's heart picked up speed. "They... just shot him? No hesitation at all?"

"I was not in the room when hostilities began, but my auditory analysis did not detect noticeable signs of hesitation or fear in their voices." Bee glanced again at Wayne. "I would like to provide assistance with burying Wayne."

He watched her waist-long black hair waver in the breeze for a minute, still trying to wrap his brain around the concept of people shooting up a roadhouse over something so trivial as paying for food... especially when they *had* the money. Stupid as it sounded, it felt like they tried to provoke a bounty on purpose. "Uhh, yeah. Sure. This is ass busting work."

Bee tilted her body to examine him. "Your posterior does not appear to have sustained noticeable damage."

Between sorrow and rage, he had no room for even a half smile.

At his lack of response, Bee stepped into the hole he'd started and got to digging with her real shovel. Kevin shook his head and attacked dirt once more with the spade, though between human muscles that got tired and poor tools, he wound up feeling more like a spectator than a helper. Bee didn't even need a pickaxe to force her shovel into the denser earth farther down.

"So who were these dead men that walked away?"

Bee paused to look up at him. "Only four of them—"

"Not now, Bee. Not fuckin' now."

She blinked. "I am sorry, Kevin I do not understand."

"I mean I'm going to find and kill the other five bastards. They're dead. They just don't know it yet."

Bee emitted a series of whirring sounds, which he imagined as gears in her head turning. "I do not know who they are. They had not been here before. All of them had the same type of jacket with the same symbol on the back."

That should make it easy enough to find something... biker gangs aren't exactly subtle. "What symbol?"

The android grasped the shovel midway along the length and held her arm up with the handle horizontal. "A white fist holding a sword by the blade like this with a circle around it." She resumed digging.

"Hmm. Never heard of that before."

Bee blinked. "How does one hear a symbol?"

Kevin screamed in frustration. He grabbed his .45 but couldn't quite draw it on Bee, so he settled for kicking a clod of dirt into the distance.

"I am sorry for causing you emotional distress." Bee hung her head.

He sighed and patted it on the shoulder before remembering 'she' was a machine. "Uhh... it's okay."

Tris appeared at the back door and ran over with her Beretta drawn. "What happened?" She did a double take. "Bee?"

"Hello, Tris." Bee smiled. "It is positive to see you."

Kevin picked at the dirt under his nails. "You ever hear of any Enclave units having a symbol of a white hand holding a sword sideways by the blade?"

Tris shrugged. "No. Not like there's thousands of them... Their military doesn't really have different units or divisions. All one group." She bit her lip. "Well, the hovercraft pilots kind of have their own little club or whatever."

"Bee, did you see their cars?" asked Kevin.

"Yes. They arrived on e-bikes."

Kevin glanced back at the roadhouse, sure that the front had been empty when he'd arrived. "How did five men drive away on nine bikes?"

"They did not." Bee, neck deep in the ground, peered up at him. "The five left in a hurry. A few minutes after, some of the News came and took the bikes. They did not go inside the building."

Kevin looked at Tris. "Anything from the cams?"

She shook her head. "No. The system hasn't worked for a long time. The flash drives were shot, and someone hacked it to hide error messages and make the diagnostic look like everything was working."

"What?" Kevin's throat dried up again. "Dead?"

"Probably for years. I can't tell when they last successfully preserved data. The oldest filename is two months ago, but I'm sure those drives have been worthless for at least a decade."

"Drives?" He *really* wanted to hit something, but neither Tris nor Bee deserved it. He settled for pulling Tris tight to his chest and squeezing. "This is beyond fucked up."

"Think of it like someone talking to you, and you writing down what they say in your notebook."

He nodded.

Tris clung to him, trying to be comforting. "Well, in this case, someone was talking to you, but your pen didn't have any ink in it, so everything you wrote never appeared on the paper."

He sent an apologetic stare at Wayne's lifeless body. "Okay, so it gets a little more difficult. Guess I'll just have to kill everyone I find wearing that damn symbol if I can't tell who did it."

"Best I can tell, they didn't steal anything. I think these guys showed up specifically to kill Wayne." Tris glanced at Bee. "Did she see anything?"

Bee repeated her explanation of what happened as Kevin moved Wayne to the hole and folded his arms over his chest. Tris reached down and helped him up out of the ground. Bee got started filling it in.

Kevin shoveled in silence at Bee's side until they finished covering the grave. He stuck the spade in the dirt and crossed his arms over the handle. "Doesn't make any sense they'd start a gunfight with a proprietor over eighteen coins when they had the money to pay. You're right. I think they wanted a fight." He exhaled. "No idea why. Wayne was a good man. Bit of a stubborn bastard at times, but good."

Tris looked down.

"What?" Kevin glanced at her.

"Uhh, nothing important."

He moved away from the spade, leaving it stuck in the ground, and grasped her shoulders. "Tris?"

She stared at his stomach. "You're going to think I'm being bitchy or trying to talk you out of the stupid idea of going after this gang."

He almost smiled. "I figured you would."

Tris lifted her head; her gem-blue eyes locked on his and widened with guilt. "Look, when I was in the office, I started looking over the books. I think Wayne was skimming coins off everyone he kept money for."

Kevin blinked. "You're accusing him of being a thief?"

"I went line by line over every job you ran for him, over every deposit he put in your 'account,' and estimated a few coins spent here and there for food and ammo. There are regular discrepancies on how much he recorded in your balance. Couple coins off each time."

He squinted. It took him a few seconds to glare his anger away from her. "I'm not pissed at you. How much?"

She managed a weak smile. "Somewhere between nine hundred and twelve hundred coins over the years you were working for him." Kevin flinched. "He didn't write down how much you spent on ammo or other crap, so there's a lot of variability possible."

Kevin kicked at the dirt. "No."

Tris looked up. "Huh? I'm sure… I'm not just saying that to make you not want to go off and avenge him. The ledger shows it."

"Not that." He grabbed the spade and stomped toward the building. "There's no way anyone would've been able to read that book while Wayne was alive… and even if they could, I doubt anyone would've found it." He stopped, gazing at the ground between his boots. "Maybe it was interest or some shit… a service charge for holding our money."

"Hmm." She shrugged. "Could be. Did he ever tell you he was going to take a couple coins off each transaction?"

Kevin smiled. "Nah. Knowing Wayne, he just decided to do it figuring no one would notice."

She followed him to the door. "You don't seem too upset over it."

"Wayne could be a bastard." He chuckled, pulling the door open. "Out here, a guy does as much as he can get away with. I've only known two people who *didn't* look for every opportunity to get one over on everyone they met… one of them was my father. That attitude got him killed."

"Who was the other one?"

He kept walking. "You."

"You missed one." She tugged on his arm so he stopped half in the doorway. When he looked back at her, she smiled. "*You're* surviving okay."

"Yeah…" He let his head hang, and sighed. "I suppose I am."

"So now what?" She glanced over her shoulder at Bee tottering over with the shovels.

"Now…" Kevin patted her on the back and eased her inside. "Now I'm gonna go see if Alamo remembers."

10

ALAMO

Wayne's Roadhouse hung in silence, save for the faint sizzle of the grill in the kitchen. Kevin hovered in the doorway, gazing out over the front porch at the dusty emptiness of Hagerman. A dark band of ominous weather spread across the sky at his right, lit by the occasional flash of horizontal lightning. The tempest amid the clouds remained as silent as the room behind him, far enough away not to rumble. A steady wind from the northwest carried a hint of rain and ozone.

Tris slid a mason jar back and forth between her hands across a round table near the middle of the room. She'd salvaged a short-sleeved black tee shirt with a faded print on it of some pre-war music group. The name had long since flaked off, but the spiked skull graphic between her breasts suggested something dark. Her new (relatively) black leather skirt stopped at less than a hands' width below her crotch, so she'd added a pair of fluorescent green leggings. Despite her slender build, they clung so tight it looked like her legs had been dipped in paint.

Her still-wet hair lent her expression a forlorn quality, as if she'd blown in out of a rain that hadn't started yet. A shared shower had brought back memories of their last time here. She'd respected his grief over the old man; neither had been in the mood for doing anything more than cleaning up. A long, soapy embrace had managed to make him feel better. Tris caught him glancing back at her and offered a somber little version of a smile.

He fired off one last, long look down the road in the direction of the Bobcat market. As he expected, it didn't take long for the News to show up once a car appeared out front. The last he'd seen of them prior to an hour or so ago, they'd not given him the feeling of continued trouble. It'd been Juan and Rash rolling up on their e-bikes… the two with the biggest grudge. Most guys didn't react well to having their asses kicked in front of their friends, especially not twice by a little woman, once with her hands tied behind her back.

Kevin shook his head with a chuckle and meandered to the table.

Within a second of his grasping the chair to pull it back, Bee entered from the kitchen area carrying two plates loaded with dust hopper burgers and fries. Wayne was nothing if not consistent. Variety, at least in terms of menu, had been a dirty word. His ass hit the seat in time with the plates touching down on the table.

"Thanks, Bee."

The android nodded at him. "You are welcome."

"That leg looks good." Tris leaned around to examine the artificial woman. "The actuator giving you any trouble?"

Kevin gathered the burger in both hands and raised it to his mouth. It smelled the same as he'd grown used to. Meat, pepper, salt, a hint of metal, and an indefinable quasi-chemical aftertaste not quite sweet or sour. He'd always thought Wayne had some special recipe, but it had been Bee all along. The fifteen-year-old in him slunk off to a corner to hide tears while the last twelve years kept his face stoic and his mind focused.

Bee faced Tris, hands on her hips. "If I bend at a greater than ninety degree angle, it sticks. The brief period of increased resistance prior to resuming full mobility suggests a burr or imperfection in the servo rotator."

Kevin took his usual measured bite, chewed three times, and tossed a fry into the mix. The hot starch, drowned in salt, combined with the meat-bread mush and hit that flavor point he used to spend hours behind the wheel dreaming about. Having his own roadhouse and six months of not driving runs anymore hadn't struck him with how he'd never wind up looking forward to one of these meals like that again. In truth, he hadn't thought once about the food here in all that time. Finding Wayne dead put him right back in the driver's seat, thirteen hours away from food and a real bathroom.

Well, as real as 'not sling-assing it over a guardrail' can be.

"I'm not sure how long we're going to be here, but I can check it." Tris took a pinch of black pepper from the bowl at the side of the table and dusted her fries. She looked at Kevin and paused, no doubt at the faraway stare he knew he had. "You okay?"

A few seconds after she spoke, he broke eye contact with nothing and glanced down at the burger before looking her way. "Ain't no amount of feelin' bad gonna bring Wayne back or make it right what was done."

Bee swiveled her head to look at him. Even without the thumb-sized hole in her cheek exposing steel, she looked too artificial to think of as female. Her skin had a not-quite-right shade and a somewhat-rubbery quality to how it moved over the metal underneath. He almost smiled remembering a few times some random driver had gotten blind off moonshine to the point of mistaking Bee for a real woman, and forcing Wayne to physically separate them.

The android looked at the door and back at him; a quick *whirr-whirr* noise emanated from her neck. "Will you be operating this place now?"

Kevin stared at the tip of a fry an inch from his lip. He leaned his arm back, raising the potato shard vertical. "Bit sentimental. This place doesn't do bad, but I'm up in Rawlins now. Lot more traffic there. Easy I see in two days what Wayne got in a week." He nibbled on the fry. "Don't feel right not to, but don't make sense either."

"Bee, did Wayne ever give you the combination to the safe?" asked Tris. "The ledger's got six drivers he'd been keeping accounts for."

"You're not?" Bee slow-blinked with a *click-click*. "I had not anticipated that outcome." She shifted to face Tris. "Wayne did not provide me with the numeric sequence."

She slouched.

"Sounds like Wayne. He didn't even write it down, I bet." Kevin ate another few bites. "If anyone shows up for their money, they can worry about how to get it."

"However." Bee held up one finger. "I may be able to open it given proper analysis of the rhythmic acoustics. The mechanism is old."

"What's the Code say about those coins?" Tris shifted her gaze to the side. "Someone's coming."

"Since I'm a proprietor, I'm supposed to keep the accounts active. Different if a site inspector finds it."

"Oh?" Tris took a huge bite of her food.

Hard boots tromped over the wood of the front porch, reverberating in the floor.

Bee spun, wobbled, and teetered off in the direction of the back room. "Site inspector would declare all assets Amarillo's."

Tris grumbled into her burger.

Kevin popped the last bit of meat and bread into his mouth and glanced at the door.

Alamo strode in, belt-long, straight, black hair trailing after him. Plain white tee, jeans, and cowboy-style boots matched the other three News behind him. A silver .44 revolver wobbled at his hip as he sidled up to the table. High cheekbones lent an air of imperiousness to the expression aimed down at Kevin, though the mood behind it could've been amusement as easily as scorn.

The head of the New motorcycle club hooked his thumbs in his jean pockets and nodded at Kevin, then Tris.

Weed, the same height though probably half the weight of Alamo, kept a decidedly unhappy stare leveled at Tris. The skinny man scratched at a couple days' worth of dark beard stubble. Four well-worn handguns, two on his belt, two on his chest, clattered with his motion.

Juan, the short-but-thick New, hung back a step or two. He crossed his arms, making his leather cut creak from strain. He had a combat rifle across his back and a 1911 on his hip, but didn't reach for either one. Like Weed, he kept a dour frown locked on Tris. Kevin hadn't seen the fourth man before. Later twenties, dark skinned and pudgy, but the kind of pudgy that hides a shitload of muscles. The lower three-ish inches of a hairy, dark stomach poked out from under a stained tee shirt. He had a serious look, a square, nearly cube-shaped head, and a neck wider than his jaw.

Kevin found himself grinning. The compulsion to throw stuff at the new guy's afro to see if anything would stick in it proved too tempting to resist. Pity he had nothing but a plate in front of him; throwing that *would* start a fight. He stood, shifted to face the four men, and raised a hand to shake. "Alamo."

The tall Native American gripped forearms and shook once. "Kevin."

The 'I just slept with your sister and you don't know it yet' smile that had gotten him in so much trouble reappeared. "Looks like those two want a rematch with Tris."

She glared at him. "Do we *really* have to get into a fight with these guys every single damn time we're in Hagerman?"

Alamo's rock-melting stare broke apart as he leaned back with a window-shaking belly laugh and slid into the seat to Kevin's right. "So, I hear you got your own roof these days. You ain't been 'round here for a while now."

Kevin sat, made eye contact with the other three News, and gestured at the adjacent table. "You boys hungry? Beer?"

Weed and Juan murmured to each other, seemed to relax a tick, and moved around to sit. The dark roadblock followed, but kept the same intensity. He looked like he could go from zero to 'beating-a-face-in' at a finger snap. Kevin fidgeted, trying to mask his unease with a smile.

"Bee?" yelled Kevin.

The android poked her head out through the curtain separating the area behind the counter from the back room. "Yes?"

"Would you please bring out some beer for us?"

Bee emerged from the curtain and set her fists against her hips. "Are you charging them?" Her head shifted with a whirr to stare at the gang for a few seconds before facing Kevin again. "I do not know if... are you paying?"

"Shit don't last that long. Gonna go south if it ain't drunk." Kevin gestured at her. "Please?"

"Okay." Bee's torso whirled to face back the way she came a half-second before her legs followed, and she tottered out of sight.

"So, what's this meeting all about?" Alamo laced his fingers together, forearms braced on the edge of the table. "I hear you wanted to see me?"

Kevin dropped his smile and un-slouched. "Someone killed Wayne."

All four News leaned back. Weed gasped.

Alamo tilted his head to the right. "No shit? We figured he'd gone on a trip."

"Nope. Couple drivers took a run from me a few days ago. Said the place was deserted. Couldn't get Wayne on the radio, so I decided to come take a look." Kevin massaged the bridge of his nose, eyes closed, for a few seconds. "Found him in the basement."

"That ain't good," said Alamo. "Gonna be some heavy coin on someone's ass."

"Yeah," said Weed.

"*Asimismo, puta madre,*" muttered Juan.

The table shifted toward Kevin.

"You got any idea who?" asked Alamo.

Kevin opened his eyes; the big man had leaned forward, looking *interested.* Fair bet since the News thought themselves the 'law' in this area, they'd be humping after that bounty big time. Course, that also meant they probably wouldn't hire any extra muscle out of Roswell and try to deal with Amarillo directly. *I hate mercs.* "You guys didn't notice?"

"Evidently not." Tris glanced to her right as Bee entered carrying a tray of mason jars filled with thick brown homemade beer. "Sure looked surprised to me when they heard about Wayne."

"Guns go off all the time 'round here." Weed paused to give Tris a challenging stare. "Didn't think nothing of it."

She met his glare and hardened her eyes. "Something wrong, Weed?"

He looked away.

"Didn't think so."

"Look." Kevin slapped the table. "This whole thing started when you boys got it in your head she was some bounty and you tried to poach her from me."

"Operative word being *tried,*" said Tris.

Alamo raised a stalling hand at Weed. "The matter is over. If you open another bottle, what it holds is yours alone to drink." He looked at Kevin. "What do you know?"

"Bee got a good look at them. Sounds like another club. Bikes, cuts. Hand holding a sword sideways in a circle. All white."

The android recounted what she saw again while handing out beers.

"We know this group. The Redeemed," said Alamo. "Strange that they roam this far."

"Guess so. Can't say I've seen them before." Kevin raised an eyebrow. "How far outta their territory are they?"

An appraising frown curved Alamo's lips. "Usually find them down around Las Cruces. We had a few *disagreements* with their idea of territorial boundaries. They dick with the Olds the same as they do with us, maybe more. Ain't no bad blood. Business."

Kevin chuckled. "Why do you go after each other?"

"News and Olds?" Tris failed to hide a smirk.

Alamo sat up tall. "Olds think they're the Mexican Army, and Sandoval..." He raised a hand in a 'wait a sec' gesture. "Sorry, *General* Sandoval"—the other bikers laughed—"thinks it's his duty to re-take land the U.S. 'stole.'"

Still laughing, Juan and the potbellied roadblock clinked mason jars and drank.

Kevin blinked in disbelief. "Uhh, has anyone bothered to tell them there's no U.S. anymore? There's no damn Mexico either."

"They're trying." Alamo took a long sip of Wayne's beer. "Damn, this stuff ain't bad. You know how ta make it?"

Kevin shook his head.

"Pity." Alamo drank another gulp. "They got nothing else to do down there. Bunch of 'em raided an old fort. Got all the uniforms and crap. Weapons. Ain't no countries left to fight for, but we let 'em in, and they're gonna start trying to collect taxes, impose law, make everyone 'Mexicans.'"

"Sounds like Sandoval's been out in the sun too long." Kevin stared into his beer. "Wayne's dead. I'm going to find who killed him."

Alamo flicked his thumbnail over the ridge at the top of the mason jar-turned-beer-glass. "Spirits tell me you not after no bounty."

"Your spirits are wise." He looked away from his wavering reflection and took a long pull. Maybe he didn't want to know how Wayne managed to impart a hint of fruitiness to his beer, but he'd miss it... even if it came from beetles or flies.

"Guess that means you ain't gonna call it in?" Alamo narrowed his eyes.

They can't claim a bounty that doesn't exist... I can't find these fuckers without help. He glanced to his right at Tris, her eyes wide with concern. He had a Roadhouse to run. He didn't go out and do this shit himself anymore. He was Wayne now. He paid guys to do stuff. He stayed home... with his girl. *Fuck it.* Kevin sipped again, letting the beer swirl around and over his tongue, savoring the fizz. "Guess it don't matter much who gets 'em as long as they go down. Yeah. I'll call it in, but I need information. Where are these 'Redeemed' coming from? How many? You recognize anyone specific from Bee's story?"

The News shrugged and muttered.

"We're not that friendly with them." Alamo smiled. "Try around Las Cruces and west. We never bothered chasin' 'em down, but they're 'round there. Maybe south or Juarez."

"Nah, man." Juan set an empty mason jar on the table. "Them shits ain't in no Juárez. That place fulla Olds."

"What's their deal?" asked Tris. "What would make them come all the way to Hagerman and pick a fight with Wayne?"

"Maybe they gettin' too fat for their own good." Weed scraped a few fingers at his ratty moustache and pulled a hand down his face, making it seem even longer for a second. "Maybe it ain't so much Wayne as they wanna start a war with Amarillo."

"The hell for?" asked Kevin. "Are they *that* stupid?"

Juan leaned his head side to side, cracking his neck twice. Kevin suppressed the urge to wince. "Dat *pendejo* from San-An say some people out lower Cali thinkin' the Roadhouse a jaguar with no fangs." He flared his eyes. "Look all scary, but"—he curled his lips over his teeth and mimed toothless biting—"can't do shit."

"There's cameras." Tris gave Kevin the 'side-eye.' "Amarillo will know exactly what those men look like. They won't be able to go within two miles of any Roadhouse location without ten people clambering for money."

"The damn hell's a camera?" asked Weed.

"Pre-war electronics. You know what a picture is?" Tris glanced at him. He nodded. "A camera is what makes a picture."

"So you have this?" asked Amarillo.

"No." Tris sighed. "The data is encrypted. Can't be looked at or erased on site. It would be stupid if they allowed that since someone who caused trouble could just get rid of it."

"You think these people know what technology is?" Alamo chuckled.

Kevin's fingers dug into his knee. *Damn.*

"I didn't design it," said Tris, calm as anything. "Data's already *at* Amarillo over radio, but it all goes into a storage farm. No one looks at it unless they have a reason to. As soon as Kevin calls in the explanation, every Roadhouse operator will know what they look like."

Where is she getting this shit from? Kevin thought about Wayne's last facial expression so he didn't laugh. "Look, guys... I'm. I dunno. I was all kinds of pissed off. Ain't sure I'm really going to run around out there and get my ass shot up when I don't even know who I'm looking for." He let out a long sigh while surreptitiously grasping Tris' hand under the table. "I could spend the next four years roaming around and maybe never find these bastards. Maybe get shot in the back for asking the wrong question to the wrong person. Ain't gonna bring Wayne back outta the ground, and you boys look like you need the bounty more than I do."

Tris blinked at him. The shock on her face melted to a look of confused relief.

Alamo pursed his lips and tapped a finger on his chin. "It is difficult to slay a man you cannot see. Perhaps you are sincere after all, though I saw the kill in your eyes."

Kevin drummed his fingers on the table. "If I knew who did it and where they were, I wouldn't still be here. I owed Wayne a lot, nothing coins can buy, but..." He stilled his hand. "I've got a 'house to run now. Can't spend months driving around in circles kicking a hornet nest in every settlement."

Alamo pondered.

Juan yelled for Bee to bring him a refill. The android gave him a questioning glance until Kevin gestured at her to proceed. At that, Weed waved his empty mason jar at Bee as well.

"You won't be here then." Alamo lowered his hand from chin to table.

Kevin shook his head. "Nah. Can't. Lotta memories here, but..."

"Not all of them good." Tris squirmed.

Some were. He thought of their first shower together. "True."

"Alright. The place is ours now." Alamo bumped the table with a fist like a gavel.

All the times Wayne sparred with the News flooded back into Kevin's mind at once. The very idea that *they* would occupy this building locked every muscle in his gut. Sitting naked in a bucket of room-temperature oatmeal would've been more pleasant. *No fucking way am I... going to get into a gunfight over a place I can't even keep.* He sighed. "You know Wayne's ghost is going to hate that."

Alamo chuckled. "Reckon he might. I'll leave it up to him to object."

Kevin twisted his empty mason jar around in his hand a few times before making eye contact with Alamo. "Do one thing for him? The armor... in the case by the bathrooms. Leave it be. Don't let anyone fuck with it."

"Done." Alamo held out a fist.

Kevin touched knuckles with him.

"If we find anything solid, we'll send word, get you down here if there's time." Alamo lowered his arm. "Get you in on the kill if there is to be one."

Tris cringed a little, a dire glare of worry aimed at Kevin.

"'Preciate it." Kevin lowered his arm.

Bee arrived with two beers and a large green ammo can. The way she handled it, it appeared empty, but Tris' eyes bulged when it landed in her lap.

The News all glanced at it.

"What's that?" asked the formerly silent man with a neck wider than his head.

Bee spun about to face him. "Some papers pertaining to Roadhouse business. I do not predict that you and your fellows will be operating this establishment as a franchise holder."

Alamo leaned back and flicked at the holster of his .44, more a nervous habit than a threat. "Hearin' enough I think it might be worth the risk. If they come knockin', we buy in. If they don't, well…" He smiled. "Then y'all come down and 'ave a burger on me."

Shit. "The Redeemed have to be starting those rumors. Why would they want war?"

All four News shrugged.

Bee squared her shoulders, facing Kevin. "Mister Kevin. As my previous owner is presently inert beneath five-point-six feet of earth, I am without purpose. I would like to accompany you, perhaps reprise my original function at your new location."

"Wait. We need a waitress," said Juan.

"Weed'll look okay with a dress an' a shave." Big-neck grinned.

"Eat shit, Ty." Weed picked his eye with his middle finger.

Alamo waved at them. "We got plenty of girls willin' ta help out. No gripe from us you takin' the android. Ain't natural anyway. Better it's off our land."

Bee bowed at him.

Tris squeezed Kevin's hand before she got up, holding the ammo can as though it weighed little. Ty appeared to lose interest in the can after one more look at the sylph of a girl carrying it with no effort. Weed and Juan squinted at her.

"Yeah." *Damn good thing I trunked the ammo and guns already.* As much as he hated to admit it, nothing about Alamo made him wary. "We'll be heading out in the morning. Hope you got no problems with us usin' a bunk."

"*Me casa su casa.*" Alamo held his arms wide.

11

FEAR, UNCERTAINTY, AND DOUBT

Interstate 285 slid beneath the Challenger's hood amid the mesmerizing, repetitive *thrum* of wheels on pavement. Kevin couldn't place the exact reason he hadn't slept well. Anger at the Redeemed, or whoever'd killed Wayne, unease that the sanctity of the Roadhouse had been breached, worry about the Challenger outside, and an unstable truce with the News all conspired to keep his mind racing.

He squeezed his fingers into the worn leather wrapping on the steering wheel. The Hastings Roadhouse had been bad, but it didn't unsettle him as much. Infected didn't care about the Code, and even if they had enough powers of reason left in their tapioca brains to be worried about it, who would bother putting a bounty on one? No, what happened at Wayne's was something else. A deliberate act. Perhaps not even against Wayne personally.

No, this had been a giant middle finger thrust straight up Amarillo's nose.

Alamo and his boys had played dumb. Hell, even Irwin the mechanic acted surprised to find out Wayne had been killed, but he had to have seen it go down; the garage sat across the street. Without the threat of the Code, nothing had protected the car parked out front, or his ass sleeping in a bed.

He yawned and drifted into the oncoming lane… not that it mattered.

"You okay?" Tris reached over and rubbed his shoulder.

"Kevin appears to be suffering an acute lack of sleep," said Bee from the back seat.

He rubbed his face, one eye at a time, and yawned again. "Yeah. Probably would've been better to drive a couple hours north and camp. Least I'd have been able to rest."

He hooked a left, following signs labelled: Roswell-Byp highway. The last thing he needed was a tangle with those people. As humanity's 'phoenix-from-the-ashes' act went, Roswell hadn't been doing too bad. Even Tris couldn't explain why the Enclave spared it from a Virus drop, but the city boasted a population of at least four thousand and had somewhat of an organized military. Word claimed they didn't have a lot of love for drivers, regarding them as smugglers up to no good. All it took was one story of a car being 'confiscated,' and he steered clear.

If Roswell wanted to make itself an island, far be it for him to challenge them. Of course, most of the drivers who bitched about Roz *were* smuggling things he figured a place trying to be 'civilized' might have a couple of objections to. Hell, the News went in and out of there all the time.

"So where'd you come up with all that?" He grinned at her.

Tris covered her mouth to hide a yawn. "All what?"

"The crap about the security you fed Alamo."

"Oh." She stretched. "It's what I'd do if I designed it. Took a gamble that none of them knew anything about computers."

"Not much of a gamble there. Those guys need a couple hours of training to figure out the fly on their jeans." He laughed for a few seconds before giving her a serious glance. "Think it works like that?"

"No way. There's no Internet left, and I didn't see any kind of modem capable of transmitting data over the radio. That, and there's the bigger problem."

"Bigger problem?" He steered around large chunks of crashed aircraft dotting the road. A mangled engine almost as big as the car jutted out of the dirt to the left of the road.

"Not having the ability to transfer data back to a central server isn't a big deal when your system isn't recording any data in the first place. The cameras looked functional, but the storage media has been dead for a while. Probably a few years."

Kevin squeezed the wheel. *They can't all be broken.* "The site inspectors are supposed to check that shit."

She shrugged. "Who inspects the inspectors? All that tech is somewhere between fifty and seventy years old. It's not like anyone but the Enclave has the ability to manufacture equipment like that anymore."

"So what you're saying…"

Tris swiped hair off her face, trailing her fingers through long, snowy strands. "I'm saying that we're probably at least a century or two away from being able to make the kind of computers that existed in 1970, and that's assuming anyone bothers enough to try."

"Hmm. We invented computers once… and the people who did it the first time didn't have old shit to scavenge." He accelerated up to 120 mph and flew down an off ramp to I-285 north again. "I'm not liking the sound of where this is going."

She gave him the kind of look a mother might give a small boy who'd just found their dog dead.

"Hardware in Hastings was shot too. You said ours is on its last legs. Now you're saying Wayne's system was worthless." He stared at her, causing the consoling look in her eyes to dial back a bit to mere worry. "Do *any* of them work? Does anyone *know* the whole damn thing is bullshit? I…" He slapped his hand on the wheel. "I mean, it's shitty enough if Amarillo was installing dead hardware not realizing how short-lived it would be… but, fuck, Tris… if they knew?"

"Kevin… you're doing 170. Might want to slow down." She smiled. "Please?"

He took a few calming breaths and eased back to 118. "Shit."

"Wayne did not routinely perform the specified maintenance functions for the camera system." Bee's eyes clicked. "It is likely he was unaware how to do it, however, it is equally likely he did not care."

"Option two." Kevin shook his head with a sad smile. "Fuckin' Wayne… He was too much of a badass for his own good. No one messes with Wayne."

Bee's eyes clicked again. "Except for the men who shot him."

Kevin snarled, squeezing the wheel. "Yeah… except for them." He looked at Tris once the urge to punch Bee subsided. "Whadda you think? Is it all horseshit?"

She stared at her hands in her lap, silent for a moment. "I don't know. Considering the state of the world, it's possible the people in Amarillo don't understand the functional lifespan of solid state drives. This kind of technology has its limits. Maybe back when they started the Roadhouse, it all worked and it never occurred to any of them that their hardware could fail. Could be that they found out at some point and kept their mouths shut since rumor already carried the weight of the Code. Sufficiently advanced technology is considered magic by those who don't understand it."

He chuckled. "Yeah…"

"But that hack to the diagnostic." She sighed. "It… I think they knew, and more than likely right from the start. Someone had the skills to try and hide the failure."

Blaming it on dumbassery made him feel better than the idea of a deliberate attempt to send out bad cameras. Better in his mind that the people in Amarillo had no clue. He looked to his right, catching Tris nod off. He decided to shut up and let her sleep. As much as it terrified him to think he'd been lied to, he trusted her enough to accept her theory. A deliberate modification to the system to conceal its flaws had only one explanation.

He sighed, gazing out at the road. If he gave Denver enough of a wide berth to mollify his phobia of Infected, they had a fourteen hour ride ahead of them. Maybe thirteen if he hauled particular ass where the paving allowed.

"Bee?" whispered Kevin.

"Yes, boss?"

He tensed. Some part of him didn't feel right being called 'boss' by Wayne's android. Wayne was 'boss.' A sigh slid past his teeth. "What time is it?"

"The current time is 8:12 a.m."

"Let her sleep for now. Gimme a holler when it's 'bout one or so."

"You got it, boss," said Bee, her voice volume down to approximate whispering.

<hr />

At 10:09 p.m., Kevin backed the Challenger into the garage and ran his finger across the six glowing blue rocker switches along the dashboard over the steering wheel. All the lights went out. Tris had taken over driving at one, and kept on until eight. The grim pall of silence that hung over the bulk of their ride lifted as she let out a loud yawn, stretched, and climbed out of the car.

Kevin groaned and got up. "What?" He nudged the door shut with his knee, and stifled the yawn he caught from her. "You've had this look on your face for the past two hours."

She traipsed around the front end and leaned against him. "I didn't want to worry you."

He buried his face in her hair for a few seconds before kissing her ear and whispering, "Too late. I'm already worried."

A weak laugh muffled into his chest. She leaned back enough to look him in the eye. "I was thinking that maybe those Redeemed guys know the security systems are geriatric."

He cringed inside. "That makes them a significant problem. The whole reason the Code keeps the peace is everyone dreads having Amarillo put a bounty on their head. None of that works if they don't know who to put it on."

Bee emerged from the passenger side and closed the car door. After a quick glance at them embracing, she tottered out of the garage and set her hands on her hips. "There is not much here."

"That's why I chose this place, Bee. Nearest other 'house is a few hours away." Kevin smiled down at Tris. "And I've got everything I need here."

She rolled her eyes a little, grinned, and leaned up to kiss him.

Bee remained quiet and patient for several minutes while Kevin lost himself in Tris' mouth.

Tris sucked on his lip for a little while before pulling back and looking up at him. "Do you really mean that or are you just trying to get into my pants?"

He grinned. "Is 'yes' a valid answer?"

A cute, short laugh came out of her. "I'll take it into consideration. Why don't—"

Brzaap.

"Ouch," said Bee.

The android fell over.

"Bee?" asked Tris, whirling about to look in the direction of a thin cloud of white smoke.

"Power fault in gyroscopic stabilization unit and left knee actuator." The *click* of her eye blink came from out of sight in front of the Challenger. "I am pleased that I cannot experience pain in the sense that humans do, but I find it most disconcerting that I am unable to stand."

Tris hurried over. Kevin followed. Each took one of Bee's raised hands and lifted her upright. While Kevin held on to keep the android balanced, Tris opened up a panel of false skin on her back, releasing a thicker cloud of smoke.

"The insulation burned off of the wire and the copper melted. I can fix it. Fortunately, it's only a wire I need to replace." Tris shut the panel and picked Bee up. "Might as well go in and make sure Sang is still okay."

"Yeah." Kevin turned back to lock up the garage.

With that done, he jogged to the main building. Three drivers sat around the tables working on food or drinks: a squat, fat man in road leathers, a waifish preteen boy with short red hair, and a longhaired man with dark skin and a blue Adidas shirt. Kevin took two steps to the counter where Fitch stood like a bartender, stopped, and looked at the boy, specifically at *her* miniscule, but evident breasts.

Boys don't have tits. That's a tiny woman. He rubbed his eyes. Yep. Still a girl. Well, that certainly bothered him less than a twelve-year-old being out on his own. Still, she didn't look much past sixteen. He chuckled to himself. Of the three cars out front, an armored teal compact, a lo-rider sedan with spikes everywhere one could conceivably put spikes, and an enormous white pickup truck with a plow covered in welded rotary-saw blades, he bet the huge truck belonged to the girl.

The longhaired guy muttered to himself in what sounded like Hindi and used a match to light an incense stick. The pudgy driver made a show of coughing as soon as it started emitting smoke, though no one paid him any mind.

"Hey." Fitch nodded. "How'd it go?"

Kevin crossed the room; the *thunk-thunk-thunk* of his boots attracted three pairs of eyes, though none gave him anything other than mild curiosity. He leaned against the wall behind the counter and bowed his head. "Wayne's dead."

"Aww, fuck." Fitch looked down. "Sorry man. That's some bad, bad alchemy right there. Figured things got twisted when I saw yer lady bring Bee in. He wouldn't 'ave sold her no how."

Kevin gripped the shelf on either side of his ass and nodded. "Yeah. Old weathered bastard liked that thing more than he let on."

Fitch's expression edged toward horrified. "You ain't sayin' he..."

"Hah!" Kevin found an honest laugh under the gloom. "No way. Bee ain't even equipped for that."

"You *back* back, or you just stoppin' for supplies before goin' off on a hunting expedition?"

Kevin smirked. "Why does everyone assume I'm going to run out the door, guns blazing?"

"Because we know you." Fitch winked. "Oh, that pretty little thing came back with your veggies. I settled up with her. Said she's goin' ta

Ween's now." He pointed at the marble notebook. "Pretty sure I got the hang of loggin' stuff the way you do."

"Cool. Hey, you ever hear of a biker outfit, The Redeemed?"

"Only by way of stories. Heard they hit a convoy south of Los Gatos couple months back. Whole settlement's worth of slaves bein' brought down ta Nogales."

"You ain't got the whole story, pops," said the girl. Standing, she looked even more like a boy on the younger side of teenaged. The thigh pockets of her green camo fatigue pants jostled with the tinny clatter of assault rifle magazines as she approached the counter. "I was on that ride. Wasn't no slave run."

"Oh?" Fitch raised a steel-wool eyebrow.

She nodded at the shelves behind the counter. "Trade ya the info for a shot."

"How old are you, kid?" asked Fitch.

Kevin raised a hand and winked at her. "S'okay. How old ya think he is."

Fitch studied the driver for a few seconds, scratching at his stubble. "Fourteen, bein' generous."

Kevin smiled. "I think *she's* probably seventeen."

Fitch blinked.

The girl leaned back and attempted to thrust her breasts through her tank top. "Twenty-three actually."

"Them's some nasty bee stings." Fitch chuckled, but filled a shot glass with someone's attempt at distilling scotch. "You got a name, kid?"

"I… uhh…" Neeley grinned like an idiot and scratched the back of his head. "Be happy to rub some itch cream on those bug bites."

"Saoirse." She downed the liquor without a trace of flinch, and frowned at the glass. "Please tell me that wasn't in your septic tank an hour ago." A second later, she thumped a hand on her chest and coughed.

Fitch laughed.

"Okay." Saoirse set the shot glass down with a *clunk.* "So we're runnin' this semi full of idiots who tried to set up a settlement in the outskirts o' Juarez, southeast side. Guess they got tired o' getting stuck 'tween Mex-Ar and 'Fected and wanted out. Was a merc contract outta Roswell. I head down there with a bunch of other drivers, heavy on guns and short on cargo space. Escortin' this big rig. Fine for a couple days, then these bikes come outta nowhere. Them Redeemed bastards got *told* we was transporting slaves, but 'twas the damn settlers themselves what hired us."

Kevin tilted his head.

"Yeah. That's about how I felt." Saoirse nudged the shot glass at Fitch with a hopeful glint in her green eyes. "Someone set them after us. Course, at first we thought they were raiders, they thought we were slavers... got messy. When the dust settled, it took the settlers tellin' 'em to believe."

Fitch refilled the shot. "Mex-Ar?"

"Mexican army." Saoirse slammed the cheap liquor and winced.

"Olds," muttered Neeley.

"Shook it this time." Fitch grinned. "Ain't a real shot 'less ya have ta chew it."

"So..." Saoirse exhaled, waving at the fumes. "Komodo figures out the guy who acted like he'd had his wife and kid taken is really a Mex-Ar officer. Loses his royal effing shit." She slapped herself in the forehead and twirled her hand into the air. "So everything's a total shit show. Next thing we know, there's Redeemed and Mex-Ar going after each other all around us. Got settlers crawlin' under the truck not to get shot. Them 'Deemed chased those tan-coated bastards all the way back ta Durango for all I know."

"Who's Komodo?" asked Kevin.

She shrugged. "Seemed like he'd been the one runnin' the pack. Big boy, has this whole Apache war chief thing going."

"Hmm." Kevin hooked his thumbs in his jean pockets and gnawed on his lip. "So how do they go from bein' inclined to free slaves to shooting up a roadhouse for jollies?"

Saoirse regarded the empty shot glass with a smirk. "Probably on account o' gettin' served this shite." She flashed a mischievous grin and set the glass down.

"Hell if I know." Fitch collected the glass and dropped it in the 'dirty' bin under the counter. "All you know, guys who shot up Wayne's place mighta been some pack of scavs what found Redeemed dead on the side of the road and took their threads."

Kevin blinked. "Shit. Never thought of that."

"Or they had a change of leadership." Saoirse fished out five coins and set them on the counter. "Clubs like that can sometimes change 'pendin' on who's wearin' the leader patch. Need a room, charge on number three and a refill on the beer."

"One short," said Fitch.

Kevin burst into laughter.

Both of them looked at him until he could breathe again.

"What?" Saoirse narrowed her eyes. "What you laughin' at?"

"The F-350."

"Yeah, so?" She bristled.

"Nothin'." Kevin forced himself composed, but couldn't stop smirking.

Fitch stifled a laugh. "Smallest driver, biggest ride."

She fished out a penny and added it. Her eyes wanted to laugh, but she kept a stoic face.

Kevin leaned back to turn on the charging station while Fitch refilled a mason jar. As Saoirse headed back to her table, Fitch gave him a look.

"Didn't you have some kinda thing with redheads and pickup trucks?"

Kevin scowled at the floor. "The Marauder wasn't quite that big, and the bitch had real long hair, and a giant pair of..." He grumbled. "I'll be back in a bit."

"Take your time." Fitch grinned.

Kevin clapped him on the shoulder. "Thanks, man. Gotta deal with some crap. Mind watchin' the front for a few minutes more?"

Fitch leaned one elbow on the counter top, grinning. "No problem. Shit, I don't know how you tolerate not gettin' shot at every twenty minutes. Just standin' around watchin' people drink, brokerin' jobs..."

Kevin faked a wince. "Yeah. Life just ain't the same without wondering if I'm going to live through the next twenty minutes."

"Shame." Fitch chuckled. "Ah well, s'pose a man's gotta do..."

"Yep."

Kevin ducked into the rear hall and poked his head into the kitchen doorway. Sang sat on his cot reading; the scent of something meaty hung in the air. "We're back."

The old man looked up with smiling eyes. "Kevin. Good to see you. How was trip?"

"Trip's okay. News ain't so good."

Sang lowered the book to his lap. "Want to talk about it?"

Kevin pondered for a second or four. "Maybe. Not right now. Got stuff to do. Wayne's dead."

"I am sorry." Sang brought his hands together and bowed his head.

"Thanks."

Kevin sighed and remained a few seconds longer before heading across the hall to the office. Bee lay prostrate on the secondary desk against the rear wall, shirt off, back wide open to expose her metal internals and wires. A thick plume of whitish smoke trailed upward from an open panel on a black box mounted to the spine about where a person's intestines ought to be. The android rested her chin on her crossed arms and made idle conversation with Tris about the pros and cons of skirts versus pants.

Tris, standing at a workbench full of junk, twisted around to look at Kevin as he entered. She looked calm, though her face bore the frustrated glower of someone engaged in a tedious task. Merely seeing her lifted his mood enough for a smile to happen. She returned it, and resumed rummaging around through assorted crap they'd torn out of the former rest stop restaurant. Mostly coin-operated mini-jukeboxes that had been installed at each table, though a couple of computers and two floor-polishing machines joined the tech graveyard.

"How goes it?"

"Fine," said Tris. "Trying to find some eighth-inch wire before I have to make one, but all the wiring in this crap is sixteenth."

He gestured at a rotary polisher head. "What about that thing?"

"Probably does… but I don't have the right size socket driver to get it open."

"I can assist you in braiding wire," said Bee. "My sense of balance does not exist, but my arms work."

Kevin chuckled and headed over to the security console/radio desk. He let his weight fall into the green cloth chair, launching a cloud of dust. Landing there felt as though the weight of the past two days' anxiety had been packed into an enormous water balloon balanced on his head, which burst.

He leaned forward, face in his hands, and exhaled. Home. Safe. As angry as he'd been about Wayne, what good would it do to get himself killed? Even if he *did* manage to find the particular individuals responsible for killing him—without dying in the process—it wouldn't resurrect the old bastard. The world wouldn't notice or care one way or the other that Wayne had been avenged, and it wouldn't give a mustard-covered fuck if Kevin took a bullet in the head for his troubles either.

After a long five minutes of staring at the floor while listening to Tris grumble under her breath, he reached out and took the radio mic. Two breaths later, he pushed the button. Tris went quiet at the pop of static from the speakers.

"This is Kevin outta I-80, Rawlins. Anyone awake?" He let off the button.

"Ya. I'm here," said Gertrude.

"Hey, cutie." Beth purred.

Kevin shivered, remembering the woman old enough to be his mother.

"Kevin," said the gravelly voice of Harold, somewhere in western Ohio.

Seven or eight new voices answered, from roadhouses scattered from the northwest down to this guy Enrico in Florida.

"Whazzat?" asked a creaky old voice.

The radio channel erupted with laughter.

When it settled, Kevin squeezed the talk button and brought the mic to his lips. "It's important. What I'm gonna say needs to make it to every 'house."

"*¿Que esta?*" asked a baritone voice.

"Sounds *nicht so gut*," said Gertrude.

Tris set down a tool with a soft *thunk*, braced her hands on the worktable, and twisted around to watch him.

Kevin waved her back to her task. "I'm okay. Keep fixing Bee." He winked and pushed the button. "I'm just back in the door from takin' a ride to Hagerman. Wayne's been killed. He—"

The radio erupted with too many voices at once to make sense of any of them.

Kevin waited until the channel fell quiet. "He had an android waitress who they didn't bother destroying."

"I behaved as though I was a simple cleaning unit without personality," said Bee.

"Yeah… what she said."

"Oh." Bee covered her mouth with a hand. "Kevin. Thank you."

He let off the talk button. "What?"

"You called me 'she.'" Bee smiled.

He rubbed the bridge of his nose, eyes closed. *Screw it.* "Anyway, she told me a pack of bikers came in, refused to pay, wound up shooting him. They all had the same symbol. White hand inside a circle, grabbin' on a sword by the blade."

"Ain't never heard o' that," said Earl.

"Yeah, but you's near Topeka. Ain't nothin' there." Harold laughed.

"Wayne's dead?" Tears saturated Beth's voice.

An awkward silence settled over the channel for the better part of a minute.

"Redeemed," said an unknown girl who sounded on the young side. "Seen 'em in here a couple times, but they ain't caused no problems."

"Who is this?" asked Gertrude. "I do not recognize your voice, *Schätzchen.*"

"Uhh, I'm Maribel. This is my dad's roadhouse. He's busy with the front, so he told me to get the radio."

"Language check," said Harold.

"Kid alert," added Enrico.

"Whazzat?" asked Whazzat.

"I'm not a little kid; I'm eleven." Maribel huffed before her transmit cut out.

"Right…" Kevin smiled for an instant, but his stomach roiled. *If those fuckers start shooting up roadhouses…* "Look, there's something else."

"Oh, this is great." Harold grumbled. "Worse than killing Wayne?"

"Yeah." Kevin rubbed his forehead. "The camera system in Hagerman was toasted. Hasn't worked in years."

"What's wrong with it?" asked Gertrude.

"Whole thing's fffffudged," said Kevin.

Enrico and Harold's laugher collided on the channel.

"Easy on that technical talk, boy." Mac clucked his tongue. "You know I can't understand it."

More chuckling.

"I'm *not* a little kid," yelled Maribel.

Tris swooped over and took the mic from Kevin's hand. "Hey. It's me. I'll try to use small words." She let off the talk button long enough for another round of chuckling to simmer down. "The cameras record digital video to a solid state hard drive in the main component cabinet. That's the dark grey box with the word Dell on it or maybe the initials HP. Problem is, those types of drives don't last forever. They wear out and stop working. Maybe millions of rewrites, but these cameras have been recording constantly for years. All of this hardware predates the war. It's old, and it's going to fail soon if it hasn't already."

"So what you're saying…" Harold coughed and stopped transmitting.

"Shit," rasped Mac. "Uhh, crap. Sorry Maribel."

"I'm okay," said Maribel in a tiny, frightened voice. "The bad words are only a little scary." After a second, she laughed.

Kevin did as well, though he didn't send it over the radio. He grasped the mic and Tris' hand, pushing her thumb into the button while drawing it closer to his mouth. "She's saying that all of our security systems are probably dead or about to be dead. Is anyone from Amarillo on?"

Dead silence.

"Amarillo, come back?" Kevin waited thirty seconds. "Amarillo?"

Her stare said 'oh shit.'

"Roger, Kevin." An oldish man cleared his throat twice. "Copy. This is Amarillo. Proceed."

"Whazzat?" asked Whazzat.

He imagined a collective sigh of relief throughout what had once been the United States... well except for the northeast. No one went there anymore. So many Infected, not even the Infected lasted long. Kevin rambled over a detailed retelling of the events of Wayne's demise, and spent a good six minutes complaining about the dead hardware.

"Understood," said Amarillo. "Couple of those HP units had an issue with crappin' out. Part-a the routine checklist no one bothers ta follow. I shouldn't need to remind all of you to not advertise to the run of the mill if you're havin' technical difficulties wit yer security monitors. If yer unit's down, disconnect the cables from the back and send it on back to us"—distant gunfire echoed, as if on the other side of a thick wall—"under the code of 'scavenged tech.' We'll fix 'em up and get 'em back to you." The start of a coughing fit cut off after half a second.

"I have no idea vot ze hell I am looking at back zhere," said Gertrude. "Is all blinking lights and vires."

"Copy that, Brownstown. Confirm, you're on I-70, right?"

"Ja," said Gertrude. "I am trying to get *die maschine* to play ze recordings, but *es ist nur* screen filled vith grey sparkles."

"Snow," said Tris. "Same thing I saw at Wayne's. Your SSDs are dead."

"Hell Trude, that's what you get for not usin' protection. SSDs." Mac roared with laughter.

"Eww," said Maribel.

"Whazzat?" asked Whazzat.

"Have you seen Gertrude?" asked Harold. "She *is* protection."

"I know vhere you live," said Gertrude. "You are not ze shpring chicken either."

"A site inspector will be there soon." A few more gunshots snapped like popcorn in the background of Amarillo.

"Central, what's all the shooting?" asked Enrico. "You boys havin' a party in Texas?"

The old man let out a dry chuckle. "Training. Just some of the recruits on the firing range practicing."

"Amarillo," said Kevin. Tris released the mic and wrapped her arms around him. "Hastings Roadhouse, on I-80. We found a site inspector there, dead."

Several gasps came back over the radio, but the old man remained quiet.

"Someone's got a damn death wish," said Mirabel. "Killed a site inspector? They'll cut someone's balls off for that."

"Oh, she's adorable," said Harold, with extra gravel.

"Kevin. This is Amarillo," croaked the old man. "Do you have any information on who killed him?"

"He was infected." Kevin waited for the chatter to die down before continuing. "As best I can tell, he's the one who brought the Virus to the Hastings Roadhouse. Gave it to some prostitutes who shot him dead, but they didn't tell anyone and well… you can figure out what happened. Didn't look like anyone made it out of there alive."

"Oh, poor Sierra." Beth sighed. "*So eine Schande.*"

"Got any more inspectors?" asked Mac. His voice sounded mirthful, but no one laughed.

Kevin flicked his thumbnail over the talk button, waiting for Amarillo to reply. The entire radio channel waited as well. It took a little over three minutes for someone to break the tension.

"That a no?" asked Beth.

Another forty seconds passed.

"Whazzat?" asked Whazzat.

The channel erupted with laughter.

"Amarillo?" asked Beth.

"Yeah, yeah," said the old man from Amarillo, sounding annoyed. "Keep your panties on. Got a private channel for inspectors. Got Larry headin' your way now, Brownstown."

"*Gut,*" said Gertrude. "He can make *die maschine* work, *ja?*"

"Or replace it, yes."

The radio chatter gave way to multiple reports of non-working systems, though Mac, Earl, and Clive claimed their hardware appeared fine. Kevin leaned away from the radio as Amarillo ran the three through a test upload to see if the camera data would make it intact. Apparently they *did* have a way to send the video files over the radio. Tris hadn't recognized the modem as the tech would've been considered old even in 2017.

"Yo Kev," yelled Fitch. "You busy? Got a full house."

Tris sighed and started for the door, but Kevin grabbed her by the wrist.

"Hey… You're better with this shit." He stood, pulling her into a kiss. A minute later, their lips parted. "Why don't you stay here and get Bee back on her feet. I'll go."

"Okay." She hugged him, cheek to his chest. "As long as you're happy."

"Couldn't be happier." He touched foreheads with her for a second before winking.

TRIS LEANED AGAINST THE DESK AS KEVIN WALKED OUT. *He's a shitty liar, but he's trying to make me feel better.* She looked down, kicking the toe of her black sneaker at the floor until a faint whirr from Bee's internals got her attention.

"Oh, Bee. I'm sorry." She hurried over to the worktable.

"It is okay. I am incapable of becoming either bored or sore from lying on a table."

Tris picked among the random junk until she found an old microwave oven, which yielded a length of wire close enough to one-eighth inch thick. After removing it from the appliance, she crossed the room to Bee and compared it to the lead that ran from the main power cell to the gyroscopic unit bolted to the robot's spine. Her salvaged wire wouldn't have any slack, but the gauge of wire appeared perfect.

She spent the next half hour clearing bits of melted copper and insulation from the contacts before soldering the replacement in. Fortunately, she'd managed to swipe all of Wayne's tools—at least anything useful for electronics work—while Kevin worried about guns and bullets. Even if Alamo and those idiots had noticed, they probably wouldn't have considered the tools worth much. She eyed the ammo can full of coins and Wayne's ledger that Bee had smuggled to her. Though she thought it silly, she respected Kevin for being true to his beliefs and wanting to hold those accounts for the drivers.

The gyroscope housing vibrated and emitted a faint scraping noise for a few seconds before it faded to an almost inaudible whirr.

"That feels good," said Bee, wagging her head from side to side.

"Just a bit longer… and I'm sorry." Tris flipped the android's skirt up over her back to expose her from the waist down. Aside from two scuffmarks and a .22 bullet hole, Bee's nether regions were smooth and featureless.

"Why are you sorry?"

"For taking your pants down." Tris pressed at the thigh until a previously-invisible seam appeared and a long narrow hatch opened to expose the femur and surrounding components.

"I do not understand. You seemed quite pleased to remove your clothing before. Perhaps someday you can explain the meaning of—" Bee's speaking voice cut out to a recording of Tris emitting orgasmic moans. "I was unable to determine a language for those vocalizations."

Tris covered her red-hot face with both hands. It took her over a minute to find where her voice ran off to hide. "Uhm… Bee… It's not a language. It's an… umm, involuntary noise triggered by a biological process. It doesn't really mean anything."

Bee's head rotated back, farther than a human ought to be able to, but not quite backward. The android smiled. "I am teasing you."

Tris burst out laughing. She peered into the hollow leg, at a loose wire with a flat four-prong plug. "Oh, there's your problem. The connector popped loose."

"One of the men who attacked us threw me to the floor." Bee drummed her fingers on the table. "If not for the first law, I would have shot him."

"First law? Oh… that whole cannot harm humans thing? Asimov?" Tris scratched her head for a second before sliding her hand into the narrow space and grasping the connector between two fingers. She bit her tongue while trying to ease the thing back onto the four naked pins jutting out of the knee actuator. "Damn, there's not a lot of space in here."

"No, Tris. Wayne's first law of robotics."—Wayne's voice played out of the android's mouth—"If someone starts some shit, use the biggest god damned gun you can get your hands on and blow his god damned head off." Bee's eyes blinked with a *click,* and her normal voice returned. "The handgun on my belt was a .357 Sig. A 12-gauge shotgun loaded with solid slugs located under the counter was the largest weapon in the area. I was shot while attempting to retrieve it. Alas, I was unable to determine the weapon's relationship with a theoretical higher power."

"You shouldn't have taken him literally, but I suppose that's not your fault." She twisted her entire body up on one foot while seating the connector. After nudging it with one fingernail until it clicked, she relaxed.

"I'm reading everything online. You are wonderful to me, Tris."

Tris closed all the panels and adjusted the android's clothing back in place. "Since Wayne isn't around anymore, I'm giving you a new, uhh, prime directive."

Bee climbed off the table and tested her limbs' range of motion. "Programming mode on."

Is she kidding or did I open the firmware? "If anyone threatens Kevin or me, or any innocent people in your vicinity, use the closest weapon at your disposal to protect them. Firearms take priority over melee weapons, but only if it is safe to discharge a firearm in the area without harming the innocent."

Bee blinked. "I understand."

"Great. Let's go see if the boys need help." Tris examined her filthy hands. "After I clean up."

⁘⁘⁘⁘⁘⁘⁘

KEVIN NUDGED MEAT PATTIES AROUND THE GRILL, WORKING ELBOW TO elbow with Sang. The old Korean tended to another four burgers as well as the fryer. The oil smelled a little off. He'd need to see if Carver had any fresh stuff soon… without Sang's increasingly famous fried potato discs, he'd probably have a riot in the restaurant.

He grinned, though the humor faded before the sound of a laugh could escape his mouth. Scary as it was, someone *might* actually pull a gun over them not having fries, especially if word got out that the Roadhouse security system was faulty. *Sounded like people had a seven-in-ten chance of finding a 'house where the security's as useless as a blind dust hopper.* He flipped patty after patty, poking them back into place one after the next so they remained in neat rows. *Pretty stupid of me.* He sighed, thinking of how he once regarded the Code as this mythical law that protected drivers and 'house operators… as if the mere instant someone so much as thought about doing something, the entire Roadhouse network became aware of it and would come down on them with a hammer. *That's how a little boy looks at it. Ol' fuckin' Road House Santa Claus will just know who's the asshole.*

Sang handed him a plate of bottom-buns, toasted.

"Thanks."

Sang nodded.

Kevin set the plate at his side and scooped burger after burger onto the bread Sang had likely baked that morning. He stared at the giant spatula, wondering at what point in the past seventy-two hours the thought of making his living with it instead of a .45 felt *more* dangerous. *At least on the road, I* knew *someone was trying to kill me.* He glanced at the little hole in the wall to the main room. Days… weeks… months could go by of total quiet. One kook having a bad day and *blam.* That's that. Shot in the back without warning. He used to have faith the Code would keep people too scared to dare try.

Not so much now.

Sang started flicking top-buns at him across the grill from where he'd set them to toast. "Need ta buy more cheese from Cahvah. We out."

"Yeah." He plucked the sliding bread domes from the grill and covered the burgers one after the next. "Maybe I'll run over there myself tomorrow."

"Sound good." Sang nodded. "Mister Fitch good man. Otha driver respect him."

Kevin shook his head at the grill while chuckling.

"Oh. They respect you too." Sang grinned.

"Oh, sweet Laird Jeebus," yelled Fitch out in the front room. "What in the hell is that?"

"My name is Bee."

Kevin aimed his voice at the passé-plat. "Fitch, it's okay. She's here to help."

Tris popped in through the door, wiping her wet hands on a small beige towel. "Hey. Need any help in here?"

He carried the plate of twelve burgers to the hole, and passed it to Bee. Tris trailed after him. Kevin sidestepped Sang coming in with a giant wire basket of seasoned fries, which Fitch grabbed.

Damn those smell amazing. Tris put a hand on his growling stomach. He stared into her eyes. Rather than the upwelling of adoration the sight of her usually stirred within him, he felt dread. His brain seized upon her small frame, delicate features, and the concern in her eyes. All at once, his world came crashing down. Could his dream be a tomb? He found his hands shaking as he threaded them around her neck and drew her close. If the Code had holes in it, anything could happen to her.

We're sitting ducks on the side of the road… out here, alone. He couldn't find a way to force words out of his mouth, so he held her in silence.

"Kevin?"

Her voice stalled his mind. *She's not as helpless as she looks.* He smiled. *Still… What if she doesn't see it coming?* "Yeah?"

"You okay? I... know losing Wayne wasn't easy on you."

"I'm okay." He loosened his grip to clasp her shoulders at arms' length. "Just thinking about everything going on."

"You two hungry?" asked Sang. "I can hear your stomach across the room."

Tris ducked her head between Kevin's arm and chest to peer at Sang. "Yes! Starving."

"Yeah," said Kevin. "Food sounds good."

She popped upright and grinned at Kevin, who eyed the outer room past the hole in the wall where the din of over ten people rumbled. "Be right back. Gonna make sure everything's under control out there."

DEAD CODE

Tris stretched her arms up over her head, basking in a warm breeze washing over her naked body. The stretch evolved into a lazy yawn. After, she rolled onto her side, gazing blearily at the open window near the bed. Subdued scratching and the muffled grunt of Kevin attempting to rummage around for his clothes without waking her made her smile. With a soft moan of contentment, she stretched again.

"Morning." Kevin leaned over the bed, shirt still unbuttoned, and kissed her.

She ran a hand up his chest to his neck, drinking in the smell of him. "Mmm. Where are you rushing off to?"

"Just a quick run over to Carver's farm for supplies. Fryer oil's old enough to demand pay, and we're going through potatoes like hell."

Tris closed her eyes, grinning at the soft scratch of a calloused hand sliding over her breast and down her side, settling on her left hip. "Okay. I'll be up in a little bit."

He patted her butt twice before drifting away. A moment later, he drew in a long breath. "Love the smell of morning."

Tris laughed, one eye popping open. The mattress hovered as an off-white blur a few inches in front of her face. Sweat and musk filled her nose. "Smells like sex over here."

The bed shifted from his weight settling at the edge. She crawled closer and rested her head on his thigh. Her limbs got heavy when he ran his fingers through her hair, her body losing what little urge she had to get up. For a while, she lay in blissful silence as he stroked her back, butt, and thighs in a continuous, gentle caress.

"I never thought I'd ever really know what it's like to be happy." He continued running his hand over her head as though she were a cat. She half considered purring. "Every day, I wake up expecting it all to be a dream, but there you are."

Her brain sent 'I love you, too' to her mouth, but only a soft, "Mmm" came out.

The next thing she knew, she lay on her chest, cheek on the mattress, a sheet covering her up to the neck.

Tris pushed herself over onto her back, took a deep breath, and sat up, squinting at the room. The light hadn't changed *too* much, so she figured she'd lost only twenty minutes to passing out again. After a yawn, she scooted to the edge and got up, stretched again, and reached for a shirt. The instant cloth settled around her shoulders, she got overwhelmed with 'feeling sticky everywhere.' Deciding to have a quick shower, she pulled it back off.

She clutched a black tee with a faded ankh silkscreen and one of the new items she'd liberated from Wayne's—a mid-thigh denim skirt with only one dried bloodstain—to her chest. After peering into the hall to verify it free of prying eyes, she streaked across to the little private bathroom they'd installed in what had once been a huge storage closet.

Plastic tubing carried water in from the well pump to a bright orange nozzle with a butterfly valve. An upside-down spoon tied on with wire and bent under the spigot sort-of made it a showerhead. She set the clothes on a steel shelf and stepped over the edge of the kiddie pool up on cinder blocks. An improvised drain of radiator tubing ran through a hole in the wall.

A few rapid breaths prepared her for the cold water, and she hurried the process of cleaning herself with some of the tiny soap bars Kevin found in an old hotel years ago. By the time she'd rinsed free of suds, her teeth chattered.

Tris stepped into the skirt, pulled it up, buttoned it, and let go. It fell straight to the floor around her ankles. She leaned back and sighed at the ceiling. "Crap."

The tee shirt didn't cover enough to act as a dress, so she held the skirt up by hand and scurried back to the bedroom. A few minutes of knife-and-thread surgery gave the garment a new buttonhole that kept it on.

Two sneakers later, she added her gun belt with the Beretta and went downstairs to an empty room.

Sang mumbled to himself in the kitchen, a usual sign that he'd lost himself in a novel. She poked her head in.

"Going out for a little air. Been putting off checking that shack long enough."

"Okay." Sang looked up and nodded.

Tris wandered to the end of the inner hallway and into a small bare concrete room where a few stacks of old pallets had piled up against the wall. Two roll-top doors led out to a tiny loading dock. She went for the pedestrian door to the right, crossed the deck in three strides, and descended a short concrete stairway to the paved lot behind the building. Warm air rushed under her skirt, making her self-conscious about her lack of underwear. Not since leaving the Enclave had she even seen another pair to scavenge.

Probably why all the other women I see have pants... or long dresses.

Brown field stretched as far as she could see into the distance toward mountains, dotted liberally with green scrub bushes. Off to the left, a group of picnic tables held the ghosts of prewar travelers. A minute or two outside, and the sun had dispelled the chill from the shower

She closed her eyes at a sudden pickup of dusty wind and flapped her shirt to let the moving air pull dampness away. Once the wind died down, she headed to her right along the back wall toward the west end of the property.

The old central air unit supported a colony of brown and green beer bottles, likely there since before the nukes. She could almost hear the teenagers who'd worked here half a century ago complaining about wanting to get out of the middle of nowhere, or how poorly they were paid. The Enclave understood the concept of money as it had been before, and taught it to her as a child. She daydreamed about being eleven again, listening to the nameless instructor explain how foolish humanity had been for allowing a small minority to control most of the wealth instead of allocating it efficiently. Tris frowned. 'Instructor' had been the only name ever used to refer to the teachers, as if any dose of humanity in the classroom would've been some kind of terrible crime.

Blaming money in large part for the nuclear war that devoured the civilization that spawned it, the Enclave didn't use currency, per se. Everyone had a job and responsibilities. Everyone got what they needed. *And the Council of Four got a whole lot more. Funny how that works. I wonder why Tier 1 'needed' luxury.* She felt a bit of the hypocrite as she walked past the corner of the building and hooked a sharp curve along a walkway of red patio tile to the parking lot out front. Her father—before she had been re-homed—lived well. While she couldn't recall anyone in the Enclave being 'poor,' some people definitely had it easier. As she thought about her father, an odd realization leapt to mind. She remembered cars on the roads when she was six, but couldn't recall seeing one much past that, not since the night he'd woken her up early, excited to be able to bring her to work. Some kind of company event where everyone got to bring their kids in.

He drove us to work, but security drove us home...

The walkway veered left, running along the inner edge of a massive parking lot that had to be at least a half mile from end to end, where ramps connected it to I-80. Two-thirds of the length of the rest stop had been devoted to the gas station. Near the far end, a modest beige shed stood next to the rusted hulk of a dump truck. For months, Kevin had been meaning to check out what was in it. Somewhere between the long walk and having so much other stuff to do, they'd never gotten around to it.

She paused, fists on her hips, and twisted back to stare at the decaying pumps, the crumbling canopies over them bearing an Exxon logo. Much of the area taken up by the gas station appeared intended as a queue. She tried to imagine a society where so many cars existed that they needed *that* much space to let them line up to wait for fuel. Her childhood memories consisted of a small suburban street with infrequent traffic passing by.

Her thoughts returned to the historical documentaries. A few sounded far too serious to have been fiction, as Kevin maintained. Some of them had scenes of cars upon cars, too many for the road to handle. "Oh, what did they call it? Grid... something."

She muttered to herself, grinning, remembering an argument between a married couple while they sat in standstill traffic behind a truck carrying a massive boat on a trailer. Wealthy people partied on the trailer-bound sailboat despite it being in the middle of a New York street.

"Gridlock!" She called to the clouds.

Her smile lasted only a few seconds before she let out a sad sigh. *All those people...* Again, she trudged forward, eyes downcast. Long skid marks on the blacktop traced lines from parking spaces. Some curved, some squiggly, some short, and some long. Ghostly travelers appeared in her daydream; parents screamed at small children to get in the car. The skies to the east and west turned orange with nuclear fire. *Did they fight each other to get away faster? Where would they have gone?* She crouched to pick up a corroded shell casing from the nook where parking lot met curb. It looked like a 9mm, but whether or not it had been fired *that* day, she couldn't tell. Darkened to saddle-leather brown by the elements, it could've been a few years old as easily as forty.

"Did you kill someone the day the nukes fell? Or did you show up later?"

She turned the brass over in her fingers for a moment before dropping it.

"Okay, that's enough." She stood and marched forward to the shack. "War happened. It sucked. They're all dead, and I'm not going to change that."

She kicked at a rusted padlock for a little while without getting anywhere. The keyhole had too much corrosion for her to consider picking it. Out came the Beretta. Tris aimed, unable to decide if she wanted to shoot the shackle or the body, or if it would even be worth using ammo. Wayne had sold 9mm for two coins a bullet, highway robbery according to Kevin who wanted to let them go for one coin per two. She'd talked him into one each. It wasn't as if they had an unlimited supply.

She holstered the weapon and went left to the dead dump truck. The cab smelled like an old sneaker left out in the rain for decades. No glass remained in the rusting frame, bits of diamond-like sparkles shimmered in the dirt around it as well as the rotten seats. Its door let off a crunchy *creak* of protesting steel when she pulled it open. A brief look around yielded a tire iron under the driver's seat, which she used to pry the old Master lock off with ease.

Tris flung the two barn-style doors to the side and stared at a huge pile of whitish crystals, more than what could have fit in the dump truck. A hesitant sniff, and reluctant taste later, she blinked in astonishment, recognizing the substance. "What would anyone need this much salt for?"

Bang!

Tris flung herself to the ground, holding as still as she could while the echo of the heavy gunshot rolled off into the distance. The rapport sounded like a huge rifle; her mind leapt back to a sniper catching her with her pants quite literally down. Four seconds after the rumble faded to silence, 'the sniper' in her memory became Zara. Someone else from the Enclave who had been sent to kill her, and almost did.

She picked her head up enough to look around. Rapid breaths echoed in her skull. After their last meeting, she doubted Zara would come after her again, but couldn't imagine sniper rifles that big (or loud) being common. Then again, the soldiers defending Dallas had .50 cal sniper rifles too, so maybe a handful of them did exist out in the Wildlands.

Arm over arm, she crawled against the rusted heap of dump truck. It might never drive again, but maybe that much steel could stop a bullet. She pushed at the ground and got her feet under her, squatting half under the fender. No motion broke the endless placidity of the barren land.

On her third visual sweep back and forth, it hit her that the roadhouse's windows looked too black. A thin wisp of smoke rose from the roof amid the solar panels. Not a gunshot—something exploded.

Fear evaporated.

"Shit." She stood and rubbed her forehead. "Now what? Oh, please tell me that bang wasn't the power controller blowing up."

Tris jogged back to the building, finding the restaurant area dead and silent. Nothing electric (including the charging panel) showed any sign of life. Grumbling, she trudged upstairs to the grey metal ladder leading to the roof. The hatch opened with a spine-wiggling squeal, and fell against the roof with a loud *clang*. Her next breath flooded her senses with molten plastic and charred meat.

Beretta out, she stalked around the housing of an HVAC unit and aimed down the row of solar panels. The smoke appeared thicker one row to the left. She edged sideways until the remains of a flaming squirrel came into view, teeth still clamped on the half-inch cable it had chewed on.

"Oh, son of a bitch." She let her arms drop and shook her head.

After shutting off the main switch, she took a knee by the dead, smoldering critter. Its right forepaw had fused to the housing of the adjacent panel's electronics, teeth in the wire. She knocked it away with the Beretta before holstering the weapon. A three-inch patch of insulation had melted off, and one corner of the cabinet had blackened before the fuse had done its job. That appeared to be the extent of the damage.

Hopefully, that bang came from the breaker going.

She headed down the ladder to the kitchen, where Sang furiously worked a towel over a section of counter between the fryer and a sink.

"Damn squirrel," said Tris.

Sang whirled around. "Sorry, miss. I spill water into the wires and it go bang."

She walked over and peered into a gap between the wall and the steel fryer. "Those are old wires… they don't even have any power in them. Damn squirrel chewed one on the roof."

"Oh." He smiled with relief. "I thought I'd broken things." He gestured at the wall. "It went dark as soon as I spilled. This heart can't take such a scare."

She patted him on the shoulder. "It's okay." For whatever reason, Kevin had appropriated a non-working industrial fridge as a storage cabinet for 'various random shit' that might be useful, including the box of spare fuses Amarillo'd soaked him another hundred coins for. She pulled the door open, inhaling a mixture of rubber, plastic, and must.

"Can you fix?" asked Sang.

She pulled two dented toolboxes—one red and one blue—out and opened them. "Probably. Depends on if the main breaker tripped or exploded. I also need something to reinsulate some wire with or the whole thing is gonna fry as soon as it rains." When neither toolbox offered anything useful, she grabbed for a cardboard one she recognized from the Challenger's trunk, and dragged it off the shelf to the floor. Among stray sockets and a bunch of spare cables for an e-car motor, lay a healthy spool of electrical tape. "Aha!"

Tris jumped up to her feet.

"How much of squirrel is left?" Sang raised an eyebrow.

She shivered. "Not enough to cook. It's char."

He snapped his fingers. That she couldn't tell if he was joking caused a slight shiver as she hurried back to the ladder. Replacing the fuse took all of five seconds. Fifteen minutes later, she'd cleaned and wrapped the wire enough to trust. By the time she finished and bit off the tape, the char-squirrel had cooled to the point she could touch it without burning herself. She chucked it off the roof on the way back to the hatch.

In the hall, she paused by the breaker box and meditated. *Please don't be fried. Please don't be fried.* The door emitted a faint metallic squeak when she opened it, exposing a giant four-span switch at the top, the main, which had flipped down. A sniff test got a nose full of plastic and dust, but nothing alarming.

She shut off all the sub breakers and eased the main to the on position before heading back up to the roof to turn on the panels' master switch. A few minutes of watching later, when nothing caught fire, she climbed down and flipped the smaller breakers on one after the next. On the fifth, Sang cheered.

Tris shut the circuit box door, but left her hand on it for a few seconds, waiting for something else to go wrong, but everything remained quiet. No one had arrived out front, so after a brief glance, she headed for the office and fell into the chair by the security computer.

"Okay, thing." She poked the button to wake the screen. An OS desktop appeared for less than a full second before it flickered to a hand-drawn Roadhouse logo and the camera system came up.

Expecting the same situation she'd found in Hastings, she broke out of the camera OS and hunted down the modified configuration file. Sure enough, it contained the same commands to always display the self-diagnostics as passing for all components. Tris un-hacked the file and started the diagnostics before leaning back with one foot up on the desk. When the progress ticked up to 4%, she remembered no one outside of the Enclave apparently had any idea what panties were, and anyone walking in the office would've gotten a hell of a show.

She put her leg down.

"I'm going to go back to the Enclave for no other reason than to get some god damned underwear." She huffed.

A sixty something year old cloth-cushioned chair with three out of five wheels broken wasn't a terribly comfortable thing to sit in for twenty minutes. She pivoted away from the door and put her legs up on the desk in the other direction (away from the entrance), ankles crossed.

Error message after error message popped up.

Twelve of the twenty two-terabyte SSD units in the memory box reported data sector failures, with a third of those having less than 15% of their sectors reporting writable. Two showed as completely dead. For each of those, another popup notified her that the system had auto-removed them from the ZFS RAID filesystem and adjusted to run on the remaining eighteen. She spent the next twenty minutes looking at frozen data, camera recordings from some other roadhouse where this hardware had been before Kevin's place... unable to erase or write over it.

"Crap." She sat up, feet on the floor, and paged through the remaining diagnostics. One of the cameras showed 'fault,' and some of the RAM in the primary computer failed randomly. She ran the test four times, each one coming back with different bad memory addresses. She exhaled in frustration. "This thing is so flaky I should butter it. It's gonna die any damn day."

"Hey, anyone," yelled a male voice from the radio with gunfire in the background. "This is Nash, Roadhouse on I-10 west o' Lordsburg. Under attack"—four loud gunshots came over the channel accompanied by screams of pain and howls that conjured image of drunken Viking raiders— "Bobby and Dan are dead. Lauren's makin' a run for it with the"—a loud male scream of anger cut off in a half-second with another tremendous gunshot—"kids."

Tris leapt from her chair and grabbed the mic. "Nash, this is Rawlins. Who's attacking? Why?"

Her heart sped up, though her breath caught in her throat. Five seconds of silence, timed in heartbeats.

"No fuckin' idea why," yelled Nash. "Bunch of goddamn bikers. White fists on their backs." He let off a garbled roar, and a rapid flurry of gunfire erupted over the speakers, followed by a heavy *thud* and gurgly wheezing.

"Nash?" yelled Tris. "Nash!"

"Mother of God," whispered Clive, safe somewhere at his 'house in northwest Colorado.

"Yo, Nash, man. What's goin on?" asked Mac, amid a crackle of radio static.

Silence.

Tris stared down at her shaking hand, clutching the black mic. The Motorola logo in the middle blurred. "N-Nash?"

A louder wheeze and the heavy *thunk* of slow-walking boots came over the speakers.

The weak, gurgling whisper had a hint of Nash's voice. "P-please let my kids…"

Bang.

The heavy boot steps clunked into the distance, accompanied by the rhythmic tapping of a swaying microphone against the side of a desk.

Tris buried her face in her hands, shaking.

Some minutes later, Harold's gravelly voice ventured soft and hesitant into the silence. "They just pissed all over the Code."

"Who are these sumbitches?" roared Mac.

She sat up, arms crossed limp over her lap. *It's falling apart out there.* Her thoughts filled with a woman running for her life with a child under each arm. She had no idea how old Nash's kids were, but her waking nightmare filled in a pair of five-year-olds.

The clatter of the front door made her jump.

"Yo, anyone here?" yelled a man out in the front room.

Soft *thumps* of multiple sets of boots followed.

Tris stood, checked the Beretta on her hip, and eyed the door. *Relax. They're just drivers looking for food and a charge.* If she saw Redeemed symbols, could she open fire right away?

She put on a calm face, trying to ignore that she'd just heard a man die on live broadcast begging for his children's lives. Did they get away? What would happen to them if the bikers caught them? For once, Tris regretted watching the historical documentaries.

Three men stood by the counter out front. As soon as she appeared in the hallway, they smiled with a hint of surprise. All wore leather riding armor and jackets in various degrees of black and scuffed to hell. The nearest man had his two friends by a touch over a foot in height, putting her eye level with his sternum. A dark brown man on the left with long dusty hair stared at her thighs with a huge grin while the other guy, a ruddy ginger, kept eye contact with an equally frightening 'hungry' look. Fortunately, none of them wore the symbol of the Redeemed.

"Hey." She walked up to the inside of the counter. "What do you need?"

The dusty-haired man gestured at her and muttered in Spanish at the ginger before winking at her. "Nice legs, mama."

"Yo, bitch is white like a china doll." Ginger licked his lip. "This gonna be a funner stop than I thought."

Her jaw tightened, eyes narrowed.

"Lemme have three of the closest thing you got to beer."

She relaxed a little.

"And"—he pulled a gun from a holster, but didn't point it at her—"all the coins you got on hand. And, oh yeah... why don't you take them clothes off. You won't be needin' em."

13

BOUNTY

Kevin frowned at the dashboard of Bull's SUV. Why anyone would have an otherwise beautiful machine like this… and not even have *one* mounted weapon on it boggled him. Without a combustion engine, the space under the hood had enough room for battery pack as well as at least two .50 cal machineguns. The roof rack would work for M-60s. The windows ought to have been armored up, and the back had a crapload of room for who knows what. Hi-torque motors could haul a lot of weight, but sucked for speed.

"Bull, you're a damn idiot." He sighed.

Of course, Bull had wanted his truck to 'look good,' and be as close to prewar bling as he could get it. The idiot figured a crew with rifles could do the work while he focused on driving. Kevin raised both eyebrows as he turned on to the dirt road leading to the Carver farm. A modest field of green spread out behind a massive Quonset hut made of mismatched pieces of corrugated steel and some plyboard.

"S'pose he did have a point. Not like he died in the truck."

Kent Carver, a hard-bodied man in his early sixties, sauntered off a porch of dusty wooden boards, a guarded expression on his face. Pale blue farmer's shirt and white pants made him look like he belonged back in the year he'd been born. Soon after he appeared, two of his sons, both near in age to Kevin, walked out onto the porch with bolt-action hunting rifles.

The truck bounced and rocked over a dirt lot full of crisscrossing tire marks before Kevin brought it to a stop a few paces away from the old man. Once Carver got a look at him, he warmed up, and his sons relaxed.

"Dammit boy." Carver waved dismissively. "I know the damn fool what used'ta drive that thing. Do an old man a good deed and tell me that sorry son of a bitch is dead."

Kevin hopped out and gave the door a shove closed. "Yep. Though weren't my doin'. Had a convoy crew with a pretty daughter… and assault rifles."

Kent spat to the side. "I had ta run that man off month ago. Tried ta play grabass with Laurie."

Kevin stared. "Laurie's what, like twelve?"

"Thirteen." Kent glared at the SUV.

A girl with curly brown hair and a precociously developed figure peered out of a large window. Her breasts looked larger than Tris'. "Did you call me, gran'pa?" She eyed the truck and lost a little color in her cheeks.

"Naw." Kent smiled at her. "Idjit's dead."

She exhaled, smiled, and disappeared back into the Quonset.

Kevin walked up and shook hands with Kent. "Glad ta at least bring good news."

"What'cha need?"

"Take three boxes o' tatoes, and a mix of whatever other veggies you have in another box. Hopin' for maybe twenty or thirty pounds of meat. Beef if you got it. And I need fryer oil."

Kent grimaced. "Beef gettin' light. Have ta kill and process and I'd rather not on account o' needin' ta breed. Got plenty of hopper. Them things breed so damn fast."

"That's fine," said Kevin. "No sense risking your herd."

Kent nodded at the younger men who headed into the hut with purpose in their stride. The story of Bull's death became a detailed conversation, which Carver relished. A dark-haired woman not quite old enough to be Kevin's mother brought him a cup of cold water. Aside from remembering she worked on the farm and had four sons, he couldn't place her name.

"Thanks." Kevin held up the glass in salute.

She smiled at him before disappearing back inside. Soon, one of the Carver sons beckoned him in. A long wooden table near the door held five wooden boxes about the size of milk crates. Three contained potatoes, one a mix of green, orange, and red vegetables, and the last a bunch of salted and cured dust hopper meat. At the end stood a large metal can that looked like it belonged on the back of a military jeep, likely the oil for frying.

"G'won, check it out, make sure it's to your likin'." Kent smiled.

Kevin examined the food, finding it reasonable. Sure enough, the giant can contained vegetable oil. "Looks good."

"Eighty-two coins then." Kent nodded.

Kevin opened the inner pocket of his armored jacket and grabbed a handful of pennies and dimes. Counting took a while.

"Thank ya kindly," said Kent.

The sons, plus Kevin, carried the stuff out to the SUV and loaded it. Kent approached as Kevin closed the doors.

"Say, if you got a driver lookin' for a job, I got a guy up near'bouts Belfry offa 72. Sent word he's got a bunch of seeds I'd be sorely tempted in. Ain't all that much value, and it's a bit of a haul, but it's important to us."

Kevin nodded. "Go up to your guy in Belfry, pick up the seeds, then bring 'em back here. What's he askin' for the seeds?"

"Six hundred."

"Hmm." Kevin scratched at the back of his neck. "Drivin' a person there, I'd charge 'bout 150. Usually post the run for 720 coins, twenty percent of the value. I doubt a driver's gonna touch a run that long for a hundred coins after I take my 20." He chuckled. "I'll see what I can do, but I might need to post 750, and I'll waive my bit in exchange for a decent bit of steak whenever it comes 'round. 150 might get you wheels."

Kent considered, his expression cycling among contemplative, grimacing, wincing, and annoyance before settling on resigned. "I'd appreciate it. Okay, if you gotta go to 150, do it."

They shook hands.

"I'll post it. Normally, I'd take the 750 to hold, but I'd feel bad sittin' on that if no one picks up the run. If someone signs on, I'll run down here again. Hell, I'm here often enough as it is."

Kent laughed. "Take care of yourself, Kevin."

"Will try."

He climbed back into the SUV, once more frowning at the dashboard. One power switch. One point of failure. "Idiot."

Kevin jammed a finger into the rocker switch, which lit up orange with a sharp *click*. He eased away from Carver's farm, making an effort not to kick up too much of a dust cloud out of courtesy. At least the truck didn't handle too bad on the dirt; in that respect, it had an advantage over the Challenger. Of course, without armor, its lack of speed made it a death trap.

A rhythmic rumble vibrated the cabin once he hit paved road. The knobby treads turned the seat into an ass-massager. Route 789 heading north offered a breathtaking view of endless nothingness. He shifted his gaze from mirror to mirror and ahead again, waiting for a worst-case scenario: pirates or raiders coming after an unarmed truck with one driver.

About twelve minutes later, he hit the on-ramp for 80 without seeing a single other vehicle and felt paradoxically *more* nervous, as if the world lured him into a trap. He avoided a crashed bus and a pair of burned Humvees, wincing at the sight. Every time he passed that wreck, he honored a moment of silence for the two destroyed machineguns on the back ends. Both had been smashed when the vehicles rolled over. He wasn't sure what they were—other than being larger than .50 cal.

"Whoever scavved that ammo got a rude surprise. No one can use it. Ehh, probably popped 'em open for the powder."

Five minutes east on I-80, the rearview mirrors remained clear and nothing lurked up ahead.

"Maybe this really *is* the ass crack of nowhere. So much *nothing* here that no one thinks there's anything to steal."

He allowed himself to calm a little. Seven minutes later, (due to the truck taking umbrage with any attempt to drive faster than sixty-five mph), his roadhouse came into view. Kevin smiled. *Okay, maybe I am being paranoid.*

A nudge of the wheel made the truck nose onto the approach ramp, past a few shot-up blue signs announcing the rest stop. He wasn't sure he wanted to know what a grinning cartoony red-haired little girl had to do with food, but the pre-war world was almost another planet. A boy he'd befriended when they'd both been about ten had some old comic books that told a story of humans inhabiting a world once controlled by advanced aliens that had died off. Civilization sounded an awful lot like those aliens now. Humans running around discovering mysterious and indecipherable things that only made sense to the aliens.

I wonder if Keith's still alive? He grumbled, not having seen him since his adoptive parents decided to strike off on their own.

The sight of three e-bikes parked out front got his blood pressure up, though he calmed at not finding any sign of a Redeemed logo on them. A sad, sad attempt at an eagle decorated the saddlebags on the middle bike, but the other two had no discernable colors.

Shit, I'm on edge. Just some travelers.

He pulled up to the main entrance and backed around in a turn that lined the rear up with the door. Up onto the grass he went, rolling uphill until a stairway plus a row of bright yellow concrete pylons kept the back bumper a 'safe' distance away from the front of the building. He caught a glimpse of Tris' white hair moving around inside via the door mirror and grinned.

"Home at last."

TRIS STARED AT THE MAN WHO'D DEMANDED SHE STRIP. HE HAD THE KIND of cocky, self-assured smirk that said he had no expectation some delicate little woman would do anything other than as she was told. "I'm sorry; I didn't quite hear that right. Did you just ask me to take my clothes off?"

He grinned. A slight wag of the head seemed to pass down his body into a wiggle of the arms, and his handgun.

"You a virgin, girlie?" asked the ginger. "If you're real nice, we'll keep it gentle."

"How many coins you got back there, Roadhouse girl?" asked the dusty-haired man. "Your pretty little ass gotta be loaded."

"Heh. If it ain't, it will be in a couple'a minutes," said the big man.

Tris raised an eyebrow. "Out. Get the hell out. I'm not in the mood to clean up blood today."

"Oh, shit." Ginger raised his hands. "Little lady's not in the mood."

The instant a shift in Big Man's expression turned angry, Tris kicked on her reflex booster. His gun arm rose in slow motion as she whipped the Beretta out of its holster. She fired at Ginger first, his laughing face showing no reaction to the creeping bloom of orange muzzle flare. Her left hand went forward, catching Big Man's arm at the wrist and pushing his 1911 to the side. She aimed at Dust Hair's forehead, firing a second round with the first bullet still a few millimeters from contact with

Ginger. The spinning lead slug burrowed into the skin a half inch left of the bridge of his nose, slipping around the eyeball before disappearing.

Dusty hair's face began to react to the gunshot that killed Ginger as the second projectile drilled into his skull a finger's width above the left eye. A 9mm thick geyser of blood spurted forth in what to her felt like three seconds before a matching one erupted from the back of his head. She jammed the tip of her Beretta in Big Man's cheek, forcing his jowls around it.

A frown spread over her lips. "Fucking idiot."

He fired, putting a bullet into the wall several feet to her left.

She painted the tile floor with his brains; he fell away from her upraised arm and landed flat on his back. Time returned to normal when her reflex boost shut down. She stared over her gunsights at the door, where a tiny hole gave away the bullet's final destination. One advantage to solid ball ammo, less splatter to clean up.

Tris lowered her arm and sighed. She trembled from a squirt of adrenaline, though it came more from fear things would only escalate rather than any sense of guilt or thrill at killing three men.

"Tris?" yelled Sang. He popped up in the window between restaurant and kitchen with his shotgun. "You okay? What happened? How you get your pistol to fire like machinegun?"

"I'm fine. Just some idiots trying to rob us."

He gave her a paternal, chiding look. "I hear what they tell you to do. Already grabbing my gun when you turn into blur. How you do that?"

"It's a long story."

Sang relaxed out of his combat posture, and smiled. "I like stories. I make tea, we talk."

She couldn't help herself but smile a little. "Ugh. I'm going to need a new mop."

A distant buzzing noise drew her eyes to the window. The red SUV Kevin drove off in sailed up the access ramp, tires buzzing on the pavement like the wings of a giant wasp. She could practically hear him cursing the speed governor. *Bet he's going to ask me to remove it. That thing's lifted. If he drives it as fast as he wants to, it'll roll.*

Holstering the Beretta, she meandered out from behind the counter and stepped over Big Man on her way to the door. The ass end of the SUV crept to a halt about twenty feet away where a short flight of stairs in the sidewalk flanked by yellow pylons proved impassable for cars.

"He's gonna *love* this." She put a hand on the door and glanced over her shoulder. *Maybe I shouldn't tell... No. I have to.*

KEVIN SLID OUT OF THE DRIVER'S SEAT AND TROTTED AROUND TO THE BACK doors. *This thing might be useful after all, but next time I'll bring her along so I have someone to work a rifle.* He leaned in and grabbed the meat box, tugging it to the back bumper before getting both hands on it and hefting it with an "oof."

An aluminum scrape behind him announced the door opening.

With a face full of salted, smoky dust hopper meat, he rotated to face the building and hefted the box as if to hand it to Tris, who plodded up to him. His wide grin faded at the strange look of sad worry on her face. The weight of the box settled against his chest.

He tilted his head like a confused dog. "Tris?"

She headed toward him with such deliberateness of stride he knew something was wrong. No sooner had he shoved the box back into the SUV did she clamp on and bury her face in the crook of his neck. She wasn't crying, or even making a sound, but the tension in her muscles said all.

He held her in silence for a few minutes, considering a lame joke about her being safe now because he'd returned. Again, he glanced at the e-bikes; nervousness crept in. "What happened?"

She took and released a heavy breath and pulled back enough to look him in the eye. "Three men tried to rob us... and..."

He grabbed her shoulders. "Are you okay?"

Tris pulled a strand of hair out of her eyes and hooked it behind her ear. "Yeah. I'm fine. They made it clear what they wanted to do to me. Told 'em to get out, but they went for their guns, so I shot them." He pulled her tight against his chest. "Ugh. Air please." He eased off a little, and she kept talking into his shirt. "Nothing happened. I know what I look like, but I'm not some helpless little waif. I'm glad they told me to get naked. All that did was get rid of my guilt."

He cradled the back of her head for a little while before they leaned back enough to look at each other. "Okay, so why do you look so..." Kevin waved his hand about in a circle. "Upset."

"What do you want first? The bad news or the awful news?"

"You're sure you're okay?"

She nodded. "Yeah, just worried. Look, better get that meat in to the cooler before it goes." Tris snagged it, showing no visible sign of struggling with its weight.

Kevin took the mixed vegetable box and walked at her side to the door. "Hit me with the awful…"

"Nash is dead. I-I…" She breathed. "I was in the office checking the computer after a power crash, and he came over the radio yelling that someone was attacking his 'house. He… died on the mic."

Fuck. Kevin clenched his fingers into the dry wooden box. "Just like Wayne."

Tris hooked the door handle with her shoe and pulled it open before kicking it to the side and ducking in. "Not quite. I mean, I only heard the last parts, but it didn't sound like they even bothered to set up a fight. They just went in there shooting. And…"

"Redeemed?" He followed her down the hall to the kitchen.

She set the box of meat on a steel table in the middle, between two cutting boards. "I think so. Nash said they had a white fist on their jackets. Didn't mention a sword but… I'm not sure I'd be too observant if I was being shot at."

Bee entered carrying a box of potatoes. Sang hurried over and began unpacking the meat box, sorting different cuts into piles.

"Thanks, Sang, Bee." Kevin gave them both curt nods. "Be right back with two more boxes of 'tatoes and a big can of oil."

"I got it, boss," said Bee. "I don't get tired."

He smiled at her.

"Not bad. Not bad," said Sang. "Fresh. This'll last a good while."

As the old man loaded the working fridge with meat, Kevin headed across the hall to the office. The radio remained silent, though a somber gloom hung in the air. Tris came up behind him and clung.

"And the bad news?" asked Kevin.

She gestured at the computer equipment. "It's dying. I can't really tell how much longer it's going to last. It could fail five minutes from now or five months from now, but it's definitely on the way out."

"Shit." He took a seat in the office chair and pulled her into his lap.

"Amarillo didn't say a damn word." She glared at the radio. "Nash was screaming, and they just ignored him."

Kevin closed his eyes, offering a moment of silence to a fellow proprietor. "That's not how they work. They usually don't reply; they'll post a bounty. The radio goes between 'houses. Not like all drivers hear that and help could've gotten there in time." *Yeah... we're on our own.* "They're going to download the cam data and—"

"What if it's dead? How are they going to put a bounty on screen snow? Amarillo answered Gertrude the other night."

He swayed side to side with her, feeling a bit like a child with a teddy bear. His brain refused to accept everything he'd ever believed and worked for had all the substance of a rainbow. His beloved Code couldn't be disintegrating. The Roadhouse network had been strong for years... maybe he'd taken too long to get on board? Wayne used to say everything ended sooner or later. *Spend years busting my ass for a dream. Figures it takes a shit a couple months after I get here.* He pulled Tris close and held her in silence for a while. Being with her tempered the crushing dread of his life's ambition collapsing.

"Word'll get out. Someone'll look to drag some Redeemed back to Amarillo for a reward."

She shifted her weight, lifting her head to stare into his eyes. "Do you really believe that?"

Kevin glanced at the computer table, the workbench, the wall, and the door to the hallway. "I used to. Couple years ago, the 'house was like... I dunno. Like a crotchety old dad that wanted to do right by his son, but wouldn't tolerate the tiniest bit of disrespect. I've seen grown men turn white in the face when they dented someone's car by accident at a 'house." He sighed. "'Course, I don't got any sort of idea what's going on now." He closed his eyes. *She's tougher than I am. I don't need to bullshit her.* "I'm worried."

"I know." She patted his thigh. "You've been worried for a while. All your life, you've wanted this, and now that you have it, you're afraid someone's going to take it away." Tris studied her shoes, legs swinging free like a little girl on a chair that didn't let her feet reach the ground. "Since I'm not going to save the world, I guess I can settle for saving one roadhouse."

He opened his mouth to speak, but his brain struggled to come up with something comforting to say about the whole Virus thing.

She flashed a playful grin before he could get a word out.

They kissed.

"Things are changing," said Kevin. "Maybe I oughta see if Fitch and Neeley will hire on as security."

Tris feigned insult. "You don't think I can handle it?"

"Of course I do." He pecked a kiss on the tip of her nose. "But you have to sleep."

A knock at the door broke the mood.

Bee, her arms filled with a bundle of clothes and boots, peered in. "Hi, boss. I got them bodies cleaned up. What you want me to do with the remains?"

Kevin lowered his forehead onto Tris' shoulder, and laughed. "Finally, something feels normal." *Just like I'm back in Hagerman.*

14

BASTARD

Moonlight streaming from the window made Tris' bare skin glow, as though she'd become a creature of pure energy. Kevin arched his back, gripping her thighs while adding quick thrusts in time with her moving up and down on top of him. Her waist-long hair swayed side to side; her fingernails dug into his pectorals.

He slid his hands up over her hips, along her prominent ribs, and cupped her breasts. She stifled a moan as he massaged her areolae, shuddering whenever his thumbnails grazed her nipples. As much as he tried to stay focused, every time he closed his eyes, he'd see Wayne lying dead or imaginary bikers kicking in his front door.

"You're not in the mood." Tris sensed his… lack of focus, and slowed.

"I *am*. I just… I know it's been quiet for a bit, but—I can't stop worrying. If anything happened to you…" He tried to tune out the world, staring at her face.

She bent forward; their tongues entwined.

The entirety of her engulfed his senses: from her sylph-like curves to the warmth of her skin, the scent of her being, the taste of her, everything. He surrendered to the moment, refusing to let dark thoughts cloud his mind. At his sudden re-inspiration, her eyes shot open.

GASPING FOR BREATH, TRIS SLUMPED OFF HIM TO THE SIDE AND CURLED UP to put her head on his shoulder. She stroked her fingers across his chest hair, her warm breaths puffing over him. He raised a leg to pull the sheet and blanket up to cover them both. She snuggled in closer.

Kevin glanced to his right at the .45 within arm's reach on the file cabinet turned nightstand. At least with Bee here, he felt more secure. She, it, or whatever, was like having a 24/7 employee that never had to sleep and didn't even want to be paid. If anything happened in the middle of the night, the android would at least make enough noise to wake him.

If nothing else, spending ten some odd years on the road taught him to sleep light.

"So what's really bothering you?" whispered Tris.

He reached up and held her hand atop his chest. "Still have half a mind to shoot the sons of bitches what killed Wayne…"

She shifted to look up at him.

"Half a mind." He smiled. "No idea who to even look for."

Tris laid her head back on his chest. "I understand."

"Wayne was like the asshole father I never had." He tapped his foot on nothing. "Maybe more like the begrudging uncle. I'm still not sure why he decided to take me under his wing when I got it in my head to be a driver."

Eyes closed, she cuddled tight against him. "How'd that happen? That you wanted to drive."

"Guess 'cause I'd been workin' on machines for as long as I could hold onto a tool. Hemi did most of the fixin' for the settlement before we left. After they took me in, he got to teaching me things. I think I might've been thirteen when I found this old e-conversion Impala. Thing was in such bad shape it took all four of my friends plus a horse to pull it back to town. Spent a couple years rebuilding it for fun. Almost burned down the work shack a few times."

Tris emitted a soft half-asleep chuckle.

"Electrical fires suck." He rocked his shoulders and settled into the mattress. The pocket of trapped air under the blanket reached perfect coziness. "Back then I had no idea 'bout roadhouses or anything. Driver came in to drop somethin' off for Grizzle, guy who ran the only store in town. He made it sound like the kinda life a boy dreamed about. Freedom, adventure, playing with guns. Decided to take a stab at it when I turned seventeen. Hemi figured I'd be back in a couple days, but I guess I got lucky. First run, five cans of coffee. I pocketed almost 250 coins. Gave 200 to 'Mom an' Dad,' and like magic, they both decided driving was good for me."

"Now you wanna stop getting shot at for a living?" muttered Tris, a hint of smile on her lips.

"I ain't seventeen no more." He sighed. "Immortality doesn't last forever."

She took almost a minute to reply, her voice slurred with tiredness. "If you had one wish, what would you use it on?"

He rolled a heavy marble of thought around inside his skull for a few minutes. "Well… if you were an ordinary sort of woman, I might be tempted to wish that nothing ever hurt you." He kissed the top of her head. "But, you're actually kinda hard to kill. I think I'd wish for the Virus to stop. Oh hell. It's a wish. I'd wish it never happened. The whole war."

Tris lifted her head again, tears in her eyes. She didn't say a word, just stared at him with a heart-melting expression for a long moment before hugging him. He put an arm across her back, holding her. One of her tears trickled over the side of his neck.

Soon, she slipped off to sleep, leaving him staring at the ceiling again. Too much went on out there for him to merely sit here and hope things sorted themselves out. *Things never sort themselves out,* said Wayne's voice in his head. *Sortin' things out usually takes slappin' idiots upside the head. Sometimes it takes shotguns.*

"Yeah, you're right on that, old man," whispered Kevin. "Maybe I should take a ride to Amarillo."

PAULINE

L ate morning sun sent shimmering beams of dust particles among the tables. A murmuring din suffused the room from scattered conversations maneuvering around food. Two of the three drivers he'd sent on a run, Roy and Kira, quibbled about the payout... their buddy Pills didn't come back. *They didn't seem too upset. Probably told him to get lost.* Two tables over, a massive, dark-skinned man with black leather pants, armor-plated boots, and no shirt sat next to a giant sword. The guy reminded him of an old movie. *Heh. Post-nuclear Conan.*

A large group from a bus packed all five tables nearest the window. Aside from his 'escape from Chicago' run, Kevin couldn't recall ever seeing another functional bus. Apparently, this guy Darius and his sister Rebekah (with a K, as she'd pointed out at least six times during their conversation) found one and decided to start up a one-bus line, transporting people between settlements. Tall and lanky Darius had a complexion like creamed coffee. His sister, shorter by a full head, wore a huge mass of butt-length dreads and was perhaps the darkest-skinned person he'd ever met. Aside from her neurotic fixation on the spelling of her name, she struck him as one of those too-sweet people who'd be easy to take advantage of. Granted, her rapid retreat when Tris walked over and put an arm around him forced him to look away instead of laugh.

He grinned at the almost-full room. *I'm gonna have to hit Carver's again soon. Has it already been a week?* Contentment died a few seconds later when he wondered if any of these people might get it in their heads to thumb their noses at the Code. Wayne could've stared down anything without a scrap of worry showing on his face. Kevin thumbed the back end of the .45 on his belt, hoping he'd be fast enough.

Tris had gone up to the roof again to double-check the panels. She'd mentioned something about the inverter worrying her, and wanted to make sure it didn't burn out or worse—start a fire.

Sang appeared in the kitchen pass-through, sliding a tray of plated fried potatoes toward him. "Too many order to cook at once. Rest be out in a few minutes." He peered around. "Where's Tris?"

"On the roof." He took the tray. "Something about AC from DC and lots of fire."

Sang's grey-black caterpillar eyebrows shot up. "Oh. That does not sound good."

Bee retrieved the tray, smiled at Kevin, and headed over to the bus people.

Kevin edged back from the counter, talking low so only Sang could hear. "Been some hardware issues at a couple of roadhouses lately. She's triple-checking everything."

"Aye. Good idea." Sang nodded. He patted the linoleum in the wall gap. "Ah well. Need more fries."

'Conan' got up and approached the counter. Kevin didn't bother to un-lean from the back wall, preferring a little distance.

"Hey man. I hear you're the one ta talk to 'bout movin' stuff."

Despite his imposing pectorals, the man's calm demeanor let Kevin relax. "That's right."

"How's this thing work?" Conan gestured around at nothing in particular.

"Depends a bit on the circumstance, but usually the sender leaves the cargo here. I find a driver willin' to take on the job. They bring said cargo to the destination, collect payment, and bring it back. I'd hold the coins 'til you come an' get 'em. Cost for the run's based on distance and danger. If you're movin' somethin' everyone an' their mother's going to come after, it'll cost more."

Conan leaned two meaty hands on the counter, tapping one finger for a little while in thought. "Got a guy in Glimmertown workin' for me. Settin' up a place. Found a stash of magic muscle powder." He flexed his chest; muscles Kevin hadn't known existed before undulated under the giant's skin. "Need somethin' the size o' that bus ta move it all, and even that thing'd need a couple back and forths. Thing is, I know you gonna charge more an' I got for movin' that much right now. Lookin' ta get an idea on cost. I'm takin' couple bottles at a shot myself, but I'm getting all kinds-a nervous leavin' the place empty with that much product sittin' there."

Kevin raised an eyebrow. "Magic powder? Drugs usually cost more on account of risk."

Conan grinned. "Ain't drugs. Pre-war muscle powder. Vitamins, protein... crap like that. Takin' that stuff and keepin' active'll give you a body like this." He pointed both thumbs at his chest.

And who has time for that? He smiled. "Well... I can't think of anyone runnin' a big rig around here, at least one set up for cargo hauling." He gestured at Darius and Rebekah. "They've got a bus, course they're transporting *people*. Closest I can think of is a van. Couple of them out there. This guy Henley's probably your best bet. Vans aren't exactly nimble, but he's got a pair of bikes riding escort. Only seen him down here twice in the past six months. Usually haunts Jenny's 'house, on 90 east of Gilette."

Conan pursed his lips, apparently lost in thought for a few seconds. "So how'd that work?"

Kevin moved away from the passé-plat as Bee came to collect the next plate of fries. "Well, you could go up there ask around for Henley... or I could put the word out on the Roadhouse net for him. Might cost a few more coins to have him come down here, but if you've got *that* much shit to move, and it turns into a regular sorta gig, they might not care."

"Aight." Conan nodded. "Im'a head back an' keep an eye on my stuff. You do that 'puttin' the word out' thing, and I'll be back in a couple days."

Kevin shook hands with the giant.

Bee tottered over to the bar. "Need five beers, boss." She dropped ten coins on the counter.

He filled glasses, set them on a tray, and swept the coins into his hand as the android carried the drinks off. *As sane and normal as this feels... why do I think something's going to blow up?*

The door opened a few inches and stopped. He reached for his pistol, but relaxed when Athena pushed it in the rest of the way. He couldn't help himself but grin at seeing her wearing the armored jacket he'd given her. His smile flattened as she approached, a little too stiffly, and a little too lacking in her usual attitude. The blonde 'angel in white' wore a face of determined calm, like she forced herself stoic.

She reached the counter and rested her left forearm across the edge. "Hey. Lemme get a burger, fries, beer, and a charge on number nine."

"Alright. Got the sack from the Spring Creek run?"

"Oh. Yeah." She gripped the counter edge while slipping her right hand into the armored jacket and extracting a dingy cloth pouch. The clatter of coins attracted a few curious glances from the room, but nothing severe enough to get Kevin on edge. "There. Twenty like you said, right?"

"Right. This is for the job. 'Nother ten for food an' charge."

She swung her right arm back and forced her hand into the pocket of her tight white jeans. "Ten's a little steep, ain't it?"

"Fries are three now. Demand." He winked.

She closed her eyes, letting the counter hold her upright while picking a bunch of nickels and pennies out of her pocket and dropping them one after the next on the wood.

"Something wrong, kid?"

Her right eye opened a sliver. "Other than getting gouged on potatoes and you calling me 'kid,' no."

He stared at her chest, specifically at the dark grey scuff two inches outside and south of her left breast on the white jacket. Kevin smacked his lips, looked down, and counted the coins into his waiting palm by sliding them off the counter two at a time. "How bad is it?"

"What?" She leaned both arms, crossed, against the bar.

"That bullet you took." He gestured at the scuff.

A little trace of her usual pride returned, though she broke eye contact first. "Lucky ricochet. I'm okay."

He smirked, feeling the echo of a handful of similar past wounds. "Want someone to check it? Sang's got some experience with that sorta thing. Used to be a medic for his village. Probably where he learned how to work a knife."

Athena raised a hand. "I'm good."

Kevin put two coins back on the counter. "Humor an old man?"

"Thought you had a chick?"

He smirked. "I'm not tryin' ta see your tits. You look like you can barely move. I'd feel all sorts of bad if you died in your sleep in my roadhouse."

She sighed. "Fine." A grimace took over her face when she put all her weight on her legs and lifted her shirt up enough to expose a large mottled bruise wrapping around her left side.

Damn that looks bad. Kevin leaned back toward the hole in the wall.

"Sang." When the old one appeared, he waved him out. "Need your medical experience. Check this out."

Athena blushed.

Sang, wiping his hands on a towel stuffed in his belt, emerged from the back hallway. Kevin gestured at Athena standing there with her shirt wadded at the base of her breast. Sang gasped at the sight of the bruise and hurried over.

She cringed and stifled a whimper as he examined the area, stumbling into the counter at the touch of a light prodding finger.

"Rib broken." He offered an apologetic smile. "Does it hurt to breathe?"

"Yes." She forced her voice past clenched teeth.

"Hurt too much to breathe all the way?"

She tilted her head side-to-side.

"Probably only cracked then. That good. Splinters can damage things." He laid his hand flat on the area, making her whine out her nose and shed a few tears.

Once he stopped touching the spot, she shot Kevin a stare half-pleading and half-accusatory.

Told you so. He couldn't quite bring himself to mock the destruction of her sense of immortality—yet. He'd save it for a later upwelling of teenaged idiocy. He eyed Sang. "What's the verdict?"

"Not much to do for crack rib but manage pain. Should heal on its own in a month or two. Be painful to breathe, twist, move, lift for a while. Girl should take easy. Less she move, faster she heal."

Athena rolled her eyes and grimaced. She let her shirt fall. "Okay, show's over. How 'bout that food?"

"Sang, why don't you set her up in Room 18?" Kevin tried to keep smugness out of the smile he directed at her. "You're not in any shape to run jobs. Won't be for a month at least. G'won an' take the room 'til you're feelin' back to normal."

After a flash of indignation, likely at being treated like a child in need of help, she looked downcast. "I... can't afford that. Two coins a night for months? And what am I gonna do on my back for two months?"

Kevin suppressed the joke that leapt to mind. "Didn't say I was gonna charge you for the room. Long-term rates are different. And Sang's got a pile of books I'm sure he'd let you borrow."

"You're doing the dad thing again." She frowned. "Thanks but... I can't read."

"I can fix," said Sang.

Kevin leaned on the counter. "Look. It ain't a common thing out here when someone's willin' to *not* take advantage or use any opportunity to get something. When someone *does* try to be nice, you should accept it. Of all the things in the world that'll kill you, pride and stupidity are the sneakiest."

Tris glided in from the back hallway, humming to herself. *At least she's in a good mood.*

"Hey." Kevin waved her over. "'Thena here took a bullet. Probably at least a 7.62 by the size of that bruise. Glancing... didn't get past the armor."

Athena rolled her eyes. "Yeah, yeah... Thanks for the jacket. It went through the damn car first, too."

Kevin explained his suggestion to let Athena recover in Room 18. Tris rounded the counter and all but dragged the nineteen-year-old away from the restaurant area to the rooms.

"I'll send the food when it's ready," yelled Kevin.

Sang nodded. "I can get her to read. Now more cooking."

A few minutes after the old man disappeared into the kitchen, Tris returned. She perched on the office chair in the space behind the counter, setting her heels atop two of its five wheel spars while gripping the cushion between her knees. "Solar panels look okay. Things will probably last at least another ten or twenty years."

He smiled. "Finally, some good news."

She stared at the crowd for a while before looking up at him. "What would you do if some guys carried in a tied-up girl?"

Kevin filled a mason jar halfway with beer and helped himself to a long sip. "You mean like the way Wayne ignored you?"

She chuckled. "Yeah. Like that... or like someone trying to keep a slave. Would you just sit there like Wayne did and claim the Roadhouse forces you neutral?"

He sucked air in his nose until his lungs couldn't hold anymore, and held it. The Code could be notoriously arbitrary when it came to that sort of thing. Some settlements tolerated kidnapping, usually small ones where the slaver had bigger guns than everyone else. Others where something of a local militia tried to keep the peace often treated it as one of the worst of crimes. Hell, even Glimmertown got out of the biz, but only because Mr. Petersen got tired of dealing with angry parents and older siblings with guns. Wayne took the concept of 'neutral' to dizzying heights. Of course, pirates and raiders would often stop in Hagerman for a charge and a bite and not start any shit while inside. Given the somewhat flimsy state of things as of late, perhaps it would be better not to have an environment that attracted such people.

"You saw how I handled it already." He winked and sipped his beer.

She looked down; her hair formed a curtain of snowy white obscuring her face. "That's different. Wasn't your roadhouse then."

"Nope. No, it wasn't. Wayne made his own set of rules. Guess one could argue getting involved is a breach of neutrality. Proprietors aren't supposed to up and shoot people unless they're being threatened. Course... with the cameras dead and the slavers dead... s'pose the girl'd have to go complain to Amarillo that I interfered with her bein' sold."

Tris raised her head hard enough to fling her hair over her shoulders. After staring at him for a few seconds, she laughed.

I love the way she smiles.

The bus crowd all got up at more or less the same time and shuffled out. Bee set about collecting dishes.

"Heh." He sighed. "At least we got a good deal on those plates."

Tris filled a water glass for herself. "Yeah. Only about twelve bullets spent in Rawlins. Wasn't too bad."

He thought back to their house-to-house scavenging trip and the pack of marauders that wanted the Challenger. "Yeah." *I'd expected at least a few Infected but... guess we got lucky this deep in the middle of nothing.*

A tall woman with long, straight black hair, light brown skin, and prominent cheekbones entered. She wore a blue BDU with police markings and carried an M4 rifle as well as a handgun. Except for the obvious age and wear on the uniform, she looked pre-war. She shifted the rifle to a shoulder strap as she approached the counter. "Afternoon."

"Nevada." Kevin nodded in greeting. "Usual?"

"Yep. You got any 5.56? I'm down to my last mag."

"I'll check." Tris stood and drained two gulps of water before putting the glass down. "And I'll ask Bee to count our inventory so she has it in her head."

Kevin leaned toward the kitchen hole. "Need a hopper leg and a double order of fries."

"On the way," said Sang.

Nevada turned to face the front windows, one elbow on the bar, watching people filing onto the bus. "What's the story there?"

Kevin explained Darius and his sister Rebekah (with a K) trying to start up a transportation service.

"They should hire some guards. That's a box full of misery if they make a wrong turn." Nevada dropped a sack of coins on the counter. "So why did that idiot pay so much for a gun that doesn't even work?"

Kevin shrugged and took the pouch. He tucked Athena's under the bar—he could count it later—and spilled the contents of Nevada's out. "Collectable or some bullshit like that. Up for a quiet run?"

Nevada glanced at him for a second before shifting her gaze back to the bus. "If by quiet you mean not having to burn through sixty rounds of ammo... maybe. Is this quiet safe or quiet boring?"

He explained the seed run for Carver. "I'd need to run down there to pick up the initial payment so the old man knows it's legit, but a trunk full of seeds shouldn't get you shot at too much. Long trip is the worst part."

"I'll think it over."

Kevin counted 120 coins into a pile, pulled away four for food, three for a charge, and put his fingers on two more. "Room too?"

Nevada nodded. "Got enough water for a shower?"

He flicked the two coins into his hand, leaving 111. "Yep. Six coins or one per minute."

She glanced back at him with a hint of a smile. "Free if I let you watch?"

Kevin laughed. "Well that's the first time I've heard that from a woman I'd actually *want* to watch shower. Heh. For a second there, I thought you were serious."

She offered a subtle shrug that could've meant 'I was' or maybe she'd been impressed he hadn't drooled. "If the water's hot, I'll take the six. If not, by the minute."

"By the minute then," said Kevin. "Still need to scav a decent water heater."

Tris emerged from the back hallway. "Got forty-seven 5.56 in stock."

"Two apiece," said Kevin.

"They work?" asked Nevada.

Kevin nodded. "Of course. I got 'em from Ween. If they don't fire, bring back the dud and I'll give ya two coins."

"If they don't fire, I won't be coming back to complain." She narrowed her eyes at him, seeming annoyed or suspicious, but with a hint of a smile.

Kevin held up his hands. "I use his ammo too. Never had an issue."

"Thirty."

He pushed the pile of fifty-one coins back to her.

Nevada grumbled. "I'm gonna need to do something with a bigger payoff. Barely breaking even on these last three."

Kevin sighed. "Okay, shower two minutes on the house. Payout for that seed thing is 120. I'm not takin' a cut there as a favor to Carver. Should be an easy back and forth. Even throw in a free charge when you're back from it."

"Still thinking about it." Nevada grinned and headed to an empty table by the window.

After collecting his percentage of the run and retrieving Athena's pouch, he headed to the office. Tris took position behind the counter without a word.

He lockboxed the loose coins and counted what should've been the twenty coins Athena brought back... but found 61. *Paid me for the armor.* "Bah. The girl's bad at math." He rebagged the 41 coins and grabbed the radio mic. "Howdy all. Kevin in Rawlins. Got a man lookin' to move a large amount of cargo. Anyone got knowins' on a hauler with a rig? Jenny, you seen Henley lately? He might want this one."

"Saw a rig go by the other day, but it was someone's house," said Clive. "Whole family."

"Yeah." Kevin laughed. "Saw 'em too."

"Henley's on a run up north a ways. Sent him up there," said Jenny. "Feel kinda bad for his ladies on bikes in that weather. They ought'a be back inside of a week. What should I tell him?"

A few more replies came in back to back, all saying they hadn't seen a functional semi in years.

"Quite a few runs between an undisclosed location and Glimmertown, movin' some kinda muscle powder."

"Holy shit," said Harold. "Someone's gonna try and sell fifty-year-old creatine?"

"What the Sam Hill is creatine?" asked Mac.

"Is 'Sam Hill' a dirty word?" Maribel's over-innocent voice silenced the radio for a moment.

"Nope," said Kevin.

"Whazzat?" yelled Whazzat.

"Hey!" yelled a ragged female voice. "Fuck... fuck! Anyone... this is Pauline. I need help!" A distinctly inhuman moaning growl came over the radio. Pauline's scream drowned under a pair of rapid gunshots. "Fuck... Infected... everywhere."

Kevin's muscles locked.

"I'm getting off the radio," said Maribel. "I might like suffer permanent harm hearing that language." Pauline started to shriek for help again, but Maribel's signal overpowered her. "Kidding. Geez, guys, I'm like *eleven*. I can handle words."

"... coming in the windows," yelled Pauline.

"Where you at," replied Mac.

"I40... pissing distance from the border. Hang on." Pauline's transmit stopped.

"That's pretty god damned close to Amarillo," said Beth. "I don't like the sound of that."

"Yeah..." The normal gravel in Harold's voice grew into boulders. "Thousand people there at least. That'll get ugly fast."

"Not as ugly as your mug, Harold." Somehow, a large grin came through clear in Clive's voice.

"Back..." Pauline gasped, breathing hard over the radio. Automatic gunfire rumbled in the background. "There's too god damned many of them. Blood's fuckin' everywhere. I'm... we're running. *If* we can get out. Everyone... stay the fuck away from here. This ain't no Roadhouse now... it's a god damned apocalypse."

Kevin stared dumbfounded at the radio for a full five minutes before it occurred to him to move. A steady, muted conversation had been going on among other proprietors, but it had all become meaningless warbles to his brain. He got up and shuffled out to the counter, leaning both hands on it and staring into space.

"That girl's having trouble believing you really intend to be nice to her. Lot of attitude on that one. Guess that can keep you alive sometimes." Tris turned to say something else, but her smile fell away. "What's wrong?"

"Roadhouse on Interstate 40... Infected." He bowed his head. "Pauline... might make it out."

"Oh, no... not again." Tris put an arm around him. "Do you know what happened?"

"Other than screaming and shooting? No... not really."

She squeezed him. "We should check it out."

He shook his head. "No... no way. It's not my problem. She sounded pretty confident they'd make it out. Either way, by the time we got there, they'd already either be safe or dead."

Tris waited for Bee to come collect food from Sang at the window and walk away before she continued. "Pauline? Her 'house is the one we stopped at when we went to Amarillo, isn't it? 'Bout five minutes into Texas."

"Yeah." He shut his eyes and bowed his head.

"Kevin... Amarillo had a lot of people. Infected that close..."

He looked up at her. "I know. I know." He exhaled hard.

"If Infected got in there... Amarillo could be gone." She lowered her voice to a near-whisper. "If Amarillo's gone. The Code's gone. That *is* our problem."

Kevin pushed away from the counter and faced her. "What're you planning to do? Run into a city with thousands of Infected and pour moonshine on everything?" He waved a hand about, his mind grasping for words not quite formed.

"You're white as me and shaking..." She clasped his cheeks in two hands, body pressed to his. "You're terrified."

"You know how I am about Infected." He shivered. "I... can't even think sometimes."

"Fear is worse when it's theoretical." She slid her hands around his head and grasped her wrist behind his neck. "You're brave when you need to be. It's scarier to sit here thinking about them from a distance and getting worked up. Someone who was paralyzed with a phobia wouldn't have jumped off that bus in Chicago to save Star."

"I wasn't thinking... that was different. A little girl." He hooked his thumbs in his pockets and glanced down.

"You *are* a good man."

"If it wasn't a kid, I'd have been like, 'sorry pal, sucks to be you.'"

She poked him in the side and whispered, "Asshole."

He chuckled.

They held each other for a few minutes in silence until Fitch shambled in the front door with a huge olive-drab duffel bag over his shoulder. He chucked a canteen case full of coins in Kevin's direction and headed for a table.

"All done. When you got a minute, scavved a bunch of crap you may wanna have a look at."

Kevin waved at Fitch. "Damn, you ran that shit fast. Course, twenty pounds of weed... I'd haul ass too. Any new dents?"

"Alls good." Fitch smiled. "Your baby's just fine. All cozy in the garage. Remind me to have a chat with Neeley 'bout punctuality when he gets back."

"I thought we agreed not to broker jobs with drugs." Tris smirked and crossed her arms.

"We did, but that wasn't drugs... it was weed."

She rolled her eyes. "What about Amarillo? We can't just do nothing... sit here, waiting for whatever's coming."

He peeked at the mass of coins in the canteen carrier for a second and set it down, keeping his hand on it. "We're out here in the middle of nowhere. I can't see an Infected walking a hundred miles of desert to come here."

"No, they'd take a van," called Fitch from his table.

Kevin cringed.

"What about those Redeemed people? We're out here in the middle of nothing, like you said." She fidgeted. "Like Nash. If something happens..."

Kevin smiled, lifting her chin with a finger. "Yeah, but Nash didn't have you. Bet you could take out five Redeemed before they even had their guns drawn."

Nevada coughed to announce herself. That she had gotten within arm's reach of the counter without him noticing made Kevin jump. "Is your cook chasing a dust hopper around back with a knife? Any chance of that food before midnight?"

"Sang?" yelled Kevin.

The old man rushed over to the window. "Sorry. Hopper very salty. Too salty to cook. Soaking for a bit to make more edible. I will hurry it along."

Nevada raised her half-gone beer in a toast at Sang. "Okay. You said something about Redeemed?"

"You know them?" asked Kevin.

Tris peered around him at her.

"'Know' is a strong word. I ran into some of them at a 'house near Veil. Didn't seem like bad people."

"How long ago?" Tris gestured for the woman's glass. "I'll top you off for the delay on your food."

Nevada smiled and handed it over. "Two weeks? Give or take a day. What makes you think they'd be trouble?"

Kevin scowled at the wall. "Veil... Arizona? That's off I-10. Southerly. Couple of 'houses got shot up by Redeemed."

"Probably a turf war or something." Nevada thanked Tris with a single nod and took a sip of her beer.

"I don't think so." Kevin hesitated, but he knew Nevada enough to trust she wouldn't go starting wild rumors. "They were shooting at the proprietors. Men flying Redeemed colors killed Wayne."

Nevada raised one eyebrow. "The guys I saw in Veil looked more interested in beer and cards than trashing the place." She shrugged. "Who knows? People do weird things sometimes." She headed back to her table.

"Five minutes," yelled Sang.

Kevin frowned. *That doesn't make any goddamned sense.*

A MATTER OF JUSTICE

T he rumble of a heavy vehicle shook the ground a few seconds before the grind of tires on blacktop made it to Kevin's ears. Fitch perked up, sporting a grin that could only mean he recognized his truck returning. Tris continued to pick at her fingernails, perpetuating the awkward silence hanging between them for the past ten minutes.

Neeley's scrawny figure, covered in tattered grey pants, grey sleeveless shirt, and lots of grime, sauntered in with a cat-that-got-the-canary smile. A dark green ammo can dangled from two fingers of his left hand. He set it on the counter, flashing a victorious smile. "All done. Ween almost fainted when I walked that box in."

Kevin seized upon the chance to think about something other than the possibility of Amarillo being gone. "Great." He opened the can and blinked at the coins. "I almost never do this but…" He glanced left and raised his voice. "Bee?"

The android hurried over. "Yes, boss?"

He pushed the can toward her. "Please count that."

Bee's eyes blinked with a *click*. "There is one can."

Kevin stared. Neeley guffawed.

"Bee…"

"Tris has been attempting to demonstrate sarcasm." Bee blinked again.

"I take things too literally and am trying to reconfigure my logic algorithm to be able to process humor."

Bee carried the ammo can into the back, coins clinking.

"I am in *dire* freakin' need of some foodage." Neeley pointed two index fingers at the hole in the wall. "Yo, Sang, my man. Hook me up."

"You got it," yelled Sang, followed by the soft *thump* of a book closing.

"Beer too?" asked Kevin.

"Not yet. I'm too damn thirsty for beer. Gimme two waters and a beer after."

Kevin handed over two waters. As soon as Neeley headed over to the table where Fitch waited, he looked at Tris. "I know… I know. Sitting here seems like a bad idea, but I'm not sure what good it would do for us to go there. If the place is teeming with Infected, I don't have enough damn ammunition to clear it out."

Tris' gaze roamed around for a few seconds before locking on to him. "Wait. We don't have to take them on alone… Let's go scout. See if there even *is* a problem. Worst case scenario proves true, we haul ass out of there and get on the radio. The world needs the Roadhouse network. If Amarillo got wiped out, someone should put it back together… and it's gonna take a small army. I'm sure every proprietor is going to want to keep this quiet, and to keep things going."

He tapped his foot. *Didn't think of that… raising an army? Deliberately going* into *a city full of Infected to clear it out?* "I dunno. Something like that's gonna need to get talked about and thought about."

"You're afraid." Tris stood and took his hand. "I understand. Thinking about it is worse than doing it."

"We still don't know for a fact anything even happened. I'll try to get Amarillo on the radio later."

She smirked.

"I will. Really." He smiled.

Tris opened her mouth to speak, but stalled at a wash of headlights sweeping over the front door. Outside looked unusually dark for the time; perhaps the night would bring rain. Boots hit pavement outside, followed by the *clunk* of two automotive doors. Seconds later, the *clang* of an old pickup truck's tailgate followed.

Marty, still wearing the trench coat he'd had on in Chicago, entered ass-first, carrying two wooden crates full of vegetables. His SPAS-12 rattled against his back on a strap. Zara followed, also with two crates in her much smaller arms. She got a couple stares from the room.

A prickle of pins and needles ran up and down Kevin's body at the sight of the black-haired Enclave sniper who'd shot him with the metal spiders from hell. Despite her having decided to stay at Nederland, he'd still trust her more bound and gagged. *Never did get that bitch back for that... shock thing.*

"Hey," said Tris.

Marty set the crates on the counter and shook Kevin's hand. "Hey dude. Sorry it took so long. Emma snuck onto the truck. We had to turn around and bring her back."

"She wanted to help 'guard the shipment,'" said Zara. "Honestly, she's not a bad shot... for a kid with no implants."

"Thirteen," said Marty. "Her parents would've cut our balls off."

"Speak for yourself." Zara winked at him and set down her two crates. "All the vegetables you could want for a while. Fresh grown from Ned."

Tris leaned on the counter. "How's it going there?"

"Boring." Zara shrugged. "Farm's doing well. Get the occasional Infected wobbling up the road from Boulder, but it's been quiet." She laughed at a sudden thought. "Some idiots tried to raid us two months back, but they took one look at the gate and changed their minds."

Kevin thought back to the pair of flipped heavy-duty dump trucks and chuckled. "Yeah... good luck moving that." *Ned...* He looked around at the room, then out the window at the long strip of empty highway. *High up in the mountains... giant freakin' gate.*

Marty patted Zara on the ass and started toward a table. She grinned and trailed after, dragging her hands over the counter as she departed. Tris followed, trying to start a conversation to catch up on what her 'Enclave friend' had been doing since they'd last seen each other.

Neeley waved at Kevin. When he looked, the skinny man beckoned him over.

Kevin, eyes on the room, meandered to their table. "What's up?"

"Forgot to mention," said Neeley, "Ween was lookin' for whiskey. Said he's willin' ta pay sixty coins for any unopened bottles."

Kevin scratched his eyebrow. *Usually get about fifty coins on a bottle, sellin' shots at three each.* "Okay... I'll put the word out, but I need my stock."

Sang whistled from the kitchen portal.

It took him a moment to remember Bee was in the back counting coins. Kevin retrieved Neeley's dust hopper steak and fries from Sang, and brought it out with a beer.

"You're too kind." Neeley all but drooled on himself.

Kevin eased himself into a chair. "Part o' Fitch helpin' out while I went runnin' off. Hey... you two know much about an outfit callin' themselves The Redeemed?"

Neeley moaned with ecstasy as while chewing on a hunk of dust hopper meat.

"Some rumors." Fitch twisted his mason jar glass side to side. "Same sorta rumors you hear about any bike club."

Neeley held up a finger, wanting the savoring to last a bit longer.

"Any idea what kinda bug they'd get up their asses about roadhouses?" asked Kevin.

Fitch mumbled something inaudible. "Nothin' comes to mind. Only odd thing I heard once someone sayin' they think they're some kinda outfit what 'helps people,' but they ain't no different from any other roving group like that. They do whatever suits their purposes at the time."

"Mmm." Neeley frowned, chewing another hunk of meat. He shook his head while trying (and failing) to talk with a full mouth.

"Fuckin' Wayne, man." Kevin flung his weight back in the chair. "I don't get what happened there."

"Wmmpnd?" asked Neeley.

Kevin's gaze drooped, though the rest of him remained motionless. "They killed Wayne. I'm half tempted to shoot anyone comin' in the door with that symbol on."

"Whmm smmbl?"

"Redeemed symbol," said Fitch.

Kevin traced his finger around in a midair circle. "White fist holdin' a sword in the middle of a ring."

Neeley coughed and spat up an unrecognizable brownish-red lump. "Shit. Wayne? Fuck. I saw a bunch of them dudes in a 'house off 84 on my way outta Ween's place." He froze for an instant, all the anger evaporated from his face to a serious look. He pointed at Kevin. "Fuck that guy. Living up at a mountain lake. That's an annoying ass ride." His eyebrows shifted to a glower. "So I'm on I-84 comin' southeast through the gap and I stop for the night. There's a couple guys wearin' that symbol at a table... one of 'em had this hat on that looked *just* like Wayne's."

Kevin's cheeks flushed with angry heat. He leaned forward. "How many?"

"Three. They was talkin up some shit too 'bout how they killed someone they had a real hate on for." Neeley plucked the chewed lump off the table and ate it.

Wayne'd never forgive me if I don't take this chance. "Could you recognize those guys?"

Neeley rocked his head left to right. "Yeah." He nodded. "Yep."

"Little man does have an eye for details," said Fitch.

Kevin drummed his fingers on the table. A hunting expedition sounded more plausible now. There could be dozens of Redeemed, but only five that needed to die. Fair bet the two Neeley hadn't seen were either bleeding out somewhere, dead already, or trying to recover. Of course, they could've gone in any direction from the 'house Neeley spotted them in. A trip like that could take a week or two... or longer. Maybe the Redeemed hoped to start some kind of war. Maybe they somehow had a personal beef with Wayne. Didn't make sense that Nevada had seen some of them at another 'house behaving themselves when others had all but kicked in the door at Nash's place shooting. *Factions? Ugh. Tris isn't gonna like this. I can't leave Sang here alone for two weeks... and mixing gangs with Tris... that'd start a pile of trouble.*

"Fitch... Neeley..." Kevin stilled his fingers. "I'm sorely tempted to find the sorry sons of bitches who killed Wayne. Seems like a pretty dumb thing to do alone."

"Pretty dumb thing to leave this"—Neeley waved a fry around at the room—"to go off on a bounty."

"But it's the right thing to do." Fitch took a long, slow drink. "Surprised you hadn't gone already."

"Didn't know who to go after." Kevin tapped his boot. "Security system at Wayne's didn't work. If Neels can ID the fuckers..."

"Yep." Neeley offered an eager nod while jamming fried potatoes in his mouth. "Damn, I love these."

"Slow down there, boy." Fitch laughed. "You might get up to human weight." He eyed Kevin. "You're circlin' 'round askin' us if we'd sign on ta help. Well... yeah. Count us in. Gotta send a message."

"Five grand don't hurt neither." Neeley's attempt to laugh sounded more like a donkey getting kicked in the balls.

Kevin chuckled. "About that..."

IMPERATIVE

Kevin glanced up when a flash of Tris' snow-white hair caught his eye. She retrieved a room key from behind the counter and brought it over to Zara and Marty. The two hurried off like a pair of teenagers who couldn't wait to get naked. *Wow. Never imagined that...* The idea of Zara wanting to be that close to a 'dirty wildlander' was even more far-fetched than a woman with looks like hers having interest in the thick-bodied, quick-triggered, trench-coated, shotgun-toting Marty. Then again, the dude was all right despite his strange fascination for video games.

Takes a certain kind o' fucked up ta yell, 'head shot, fatality' when ya kill a man, but everyone out here's a crazy in one way or another. "Hmph." He looked at Fitch. "Gimme a bit. Not gonna run right out the door, probably be at least a day of prep."

Fitch nodded over his beer.

Neeley dropped three coins at him. "More fries."

Kevin grinned and slapped his hand down on the coins before they rolled to the floor, unsure if he would've asked for them... but since the man offered. "Be right back."

"What're you gonna do if she says no?" asked Fitch, a hint of smile in his eyes.

Kevin rolled the coins about in his palm, staring at them. "Depends on how she goes about sayin' it."

He walked back to the counter, where Tris perched. "Of all the things in this world I don't understand, how you're so friendly to that woman is near the top of the list."

"We went to grade school together."

Kevin blinked. "She tried to shoot you and cut your head off."

"She was confused. Zara didn't mean it. And she *did* shoot me. She didn't *try* to."

"How do you 'not mean' putting a bullet through someone and reaching for a machete? Oops, sorry I shot you in the back then hiked a hundred yards over to finish you off on accident."

Tris chuckled. "She didn't believe the Enclave was full of shit until they abandoned her out here."

"I don't know if I can trust her."

"You could probably tie her up again." Tris gave him a coy wink. "After we left her like that for hours, she got to liking it. Apparently, Marty's into it too... that's how they—"

He raised his hands. "Okay, fine. Forget it."

"What aren't you telling me?" Tris slid over to him, hip against the counter.

Kevin sighed. "Neeley saw the men who killed Wayne. Three guys in Redeemed colors. One had Wayne's hat on... and they were bragging about killing someone."

She crossed her arms, displeasure clear on her face. "And you're thinking of going after them."

"The thought had crossed my mind."

"What if you get killed?" She stared at him. "Yeah, you're going after three guys, but they're part of a gang. They have friends who won't give a shit what they did. You go in there, you better be ready to kill everything that moves. And... and..."

He grasped her by the biceps, pulled her close, and kissed her. "I'd be taking Fitch and Neeley with me. Neels can pick out the guys who did it. I'm not going to do it stupid like with Tyrant."

"You think you're going without me?" She raised both eyebrows.

Kevin took one step back, raising a placating hand. "Tris... One, you're astoundingly beautiful. Like, cause these idiots to drive straight into walls because they're staring at you hot. Even if we find Redeemed, and they're not the right ones... we couldn't just walk away because they'd probably try to grab you. Two, if you see them doing some shady shit, you're going to want to get involved, and that's going to set off a shitstorm... there'll be bullets, screaming..."

She grumbled. "You're still upset at me for Cloud 9?"

"No. No... I wanted to help those women too, just too worried about the kinds of things that go wrong when lead starts flying around a crowded room. What if one of the girls stuck in a cage took a stray bullet 'cause she couldn't hit the floor?"

She stared down, grinding her hands into her flannel shirt. "There's been how many roadhouses attacked now? Wayne's, Hastings, Nash, now Pauline? And nothing at all from Amarillo. Isn't that a little odd?" Tris rose up on the balls of her feet to get to eye level with him. "Not one damn word about a bounty, or asking for a status update, or putting out a notice to kill Redeemed on sight. Nothing."

"That's not how it's supposed to work." He looked anywhere but at her, grumbling. "They... bounty." He sighed. "Okay. Yeah, that *is* fucked up."

"How do they put out a bounty if they don't talk to anyone?" She grabbed his cheek and forced him to look her in the eye. "I'm sorry, Kevin. I hate seeing you so twisted up over this. I know how close you were to Wayne, but maybe there's bigger problems than revenge right now."

He hooked his thumbs in his pockets and studied the floor for a good minute. "You're right. I want you to stay here so you don't get hurt. I still can't quite look at you and not see this woman who I'd do anything to keep safe. If we find those bastards, it'll send a message that might just keep us safe here. Keep the Code alive."

She shivered, though between frustration, exasperation, or anger, he couldn't tell. "What do you love more... that Code of yours or me?"

"You." He suppressed the urge to blink in surprise at how easily the answer came out.

Tris, too, looked stunned. The accusatory glint in her eye vanished in an instant.

He half-turned away, eyes downcast. "Only reason I give a shit about the Code is it's what's keeping you safe here. Without it, we're sitting damned ducks on the road. If no one cares about repercussions, people are going to try and take whatever they want."

She leaned against him. "You said most people aren't like that."

"They're not." He kissed her, tongues entwined. Eye contact lingered for a silent few seconds after they pulled apart. "But all it takes is one, and 'most people' don't drive around. The kind of idiots willing to leave the safety of a settlement are more likely the kind of idiots to try an' take shit by force."

"Okay... but, please think it over for a day. You're pissed off right now and not thinking clearly. If you still want to go hunting after a day, fine... but I'm going to be up all night sitting at the windows crying into my coffee until you come home."

He stared at her. It took about twenty seconds before she smiled.

"Fine. I won't cry into my coffee until you're past two weeks." She grumbled, though it sounded half-playful. "I'm gonna try to get Amarillo on the radio."

"Okay."

Tris drifted off into the back. Kevin rolled to the left and planted his elbows on the bar, face in his hands. Fitch's deep laughter rose over the din. *Ugh.* Both going after Wayne's killers and *not* going after them sounded like equally the wrong thing to do. *What would Wayne say about this one?* He stood with a sigh.

"Get them sum-bitches."

TRIS HURRIED DOWN THE HALL TO THE OFFICE AND FLOPPED IN THE CHAIR. Bee stood by the worktable counting coins with such speed her right hand appeared to be a clicking blur. *He's gonna get himself killed.* She held back the urge to cry—barely—and wound up meditating for a few minutes. *He made it twenty-seven years without me... he's not helpless.* She grinned at herself. He thought she was a helpless woman because of her delicate build, and she thought him helpless because he didn't have any cybernetic enhancements or nanites to repair his body.

Guess we are perfect for each other. A tiny laugh escaped her along with one tear.

Guilt didn't work. Logic also felt like it didn't work. She couldn't tell him she didn't really care all that much about Wayne. The ass was ready to regard her as 'dropped property' and claim she belonged to him because her owner had died in his roadhouse. She smirked, thinking back to that 'waitress' at Cloud 9 who had to serve tables in shackles because she tried to escape. *That wouldn't have been me. I'd have acted as meek as everyone thinks I looked until I could get a hand on a weapon and then I would've killed him myself.*

She grumbled. No guarantee Wayne would have actually treated her like that. Maybe he was all gruff on the outside. Kevin certainly thought so.

"Ugh. No sense dwelling on that now." She grabbed the mic. "This is Rawlins. Is there anyone out there from Amarillo?"

She swished side to side in the old office chair, listening to silence for a few minutes. Bee finished counting and looked over.

"Can I get you anything?"

"Nah. I'm okay right now. Thanks, Bee."

The android nodded and walked out.

"Amarillo? Please reply. I don't care if this is against procedure. Pauline's place is damn close to you and if Infected are there... We need to know if you still exist."

Radio silence, barring the intermittent pop or snap, persisted for two minutes and eighteen seconds according to the display on the computer monitor. A six-split screen showed views of the building interior. She spent most of the time watching the restaurant. The cam in the hall by the bedrooms picked up a rhythmic feminine squeaking.

"I do not like ze sound of that," said Gertrude. "Infected in Amarillo? *Das ist sehr schlecht.*"

Tris squeezed the button, mic to her lips. "I don't want to scare everyone, but we have to be realistic. Infected are drawn to large population centers. There've been several roadhouses attacked by the Redeemed these past few weeks, and what response have we seen? Not a damn word. Did you all check your security systems?"

"Dad got pretty pissed off at the computer last week," said Mirabel. "He used a bunch of those words you all don't think I'm old enough to hear."

"She ain't gonna let that go, is she?" asked Clive.

"Mine's screwed," said Mac. "Damn thing doesn't look like it ever worked."

A few indecipherable voices came over at the same time, though it sounded more like grumbles of assent.

"She's right. Anything like this happened a year ago, an' there'd be all sorts of chatter comin' out of 'Rillo with bounty notices." Clive went silent, probably cursing off-mic. "This ain't good."

"What are we gonna do if Amarillo's full of zombies?" asked Jenny.

"They're not zombies," said Tris. "Infected are still biologically alive.

They're as easy to kill as anyone else... easier because they tend to be stupid. They can't even figure out ladders."

"And they strong as shit," said Mac.

"Shit isn't strong," said Mirabel in a somewhat haughty tone. "It just kinda lays there in a lump, sorta like my brother."

"Yo, kid, this is serious. It's about to get all sorts of fucked up for us," said Earl. "If Amarillo's gone dark, it won't take forever for word ta get out. No Code, and raiders will come swooping right in, tearin' shit apart. Fuck anything they can catch, kill anything they can't fuck, and steal anything they can't fuck or eat."

"Whoa," said Mac. "That's a bit paranoid. Shit ain't that bad everywhere."

"Maybe not." Earl paused a tick. "But are you gonna wanna sit out on the highway or head somewhere with a wall... and people."

"Hey, *vato?*" said a new male voice. "What did you say to my daughter? She's hiding under the damn floorboards saying she doesn't wanna have sex with anyone."

"Smooth, Earl, real smooth," said Harold.

Tris repeated a summary of what had been discussed. "Still nothing from Amarillo."

"Shit," said Mirabel's father.

"Hey, Jose?" asked Clive.

"What?"

"You check your cams yet?"

"No. I ain't go to time for playin' with this shit." Jose's voice muted as though he held the mic to his chest but didn't let off the talk button. "Mira, get on outta there. No one's comin' for you."

"Everyone, can we get a little quiet in case Amarillo's tryin' to break through?" Tris sighed. "If they don't answer tonight, I'm going to go there and see what's going on. If... the worst has happened and the place is full of Infected, we have two choices."

She let off the button and waited, but no one interrupted.

"One, we try to keep things quiet while we put together some kind of group and go in there to clean it out. Retake the city and re-establish the Roadhouse network. Someone's gonna have to stay there and basically run the whole show. No, I don't want to be in charge. I'm saying that now so no one thinks that's why I'm suggesting it. I don't care who does it, but it's not going to be me. Two, we forget Amarillo, and the Roadhouse as it is now dies. Everyone's running their own show."

"Uhh," said Harold. "No idea if that would work. Earl's got a point. Most of us are alone, maybe a wife or a kid... I know Clive's got two brothers workin' for him. Think Jose's the only one with any kind of real manpower 'cause of that farm. If we start headin' for the hills and safety of settlements, there goes the infrastructure. Won't be easy to drive cross-country no more without charging stations. Them little portable shits take all day."

"Yeah," said Earl.

"I got twelve men." Jose sounded proud, but nervous. Mirabel whined 'I don't wanna come out' to someone in the background. "We can defend what we got."

The radio hissed silence for another five or so minutes. Bee appeared on camera, navigating the hallway past the small rooms, carrying food to Athena. Tris stared down on her from above until she disappeared into Room 18.

"Amarillo? Is anyone there?" Tris let off the button.

She bowed her head against the mic, and a tremble of dread started in her arm. About fifteen minutes later, she sat up with a sigh and put the mic down on the table. "Maybe Kevin's right... Going there won't accomplish anything."

Tris glared at the radio, daring it to make a sound. She considered leaving; twice she leaned forward as if to stand, but hesitated fearing as soon as she got out of earshot, they'd reply. She begrudgingly lifted the mic again. She pictured the antenna at the corner of the roof, wondering if maybe a squirrel tried to eat it.

"Amarillo?" She let off the button.

A minute passed.

"If there's anyone in Amarillo, please acknowledge."

Two minutes passed.

"... hello," whispered a young sounding female voice. "Are you still there? Please still be there. Oh, you piece of trash, come on... work."

"Hi sweetie," said Tris.

"I'm not a kid. I'm just whispering. Please help."

Shit. What now? Tris pushed the talk button. "Who are you and what's going on?"

"My name's Cassie. I'm... in Amarillo. I'm sorry it took me so long to reply, but the transceiver took a bullet and I had to Frankenstein a new board from a bunch of old ones." She sniffled. "I've been working as fast as I can, hoping you'd still be there if I got the transmitter to work."

"Amarillo?!" Tris all but yelled, off the mic. She pushed the button. "What's going on there?"

Cassie replied in an even weaker whisper, tinged with a whine of desperation. "Infected... they're everywhere. Please... we need help. There's a couple survivors hiding. I don't know how much longer we can hang on. We... can't get out. We have a hiding place and we're safe for the moment, but it won't last forever. Please tell me you're real and I'm not hallucinating hearing you."

"I'm real." Tris pictured a dozen proprietors staring at their radios in rapt silence. "How many?"

"Like hundreds," whispered Cassie.

"I mean survivors." Tris grumbled off-mic. "Hundreds of survivors?"

"Oh. Sorry. No, Infected. Maybe twenty of us left."

"What's it like outside? Can't you make it to a car or something?"

"No." Cassie sniffled. "There aren't any cars that work here. Just the solar panel truck, but it's parked in the warehouse and Mr. Robertson's got the key. No one's seen him since it all happened... he might be dead. Please please please send someone to get us out of here."

Tris' gut twisted into a ball of iron. "Cassie... listen to me. I'm coming. I'm not afraid of Infected. Might be a couple days for me to get there. Try to hang on. Keep everyone calm and let them know help is on the way."

"Thank you." Cassie sounded on the verge of crying.

"Hey, Snow White," said Harold. "That's all brave and shit, but I gotta say it's not smart."

Tris stood. "This ain't about smart. It's about being human."

KEVIN GLANCED UP AS BEE WENT BY WITH AN EMPTY PLATE.

"The girl is experiencing high levels of pain, but she is grateful for the soft bed." Bee winked. "You're a lot like Wayne."

He watched her disappear into the kitchen before sighing into a chuckle. *Yeah... he would've been nice to a clueless kid. Sure let me get away with a lot at that age.* "Damn. I owe it to him."

Tris hurried out of the hallway a hair shy of jogging. "Kevin..."

He whirled to face her; he'd expected anger and threats trying to keep him from going, or worry and pleading for him to stay. Unprepared for the urgency in her eyes, he managed a series of faces without words.

She took his right hand in both of hers and looked down. "I'm sorry. Amarillo's gone. Infected."

The room spun. He felt like a kid told 'you're an adult now' and kicked out of his home ten seconds after his fourteenth birthday. Alone in the world and not ready for it. "Dammit. We... we gotta fake it. Now I *have* to go after the men who killed Wayne. They have to think—the world has to think the Code still works, or we're in deep shit."

"I need to go there." Her gem-blue eyes showed no sign of hesitation. "There's survivors. About twenty... I gotta get them out."

Kevin grabbed the wall to keep from falling over. "Twenty? That's it? That's all that's left?"

"That's what Cassie said, yeah. We don't have a lot of time."

He put a hand on his chest, struggling to breathe. "T-there's gotta be shitloads of Infected there now. Amarillo had like five-thousand soldiers. It's... suicide. Those people." He felt like an asshole, cringed, but said it anyway. "They're already dead. You can't go."

She folded her arms. "You're ordering me around?"

"No... I mean you can't in the way people can't breathe water. You just *can't*. It's stupid." He grasped her shoulders.

"Don't go after Wayne's killers."

He bowed his head.

Tris poked him in the chest. "Don't tell me that's not fair because it's the same damn thing. I don't want you to run off and get killed."

Kevin guided his dizzy-induced fall so his butt landed on the chair behind the counter. "Okay. Look. I'll come with you to Amarillo, then you come with me to nail those motherf—"

"Kevin."

He looked up at her.

"You're as pale as I am and sweating like it's a hundred and twenty in here. I don't want you to get sick. I... couldn't stop the Virus, but I can at least try to help those people."

"That's what this is about then? Unfulfilled savior of the world?" He smiled.

She narrowed her eyes. "No. I won't get sick. I... *have* to try and help those people. I'm not going in there to machinegun down the Infected... I'm going to sneak in and out." Tris' eyes flashed wide. "Zara... I'll bring Zara."

"She's immune too?"

Tris nodded. "She's Enclave. We all got vaccines as kids. They figured the Virus would be out in the world once it killed everyone and purified the earth of all the 'damaged genetics.' The whole point of it was to 'hit the reset button,' so everyone in the Enclave is made immune."

"I don't like it."

She brushed a hand through his hair. "I don't like you going after the Redeemed either, but I know you're going to. You can't even sleep."

"Fitch and Neeley are willing to go with me. Neeley's seen the guys."

"Yes, you said that already."

"Surgical. We're going after the killers. Not all the Redeemed. We'll ambush if we have to so we can get out clean. This ain't about honor; it's vengeance. It's the Code. Protects all of us." He put his hands on her hips. "I'm doing it more for you than for Wayne."

She sighed. "Yeah... I'll take that van. Should be able to fit everyone in there."

"You could take Athena's compact. By the time you get there, you'll be lucky to find two."

"That's not funny."

He looked up at her, his heart pounding against his breastbone. "Wasn't trying to be. I was trying to make you change your mind."

"I'm gonna go tell Zara she's coming with me."

Kevin stood and pulled her into a kiss. "Go in the morning? Let's make love."

She walked backward two steps. "Those people are living minute to minute... We'll spend a whole day in bed when we get back." She turned, stopped, and whirled around again. "No. That's gonna make sure one of us dies. Go upstairs. Be naked in ten minutes. I'll be right there."

Kevin chuckled as she jogged off toward the rental rooms. "Well, that sounded like an order." He glanced at the two drivers. "Fitch!"

The man got up and walked over. "Yo?"

"Mind watchin' the counter for a few minutes?"

"Wait, so you got told you ain't goin' nowhere, now you're goin for the make-up sex?"

"Not exactly. I got told she'd be sick with worry, then she's going to Infected Amarillo, and now I'm going upstairs for the jinx-breaker sex."

"Jinx breaker sex?" Fitch chuckled. "What the hell?"

"Can I watch?" asked Neeley.

"No," said Kevin and Fitch simultaneously.

"Aww," mumbled Neeley.

"She said we'll do it when we get back. That means one of us dies before we can." He winked. "This won't take long."

"Heh. So I hear." Fitch laughed.

Kevin glared at the ceiling. "You know what I meant."

TRIS BARGED IN TO ROOM 5. ZARA LAY NAKED, TIED SPREAD-EAGLE TO THE steel bed frame with Marty half on top of her, sound asleep.

"Oh, shit," whispered Tris. She ducked her head and backed up. "Sorry."

"What's up?" asked Zara.

Tris hovered at the door, holding it only an inch open and not looking in. "There's people stranded by Infected. Will you help me get them out?"

"Little tied up right now, but maybe..."

"Why?" asked Tris.

"If you have to ask, you wouldn't understand. Loverboy here fell asleep too fast." She grunted. "Damn. Hey I don't mind if you come in long enough to untie me."

"I'll... get Bee. She's an android... won't care about that."

"What about that hurry of yours?" asked Zara.

Tris walked in, staring at the floor, and took a seat on the edge of the bed with her back to Zara. Finger-thick black nylon rope wound a couple times around her wrist in a mess of a knot. She picked at it, trying to figure out where it started.

"So, what's the situation?" asked Zara.

Tris pulled, poked, and tweaked at the knot while explaining Amarillo.

"Tris? Either hurry up with that or wipe my nose for me."

"I'm gonna cut this. I can't figure out where to start."

"No... don't cut it. Took him forever to find comfortable rope." Zara squirmed.

Tris sighed. "Sorry. This is our fault."

"Don't blame yourself. I tried to kill you. I'm... surprised he didn't put a bullet between my eyes. I had a lot of time to think after you guys left me tied up in a closet in my skivvies. You were right. We don't really live in the Enclave. I guess I always sort of got a thrill out of this kinda thing... but they'd have considered me defective if I told anyone back there." Zara twisted her right wrist around. "Hey it feels looser."

Tris wedged her fingernails into the knot. "You shouldn't do this out here. It's not a great idea to be helpless."

"What about the whole *Roadhouse* thing?"

"Long damn story. Short answer is… it's gone. It won't take forever for people to learn Amarillo's off the map. The only reason anyone respected the Code is out of fear for what would happen to people who break it." Tris pulled the knot loose.

Zara whipped her hand out of sight, and a rapid snuffling-nose sound came from behind Tris. "Oh, that feels so damn good. Been itching for hours."

Tris stood, keeping her back to the bed. "Can you get yourself out from there?"

"Probably. Gimme a minute before you go in case I can't get it. This isn't exactly a great angle and I've got Marty on top of me." She grunted. "Nope. Can't reach." A loud *slap* followed. "Wake up Marty."

"Bwaa?" He coughed. "What? Where?"

"You passed out before you undid the ropes. My arm's numb."

"Oh." He yawned. "Sorry."

"Hey," said Tris. "Get cleaned up and meet me at a table in like twenty minutes? I need to deal with something real quick upstairs."

18

MERCY FLIGHT

T ris clung to Kevin, taken by a sudden refusal to let go. His hot breath pulsed over her head while hers made his chest hair flutter. She remained still until she no longer felt winded.

"Zara's going to come with me. I should go." She kissed him on the nipple, which made him squirm. "I don't want to, but those people…"

He sat up as she rolled to the side of the bed and stood. "Sang's gonna watch the place, with Bee. I don't get that man… he seems to think the android has seniority over him or something."

Tris cleaned herself up and rooted among her clothes until she found black jeans.

The bed creaked. She smiled, picturing Kevin staring at her ass. She bent forward slow, and slid one foot into the jeans, giving him a good long look before pulling them up. After grabbing the black ankh tee, she faced the bed and smiled at the hunger in his eyes. He hadn't bothered covering himself with the sheet, and appeared ready for another round.

"We're gonna head out in the morning." He didn't sound thrilled. "I gotta at least try. Look, we won't go insane with it. If we find nothing in a week or so, I'll turn around."

"Okay." She stepped into her shoes.

He tilted his head, eyes narrow. "Why are you wearing black? For stealth?"

"Yeah." She sighed. "Yes, I know my hair practically glows at night. Not like I asked for this color."

"Not a criticism." He winked. "I think it's exotic."

She threw a ratty pair of briefs at him, grinning. "I'm not a car."

He lunged to his feet and pulled her into an embrace. "Don't do anything stupid."

Tris grabbed a fistful of his chest hair, and stared into his eyes. "Don't do anything stupid."

"Can't talk you out of this?" He tilted his head.

"I'd say, 'can I talk *you* out of this?' but it's not the same. Innocent people need help."

He cradled her head to his chest. "I'll go with you."

"No." She pushed him back. "Zara and I are the best people to do this. We won't get sick… and if you…" She cringed. "If you got sick, I… Please. Stay far away from anything Infected."

He sighed and pulled the briefs off his shoulder before stepping into them.

"Hey." Tris stared at him. "How come you find men's underwear, but we haven't found a single pair for me."

"We haven't found shit. I've been wearing the same pair for six years."

Tris clamped her hand over her mouth. *Ugh.*

He laughed. "Kidding."

She glared.

"I have nine pairs… for about the past six years." His smile melted under her glare. "Next time we go to Ned, we'll ask about it. I'm sure they've got people making clothes."

She bowed her head. "I've… now I'm just looking for things to waste time. Underpants…" She sighed. "We'll come back as fast as possible."

He hurried into his jeans, boots, and shirt, before going downstairs with her, holding hands. Tris headed for a table where Zara waited, while Kevin diverted to the counter. Zara wore black from head to toe as well, though her hair matched. She also kept it in a bob; then again, the woman had been part of the security team.

"Marty's not gonna go with us. He's still got… issues about Infected. Besides, he's about as stealthy as a drunken bull." Zara smiled. "He'll be taking the truck back to Ned in the morning… Of course, this means one of you owes me a ride home when we're done."

"Easy." Tris smiled. "So you're really okay with this? I expected to have to beg."

"Call it a better apology for trying to kill you." Zara fidgeted, looking away. "How did we go from sitting next to each other in grade school to this?"

"The Enclave is twisted. We're not people to them; we're numbers on a citizen resource allocation grid." Tris put her hand atop Zara's. "Thanks. Ready?"

"I'm sitting here dressed aren't I?" Zara stood. "Actually, I should probably hit the bathroom."

Tris nodded. "Okay. I gotta pull the van around front anyway."

They walked together down the side hall, until Zara hooked a left into the former ladies' room. Tris kept going to the back door and jogged over to the grey van parked by the garage. Kevin had charged it already, but sitting a couple days unused drained a little. She drove it around to the front, got out, and plugged in the charging cable concealed under the front license plate. Kevin looked up as she walked back in; the hope in his stare stabbed her. He practically asked her to stay without even speaking.

"Plug two?" She sighed an apology at the floor.

Zara emerged from the hall, and Tris led the way through the other hallway to the 'employee' entrance for the store.

Tris surveyed several weapons on a shelf. "M-16, shotgun, or a... whatever that is."

Zara brushed past her and picked up a smallish weapon. "FN P-90. Nice gun, but good damn luck finding ammo for it. Wasn't even made in this country. Looks like about twenty rounds left in it, and they're at least fifty years old." She put it down and picked up an MP5. "This'll work. You said we're going in quiet, right? Not going to be much distance shooting. Ammo capacity is king for this."

"Okay. I got an AK. Think that's too long?"

"Well, we're not planning on distance work... doesn't mean it won't happen. Keep it, but go with the Beretta in close quarters."

Tris raided the 9mm stash, taking all 179 bullets on hand. She found four spare magazines for the Beretta, and filled them. "That's eighty-five rounds for me."

Zara held up three magazines. "Guess that leaves four bullets for the store."

Tris pocketed them. "I'm not getting killed over four rounds. Anything we don't use goes back." *Couple years from now, guns will be useless anyway. Ween will eventually run out of powder.*

"Sure."

Over the next twenty minutes, Tris carried a few water jugs, some of the salted dust hopper, her AK-47, katana, and a change of clothes out to the grey van. The whole time she loaded supplies, Zara sat playing around with the turret.

When Tris finally climbed into the driver's seat, Zara gawked at her.

"Why didn't you tell me you had one of *these*? This is so damn cool." She waved her head around, causing an answering whirr of motors from overhead.

"Great. I'll drive; you shoot. But... try not to waste ammo."

Zara pressed her fist to her left shoulder in a mockery of the Enclave military's salute.

Tris rummaged an old folding map from a compartment in the console. "Route 80 east to 25 south... skirt Denver to 70. Then we take 287 south the rest of the way."

"Damn that's a haul. What's that... seven hundred miles?" Zara eyed the GPS on the dash. "Not using the system?"

"No satellites left." Tris folded the map smaller and jotted down quick route notes. "It's about twenty minutes to midnight now. I'm guessing this is gonna take us about eleven hours, but we'll be stuck at a charging station for at least an hour."

"I'll sleep first." Zara crawled into the back. "Oh, hey, there's even a shitty mattress back here."

Tris slid to the ground outside and trudged around to disconnect the charge cable. "I can't believe I'm doing this. They better have the damn decency to stay alive long enough for me to get there."

She pressed down on the spring-loaded license plate until the charge cord finished spindling back inside, and let it slap closed before trudging around to grasp the driver's side door. She hesitated, staring at Kevin in the window.

His lips moved, probably 'I love you,' 'be careful,' or something like that.

A lump tightened in her throat. After taking a breath, she hauled herself up into the van and shut the door.

"There better still be someone there."

19

LAS CRUCES

Kevin startled awake, not entirely sure at what point his determined ceiling-staring session came to an end. Based on the way the sun hit the walls, he figured it to be close to ten in the morning. The time would probably put Tris within visual range of Amarillo, assuming nothing went wrong and they didn't stop. That he had fallen asleep at all surprised him more than he'd let her talk him into not going along.

He sat up. "How'm I suppose to go do this thing worryin' about her? No wonder Wayne never got involved with a woman. They twist your brain around in a god damned knot."

Grumbling, he slid off the bed and trudged downstairs while wiping at the right side of his face in an effort to dislodge a particularly tenacious eye crumb. A light smattering of applause startled him out of his stupor.

"Morning, boss," said Bee.

"Rough night?" asked Fitch with a raised eyebrow.

"What?" Kevin stared at Fitch for a few seconds before noticing everyone in the room had stopped whatever they had been doing to gawk at him. At that point, he looked down at his lack of clothes and the usual rigid effect of morning. "Oh. Right."

He turned on his heel and went back upstairs. A few minutes later, he returned, dressed and carrying his armored jacket. Fitch stood behind the counter with Neeley on the 'client' side, two small metal pails between them. One half-full of peanuts, the other three-quarters filled with shells.

"You still wanna do this?" asked Neeley.

"Can't sit around here worrying." Kevin grabbed a jar of water and downed it in one breath.

Sang appeared in the window, handing him a dust hopper sausage on a long roll, covered in scrambled egg. "You sure you can pick these guys out?"

Neeley nodded. "Positive."

"Wayne's hat oughta be obvious." Fitch nodded.

"Got a week of canteens in the Challenger for ya, boss," said Bee. "Mister Fitch said he had the food covered."

"Got enough MREs to handle it if we can't find 'houses." Fitch leaned back until a rippling crunch came from his spine, and a relieved grin spread over his lips. "Ahh…"

Kevin inhaled the sandwich while going over a few last-minute reminders with Sang. As much as he tried to get the old man to understand the logbook, his cook kept circling around to talk about Athena's progress learning to read.

"Fine, forget dealing with drivers. I got two out on runs now. If they come back, just tell them to wait for me ta get back."

Sang nodded. "You got it. Be careful with yourself."

"You too."

Kevin shook hands and headed out front, where Fitch muttered to Nevada by the end of the counter. He wandered over to them. "Morning."

"Nev here's willin' to stick around 'til we get back. Help out with uhh, physical security."

"I appreciate that, but… things are strange now. I wouldn't feel right askin' you to take that kind of risk when I'm not even here."

Nevada bowed at Kevin. "I respect what you are going to do. If, as you say, these people are targeting Roadhouse operators, they will not suspect me as a threat when I appear to be just sitting at a table like a driver."

"Okay." He shook her hand. "I'll owe you. Any ammo you use up defending this place is on the house."

"How you wanna do this?" asked Fitch.

"I'll take point. You two follow me in the behemoth. I'd prefer to take Route 24 down and stay well away from Denver. We can top off the batteries near Steamboat Springs, stop again on 25, little southwest of Santa Fe. At Willie's."

Fitch gave him a thumbs-up.

Neeley rubbed his hands together so fast it looked as though he attempted to start a fire with a stick and tinder. "Let's get it on!"

"Murderous little bastard, ain't he?" Kevin chuckled.

Fitch smiled. "He likes his rifle. A lot."

HIGHWAY HOUR BLURRED INTO HIGHWAY HOUR. NINETY-ISH WAS ABOUT THE limit of Fitch's war wagon, but it felt like walking when he wanted to run. They could've piled into the Challenger; however, a trip like this all but demanded a backup vehicle. Of course, that also trapped him in a potential fight he could've ordinarily run from. Right before they'd split up to their respective vehicles, Kevin made sure they knew that if he appeared to be cutting and leaving them in the dust, he would only be exploiting his speed for tactical advantage and had every intention of coming back.

Steamboat Springs Roadhouse proved quiet. The older couple who ran it, Vick and Ruby, almost didn't believe Kevin's story about what went on. Neither had received any updates as (in addition to their security computer) their radio was dead. They didn't seem too worried about being killed. Both being in their mid-sixties, as Vick put it, someone would only be sparing them the 'shitty years.' Not like they had much to steal. All the food they sold, they grew themselves. More work, but essentially free, even though they served nothing more than vegetables and some handmade cheese from their goats.

Three e-bikes and a blue Silverado covered in rusty metal armor plates came out of a ravine about two hours south of Steamboat. The pickup hung back while the bikes raced ahead. Only pirates or bandits would ride up in such an aggressive formation, and Neeley picked off two with his Dragunov before they got close enough to even try shooting back. The third man's helmet shattered at about the same instant a burst of muzzle flare spat from the front of a submachine gun mounted to the handlebars.

Another spurt of orange came out of the pickup's grille, followed by sparks from the back end of Fitch's truck. He wrenched the Behemoth into the left (oncoming) lane, and farther off onto the dirt, mowing down a series of old wooden fence posts.

Kevin eyed the little screen in his dashboard, thumb hovering over the button trigger. He nudged the Challenger left a few inches and pushed. The AK-47 and M-16 in the trunk roared to life, each spitting about ten rounds before he let off the button. The Silverado swerved but kept on. Kevin yanked the wheel to ditch the lane an instant before the pickup's machine gun went off again, skipping tracers over empty blacktop at his right. Neeley, poking out of a hatch in the top of Fitch's truck, yelled about holding it steady despite them bouncing over dirt and bushes.

Kevin stared at the screen waiting for the Silverado to adjust to line him up for a shot. The instant it did, he swerved to the right and tapped the trigger button. A short burst from each trunk gun chattered while the Silverado's grille gun fired for only two seconds, again at empty road.

This time, the blue truck kept gliding left, off the paving, and rambled out of control over scrubland, kicking up a dust cloud.

Neeley swiveled after it; a few seconds after Fitch put the Behemoth back on pavement, he fired. The rear (unarmored) window of the Silverado shattered, as did the head of the man behind the wheel. From the way the truck had been careening, Kevin figured Neeley had mauled a corpse.

Not being in any true hurry other than wanting to get back to Tris, Kevin stopped. He scavenged two UZIs and a .44 revolver from the bikers, as well as a few handfuls of bullets while Fitch and Neeley checked out the pickup. He didn't bother counting any of it.

Fitch came back with a belt of 7.62 x 51, perfect for the M60s he had on the front of the challenger. The bullets had Ween's maker's mark scratched on them, so he tossed it in the trunk for later. Both '60s had full boxes already.

"Driver had this." Neeley held up a blue Kevlar vest. "Didn't do his balls any good though."

Fitch and Kevin cringed.

Neeley laughed and tapped himself across the waist. "Some of your bullets punched holes in the firewall. Think he bled out 'fore I shot him."

"Anything else worth grabbing?" Kevin slammed the trunk.

"Couple shitty tools. Hammer, hacksaw, crowbar. All beaten to crap." Fitch spat.

The men lined up to water the ground, raided the canteens to wet their throats, and got back in their respective cars. Kevin stared over the hood at the road again and almost talked himself out of going on with it. He got underway eventually, accelerating up to 120 before he noticed the Behemoth fading back and flashing headlights.

"Yeah, yeah." He slowed to seventy until they caught up.

AROUND 7:40 P.M., THEY DIVERTED OFF TO ROUTE 25, A LITTLE OUT OF their way since Kevin intended to take 285 to avoid having to pass through Albuquerque. Eight minutes later, they stopped at Willie's. This 'house looked normal, insofar as it being a brown, rectangular wooden building with a giant red Roadhouse sign and a couple of cars parked in front. Lights on inside made everything appear the same as they had been for as long as Kevin could remember. The way he wanted everything to stay, but doubted it would. He suspected the radio here would probably be dead as well since Willie hadn't been in on any of the wonderful conversations lately.

Fitch pulled up to his left. They shut down, got out, and plugged in almost in unison.

Inside, four men in biker cuts bearing New logos sat around a table. He didn't recognize any of them, which likely meant they wouldn't know him either. News tended to style themselves as the law around New Mexico, and usually left people alone unless they caused trouble, had a bounty on their head, or happened to be a distrusting asshole who wouldn't untie a woman in desperate need of a ride.

He frowned.

Willie could've been Wayne's somewhat younger, and much larger, brother. They both had a sort-of cowboy aesthetic to the way they carried themselves, though Willie had to be a couple fingers shy of seven feet tall with a jaw so square he looked like an amateur sculptor hadn't quite finished him.

Granted, not a lot of guys wanted to start a fight with someone who had normal human thighs for biceps.

"Willie..." Kevin shouldered up to the bar. "Looks like you're doing well."

"Not bad." Willie greeted the three with a nod. "What can I do ya for?"

"Charge on six and seven and a plate of whatever's fast." Kevin nodded toward the curtained doorway behind the bar. "Your radio workin'?"

"Why? Need to call in a job?" Willie flicked two switches on the electronics panel behind him, activating the circuit to the charging ports. "Three apiece for the juice. Same for the food."

Neeley reached into his jacket, but Kevin held up a hand. He put down six coins for the charge and nine for food. "Haven't been hearin' you on the net."

"How's you hearin' the net?" Willie squinted at him.

Kevin smiled. "Got my own place finally. Up on I-80, little west of Rawlins. Look. Can I"—he glanced over his shoulder at the News and three drivers—"have a word with you quiet like?"

Willie unsnapped the leather holding a revolver in his holster, but nodded. "'Mon 'round. No shit, you got your own franchise?"

"As a fact." Kevin grinned and pulled out the laminated card he'd gotten from the old guy at Amarillo six months and a few weeks ago. It looked hand drawn, like something a grade school kid made, but so did they all.

"Well, damn." Willie relaxed and brought Kevin past the curtain into the inner hall. From there, four open archways led to a kitchen with a man and two women in it, a storage room, a small living space, and the room where he'd set up the security computer and radio.

"There's been some problems lately. That's why I'm down here and not behind my own counter." Kevin put his hands on his hips.

"Erin. Bring out three roadrunners," yelled Willie toward the kitchen.

"Fuck you, Willie." The twenty-something sounded amused despite her language.

Willie grinned. "Thanks."

Kevin let out a long breath, and explained a quick summary of everything that had happened. He paused a moment at the end to let Willie mull. "I still don't know what's going on, but these Redeemed jackasses killed Wayne, probably Nash too. And who knows how many others where the radios don't work."

Willie raised a hand. "Hold on. You said Amarillo's... gone?"

"Well the city's still there, but the only thing in it are Infected." He gestured at the table full of electronics. "You ever use your radio? We've been talking about all this for days."

"Never had anyone mess with me." Willie grumbled. "Never saw the need."

"I don't really understand all that computer shit. Tris says the systems are burned out. Cameras are watching but the thingamafuckit that keeps the images doesn't keep them."

"Oh. That ain't that hard to understand. S'like talkin' to mah wife. I say everything, but don't keep in her brain." Willie chuckled for three seconds before a tomato burst across his head. He reached up and pulled the larger mass of it away from his eye, glanced at it, and took a bite. "She's a spitfire, that one."

Kevin glanced at a wild-eyed woman with black hair and a deep tan. She muttered something in Spanish before brightening up—a little—at Kevin.

"Need ta trade 'er in for a model with a sense of humor." Willie took another bite of the tomato, and winked at her.

"Any of those Redeemed guys come in here, stay alert. They messed with Wayne first. Orderin' an' not payin'. Nash's, they just came in shooting."

Willie wandered over to the radio, toggled a switch or two, but couldn't get it to do anything. He looked somehow wrong tinkering with electronics, as if a man that big had no business coming within ten feet of anything technological. "Reckon yer right. Thing's deadern' my—"

"She's got another tomato," said Kevin.

"Car," said Willie.

The fortyish woman smiled at Kevin before returning to the kitchen, tossing and catching a tomato.

"Figure them News'll keep tabs on a rogue club." Willie returned to the front.

Kevin followed. "Careful tellin' those guys you ain't got Amarillo watchin' out for ya. I don't trust 'em not to just take the place."

Willie laughed. "They can try. 'Preciate the heads up."

"Somethin' I gotta do." Kevin nodded. "It's all our asses in the fire."

They shook hands. Kevin walked back to the front room, joining Fitch and Neeley at a table. The 'roadrunner' turned out to be half a chicken with a portion of rice laced with beans, corn, and a bright orange spicy sauce he'd never run into before. Whatever it was, it tasted good.

"Figure crash here a few hours?" asked Fitch.

Kevin rubbed the bridge of his nose, only aware of the eye-burn of insufficient sleep after Fitch mentioned it. "Yeah. Be pretty damn stupid to roll in there half awake."

Neeley jumped up. "I'll cover the rooms."

He ran off before Kevin could protest.

Fitch leaned over the table, his voice low. "This isn't an opinion, but if you want to head back any time, just say the word. We'd understand."

Kevin stared into the inch of cloudy beer he had left. "We're already down here. Only a couple miles away from Santa Fe. Besides, feels like a jinx. If I don't finish this out, something bad'll happen."

"What like Wayne's ghost getting pissed and comin' after you?"
Or goin' after Tris. "Yeah, something like that."
Kevin drained his beer.

SUNLIGHT POURED A HAZE OVER THE TERRAIN, SWALLOWING THE ROAD WITH undulating heat blur. Kevin forced a hard yawn and shook his head to clear it. Exhaustion and worry had dueled for some time before he'd slept; it felt as though he'd spent hours staring at the ceiling and Fitch appeared out of nowhere, shaking him. They'd rolled out from Willie's at 5:49 a.m. according to the clock in the Challenger's dash. He drove into the dark horizon, munching on dust hopper (or something close to it) jerky. Meaty salt. Good enough for road breakfast.

Soon after sunrise, they weaved through a section of paving riddled with tire-eating holes, and crossed a good mile and change where whatever had hit Albuquerque buried Route 285 under several feet of dirt. *Wonder what was there that someone felt like lobbing a nuke at it?* He glanced to his right as he drove past the city. *Damn that's gotta be like fifty or sixty miles away. Maybe the warhead wasn't aiming for Albuquerque.* He tapped his fingers on the wheel. "Wonder if Tris'd know if a nuke can throw dirt sixty miles." *Whatever. Not like me knowing matters.* Whatever it was aimed at, it had to be a nuke. A radial pattern scarred the ground, gouged where heavier objects slid outward from a central point somewhere west.

Fortunately, the rad meter on the dash hadn't crept past 009.

About four hours after leaving Willie's, the Challenger rumbled over the well-cracked pavement of US-70 at the outskirts of the place once called Las Cruces, New Mexico. He stopped as soon as the first buildings came into view, a beige square across a lot from a trio of rusting silos. Several prewar cars lay in a tangle by an upside-down trailer. Seeing no one around, he rolled the car forward at walking speed, scanning the area. To the left, a scenic rise of mountains in varying shades of brown lent an air of placidity to the dry, dusty place.

The beige square building looked like the corner of a formerly larger structure, which existed as a pile of scrap wood with a tangle of old power lines on top of it. Beyond it, a field of wild grass wavered in a slight breeze. Utility poles scattered randomly around dilapidated houses, as though some drunken god had been playing darts from on high.

Amid the ruin of pre-war Las Cruces, a nest of rebuilt structures formed something of a town square about a quarter mile deeper in. One bore the familiar Roadhouse sign, though made of wood and red paint rather than metal and neon. Something itched at the back of his heart being here; sparse as it was, Las Cruces had been a population center before the war, but looking at it up close, he reconsidered his assumption it would have Infected. He glanced left at a couple house trailers parked by a fence of white plastic lattice. Old washing machines, televisions, tables, and the engine block of a V8 combustion engine lay scattered about by a dinged U-Haul trailer at the end of the larger double-wide.

"Damn. I don't think nuclear war changed this place much."

Some locals emerged from the tumbledown dwellings, more curious than wary. He led their 'convoy' down a tiny grid of streets, feeling a bit foolish at having expected the place to be larger... or at least feel more like a 'city' and less like an overgrown campsite. With no sign of The Redeemed obvious, he circled back to the supposed Roadhouse and parked by three coffee-brown jeeps.

Fitch pulled the Behemoth to a halt behind him. "What's up?"

"Place seems small."

Neeley laughed. "This ain't Las Cruces."

Kevin grumbled and pulled out his maps. He trailed his finger down their route, and found a note for a town called Organ. "Shit."

"Little anxious?" Fitch chuckled and backed up.

"Yeah. A bit," he muttered as he reversed out of the parking spot and got back onto Route 70 heading southwest.

Soon after, the actual city of Las Cruces came into view, a sprawl of crumbling buildings and once-nice houses. Though it lacked the densely-packed nightmare of high-rises, it looked quite large enough to conceal a dangerous population of Infected. He pulled off the highway and slalomed a few wrecked cars on the ramp. *Gonna stay in the car... Guess I'm looking for a cluster of e-bikes.* He gazed around as he took a left at the bottom of the ramp, into the shadow of an overpass where 70 went overhead.

A quick right brought him past crumbling houses and fields of dirt. *This place is abandoned. No one in their right mind goes anywhere near a major city.* Over the next half hour, he drove by whim, turning corners whenever the mood caught him. All the while, he debated the idiocy of running around the desert hoping to find the three men Neeley spotted.

"What am I doing?" Kevin slowed to a halt and let his forehead bonk the wheel between his hands. "This is pointless."

He switched the drive system to park and got out. Fitch, unable to roll down his armored window, opened the door.

"Yo?" asked Fitch. "What's up?"

"Give it to me straight guys." Kevin, hands on his hips, stared at the road. "Is this a waste of time? Feels like we're chasing a rabbit in the desert."

"Well." Fitch scratched at his almost-beard. "If they got a 'home' ta go back to, maybe we'll find 'em there. If they keep roaming all the time, then…"

"Yeah." Kevin grumbled. "Hell with it. Maybe we should—"

"Incoming," said Neeley.

Kevin twisted to face back toward the Challenger.

Two battered ethanol-eating pickup trucks, drab green, screeched to a halt about fifteen yards from the Challenger. Six men jumped out of the bed on the left, eight from the other truck. All looked Mexican and wore a generally similar uniform of plain brown fatigues. The group pointed an assortment of rifles—some bolt action, some automatic—at Kevin. The drivers of both trucks looked like teenaged boys barely past the need to shave, in the same uniforms, whose expressions held the kind of wide-eyed eagerness he expected on a kid ready to watch his dad beat someone up. A well-tanned man in his early thirties with a hairline moustache stepped out of the passenger seat of the truck on the left, adjusting a maroon beret before frowning at the Challenger. He lacked a rifle, and made no move to draw the pistol from his belt. The stare he shot Kevin almost made him miss Infected.

Almost.

Fitch sighed.

"Well, shit," said Kevin. "I don't think the locals are too happy to see us."

LIKE OLD TIMES

Tris wrung her hands around the steering wheel, as if doing so might squeeze a few extra MPH out of the van. Cassie's sad little whisper begging for help played on endless repeat in her thoughts, along with Kevin's opinion that she'd never make it in time. Optimism had made her take the van. The Challenger could tease out 200 miles per hour if the road allowed it, and this particular stretch of flat-open-smooth tormented her. Every time she glanced down at the speed display teetering between seventy-two and seventy-four, she had to suppress a growl.

I'm driving a brick. She rehearsed in her head how to handle an attack on the road. Memories of being thrown around the passenger seat while Kevin swerved to evade bullets got her worked up. Reflex boosters only went so far behind the wheel. Maybe she could catch an overcorrection in time to avoid flipping the thing, or maybe they'd roll wheels up and die in a hail of bullets.

According to the dash clock, she had about eight minutes to go until six in the morning. Almost six solid hours of driving. They'd need to stop for battery power soon; after that, Zara could take over.

Once the road provided a nice debris-free straightaway, she wedged the steering wheel with her left knee and fumbled with the map. A tiny overhead light helped a little, but made the outside appear darker. Kevin's notes suggested a roadhouse coming up soon along 287 south, a few miles past the Colorado/Oklahoma border.

"Probably be dawn before we get there." She yawned. "Maybe I'll even be able to sleep."

A few minutes later, her head dipped and she snapped upright. Wide eyed, she white-knuckled the wheel for a little while until she felt herself sliding again.

"Zara," she yelled.

"Mmm?" A yawn came from behind her. "What? You don't have to yell. I'm up."

Tris yawned again, despite trying to stifle it with a clenched jaw. "I'm fading. Talk or something…"

Zara squeezed through the little door in the partition between front and back. She failed to stifle another yawn and fell into the passenger seat. "Hey, it's almost six… you were supposed to wake me up after four hours."

"Yeah, I know. Seemed dumb to take two hours of sleep. We're almost at Mac's."

"So, what should I talk about?"

Tris shrugged. "I dunno… anything to keep me awake. Like that time Gerald tried to say you were cheating off him in electrical engineering class."

Zara laughed into her hand. "Tris… we're twenty years old. You want to reminisce about when we were twelve? We barely talked to each other."

"Yeah I know. We sat next to each other for years though." She tapped her thumbs on the wheel. "No one really talked to anyone, did they?"

"Not much." Zara rotated ninety degrees to face forward and let her head lean back, eyes closed.

"They wouldn't even tell us the teachers' names." Tris fought off another yawn. "You ever think it strange that they had kids older and younger in the same class, and we stayed together the whole time?"

"How is that odd to you?"

"You saw the same historicals I did. That one where they had so many kids they had to group them by age? Grades, they called it. They had twelve of those, and a separate umm… high school."

"Oh, yeah. That was before the war though. The Council came up with a better way." Zara stretched and made a soft noise of contentment.

"What if they did that because there *were* only nineteen children?"

Zara looked over. "You've been absorbing too many rads. When I was in IFT, we used to run practice drills in the city core. There were dozens of children there." She raised an eyebrow. "Usually running away from us and screaming, but they were there."

"IFT? I thought you went to university." Tris pushed the button to open the window, forgetting glass had long-ago been replaced with an armored plate. "Damn."

"I did. IFT is the phase-one preparedness course for the military. Initial Force Training. They worked it in around classes. Five in the morning to seven, we did PT, seven thirty to three in the afternoon, classes. Three to six in the evening, IFT. Usually, I'd spend the rest of the day in my little octagon doing homework or sleeping." Zara held up her hand. "Maybe going three knuckles deep."

Tris laughed. "I didn't really need to know that much detail." She blinked. "Wait, did you say 'octagon?'"

Zara looked at her as though she'd called the sky green. "What planet did you go to Uni on?"

"I didn't. They paired me with this piece of shit. Three hours in the same room with the guy and he'd hit me twice. I was *not* going to spend the rest of my life being owned."

Zara gasped. "You refused the pairing?"

"Yep." Tris didn't feel tired anymore. "Got put in Detention. Little white octagon for a room."

"Yeah... some days I think that would've been better than the dorms."

A faint haze of blue lit up the horizon to the left.

Tris kept looking for signs that might help tell where she was. "Hey, Zar?"

"Yeah?"

"Did your dorm room have a toilet?"

Zara kept quiet.

Tris spotted a 'you are now leaving Colorado' sign, and smiled. A minute later, she glanced over at her friend. "Well?"

"What kind of question is that? Of course it had a toilet."

"Why'd you hesitate?" Tris stared at her for two seconds. "It didn't, did it?"

Zara rolled her eyes. "What, you think I held it for two years?"

"My cell in Detention didn't have a toilet."

"That's disgusting."

"I'm serious. Eight white walls, one monitor for e-learns, a small table, and a little bed."

Zara raised her head in a slow turn to face her. "You're starting to creep me out." She breathed hard for a few seconds. "I... I'm trying to picture the layout of my old room, but..."

"You can't think of where the toilet was." Tris tried to stomp the accelerator pedal through the floor. "Come on you piece of shit, you can do eighty five."

"It's too damn early for head games." Zara flopped back, eyes closed again.

"Think about the last time you looked at yourself in the mirror right after high school."

Zara's lips curled into a small grin. "Okay."

"Compare to now. I think we're still eighteen."

"You have *definitely* been eating some weird shit out here."

"Am I wrong?" Tris looked over at Zara again. "Unless my memory's foggy, I look the same right now as I did when I got my diploma."

"Nanites, Tris. The damn Nanites are keeping us healthy. Maybe they slow aging down too."

Tris tapped her left foot. "Okay... I didn't think of that."

"Now I'm curious." Zara sat up. "Where were you going with that whole creep show?"

Daylight intensified. The horizon to the left took on shades of pink and blue, illuminating endless fields of scrub brush and a few dead cars.

"A couple days after graduation, security forces showed up and brought me to a medical check."

"Tell me something I don't know. It's routine. Part of getting certified as an adult."

Tris held up one hand. "Bear with me here. They hooked us up to the scanner, right?"

"Right."

"What if that wasn't a scanner. What if the day we went in there, we got... I dunno... frozen or something. When we woke up, it was in VR. Everything that happened from that day until you got chosen to come kill me was all electrons." A flicker of light up ahead in the oncoming lane caught Tris' eye. "When I thought a hacker was helping me escape, he said the door to my cell would open at nine in the morning. I went to bed that night. Took me forever to fall asleep. When I woke up, the room had a toilet and my hair was damp."

"You're imagining things." Zara leaned forward. "Headlights coming."

Two white spots shimmered beneath a royal blue sky. A sedan-shaped pile of welded steel plating approached. A head and binoculars protruded from a hole in the middle of the roof.

"I see them." Tris stared at the car, noting a pair of small miniguns on the hood. "I think I was in stasis, not getting older. When I 'escaped,' they let me out and put me in a fake cell. I met up with the resistance and they plugged me in to VR for combat training. Sometimes it was so real I couldn't tell I was basically dreaming."

Zara turned in her seat as the other car zoomed past them, watching it. "I think you're brain's been going off on a wild tangent. If you're right, that would mean they put you on ice before you broke the law. Why would they do that?"

The car threw up a dust cloud as it whipped around and rocked to a halt. A second later, two geysers of sand spat out from the rear tires and it accelerated after them.

Tris shifted her gaze from the rearview mirror to Zara. "They're chasing us, and... I don't have an answer for that."

Zara reached up and pulled the helmet down over her head. "Whoever installed this thing should've put in a chair on a rotating mount." She got up on her knees to face rearward, the turreted .50 whining overhead as it followed her facing.

Tris checked the mirror again; the car raced up on her so fast she felt like the van wasn't even moving. "Shit they're—"

When the .50 cal fired, the air inside the van vibrated as though a pair of giants walloped the sides with hammers. Tris screamed from the surprise, though she couldn't hear herself. The change from machinegun firing to car exploding behind them flowed in a seamless transition of roaring.

"I love this thing," yelled Zara. "It's like a wind-up toy version of the MM-90."

"Hoplite?" yelled Tris.

"No, Gladiator or bigger. The '90s got too much recoil for a hoplite. Why are you yelling?"

Tris leaned left to check on the rear view, eyeing a flaming hulk too far behind them to make out details. She let off a breath of relief. "That damn gun is loud."

"What?" asked Zara.

Tris frowned at her.

Zara laughed and pushed the helmet off, letting the wires tug it back up against the roof. Sleep deprivation helped the mood go contagious, and Tris found herself almost in tears laughing along with her, and couldn't even remember what had struck her funny after a while. Twelve minutes later, when the wonderful sight of a red Roadhouse sign appeared against the brightening sky, intermittent chuckles still broke the silence.

Tris pulled up to a charging port and stopped. She climbed down, shut the door, and walked around front. Zara zoomed by, heading for the building. The urgency of not having stopped for six hours got worse at the sight of her friend stiff-legging it for the entrance. Tris grunted as she stooped to plug in the cable behind the license plate, then hurried inside.

An athletic black man with a shaved head, white tank top, and broad smile looked up from behind the counter. A pair of MAC-10 submachine guns hung at his sides, on crisscrossed straps.

"Hey, Mac." Tris raced across a room full of tables and square wood-paneled support columns covered in pre-war sports team memorabilia. "Be right back."

Two other people sat at tables at opposite ends of the room. A dark-skinned man in a puffy Jamaican hat who looked in his middle twenties near the back hallway, and a weathered, bearded man with a reddish tan hunched over a plate two tables in from the door.

Unfortunately, Mac's Roadhouse had one bathroom. Fortunately, someone kept it clean. Tris bounced in the hallway for a little while, waiting. When the door opened, she grabbed Zara, pulled her out, and rushed in. Tris dropped her jeans and leapt onto the bowl, ignoring Zara's laughter.

"Okay, maybe I should've stopped on the side of the road." She groaned with relief.

Soon, they helped themselves to a table against the wall opposite the bar, about halfway between front and back. A pretty girl of about fourteen, her skin as dark as Mac's, emerged from a bead curtain behind the counter, in a denim dress, white apron, and flip-flops. Reedy and graceful, the girl made Tris feel less skinny.

"Hi. I'm Denise. Can I get you anything to eat or drink?" The teen smiled, baring teeth too perfect for anyone in the Wildlands.

Tris blinked. "Are you Mac's daughter?"

The girl nodded. "Yes."

"What's good?" asked Zara.

Tris smiled at her. "Food definitely sounds good. Need a charge on number four, and beds."

"One room is fine," said Zara.

"Umm." Denise tilted her head side to side. "We've got deer and goat steak, chicken soup, bean soup, bread, cheese…"

"I'm not sure I could eat goat. They're too cute." Tris fidgeted. "Deer steak I guess and some bread."

"Cute?" Denise laughed. "Try living around them… For you, ma'am?"

"Goat's fine. Haven't had that before."

Denise nodded. "Drink?"

"Water," said both women at the same time.

The girl offered a quick bow and hurried back to the counter.

"One room?" Tris blinked. "Uhm…"

"While I absolutely can't wait to get you naked," whispered Zara, "I'm thinking more in terms of defense. Better not to separate."

Tris stared, open-mouthed.

"I'm kidding." Zara winked. "Unless you really want to."

"Stop." Tris stuck out her tongue. "Now I *know* you're messing with me."

Zara snickered into her hand.

Denise returned with two plastic cups of water, set them down, and headed over to the guy in the rainbow hat.

Mac wandered over. "You're who I think you are, right?"

"Hey, Mac." Tris shook his hand. "Yeah."

Mac joined them at the table. "So you really think Amarillo is…"

"I do." Tris kept her voice quiet. "Have you heard anything on the radio?"

"Nah. Whole lotta nothin'."

Tris put a hand on his forearm. "You've got a beautiful daughter, Mac. I hope we can put this back together so she's safe."

"Thanks." He patted the guns. "She's why I got me these."

A woman who resembled Denise in twenty years appeared in a passé-plat similar to Kevin's, and put up two plates. The girl took them with the grace of someone who'd been waiting tables for years, balanced them both on one arm, and grabbed a pitcher to refill their waters.

"Is this the goat?" asked Zara.

Tris looked at the meat on her plate and shrugged. "I can't tell either, but I'll trust the kid."

Mac chuckled. "Yeah, she got it right. So. I been' checkin' my hardware. Everything you say be right. Damn thing busted to hell. Only the radio and the panels work."

The venison steak had a hint of spice Tris wasn't expecting, but the explosion of flavor stunned her mute for a few minutes. "Oh wow, this is amazing."

He smiled. "My dad's the best cook there is. So what's your plan?"

"Right now, we're just trying to get there fast enough to maybe find some survivors. Hard to plan anything without knowing what's going on there."

"Yeah." Zara waved a fork bearing a block of goat at Mac. "If there's a hundred Infected, maybe we can clean them out. Thousand? Better waiting for them to die off on their own."

"That hasn't been happening the way it should." Tris cut off another piece of meat. "There's some kind of symbiote. Nanotech. Somehow keeps them alive."

Zara choked on a mouthful of mashed potato. "What?"

Tris set her fork down and held her hands up about two feet apart. "It looks like an... eel. About this long. Comes out of the mouth when you kill the Infected it parasitized. Tries to go down the nearest throat it can find, even a person clear of Virus. We think it's using nanite technology to repair the host's body enough to keep the Infected alive past when the disease should kill... provided it eats."

Zara shivered. "Thanks for that nightmare. You've seen this?"

"Yeah. I've also met Doctor Andrews. He confirmed it."

Her eyes widened. "You *found* him? He's like one of the most wanted..."

"He's dead. Shot himself in the head after getting hopelessly surrounded by Infected." Tris stabbed the little bit of meat she had left. "Nathan sent me out here with what I thought was a cure for the Virus, but it turned out to be music. A band called The Cure."

Zara cringed. "Asshole."

Mac stifled a chuckle, then held up his hand. "Sorry. I... That's some cold ass shit, but dayum. Kinda funny."

Tris exhaled. "Yeah, I can see how that would be funny... if the entirety of humanity wasn't at risk of being wiped out by the virus I can't cure."

Mac stared at her. "Damn, girl."

She scooped mashed potatoes up, dropped them, scooped, dropped. "Nothing to be done about it now. It was a lie. Kevin keeps telling me I shouldn't feel guilty about failing because I didn't fail; I never had a chance."

Mac's lips curled in an appraising frown.

"I still can't believe that bastard was operating rogue." Zara scowled. "I thought it was an official..." She cringed. "Sorry. I mean... I'm not like saying I wish I succeeded or anything but..."

"I know. Now you're stuck out here too."

Zara's amber eyes flickered with something... doubt? "It's not your fault."

"Hey Mac. Can you throw us a couple extra volts? We're kind of in a hurry. Also, if you could send a wake up our way in six?"

"You got it." Mac stood.

"How much for everything?"

Mac grinned. "You're not gonna let me say on the house, are you?"

Tris shook her head. "I'll take the bed and power for free since that's not using anything up. At least let me pay for the food."

"Eight then."

"I'd say ouch, but that food was damn good." Tris handed over eight coins. "You need to try Sang's fried potatoes one of these days."

"Maybe I will." Mac made finger guns at her, winked, and returned to the counter.

Denise came by to refill their water and drop off a room key.

After chugging the water, Tris headed past the bathrooms to a stairway leading up one floor. The bedroom made the 'small rooms' back home in Rawlins seem large. It wasn't much bigger than a closet an inch or three larger than the mattress packed into it, but she didn't care.

She kicked off her shoes and collapsed before Zara even got the door closed.

<hr />

TRIS DREAMED OF BEING TRAPPED IN A SMALL OCTAGONAL ROOM WITH white walls. She spent hours and hours searching for a door, but couldn't find anything resembling one. Soon after she curled up against the wall sobbing, Zara's voice came from the speakers overhead.

"Tris? Come on... it's time."

She awoke curled on her side with Zara sitting up behind her, as if they'd been spooning.

"That didn't sound like a good dream."

Tris stretched until her limbs quivered, went limp for a few seconds, and sat up.

Zara massaged her shoulders. "Mac knocked about ten minutes ago."

"Ugh. Sorry." Tris yawned.

"Hey, don't sweat it. My turn to drive now. Shall I carry you to the mattress in the van?"

"Heh. Tempting." She stood with a grunt, the muscles in her legs as responsive as pudding.

"Tris?"

"Hmm?" She glanced back.

"I'm not sure if there was a toilet." Zara bit her lip. "I... It's a blur."

"Later." Tris rolled her right arm around to stretch her shoulder. "My brain isn't on yet."

Zara led the way downstairs, but Tris darted ahead into the bathroom. She waited for Zara afterward, and they entered the main room together. Based on the angle of the sunlight, she guessed it to be after noon, likely closer to one. Zara headed for the door, but Tris snagged her arm and pulled her over to the counter.

"Hey Mac." Tris smiled. "You got any like sandwiches or burgers… something we can walk out eating?"

"Yeah. Be a minute or two. Chicken or burger?"

"Chicken," said Tris and Zara at the same time.

"Hey pops?" Mac leaned toward the window behind him. "Two chicken burgers."

"Four coins?" asked Tris.

Mac opened his mouth, hesitated, then nodded. "Yah."

She put down six. "It's okay. If it's anything like the steak."

Something crashed in the back with a cacophony of ringing tin.

"Goddamit," yelled a woman.

"Oy! What ya doin' back there?" Mac held up a 'wait a sec' finger before darting past the bead curtain.

Tris let her eyes droop closed, leaning on the counter for support. More sleep waited only a few yards outside the door. Whiskey fumes washed over her face a few seconds later.

"Hey there," said a slurred male voice. "You two available?"

"No," said Zara, her voice cold.

Tris looked up. Three men covered in road dust and dark leather jackets loomed over them. The nearest one looked closer to forty, with a thick, black moustache.

He stared at Tris' crotch. "C'mon, bitches. You're always workin'. Give ya five apiece. There's three of us so's that's fifteen."

The man on the left, who looked even more inebriated, raised two fingers. "Five's with anal."

"No, it isn't," said Zara. "We're not 'for hire.'"

Shit. Her fatigue melted. "Go away."

"Bodies like that?" asked number three, a dark-tanned blond with about a month of facial hair. "You can't keep that shit all to yourselves. You two are like the hottest pussy I've ever seen. Hell with it, I'll give ya fifteen coins mah dam self for both y'all at once."

"We're not prostitutes," said Tris. "Look. Just go away, I'll buy you all a shot apiece."

"I'll give them shots." Zara narrowed her eyes.

Tris grumbled. "We need ammo for Infected. Don't waste it on these shitheads."

"You ladies is pretty funny," said the middle idiot. "Don'tcha just love it when a girl talks all sorts'a tough like she gonna do somethin'?" The other two chuckled. "Look…" He belched in her face. "We're gonna"—he attempted to point a finger between her eyes but couldn't quite hold it steady—"gonna… fuck yas. Now's your choice if'n you get paid or we take it on the house."

Tris glanced down at his belt, a pair of handguns on his hips. "You are drunk. Go away or I'm going to kill all three of you."

The center man reached both hands forward, going for her shirt.

Tris' neuralware dragged the man's lunge into a slow creep. She drove her right foot into his crotch hard enough to lift his boots from the floor. Before the look of pain registered on his face, she swiped his sidearms from their belt holsters, raising them upside down with her pinky fingers on the triggers.

She got three shots off from each at the two men standing behind him before the enraged man dug his fingers into her shirt and hauled her off the ground. The other two careened over backwards. The one grabbing her roared, a demonic, distorted sound emanating from slow-motion flapping jowls. Sweat and saliva flew from his lower lip as he pivoted and hefted her around to ram her headfirst into the bar.

Tris started to scream at the countertop rushing toward her face, but gurgled when her trajectory lurched upward before contact; his grip released, flinging her into the air away from the counter. She sailed over him, getting a perfect top-down view of Zara's leg completing a sweep takedown. Tris let the guns fall from her grip and braced her hands outward, catching the floor and guiding her body into a somersault.

Fatigue caught up to her; rather than land on her feet, she rolled sideways, her left shoulder slamming into one of the posts. A football helmet fell from a nail and cracked her on the head. The two she'd shot writhed and moaned on the floor. Tris sat up, rubbing where the helmet landed and cringing with one eye closed.

Ow. Son of a bitch.

Zara recovered from the foot sweep and spun into an arm-lock takedown that drilled the man's skull into the front of the counter hard enough to crack the wood and leave him unconscious. The blond man, bleeding from two wounds in his right leg, yanked a handgun from his belt. Tris grabbed for her Beretta, aiming in the slow motion world of combat boosters. Before she could fire, Zara's foot made contact with his hand, launching the gun up into the air.

Tris decided to save ammo.

Her friend spun around and brought the same heel down across his temple, bouncing his head off the floor and leaving him unconscious as well. The third man moaned, making no effort to get up.

"He's done," said Zara. "You got him in the femoral."

Mac raced out the bead curtain, a submachine gun in each hand. "What's goin' on?"

Tris struggled upright, head still spinning. "They thought we were for hire. We said no, so they tried to take it."

Mac spat to the side. "Surprised ya leave two alive."

"We're saving ammo for Infected." Zara winked.

Tris picked up the two handguns she'd pinky-fired and dropped them on the counter. Matching Sig 226s in chrome.

"Keep 'em. You didn't kill the guy." Mac winked.

"Huh. You're right. I guess technically, the Code doesn't kick in unless someone dies." Tris slid one to Zara.

Zara pulled the mag to check. "Nice. Twenty round mag."

Tris rummaged another pair of magazines from the guy who'd kissed the counter.

The third man, hand pressed into his upper thigh, hissed and wheezed. "C'mon... ya can't let me die. I'm... bleedin'."

Tris started to look at him, but Zara pulled her away. The wheezing stopped a few seconds later.

"Nothing you could do," whispered Zara.

Denise appeared in the bead curtain with two plated chicken sandwiches. Mac rushed at her, guiding her back into the rear hallway. A brief argument ended with Mac emerging with the food.

198 | THE REDEEMED

"Stay back there for now. There's a mess out here I don't want you seein'."

"I'm fourteen, not four." Denise barged into the room.

Zara shrugged. "It's really not that bad. Just blood. Not like someone's head exploded. Ever see what a star-frangible caseless .50 cal sniper rifle does to a skull?"

Mac stared at her.

"I'll take that as a no." Zara blew a kiss at him and took one sandwich. "It's kind of like dynamiting a watermelon. Oh, that guy is going to be hurting when he wakes up." She punted the one at the base of the counter. "I think she cracked his pelvis."

"Sorry for the mess, Mac." Tris sighed and stuffed the new sig into her left pants pocket.

"Well, damn. You two might just be able to survive the Infected after all. I never seen no one move that damn fast." He shook his head at the three men. "Be damn careful."

"Yeah. As careful as we can." Tris shook his hand. "There's no cavalry, Mac. Amarillo's gone until we rebuild it. Secrets don't last forever. Eventually, everyone will find out what happened. I know I'm about to walk into a meat grinder. Here, you think everything's under control… until it isn't. Be careful Mac."

Worry rattled in his eyes, but he offered only a grim nod as a reply.

Tris plodded outside, wedged the sandwich in her mouth, and unplugged the charging line. She had to hold the spring-loaded license plate down to let the wire spool in, all the while drooling around the spiced chicken in her teeth. Zara climbed in the driver's seat and Tris went straight to the back where a dingy, musty, lumpy, lovely mattress waited.

"We should be there in about four hours give or take," said Zara.

Tris, flat on her back, chomped as big a bite as her mouth allowed. "Mmm. Kmm."

"I'll yell if anything happens."

Swallow. "Okay."

Tris inhaled the chicken burger and curled up on her side, jostling about as the van returned to the highway. The vibration of the road latched on to her already exhausted body, fighting down her lingering adrenaline. A dull throb developed in her foot where she'd kicked the one guy.

Kevin… whatever you're doing out there, don't take any stupid risks.

21

ROADHOUSE DOWN

Kevin stood still as a tree, eyeing the fourteen uniformed men standing in a line across the sunbaked road. Nothing quite made a man feel as dumb as winding up staring down the barrels of a bunch of automatic rifles he could've avoided simply by not racing off with his balls lit on fire by a stupid and reckless quest for revenge. He locked eyes with the man in the maroon beret.

"Sorry." Kevin spat to the side. "Guess we made a wrong turn at Albuquerque."

Three of the men snickered.

"How you wanna play this, man?" whispered Fitch.

"Any way that doesn't wind up with a bullet in my ass." *What the hell.* He walked toward the apparent leader in as nonaggressive a stride as he could muster. "Something wrong? My uhh, plate expired or something?"

"I am Lieutenant Fernando Garcia Florentine Diaz of the *Ejército Mexicano.*"

Kevin winced. "I'm sorry."

Lieutenant Diaz narrowed his eyes. "The National Defense Army of Mexico."

"No... I understood you." Kevin gestured at the man's chest. "I was expressing my sympathy about that name."

Four of the men stifled laughter.

"I do not find your jokes humorous."

Kevin smiled. "Guess it's a good thing I'm not a professional comedian then."

"We are going to search your vehicles for materiel support you are providing to your allies, enemies of Mexico." Lieutenant Diaz waved at the formation of soldiers and pointed at the Challenger.

"Ugh." Kevin pinched the bridge of his nose. "Look, *Lieutenant,* I'm not working a run right now. I ain't carryin' nothin' but my own supplies. And I'm not *with* the News."

"This car has been spotted frequenting Hagerman. That's one of their installations." Diaz raised his nose with a hint of imperiousness.

Kevin chuckled, a reaction Diaz appeared rather un-fond of. "You've got a bit of a high opinion of them if you call that an 'installation.' A bunch of morons hanging out in an old grocery store ain't an 'installation.'"

Diaz pursed his lips, glancing down for a few seconds. "If you are not running guns for the traitors, what are you doing this far south? You expect me to believe you're sightseeing?" He gestured at Fitch's truck. "That you've got a truck that big with nothing in it."

"*Esta vacio,*" said a soldier by the Behemoth's bed.

Diaz closed his eyes with an exasperated leak of air from his nostrils, arm still out indicating the vehicle.

"Yeah, basically." Kevin grinned.

The Lieutenant put his hands on his hips. "What exactly are you doing in our territory?"

"I'm tryin' to track down a couple of Redeemed who put a bunch of bullets in a friend of mine. Another Roadhouse operator."

Five of the soldiers blinked and murmured amongst themselves.

Diaz leaned forward, head tilted to the right. "Redeemed?"

"Yeah. Was nine of them. Four died; three got out un-shot." Kevin shifted his weight onto his left leg and waved at the surrounding buildings. "We heard Redeemed holed up around Las Cruces, so here I am. Ain't complicated. Someone pissed on the Roadhouse, and I'm lookin' for payback."

"*Descansen,*" said Diaz over his shoulder. The soldiers relaxed and switched to holding their weapons sideways. "You're a little late, my friend. Redeemed ain't around here anymore. We chased 'em off a couple weeks ago. Last I hear, they've gone all the way to Silver City."

Kevin closed his eyes, picturing the map. *Two hours or so west, up in the hills.* "Guess I'm goin' to Silver City."

Diaz held up a hand as Kevin tried to walk past him. "Just a moment, friend. Where do your loyalties lie?"

"With Amarillo; with my damn roadhouse." He eased his left arm up, touched the back of his hand to Diaz's wrist, and pushed the man's hand out of his way. "I think you're both tools."

"Excuse me?" asked Diaz, pivoting to keep facing Kevin as he walked past. "Tools?"

Kevin stopped. "Yeah. News and the Olds. Fighting over a border that doesn't mean a damned thing. In case you hadn't noticed, there's no U.S. and no Mexico anymore. Hasn't been for like fifty years."

Diaz raised both hands, palms up, fingers splayed. "This land once belonged to Mexico, but was stolen by the United States of—"

"Doesn't exist anymore." Kevin shook his head. "You wanna know what side I'm on? I'm on the side of not being an idiot. Killin' each other over where some arbitrary squiggly line on a map goes is stupid. People ought'a be worried about rebuilding than where dead countries start and stop."

"We *are* rebuilding." Diaz swept his arm down like a whip. "We *are* the establishment. You may be correct in that our respective countries have ceased to be… but we will make Mexico great again."

Kevin forced a smile. *This guy's been out in the sun too long.* "Hear you and the Redeemed aren't eye to eye." *Maybe I can talk them into helping us out.*

Diaz grumbled. "No. They are enemies of Mexico."

He eyed the soldiers. A few peered into the windows of his car and shook their heads at Diaz in a way that said 'nothing here.' *Shit. Do I really want to start a legitimate war here? I roll in there with these guys, and bullets will fly.* "Guess you've got no problem then with us going there to have a 'chat' with three of them." Kevin patted his .45.

"*Muy bien…*" He waved down the road. "*Sal de aqui.*"

Kevin held his breath until he pulled the Challenger's door open and slipped in to the seat. He exhaled hard out his nose and sat motionless, watching the Olds mount up in their trucks and drive past, heading east.

The Behemoth rumbled up alongside. Neeley shoved the black-painted armored roof flap open and leaned out. Kevin poked a button; his window sank into the door with a faint electric whirr.

"Oi, now what?" asked Neeley.

Kevin blanked his mind and waited to see what urge hit him first. His system unwound from the tension of the confrontation. Two hours or so away could be the three men who killed Wayne. Maybe—just maybe—they could get in acting casual, find the guys Neeley recognized, and get out before they got caught up in a shitstorm.

"Let's check out Silver City." He punched the six blue rocker switches over the dashboard with his thumb one at a time. "This ain't worth weeks of chasing our tails. If it looks like we're gettin' nowhere, I won't ask you two to keep on."

Neeley hung his head and patted the outside of the door like a war drum. "We gotta get them fuckers for Wayne."

Kevin clung to his righteous anger. "Yeah."

"Right on," said Fitch.

"Whoo hoo!" cheered Neeley. He ducked back inside, slammed the hatch, and a few seconds later, popped up again with his Dragunov rifle.

"Well. I suppose if I'm going to do something stupid, I better commit." Kevin rolled up the window. "Half-assing idiocy is asking to die."

He leaned on the accelerator, pinning himself into the seat for a few seconds until he leveled off at seventy to let the truck catch up. *Hmm. Battery's at forty-four percent. This is gonna get shitty if there's no charging station there.*

⁓ ⁓ ⁓

ROUTE 180 NORTH OFFERED A WHOLE LOT OF NOTHING FOR THE LAST FIFTY some odd minutes of the trip to Silver City. Brown dirt spotted with green scrolled by with nary a trace that humans had ever existed, save for the road itself. His tires double-*thumped* over a railroad track at the end of a long, sweeping curve.

Silver City lay up ahead at the end of a short western spur according to his map. Three minutes along that route, he spotted a Roadhouse sign hovering over a building made of part white-walled trailer, part semi-truck, and part scrap. It sat at the center of a dirt lot off to the right. A more distant yellow building to the right had the name 'Vern's' in green letters on a small white sign. It might've been some manner of auto shop before the war, with three garage bays, but something had hit it pretty hard. Not even rats would try to shelter in it now.

Kevin tapped his brakes to flash taillights, and slowed while pulling a turn into the lot. He took the leftmost of four parking spaces with charge ports, and sighed at the meter showing twelve percent. *Guess I shouldn't be so annoyed at havin' to go slow.*

Fitch parked to his left.

Relief at finding a Roadhouse withered to unease at the sight of handprint in blood on a storm door. A crude porch shrouded it, made from a pair of pallets serving as walls with a car hood roof. More than a few bullet holes dotted the corrugated metal, wood, and white aluminum siding.

"Shit." *Of course. A 'house this close to these assholes...* He got out of the car with the .45 in his hand.

Neeley raised a micro-uzi as soon as he noticed Kevin aiming at the door. Fitch leaned back into the Behemoth and returned with a pump shotgun.

"What you seein'?" asked Fitch

Kevin studied the building. "A whole lot of pain."

He aimed the .45 ahead and walked to the entrance. Foulness like rotting meat permeated the air, threatening to get worse inside. One boot nudged the door open the rest of the way, and he followed his gun around a quick left. Another ninety-degree turn, this one to the right, led into the larger share of the interior.

The room had an L shape, with the short spur on the left side of the counter filled with booth seats. To the right, the longer section of the room lay scattered with freestanding tables all tossed about on their sides, chairs shot up or trampled. A handful of mirror slivers still clung to a large wooden frame behind the counter, where the control panel for the car chargers emitted a steady buzz. On the face of the counter, a hand-painted wooden sign committed first-degree murder on the art of communication:

Bat Reez Charged: 2 koins

Hamm Booger: 2 koins

Big Rabid Stake: 3 koins

Om Lit: 1 koin (if has)

Warm Sudz: 3 koins

Cold Sudz: 8 koins

Ag Wah: 2 koins

Room: 3 koins / day

Tilla Chipz: Hep Yo Sef

A huge basket at the middle of the counter still held a few tortilla chips, though they looked somewhere between petrified and fossilized. That even bugs had left them be alarmed him almost more than the dread of what happened here.

Fitch tilted his head as if looking at the thing sideways might make it clearer. "Big rabid—"

"Dust hopper." Kevin aimed to the right at the other empty end of the room. "Big rabbit."

Blood had splattered over the rear wall by a pair of green plastic swinging doors labeled 'piss room.' A head-sized chunk of flesh and a length of guts lay on the floor a short distance in front of said doors, covered in flies.

"Anyone here?" asked Kevin in a normal speaking volume.

"Don't look like." Neeley headed for the counter, and the charge controls. "Panel took a bullet. Sparkin'."

"Damn." Kevin lowered his arm and hurried over.

A hole big enough to stick a finger in pierced the steel between the switches for bays three and four, exposing wires and a flickering electric blue glow deep inside the cabinet. Kevin went wide-eyed at it, and ran to the center of the room, spun in a circle looking for a 'back hallway,' and, finding none, dashed outside.

The Behemoth's hood proved to be enough of a boost to climb onto the roof. Sheet metal clattered as he dragged himself up among the solar panels. Fortunately, the hardware was almost identical to what he had, though with smaller solar panels that looked different in a subtle way he couldn't quite place. Something about the shape or the edges... He shook the useless question out of his brain, headed for the master cutoff, and threw the breaker.

Whatever caused this whole place not to go up in flames, thanks. He eyed the clouds and the early evening sky for a few seconds before climbing back down. Neeley jogged out the door.

"I'm gonna check the rooms. Looks like this place used sep-rit trailers." The skinny man held up a fistful of keys. "Nothing inside, alive or dead... 'cept that mess on the floor."

Kevin grunted, waited for Neeley to move out of the way, and went back inside. Thumping emanated from behind the wall by the counter; the sound made him imagine Fitch kicking something over and over. The panel no longer buzzed, which he took as a good omen. He stared at it, pondering how to open it with his bare hands. "I'm an idiot."

After running back to the Challenger to get his tool satchel from the trunk, he returned to the panel and managed to get the faceplate off with some creative hammering. The bullet had smashed the switch component for bay three, exposing wires to the metal housing as well as each other.

The plastic bits of the switch had melted away from the copper elements inside, but one, two, and four appeared functional aside from severed wires.

"God dammit," yelled Fitch from a back room, between gagging heaves. "Son of a…" He coughed.

Kevin took wire snips and got to work, tearing out the bay three switch and patching other wires to clear the short. Rewiring two of the bays looked relatively simple… he copied the pattern of the untouched switch in port one.

A large flap of corrugated steel swung away from the wall in the approximate shape of a door. Fitch emerged from the hidden passage, his face a deep shade of dark chocolate and eyes watering. Kevin leaned back, holding two wires he'd been in the midst of twining together.

"Do I wanna know?"

Fitch waved him off, still trying to catch his breath. He lurched forward, hands on his knees, and choked out a few more coughs with a line of saliva dangling from his lip. Kevin cringed away, having no desire to watch that.

"God damn." Fitch sputtered, stood straight, and blew snot out of one nostril. "Don't go in there."

"How many dead?" Kevin threaded copper wire around a contact at the top left corner of switch four, and tightened it with a flathead driver.

"Fridge." Fitch's next cough mutated into a laugh. "Greenbeard's living in the damn fridge. Reckon' at least a month since anyone opened that thing. Somethin' went down in the kitchen too. Fridge was shot to hell and back, along with everything else in there."

About ten minutes later, Kevin studied his wiring job. He couldn't find anything *obviously* wrong with it, but he also didn't trust finding out by flipping the switch. Fire sucked. "Hey, Fitch. This look right to you?"

The older man ambled over and peered into the panel. "Looks fine to me."

Kevin smiled. "You don't have a damn clue what you're looking at, do you?"

"Not a one." Fitch doffed his baseball cap. "Well, save it's wires and 'lectric type stuff."

Neeley wandered in the front. "Trailers were empty save one. Dude looks like he shot himself." He mimed a gun under the chin with his finger. "Now what the shit would make a man do that?"

Kevin froze. "Did you get any blood on you?"

"Don't think so, why?" Neeley cocked an eyebrow. Two seconds later, he jumped in place amid a heebie-jeebie dance, swatting at his arms and chest. "Aw, fuck. No... I'm good." Seemingly satisfied he hadn't touched blood, he slouched, panting.

"What you sayin'?" asked Fitch. "Infected?"

"Can you think of another reason someone'd do that?" Kevin re-seated the panel cover and pounded it into place with the heel of his hand.

"Can think of a few dozen." Fitch folded his arms. "Don't mean anything."

"Okay, look at this place." Kevin pointed at the lump of gore. "You think the Redeemed stopped by for a casual disembowelment?"

"We got maybe an hour or so left of daylight." Fitch grumbled.

Kevin held his breath and went for the hidden door. Fitch gagged, apparently at the mere thought of someone going in there. The kitchen continued to the right, within the confines of a pair of old trailers grafted together. Straight ahead from the secret door, the 'office' occupied a shack built around a gap in the walls where the kitchen trailers had been placed close to the one that made up the short spar of the L-shaped restaurant. The fetid reek of rotting meat and vegetables teased at his nostrils despite him not breathing. *Ugh, damn. Smells like a bucket of shit lit on fire. Gotta be potatoes gone south.*

He expected the security system to be dead, so he didn't bother checking it. The box he *was* interested in, however, made his day. The solar panel array battery still showed a 72% charge. Despite it being smaller than the unit Amarillo sold him, that much in the main reserve would easily fill two cars. Solar panels be-damned; that it would soon be dark wouldn't keep them here.

Kevin rushed a breath, using his shirt as a breathing mask. Eyes watering from the stink of month-rotten dust hopper and some manner of fish, he ran out to the front and kicked the metal flap door shut.

"Dammit man, what the hell'd you go in there for?" Fitch waved a hand about his face.

"Main battery's got enough to charge us up. I'm gonna go flip the switch on the roof." Kevin jogged to the door.

"I'll git the cars," said Neeley. "Where's your port?"

"Wait." Kevin caught himself on the doorjamb. "If this thing explodes, better we're not plugged in when it goes."

Fitch's eyes bulged a touch. He nodded. "Good idea."

Kevin hopped up on the Behemoth's front end, stood, grabbed the roof, and hauled himself up once again. He walked down the row of solar panels, squinting from the intense orange of a sinking sun, and crouched by the master circuit breaker. "Well. Here goes everything."

Click.

"Three... two... one..." He waited, but nothing went bang.

Feeling a bit of elation, Kevin trotted to the edge of the roof, jumped to the Behemoth, and then to the dirt. Since he was already out there, he decided to connect both vehicles. Fitch's truck had its cord spindle in the front bumper, behind an inch-thick armor plate with an opening barely wide enough to get two fingers in to grab the plug. He eyed a huge pipe in the middle of the grille far too large to be a .50 cal. *Damn thing's bigger than my thumb... forward mounted flamethrower? Why? Wait, no pilot flame. What in the name of shit is that? Screw it.*

The Behemoth went into port four and the Challenger got port one.

He hurried inside, jumped over the counter, and hovered two fingers over the control box switches. "Come on, baby. Work." *Poke.*

Two lights went from amber to green.

"That good?" asked Fitch.

"Yah," said Neeley.

Kevin remembered how to breathe. "Yeah. I'm pretty low. Was at like twelve percent. You?"

"Twenty six," said Fitch.

"Damn." Kevin blinked.

"Got three batteries in parallel." He winked. "Lot of armor on that monster."

"No wonder it's slower than shit." Kevin winked.

Fitch gawked. "Who you callin' slow? Eighty ain't no bad thing. How fast that bucket of bolts you got do? Maybe ninety?"

Kevin smiled. "Ancient Chinese secret."

"Horseshit," said Neeley.

"Tris tinkered with the electronics. Fixed something I didn't even know could be a problem. I've had it up to 190." He righted a chair with his boot, eyed it for blood, and sat.

"Now you gone beyond the realm of simple horseshit." Neeley wagged a finger at him. "You're into like... uhh... rainbow horseshit or something."

"Fifty coins says I'm right." Kevin glanced at him.

Neeley drew a breath, arm cocked back as if to thrust into a handshake, and hesitated. "Uhh."

"Somethin' tha matter, Neels?" Fitch grinned.

"Well... you know. That girl. She's like... Spooky." Neeley squirmed. "Enclave, right? Who knows what kinda weird tech shit they got. Maybe... maybe it's possible she got that thing goin' that flamey."

Fitch chuckled.

"MREs?" asked Neeley.

Fitch's face turned ashen for an instant. "Ugh. I can't even *think* about eating."

"We're about four miles from Silver City." Kevin righted a table and arranged three chairs. "Might as well catch some shuteye, but bet they saw us come in. Someone'll need to stay up. Two hour shifts?"

"I'll get 'em." Neeley headed for the door. "Sounds fine."

Fitch nodded.

Neeley returned with three MRE pouches. Fitch got his appetite back after less than a minute watching the other two eat. Kevin took first watch. He perched in a red-cushioned chair with a black steel frame, leaning back against the wall behind the counter. The front door stood about twenty feet away, what he assumed to be the bathroom doors about forty-five feet to his left. Fitch and Neeley had crawled into a booth table at the end of the short spur of the L, to sleep on the cushioned benches.

He wound the spring of an old wristwatch he'd scavved from a corpse in a fancy car years ago. Well, at least the car had been fancy prior to exposure to fallout ash. Wayne had told him how such a watch might've been worth quite a bit of money before everything went to hell. Kevin held the strapless thing balanced between two thumbs and two fingers, tilting it side to side so the word ROLEX glinted.

He had no idea if it showed anywhere near the correct time, or if it ever had. Little needles spinning around pointing at identical blocks arranged in a circle mystified him. He knew the blocks meant hours according to the shorter needle, and the larger needle measured minutes. The fast-mover ticked once per second. He only bothered to wind it at times like these, where he had to *measure* time rather than tell it. Someone far off in another world before nuclear war would probably have cried at the scratches on the clear face. Soon, he listened to the soft *tick, tick, tick,* of seconds passing. When the small needle moved two blocks, he'd wake Fitch up.

The walls creaked in the wind and the chair groaned in time with his breath. Such perfect silence hung heavy in the shot-to-shit roadhouse that the rush of blood moving around inside his head played background noise.

Soon after the small hand edged up on passing the first block, a *skiff* on the dirt outside stalled the breath in his throat. Kevin pulled the .45 from his belt and eased his chair back down onto all four legs, aiming at the door. Another footstep outside sounded louder, closer than the last.

The door rattled as though a dog worried at it.

Kevin swallowed saliva; a trickle of sweat ran down the side of his head. *Please be human. They've gotta see the cars.*

A dull, metallic *clonk* conjured the mental image of someone walking into the side of the Challenger. Someone who lacked the reason to comprehend a person couldn't walk through solid objects.

Fuck.

"Fitch," whispered Kevin.

Dirt crunched at the door, though he couldn't tell if the source moved away or nearer.

"Fitch!" rasped Kevin. "Wake up."

Fitch mumbled low in his sleep.

Shit.

Fitch let off a boisterous fart, followed by more contented mumbling.

Two rapid footsteps at the door accompanied an eager-sounding moan.

Kevin put both hands on the .45 and tried to keep it from shaking too much.

A thin wild-eyed man in a blue tee and red pajama pants raced in. The instant he drooled at Kevin, he took a bullet in the forehead. Blood and brain spattered over the faces of two more men who shoved the skinny one's flailing corpse aside. One had most of his left cheek bitten off, the other had a bright yellow crossbow quarrel sticking out of his left thigh. Both dashed forward as soon as they made eye contact.

Kevin rushed his shots in the face of their charge; his first bullet winged the quarrel-pierced Infected in the right collarbone. The second shot caught him in the throat and put him down. The cheekless one made it close enough to grab the counter before a point-blank .45 to the nose ended him.

"Fitch! Neels!" screamed Kevin, as he leapt back from the body draped over the counter.

A great clattering smash came from the bathroom at the same time a longhaired man with caramel skin and a red leather jacket shuffled in the front door. Kevin aimed, but a huge *boom* came from his right before he could fire, and the Infected's head exploded. The body took one more step and teetered over forward.

The man's jacket bore a Roadhouse logo across the back.

Neeley zoomed up to the side of the counter, shaking hands pointing his micro-uzi at the door. Kevin whirled to cover the bathroom not a second before a short Hispanic woman in a skin-tight black shirt and lacy thigh-length skirt stepped out. If not for her rather large breasts and curvy hips, she'd have passed for a frightened teenager by height and face. She stopped a step from the door, head tilted, mouth hanging open.

Kevin stared over his iron sights at her mournful eyes. "You one of them?"

"Shoot the bitch," yelled Neeley, a half-second before the micro-uzi burped a rain of bullets into at least five bodies piled into the shrouded archway at the front door.

Growling and gurgling came from outside, and something *thumped* across the roof in the direction of the back.

Fitch shouldered up to a support post a little farther to the right. "He's right. She's too calm." He fired into the crowd, pumped the shotgun, and fired again.

"Are you infected?" yelled Kevin.

"I..." The girl limped another step closer; her right arm stiff at her side. "I... don't wanna..." She whined in a pleading tone. "What's wrong with me? Why is everyone crazy?" Her body trembled in place like one of Bee's fits. "Why am I so hungry?"

Neeley and Fitch firing and shouting dragged into a nonspace within his mind, muted blurry sounds that had no meaning.

"It hurts... Wanna." The innocent young woman's face warped with sudden rage. "I wanna... kill!" She flung her arm up, raising a handgun. Her expression fell to pleading once more and she didn't fire. The deep brown of her eyes faded to grey; tears ran down her cheeks. She twitched as if she'd walked into a cobweb. When next she looked at him, her face had no emotion. The young woman convulsed, coughing, and a trickle of dark blood dribbled out of the corner of her mouth.

Kevin's dumbfounded brain lock lasted until her weapon went off twice. Instinct squeezed his trigger. Her small body jerked as his slug hit her in the heart. She glanced down at herself for an instant, gave him an 'I can't believe you shot me' look, and crumpled into a heap.

"Aaah, fuck!" screamed Neeley. "I'm hit."

At his next breath, Kevin cringed. Pain rippled across his chest from his left breast. He grunted, trying to cradle the spot with his left arm while keeping the .45 aimed at the bathroom. A man with a strong resemblance to the young woman, perhaps eighteen, stared at him with baleful, jaundiced eyes.

Kevin shot him twice. The first hit somewhere in the chest, invisible against a black shirt. The second tore open his cheek, spinning his head and spraying blood from his face and gore from his fragmenting skull around in a spiral. He crumpled dead on top of his sister. The slide locked back, magazine empty.

An old man dragged himself in from the bathroom. Several shards of broken glass stuck out from his face and both of his legs stopped existing at the knee. He locked on Kevin and emitted a keening, wailing, shriek, hauling himself over the floor in a series of rapid pulls, neither of his legs moving. Kevin swapped magazines, fumbling to reload as the grunting horror shimmied at him with alarming speed. He got the magazine in, racked it, and put one shot into the top of the old man's head inches away from being bitten.

The *boom* of a shotgun going off again snapped Kevin out of his mental fog. Screaming obscenities in Fitch's voice overpowered Neeley whining out his nose and hissing similar words. More moaning surrounded them outside the wall, suggesting Infected circled the building in search of a way in. Kevin hoped—no in that moment, he *prayed* they weren't smart enough to think the front door dangerous. He asked any deity that might exist to let them be too stupid to find another entrance other than the front door, and not smart enough to understand a killing chokepoint.

"Shit." Kevin looked down at himself. A medium-sized bullet had mushroomed into his armored jacket about where a shirt pocket would be. *I love this thing.* "Neels, you okay?"

"I... Bleeding." Neeley side-walked over behind the counter, holding his left bicep up with a severe shrug to show off where he'd taken a glancing shot across the upper arm—a lot of blood, but a shallow wound.

"Graze." Kevin put the .45 on the counter and grabbed for a towel on a shelf behind him. "Cover the door."

Neeley one-armed the micro-uzi at the front entrance while Kevin improvised a bandage. Kevin jumped when the little machinegun went off, and cringed at another shotgun blast.

Three shambling men in hand-stitched leather armor collapsed on top of the pile. Two had biker cuts with Redeemed symbols on their backs.

After cinching the towel snug, Kevin pointed his gun at the bathroom. He really didn't like looking at the dead woman; she reminded him a bit of Fix... Stacy, or whatever her name was. They had long black hair and innocent faces in common, plus likely Mexican heritage. The dead woman had actual curves though, quite far from flat-chested. She probably had about five years on Stacy. Yeah, that had to be it. *Some women look young.* He preferred to convince himself he hadn't shot a teenager, whether or not it was true.

For a long while, all three men stood with guns pointed, listening to total silence.

"Damn." Kevin bowed his head.

Fitch clapped him on the shoulder. "Damn shame. Cute. Probably had no idea what happened to her. Shit, I'm surprised Neeley isn't tryin' ta get her naked."

Neeley gagged. "Aww c'mon, man. I have *some* standards... like being alive."

Fitch raised an eyebrow. "That's debatable."

"You wound me, sir." Neeley put a hand over his chest.

"Glimmertown, seven months back." Fitch gestured at him.

"Hey." Neeley pointed at him, wincing from the pain in his arm. "Tia was alive. Stoned as hell, but alive. And *not* infected."

Fitch turned aside, muttering, "Least not by the Virus," into his hand.

Kevin flicked the mushroomed bullet off his jacket. "That girl hadn't been turned long. Still had enough upstairs to use a gun." *She was fighting to stay sane. That... look in her eyes.* A wave of anger rose at the people who did this, crashing upon the shores of his impotence at being able to help her. *Is that why Tris is so...* He sighed and crept around the counter, stopping six feet away from the man in the bright red Roadhouse jacket. "Fifty coins says this guy's the one who brought it here."

"How you figure that?" Fitch stood at his right.

Neeley appeared at his left, twitching his nose like a rat.

"Site inspector. Saw it before in Hastings. *Dammit.* Amarillo was fuckin' compromised then too. I assumed he'd gotten ambushed somewhere out on the road, but now..." *Recruits on the training range my ass... that gunfire. The old bastard fucking lied.* He thought about the family with the giant semi, and again prayed—that they took his advice and didn't go to Amarillo.

"Whoa." Neeley looked around. "So, umm... Don't get any blood on us, right?"

"Not unless you wanna die." Kevin checked his mag, finding five rounds left. *One in the chamber.* He safed and holstered it before retrieving his empty mag from the floor.

"Question." Neeley shifted to face him, his back to the bodies. "How you fixin' on we gettin' outta here? There's a pile of death in the exit."

Fitch snorted, shivered, and leaned back with a deep, echoing laugh.

22

AMARILLO

S ubtle pieces of familiar surroundings awakened a brief memory of the last time Tris had been on this road leading into Amarillo. Or, at least, what passed for Amarillo after the war. Kevin had once joked that Texans must have scared the shit out of the Chinese, the Russians, the Koreans, or whoever it was that had lit the world on fire. Almost every major pre-war city in the area took direct hits. Some, like Houston, had been pulverized into sand lots with only a few scraps of anything suggesting a city had ever existed on the spot.

Maybe it's because everything the government did seemed to be controlled there. The historical documentaries sure made the place sound important. *Houston, we have a problem.*

Tris slowed the van to a creep, staring ahead at the dark shapes of distant battlements. At some point over the last fifty years, the people who'd survived or resettled Amarillo had constructed a new city in a scrap metal nod to pre-industrial forts. It even had two honest-to-goodness cannons, though she suspected they were more for show, given the horrible odds of anyone hitting a moving car with such a weapon.

Curls of concertina wire surrounded the top of a fourteen-foot wall, run in three bands above the gate. In direct opposition to the foreboding edifice, painted red-and-white letters declared, "Welcome to Amarillo!" next to a yellow smiley face wearing a cowboy hat.

Distant armored figures stood watch on the rooftops of four and five story pre-war buildings that hadn't disintegrated. Three or four soldiers paced back and forth on patrol per structure. Most of the buildings had survived only as skeletons of I beams holding up pancakes of concrete floor. A few had patches of original wall left, though a collage of mismatched wood, drywall, metal slabs, and even kitchen countertops filled in the gaps.

Tris stared at the distant armored figures. *They don't look like they're in the middle of a war with Infected. Guess they think they're safe way up there.*

Below the greeting, an enormous double door reminiscent of an old castle keep hung ajar. The gap would let a person in with ease, but not the van. Distant rattles, *snaps* and *twangs* like stray threads of razor wire slapping metal in the wind, and a repetitive stone-on-wood *clonk* filled the air. Of the perhaps thirty figures milling about in the distance, not one reacted to their approach.

"Gonna park here?" asked Zara.

Tris grumbled. "I don't like leaving it out in the open, or at the gate... too far to walk if we find someone alive. I also don't want to drive in too far in case we get cut off." She tapped her fingers on the wheel. A twinge of nausea tickled the bottom of her stomach. "Got an idea."

"Must not be a good one if you're making that face." Zara grinned.

She chuckled. "There's a mechanic place a little bit inside the gate. Fat bastard that owns it offered us a free charge if I had sex with him."

"Ugh." Zara rolled her eyes. "Probably the only way he got any."

"Well, he didn't get any." Tris laughed. "Kevin almost shot him for asking. I think if we were anywhere else but Amarillo, he would have."

"Why?"

Tris rolled up to within a few feet of the gate, stopped, and opened the door. "Spend most of your life idolizing something, then you're there... he didn't wanna mess anything up." She hopped out and hurried toward the city's entrance.

Zara jumped down, her boots hitting the road as Tris passed the front bumper. She jogged over to help pull. With both of them hauling on it, the gargantuan slab of corrugated metal, armor plates, and wood moved. Inside, the street lay strewn with bodies, most riddled with bullet wounds, a handful had arrows sticking out of them, and two or three appeared to have been victimized by swords. Somewhere between twenty and thirty men and women in various amounts of armor lay dead on the blacktop and sidewalks. One guy even had a steel colander on his head as an attempt at defense.

"Whoa." Zara covered her mouth to suppress a chuckle. "I shouldn't laugh at this, but what was that idiot thinking?"

"I don't like this at all." Tris squinted. "Someone took all their weapons, even the swords. Infected aren't that smart."

"Survivors?" Zara shrugged. "Look there." She pointed to a storefront where huge blue spray-painted letters spelled 'Gunz' over a blacked out window. "The bodies crumpled over that barricade look like Infected."

Three human figures hung tangled in a defensive wall of sawhorses and razor wire set up in front of the store; the corpses had the unmistakable vacant stare of Infected, as well as some early signs of skin degeneration.

"Come on," whispered Tris.

She jogged back to the van, waited for Zara to climb into the seat, and drove in. Eerie silence surrounded them as they passed building after building. Some had been made of house trailers stacked three high, with improvised patio porches at each level. Lines, rope as well as wire, crisscrossed the street, hung with bedsheets and other laundry. She couldn't help herself and scanned for salvageable underpants, but shied away from the thought before spotting any. Most of the garments looked filthy. *If that's what stuff looks like* after *washing it... ugh.* Still, with her jeans and dust hopper leather shirt, she didn't have to worry about putting on a show.

Strangely enough, none of the soldiers on the rooftops yelled down at them.

About sixty yards from the gate, she pulled left into the lot in front of 'Otto's Plug and Play.' Three garage-style doors occupied three-quarters of a brick-shaped building. The portion to the right of the doors looked more like an old 1950s era diner, complete with chrome walls and yellow and green neon lights. Nude-lady silhouettes decorated the windows in crude hand-painted renderings.

"It's genius." Zara gestured at the windshield. "Get your charge on while you get your fluids drained. Why haven't I ever seen a place like this before?"

Tris nosed the van into the only open bay, the one in the middle. Fortunately, no bodies lay in her path. "Because it's a bad idea. This asshole belongs in Glimmertown with the rest of the sick bastards."

The van bounced over a hydraulic lift in the middle of the space before she stopped with maybe four inches between the bumper and a large toolbox on wheels. Tris shut down the drive system and slid out of the driver's seat to the ground. She pulled her AK-47 out from behind the seat and slung it over her left shoulder on a strap. Her katana followed, going over her right shoulder. She eased the door closed before pushing it to click, taking care to be quiet.

"Maybe we'll get lucky and there'll be some juice in the batteries still."

Zara emerged from the van a moment later, having donned her Enclave armor, sans helmet. When Tris gave her the eyebrow lift, she shook her head. "Power cell ran out. Cloaking won't work without it, and I was a little paranoid about them tracking the transponder. Haven't finished putting it back together yet. I wasn't exactly expecting to need it so fast... helmet's in pieces back in Ned." She thudded her fist against her chest. "Still good armor. The Nederland militia sure likes it; we kept all the suits from Nathan's kill team."

"Oh." Tris squatted in front of the van and pulled out the charging cable.

Boom. The heavy slam of something smashing into the side of the van echoed over the garage.

Tris screamed.

She jumped up in time to catch a glimpse of Zara's hair trailing after her on the way to the floor. A person-sized crimple on the van's passenger wall showed where Zara's impact had crushed the thin metal against the armor plates inside.

Otto, the bald, pudgy, drooling (and tragically shirtless) piece of human filth who'd leered at her seven months ago wobbled on his left leg in an effort to recover from the force with which he'd punched Zara in the back. The infection made him look blobbier; his jowls draped down on his chest like a melting pizza. His belly overhung his thighs, and his flesh had either pinked or mottled with purple. Stubby sausage fingers opened and clenched. He flailed and threw his weight to the right, avoiding a fall.

Tris yanked the katana out of its sheath. "Did I mention the guy also grabbed my ass?"

Two yellow eyes rolled around trying to fixate on her.

Zara made a wheezy moan-whimper from where she laid on her front near the van. She didn't move much.

"Hey asshole," said Tris. She'd have yelled, but didn't want to attract a dozen more Infected from across the street.

Otto whirled on her fast enough for his various folds to clap, and grunted.

She ran at him, drawing the blade down his chest in a crossing slash that loosed a waterfall of blood over his undulating stomach. He gurgled and grunted, sounding more annoyed than hurt. An arm thicker than her leg swiped out. Tris ducked, barely noticing the loss of a strand of hair. The instant the massive, limb passed overhead, nana-flap wobbling, she lunged to her feet in a spinning slash that took his head off.

Expecting a symbiote, she let her reflex boosters drag time into slow motion for a few seconds. The huge body collapsed to the ground in an avalanche of flesh. No black serpent launched itself from the stump of a neck. Tris relaxed her ready pose and held the sword out at arm's length.

Zara pushed herself up to kneel, still wheezing. Blood decorated her upper lip and chin, though her nose had already mended.

"You okay?"

"Ow. Yeah. Just waiting for a rib to stop squealing." Zara grabbed the side of the van to pull herself upright.

The woman looked more worried than Tris had ever seen her.

"Never saw Infected before?"

Zara shook her head.

"They're... strong."

"Thanks for the tip. I hadn't realized." Zara spat blood.

Tris wiped the sword on a clean patch of Otto's pants and re-sheathed it. She plugged in the van before heading to the control panel on the wall next to the door leading to the 'Play' part of Otto's Plug and Play. Zara coughed twice, took a couple deliberate breaths, and strode over. With one hand, Tris flipped the charge switch to the 'on' position at the same time her other hand hit the button to activate an overhead motor.

The garage door rattled and squeaked as it closed, stopping not quite flush with the ground. Tris headed outside, bypassing the strip club portion of Otto's by way of a person-sized door between the third bay and the wall. Outside, she followed her best memory of the path to the Roadhouse main office. The AK-47 tapped against her butt in time with each stride. She waffled between resting her hand on the Beretta and reaching for the katana; her arm kept going back and forth.

"I can't tell if all these bullet holes are new or if they've been here." Tris peered among the mismatched buildings, patches of prewar masonry appeared every so often among metal and wood.

Zara swiveled to the right, MP5 raised. "I got nothing. This place is just like every other shithole out here. Was it this bad when you came here to buy the panels?"

"Uhh, I think so." She squinted at the greying sky. "Was earlier then. Not quite so gloomy. Guess the sunlight made it look nicer... or having living people around."

"Please tell me the Infected don't go crazy at night. That whole dark thing is a story, isn't it?"

Tris looked down to navigate a tangle of bodies. Another three infected, though these didn't have armor. "The Virus renders them photophobic. Victims aren't harmed by light, or even really hindered by it... but they don't like it. During the day, they might choose to stay in a dark place rather than come after someone who's out in the sun."

"But they don't get stronger or go crazy or anything?" Zara swiveled left, aiming at nothing. "Damn; I'm seeing stuff move everywhere."

"Not as far as I know." Tris hopped left onto a patch of sidewalk stained with old blood. "If any of them do that, my 'resistance training class' didn't mention it."

Metal clattering, like pipe bouncing on pavement, came from a side street beyond a building labeled 'Millie's Hotel.' Tris looked up along five stories of white masonry, fire escapes covered in torn white cloth and random pieces of spray-painted plyboard in place of some windows.

"Feels like we're being watched."

Zara looked up. "Yeah. How many did you say were here?"

"Place looked bigger last time. Kevin thinks there's thousands. Amarillo's supposed to have a huge army. Most of the people here are soldiers or their families... the ones who supposedly enforce the Code."

"Something's moving." Zara dropped to a knee and aimed at the alley.

The pipe, or whatever it was, skittered out into view as if kicked. A moan followed.

"Shit. Don't! They'll hear the shot." Tris grabbed Zara's shoulder, but her hand slipped off the Enclave suit's inflexible material. A hexagonal pattern in the black armor glimmered with a mesmerizing rainbow hologram.

Zara took the hint and leapt up, following in a dash to an opposite street. Tris skidded to a halt at the sight of a group of about a dozen

Infected midway down the block. A quick search found a fire escape ladder, and she vaulted up to it on her first try.

Her weight carried it lower; she climbed as it came rolling down, effectively keeping her in place for a few seconds until it reached the ground. Zara rushed after her. Both of them pulled the ladder up faster than the counterweights could move it as the Infected wandered closer, attracted to the metallic scraping.

Tris held a finger to her lips in a 'shh' gesture before tiptoeing around to the steps up. Five switchbacks later, they reached the top of the fire escape. She climbed the brick face to the top and dragged herself over the edge. The roof offered little obstruction beyond four pipe vents with chef-hat vanes spinning in the breeze. Tris fast-walked across the black-coated surface to a wooden defensive fortification at the corner. Zara hurried along after.

A wooden plank bridge connected from the edge over an alley to the side of another building. Other than a metal folding chair and an empty green ammo can supporting an ashtray, the 'guard station' had nothing of use. Across the street, three figures in olive drab armor and green pre-war camouflage pants shifted about. One meandered back and forth as if on patrol, while two appeared to be in deep conversation, though she couldn't hear anything from where she stood.

"Hey," whispered Tris, waving her arms over her head.

The men ignored her.

What's wrong with them? Are they assholes or drunk? Infected?

She glanced about at other buildings of similar height. As far away as a quarter-mile, every structure at least four stories tall had a roof full of armored figures. Some sat still, some paced, a few peered over the edges at the street. A brief mental count tallied over fifty men all acting as calm as if the streets

weren't packed with Infected.

"What's going on? Is everyone high? We're not gonna be able to fit all these guys in the van." She hesitated. *Cassie said there's only like twenty survivors... what is going on? Maybe she doesn't know about the soldiers up here?*

Zara started across the plank bridge, but stopped two feet out. "I see a Roadhouse sign over that way. Couple blocks."

Tris reluctantly pulled her gaze off the oblivious army, and trotted after Zara to the next building, where the roof had six canvas lean-tos over fifteen sleeping bags and a couple of footlockers. Not being in any mood to pick among the junk while people might be in their last minutes of survival, she hurried to the far end where an outbuilding offered a door inside. A cramped stairway led only to the topmost floor, ending at door that had already been battered open—from the looks of things, with a sledgehammer.

The space beyond it had the trappings of an office: a hallway with a toppled water cooler, a room full of cubes, break room, a few conference rooms, storage closet full of old copier paper, and the main stairwell access. They jogged across the room to the stairwell door, and Tris rushed in.

She'd expected an ordinary stairwell, not a wide-open metal grating stairway descending in the open through four stories of warehouse. *Whoa. Good thing I'm not too afraid of heights.* She clamped onto the railing. For at least a hundred yards to either side, tall shelves held row after row of solar panels, many still clad in shrink-wrap. Other shelves had spindles of the three-quarter inch thick wire she'd become all-too familiar with on the roof. Boxes upon boxes of new charge-plugs, not yet mounted to wires, took up a whole section.

"If we were scavving, we'd be set for life." Zara whistled. "They charged your boy ten grand for like forty of these and there's gotta be a few hundred here."

"We're not after panels." Tris eyed a large flatbed truck with a hydraulic arm parked by a garage door in the approximate middle of the building. "That's the rig they used to deliver our stuff... or at least one exactly like it."

Zara spun around in a three-sixty before pointing to Tris' left. "That way. The Roadhouse office or whatever it is." She tilted her head. "Wait, do you have any idea at all where these survivors even are?"

"Uhh... I'm thinking they're inside that building. Probably the most well-defended place in the city."

Distant moans echoed in from windows along the second story level.

Tris decided to stop talking. She walked in the direction Zara indicated, eyeballing some of the panels. According to labels and stamping on the aluminum frames, her earlier theory appeared correct. Amarillo hadn't been making new panels as Kevin always believed... they had a stockpile from before the war.

Zara swatted her on the bicep with the back of her hand twice, and pointed up when Tris looked.

A 'New Mexico Solar' company banner hung on string between the rafters forty feet off the ground. Naturally, a cartoon sun took the place of the 'O' in solar.

"What's New Mexico doing in Texas?" whispered Zara.

"Ask me if I care." Tris winked. "I don't think it matters since the world ended."

At the end of the shelves, flimsy beige walls cordoned off a small section of the first floor behind a small army of forklifts. A shelf to the left against the cinder block wall held thirteen three-foot tall canisters. Similar canisters perched on the rear ends of all the forklifts. Tris approached the doorway and peeked in to a break area with five rectangular folding tables and more metal folding chairs.

Some of the food laying around looked more recent: grilled slabs of dust hopper, gnawed-upon vegetables, and a jar of moonshine.

"You think we're too late?" whispered Zara.

Tris grumbled at the abandoned food before closing her eyes and trying to summon hope. "We still haven't made it to the head office."

Zara gestured at a door about ten yards past the cylinder shelf. "You lead, since you've got the quiet weapon."

"Right."

The red-painted door opened to a tarmac where six pre-war cars lay in various states of decay, parked in a neat line along the outside wall. *Some people had a bad last day at work.* She sighed. *Why did they blow it all up? What could've been so bad that billions of people had to die to fix it?*

"Focus," said Zara.

Tris let out an *eep*, and stopped short of walking straight into an open manhole.

"Where's your brain?"

Her face warmed with blush. "I got categorized as 'overly sensitive' in tenth grade." She indicated the cars with a nod. "Whenever I see stuff like that, I start getting all sad about everyone who died."

"Aww." Zara's pout looked eminently fake. "You're adorable."

Tris punched her in the shoulder, and shook the 'ow' out of her knuckles.

They both laughed for a second before remembering where they were, and stifled it.

A grunt emanated from a dumpster about forty yards to the left.

"Shit," whispered Tris.

She sprinted along the open driveway behind the warehouse and across the street into a narrow alley flanked by stacked pallets and huge blue trash bins. Two Infected groaned and crawled out of a mound of garbage bags. Tris beheaded the one on the left, and stabbed the one on the right in the heart two strides later.

Bang!

A wet splat followed a gunshot.

Tris whirled, cringing and ducking a flailing Infected who'd launched herself out of a second-story window. Zara's shot had killed the former woman in midair, giving Tris enough warning to get out of the way.

Moaning rose up from everywhere. Pallets fell over, plastic trash bins bumped against each other with hollow *thuds,* and shuffling shoe-scrapes set the hair on the back of her neck on end. A distant *slam* conjured the image of a bloodthirsty Infected hurling a refrigerator out of the way.

"Sorry." Zara grimaced. "Guess we go loud."

Tris pointed at another fire escape. "Not yet. They can't do ladders."

A thirty-yard sprint later, Tris leapt up to a dumpster and the bottom of a second story fire escape porch. She jumped up under the grating and monkey-barred it to the far end and the ladder. Zara fired a few more times; Tris winced inside with each shot as she slithered around the ladder onto the platform. Zara held her ground, shooting into a pack of about fourteen stumbling Infected out on the street. The wall of the building across the alley swelled outward, split with racing cracks and flaking faux stucco.

"Zara! Move!" yelled Tris. "Behind you!"

The black-haired woman whirled and let off a clipped, "Dammit." She dropped the MP5, letting it dangle on the strap over her shoulder as she jumped up to grab the bars along the underside of the fire escape porch. She followed Tris' acrobatic lead, but had to keep her legs up to avoid a sea of hands jutting up from the throng spilling out of the broken wall and flooding the alley. Tris drew the Sig she'd taken from the guy at Mac's, and shot six men and four women in rapid succession as they tried to pull Zara down. When her friend made it to the ladder, Tris grabbed her and pulled her up onto the deck, hard enough to fall over backward, dragging her away from the endless wave of moaning bodies.

Zara landed with her hands on either side of Tris' head, two inches from an intimate kiss.

"Well... I didn't know you had this in mind." Zara winked, and pushed herself upright.

Tris scrambled to her feet. "How can you even think about jokes right now?"

Zara sashayed to the ladder. "What makes you think it was a joke."

"That's not funny."

Her friend's high-tech armored boots took the metal stairs without sound. "Oh shit, Tris. I'm trying to cope, okay? I... zombies? My job used to be nabbing curfew breakers or dealing with vandals... zombies!?"

A man with almost-green skin rife with leprotic sores appeared without warning, clinging to the railing at the end with a *clank*. Zara screamed as he'd appeared in arm's reach of her. Tris shot him twice in the forehead, strode to the end of the platform and shot the one who threw him. "They're not dead. Just... vegetative, and highly aggressive."

Zara raced up, stopping at the fifth floor, the end of the fire escape. Someone had blocked off the window with a pile of furniture from inside. "I read a little about them in a briefing... Since I wanted *nothing* to do with the outside world, I didn't pay attention. I know I can't catch the Virus. *Seeing* them up close is another whole level of fuck."

"Yeah." Tris smiled. "We've got the advantage."

"What advantage? Guns?" She grinned. "Vanister was shocked I didn't put in for a hovercraft gunner given my aptitude scores."

"No. Opposable thumbs." Tris grinned and wiggled her thumbs.

Zara stared at her.

"Okay. I meant rational thought... but thumbs was funnier." Tris lost her smile a second later, and ran both hands over her hair, clutching it to the back of her neck for a second. "Shit, I hope there's still some survivors left alive... at least one person. Oh, who's Vanister?"

"Deputy commander of training division. The guy who assigns jobs. I guess I got on his bad side when I said I didn't want to go outside since everything was so perfect..." Zara pointed her MP5 over the railing, down at the throng of Infected. "Looks like about fifty or so. Scary, but nothing like you were worried about. Shouldn't there be a lot more?"

"All those bodies by the gate?" asked Tris. "And maybe that's why you got sent after me. I hope Nathan had to get on his knees for that request."

"Out front? That was maybe thirty. Plus these poor bastards, that's seventy or eighty. Where are the thousands?" She scowled. "My record wasn't bad. It had to be a random assignment."

That's a damn good question. This place should be a nightmare worse than Chicago. She pulled Zara back and stuffed the Sig in her belt. "Don't waste ammo. Let's go on the roof to get out of sight. They'll forget us in a little while."

Zara held her hands together in a boost step. "You go first."

Tris grabbed Zara's shoulders and put her right foot in the woman's hands. Zara all but threw her upward. Tris windmilled her arms and landed on tiptoe, standing on the edge of a three-foot high wall around the roof. Seven armored men milled about; two sat on folding chairs, three paced, and two hovered near the edge of the roof holding rifles.

Rifles made of wood and paint.

There before her stood four mannequins and three androids even more primitive than Bee.

Her mouth hung open. "Oh, shit."

23

THE LOWER DEEP

A little under an hour after the last Infected stopped moving, Kevin discovered a trapdoor hatch behind the counter that led down to an underground storage room. Some (probably dust hopper) jerky wrapped in burlap still smelled decent enough, and the men helped themselves. The far end offered a concrete stairway up to an angled metal cellar door. Whoever had run this place transferred the padlock to the inside, making it a relatively simple matter to batter open.

They resumed their sleep/watch rotation once they'd returned to the cars. Much to his surprise, the time between settling into the Challenger's seat and Neeley thumping on the window felt like only a few minutes. The sun peered over the eastern horizon, flooding the sky with clear blue. To the west, indigo clung to the barren earth.

"Time," said Neeley.

"Yeah, yeah." Kevin blinked and shook his head. His old life came back faster than he'd liked, years spent on the road allowed him to brush off the fatigue and discomfort of sleeping in the car with ease. "How's that arm?"

"Sore, but it'll be okay. Fitch hit it with 'shine."

Kevin glanced at Neeley's black eye. "And punched you back?"

Neeley laughed with a snort. "Heh, yeah."

Fitch walked over as Kevin got out and stretched his legs, offering a canteen. "Water?"

Kevin took a long drink, and eyed the western dark. "You two're 'bout the closest thing to friends I got. Not sure what that means seein' as how I've known your sorry asses for about four months." He laughed.

Neeley grinned. Fitch slapped him on the back.

"You two g'won back to my 'house. Help yourselves to whatever food ya need 'til I get back. I can't ask you to get dead over this."

Fitch grabbed his wrist, holding the canteen back from another drink. "You think we're gonna let you run off on yer own?"

Neeley nodded. "No way man. Your chick would kill us."

Kevin chuckled, and drank when Fitch let go.

"I kinda wanted my own Roadhouse for a while." Fitch scratched the back of his head; something fell from his afro and fluttered away to the ground—a piece of drywall. "But I didn't want it near bad 'nuff to suffer up ten grand, and I sure as shit don't want it bad 'nuff to let you walk off and die."

"Wait." Neeley took a step back, pointing at him. "You get bit or somethin'? Blood on ya? That what this is? You're dead and you wanna go down shootin' fore ya turn into one of them fuckin' things?"

"Maybe it's that pretty little woman. Guilt's a bitch." Fitch squeezed Kevin's arm. "She was already dead. If we weren't here, she'd still be dead. Might'a looked innocent, but—"

"Yeah, I know. Nothing I could've done... all that shit. Kinda reminded me of someone."

"For real you ain't bit?" asked Neeley.

"Is it going to require me getting naked to make you feel better?" Kevin winked at him.

"Nah. You's covered 'cep for your hands an' face." Neeley leaned left and right. "Don't see no tooth marks."

"Good. It's settled." Fitch clapped him on the shoulder. "Let's get going."

Kevin stared at the ground for a moment, decided to accept their continued help, and nodded.

A few miles later, a settlement spanned the road, outlined by semi-trailers, buses, box trucks, and a handful of house-trailers reinforced with scrap metal and junk. The perimeter surrounded a 'town square' of sorts, containing some-teen number of e-bikes and a group of men in leather jackets and biker cuts, all with the Redeemed symbol.

Odder still, for every Redeemed, he counted two or three settlers. Silver City appeared to be a large settlement where a biker gang had moved in. He'd been expecting something like what the News did, where they 'owned' the entire place and ran it a bit like a military encampment, only with less order.

The most shocking realization about Silver City hit him in the form of a long black-painted building with twelve e-car charging ports arranged in front of parking spaces and a Roadhouse-style restaurant/shop inside—but no Roadhouse sign. Instead, flickering purple neon letters named the place 'The Lower Deep.'

If Amarillo got wind of this, there'd be coins flying. Curiosity got the better of him, and he rolled through a gate formed by a pair of blunt-faced semi cabs, one black and one green. Both were in such awful shape he doubted they could move to 'close,' and had been set up more as a decorative accent.

Fitch followed, and parked the Behemoth in the space to his left. Neeley looked down at him, baffled, matching Kevin's mind. A couple of the Redeemed glanced at them on the way in, but none had any trace of recognition or hostility he could detect.

"Anyone look familiar?" asked Kevin.

Neeley climbed out onto the Behemoth's running board, twisting about and craning his neck. After looking at everyone in view at least twice, he shook his head. "Nawp."

Kevin slithered up out of the Challenger and stood in the crook of the door for a moment, taking in what had always been verboten. An independent place operating in the manner of a roadhouse, without being a Roadhouse. A third of his brain felt like the little boy who always told on others when they did something bad. That hunk of cerebellum wanted to run squealing back to Amarillo and point at this place, waiting for the brute squad to go out to mete justice.

Two thirds of his brain glowered, the part that felt like an utter idiot for slaving away to hand over ten thousand coins instead of just setting up shop on his own. Granted, he'd still have had to find solar panels and all the charging gear... but abandoned 'houses did exist here and there.

Angry at the guy who did this, but angrier at himself, Kevin stormed in the front door.

Music emanated from a flashing onyx and violet box on the far left side past rows of square tables tilted to diamonds. A man's voice wailed high over straining electric guitars, shouting something about a holy diver.

Three men in piecemeal armor, leather, and pre-war clothes occupied separate booths along the front wall. One had a woman with him with an eruption of dense, inky curls hanging down to her waist. A frilly black skirt, thigh-high leggings, and thick-soled shoes that looked more like bricks with straps made her look like a dark version of Alice in Wonderland—if Alice carried an assault rifle.

Kevin took two steps forward, Neeley and Fitch behind him to either side.

A tall, athletic-looking man behind the counter, shaved bald with a dark goatee, paused in his conversation with a dark-skinned woman. He stood about two inches taller than Kevin and his tight black tee shirt revealed the sort of musculature had by people not used to playing by the rules.

The woman gave Kevin the up-and-down glance before smiling. He guessed mid-twenties, despite a hint of childishness caused by large brown eyes and a button nose. Her tie-dye half-shirt left her midriff bare over faded fatigue pants loose enough to hide the curves of her legs. Toes poked out from the mottled green fabric, atop hand-made sandals of twine and wood.

"New boy," said the bald man. "You look like you just saw somethin' you'd rather forget. Maybe I can help ya do that." He flashed a grin while nodding at a row of bottles behind him. "Everything's fair."

Kevin approached the counter. Sure enough, a control panel for the chargers glowed red, amber, and green from the wall behind the man, though it wasn't the same model he'd gotten. It looked more cobbled together from random parts, probably one of a kind.

"Hey, pal. Did your ship just land or something?" The man waved a hand past Kevin's eyes. "Welcome to planet Earth... what's left of it."

An identical woman came out of a heavy, dark curtain in a doorway to the right of the counter, carrying a tray bearing plates of food. Her plain white dress hung down to mid-thigh, and she didn't bother with the homemade sandals. She almost had Tris' slender build, only the twins were taller, leggier, and had larger breasts. Except for their clothing, the women were exact copies of each other.

Kevin found himself staring at her until she set the food down by the driver with the Goth pixie clinging to him. He pulled his gaze off her and scratched his head. *Is it wrong to get a damn charge here? Oh, fuck it. Power is power.* "Uhh... Charge on six and seven. Beer?"

"So you *are* considered sentient." The man offered a hand. "Name's Dallas."

"Kevin." He shook.

"You've got that 'my world is falling apart around me' look." Dallas laughed. "I never get tired of that. Right now, you're wondering why I'm still standing here, operating this place and not getting my face adjusted by a pack of Neanderthals."

Kevin glanced left at an old pool table perched under a ceiling fan hung by loose bolts. "Yeah. Something like that."

A Hispanic boy of about nine paced around the table, idly making shots alone. He caught Kevin looking his way and gave him an 'I'd beat you easy' smile, followed by a 'c'mon over and play me' nod.

Dallas leaned aside as one of the twins filled three plastic cups about the size of beer cans with suds. "Coin each for the drinks. You, and most of the rest of those drivers out there, got the brainwash put on you. Just like those damn idiots up in Wichita who think the war was all some 'god wrath' horseshit." He leaned away to let the woman put the beer in front of Kevin, Fitch, and Neeley. "There ain't no bounty comin'. Never was. Never will be."

Kevin put three coins down. *Half the price... he must either brew his own or steal it.* "You're so sure?"

The woman took the coins with a smile, dropped them into a container under the counter, and wandered off to check on one of the men at a table.

"Been here seven years now. Figure if that story had any teeth, they'd long ago been sunk deep in my ass. I get your type in here now and then. Bet you're gonna run to the nearest 'Roadhouse' and go all 'gee wilikers' on the guy runnin' it." Dallas smirked. "I don't consider myself to be a genius, but even I can smell bullshit of that magnitude. They don't give a shit. Now, with the Redeemed around, I ain't got a bit of trouble sleeping at night. Even if some jackass gets it in their head to start some shit, they got my back."

"Yo, Mary," yelled the guy sitting closest to the machine emitting music.

The song had changed since they'd walked in. This one slower, without the wailing guitars, had a bassy-voiced singer and some woman chanting about "Some day" and "The minion" or "dominion" or something.

Both twins whirled to look at the man at the same time. The women did a rock-paper-scissors thing with a stare, and the one in the dress walked over to the table while her sister ducked past the curtains.

Kevin raised an eyebrow. "They're both named Mary?"

Dallas laughed. "Their momma wasn't the most imaginative critter on the face of the world. Guess she didn't want to forget who was who." His grin faded to a cold stare. Kevin glanced over his shoulder at the leering ogle connecting Neeley's eyes to the girl's bare legs. "I found 'em when they were around twelve or so. They're like daughters."

Neeley didn't react until Fitch slapped his head.

"Sorry 'bout him. Boy's like a dick with eyes sometimes." Fitch grumbled.

"Redeemed..." Kevin rolled a mental boulder around inside his skull, tilting his head side to side. "Don't seem like you got much of a problem with 'em. Also don't seem like there's too many here."

Fitch and Neeley took their beers and headed off to a table that left their backs to a wall.

Kevin sampled his drink. *Weaker than Wayne's, but not gonna bitch for one coin.*

The woman in the camo pants emerged from the curtain, sandals skiffing over the floor as she dragged her feet to the man farthest from the music-making box. She set a plate in front of him with a slab of meat on a bun.

Dallas squinted at him for a moment. "You're looking to start trouble with them, aren't you?"

Kevin shot an exasperated stare at the ceiling. "Not all of 'em. Couple of 'em killed a good friend of mine. Guy also happened to run a Roadhouse."

"I'm tellin' you, friend..." Dallas shook his head. "There ain't no bounty."

Kevin set the glass down. "Fuck the bounty. They killed a man who's closest thing ta family I had." A shrill warbling vocal came from the music box along with rapid guitars. "Who the fuck is doing *what* to that cat?"

"It's Judas Priest." Dallas grinned.

"Thought you said that god stuff was horseshit," said Kevin.

The bartender's eyebrows knit together in a flat line over his eyes. "Buddy, I think you're beyond help." He kept that expression for a few seconds longer before offering a blasé lift of one eyebrow. "The 'Deemed ain't unreasonable. I'm sure if they shot that guy up, there's a damn good reason for it... or someone's wearin' their colors. Doesn't sound like the way they roll."

Kevin leaned both hands on the counter. Anger got the better of him before his brain considered it dumb to attempt to 'loom' at a bigger man. "They've shot up a few other Roadhouses too. Did they have 'damn good reasons' to do that?"

Dallas gained an inch in height as he changed posture, head tilted ever so slightly to the left. "I can't speak for them. Get enough of 'em through here that I know it don't sound right. You got an itch ta go kick the Grim Reaper in his bony balls, go right ahead. F'I were you, I'd make sure I understood things first."

Kevin grumbled, pushing off the bar and pinching the bridge of his nose. "Okay. Help me understand then. Why would these guys go hunting proprietors for jollies?"

"'Deemed answer to Komodo. Bad... bad dude. Not the sort I'd wanna trade bullets with. I hear he's got a weird sense of honor. If you got the balls, to go lookin', you can find 'em up by Pinos Altos."

Three men in Redeemed cuts and a skinny maybe-seventeen year old girl in someone else's leather jacket walked in. They took a booth near the music machine, with the girl in the innermost bench seat against the wall... as if to protect her.

Kevin's brain ground its gears. "Right... How 'bout that charge... and three of whatever that guy got." He gestured at the man with the steak-on-a bun.

"Nine for the eats, four for the charge... two each."

"That's fair." Kevin counted out thirteen coins.

"Mary," said Dallas. Again, both girls turned to look at him. Camo-pants walked over. "Three number fours, please." He gestured at the table where Neely and Fitch sat.

"Sure thing, D." She smiled at Kevin long enough to get Dallas to give *her* the 'stop it' look.

He considered admitting to owning a Roadhouse himself, perhaps warning the man about what was going on... *Why? He wouldn't care if the 'house crumbles, wouldn't affect him at all.*

Dejected, Kevin mumbled something approaching "thanks" and headed to join his friends.

"How'd it go?" asked Fitch.

Neeley hissed, rubbing his arm.

"Staring again?" asked Kevin.

"Yep." Fitch grumbled. "I ain't gettin' shot on account o' your out-of-control prong."

"Pinos Altos." Kevin sat and buried his face in one hand, beer in the left. "This just got a whole lot more fucked up."

BEHIND THE CURTAIN

Tris stared at the armored mannequins, too dumbfounded by the implication of what she witnessed to move. Zara brushed past her and approached one of the pacing figures. This close, the rhythmic *whirr, click, pssht, whirr, click* of its mechanical innards couldn't have been more obvious. It didn't react at all when Zara plucked the carved hunk of wood from its grip, continuing to march about as if carrying a weapon.

"I'm not sure what they're expecting to do with this." Zara tilted the 'rifle' up to examine the underside. "Hey maybe it's magic or something and fires off energy bolts if you say the right words."

"That's…" Tris dragged her feet as she walked up to her friend, staring at the black-painted wood. "Not even funny."

Zara threw the fake gun at one of the motionless figures in a folding chair. The force of the strike broke its helmet in two pieces and knocked the false body to the rooftop. "Oh, look at that… the armor's fake too." She wandered over and picked up the 'kevlar helmet.'

Papier mâché, painted olive drab.

Tris' lip quivered. For an instant, she felt the urge to cry like a child who'd learned the 'historical documentaries' about superheroes were fictional. Before a tear could fall, she got angry. Kevin had hung most of his life on this Roadhouse thing, and the sight of his gods reduced to sticks and paper left her livid.

Zara leaned back. "You all right?"

"Bullshit."

Zara blinked.

"It's all bullshit." Tris snarled and punched the pacing android, leaving a fist-sized hole in the back of its 'armored vest' as well as knocking it over. The legs continued moving as though it walked. "The whole Code… So few Infected… It makes sense." She looked up at Zara. "There never was an army."

"How has anyone not noticed?" Zara punted the android in the head. "Not like these things are even *good* fakes."

"They don't have to be good to fool someone a half mile away at ground level. When we bought in, we went right to the office, spent the night at the hotel across the square, and left the next morning. The twenty or so soldiers we *did* see hovered so damn close they made Kevin nervous enough to want to leave as soon as he signed the ledger."

"Okay, so they chase people out quick, but no one living here let the secret out?"

Tris, grumbling, stomped across the roof to the side of the building closest to the Roadhouse HQ. "Either they didn't care, didn't think to look, or knew and didn't want to ruin their gravy train."

One story down, a six-inch thick pipe spanned the street, connected to another building. If not for the Infected below, she would've used the mannequins across the way for target practice out of spite.

"They're still moaning at the fire escape where we came up," whispered Zara. "Think they'll figure out we're on the other side of the building?"

Tris checked the retaining strap on her Beretta's holster and tightened the AK around her shoulder. "Depends on how much noise we make."

She grasped the wall, hauled her legs up beneath her, and perched like a cat on a fence. Aside from the steady groans and wheezes emanating from the alley, dread silence cloaked the post-war city of Amarillo. At best, they had another forty or so minutes of daylight, and a darkening in the sky to the south didn't bode well for weather. *Hope it's dry clouds.* From her vantage point, the shattered sprawl of a once-great city reawakened the lump in her throat. So many people died here because someone hit a button.

"Ready?"

Zara raised an eyebrow. "Thought you wanted to wait them out?"

"It's going to be dark soon. Every minute we waste is a minute someone could die." Tris shifted her weight to her hands and let her legs slip forward. She sat on the edge for a second before dropping down to stand on the pipe.

Zara grabbed her shoulder, a little too hard to be comfortable, and suppressed a cry of shock to a raspy whisper. "Be careful!"

"I'm good." Tris positioned her feet heel-to-toe on the pipe.

Zara pulled at her. "This isn't a good idea."

Tris smiled back over her shoulder. "You've got the same reflex boosts I do. This is easy. You were walking across the parking bumpers back in Rawlins."

"Yeah, but that was a six *inch* fall. Not six stories."

Tris patted the hand on her shoulder. "Five. Pipe's one down from the roof."

"Smartass."

Her muscles tensed, flooded with electrons from her cybernetic augments kicking in. A careful, but none-too-slow, stride got her across. She grasped a window ledge and climbed to the roof, pausing with half her weight on her left shin atop the wall to look back.

Zara had made it onto the pipe, but remained with her back pressed against ancient brick. She sensed Tris staring at her and looked up, mouthing "okay, okay."

Tris allowed herself a bit of amusement at watching the formerly terrifying silhouette in black struggle to tightrope-walk the pipe. When the woman had chased her in the woods, she'd seemed like a demon made of shadow; on the pipe, she wobbled like an awkward tween at her first gymnastics class.

Zara's fear proved unfounded; she hurried across the pipe with ease. A steady nervous whine leaking out her nose got louder as she approached. Tris slid over the wall to the roof and helped her up once she'd crossed.

A wall of HVAC units, riddled with bullet holes, formed a near wall between them and the remaining two-thirds of the roof of the L-shaped building. Here and there, human bones lay amid piles of windblown debris. Some more-intact skeletons had remnants of leather or cloth apparel, which had evidently been too gore-caked to scavenge.

"They've been dead a while." Tris avoided stepping on them, and headed for a gap in the HVAC boxes, turning sideways to shimmy through. "Might've been here and dead before the whole Roadhouse thing ever started."

When she emerged from the other side, the sight of a five-foot long jet-black airframe crumpled into an elevator shack froze the blood in her veins. Two of the drone's fans had sheared off during the crash, the other two remained intact at the end of their struts. The underbelly split open down the center where hatch doors hadn't quite closed over an internal weapons bay. Judging by the smell of electronic smoke and the seep of battery acid onto the roof, it hadn't been there too long.

"Whoa... what on earth is an imp doing here?" Zara squeezed out of the gap in the HVAC housings and stopped at her side. "Oh, someone's pissed. Bet the guy operating this got demoted... this drone got shot down."

Tris crept up to the wreckage; the imp had come down with enough force to smash the doors inward, not that she expected the elevator would've worked before the crash. She crouched a few feet away and leaned to her right to peer into the belly. Two parallel metal bars had circular sockets separated at two-inch intervals, about large enough to hold beer cans. Of the forty-eight slots, five still held capsules of green liquid.

Nathan... Tris bowed her head, crying out of anger.

"Uhh," said Zara.

"That bastard." Tris sat back on her heels and wiped her face. "He killed these people. I know it was him. I don't know *why*, but I know he did this. Nathan sent Virus here."

Zara, fists on her hips, twisted left and right, surveying the area. "There's a lot of rumors about how much influence Amarillo had... about how powerful their army was. We even heard it inside. Might've been the Council of Four getting to the point they finally regarded this place as a threat."

Tris sniffled. "No... he knew. He knew Kevin had a 'house, and he knew I was with Kevin. I... The only thing that makes sense is a long shot. Destroy Amarillo, word gets out that it's gone, and he hopes the people out here are every bit the savages the Enclave thinks they are." She leapt to her feet and stormed over to nine mannequin-soldiers standing guard at the roof edge by the long part of the L. "You got anything on you to start a fire?"

Several Velcro rips came one after the next from behind while Tris collected wooden rifles and paper armor.

"Yeah," said Zara. "E-lighter in the suit... for survival. Proof that the eggheads are either stupid or they never expected we'd actually use it.

Barely works. I don't think this piece of trash would even ignite dry wood."

"What about paper?" Tris dropped a bundle of fake rifles and armor and made an improvised fire pit out of a large sheet of siding from one of the HVAC units.

Zara tossed her a small device about the size of a 9-volt battery. Two metal studs on one end even made it look like one, or a tiny taser… She pushed the button on the flat face, and a little blue spark flickered between the two contacts. While it might've been laughable on wood, the device ignited a scrap of papier mâché from a 'helmet' in an instant.

Once she got a decent fire going, Tris held her breath and reached a trembling hand up into the imp's weapon bay. The Virus-containing capsules were glass, easing her initial worry they'd pop like water balloons if she touched them. She tugged with light pulls and twists, but the jars wouldn't come loose. Eventually, she noticed a manual release button near each socket. Hitting the switch let the jar slip out with a faint *click*. Tris cradled it in two hands, twisted, and held it up. Zara got the hint and took the capsule, carrying it to the fire as though it would explode and kill her if she made the slightest noise.

One by one, Tris extracted the un-dropped Virus capsules. Soon, all six sat in the center of the fire. She added more rifles and some of the paper vests, and frowned. *That's not going to burn hot enough to rupture the glass.*

She backed up and drew the Sig. Using someone else's bullets first felt more frugal.

"Quiet?" asked Zara.

"They won't know where it came from. We're up too high." *I hope.*

She aimed, trying to put a single bullet through as many canisters as possible, but wound up needing three shots to shatter them all. Soon, white smoke billowed from the burn. Both women backed away from it.

"Do you have any idea if that smoke is contagious?"

Tris bit her lip. "Theoretically, the heat should destroy the virus, but I'm not too confident that's burning hot enough. Better than leaving it sit here intact though."

"Probably. Can we… go?"

"Yeah." Tris walked backward for two steps before whirling about and jogging to the corner of the building.

The Roadhouse sign peered over a three-story pile of scrap metal impersonating a hotel a few blocks away. Across a narrow alley, the building to the north offered a fire escape to the street level, though it had been reinforced with barbed wire and corrugated steel plates.

"We're going to need to either jump that, or see if the elevator shaft has a ladder."

Zara backed up a step. "That involves getting closer to the fire of deadly smoke."

"We don't know for sure that it's dea—"

The black-haired woman sprinted by and leapt off the edge. She cleared the alley with a healthy distance to spare and landed one story down atop the other building in a tumble. Tris unslung the AK-47 from her shoulder and held it sideways in both hands, then backed up to get a running start. She charged with all the speed she could summon in a short sprint and flung herself out over the gap. The alley, scarcely wide enough to accommodate a single car, passed in a blink, and she landed in a clomping run on the far side, her katana almost bouncing out of its scabbard.

Zara offered a slow clap. "Nice."

She breathed heavy for a few seconds before tossing a nod toward the fire escape. Tris led the way down, past barricades, chairs, and the smallest folding table she'd ever seen loaded with playing cards and bullets. The arrangement of the ammo made it look like they'd been used as chips in gambling. Despite them being .40 cal, and her not having a weapon for it, she pocketed all twenty-seven rounds.

They descended to the street level in silence. Tris gestured the AK in the direction of the building and waved Zara to follow. Her friend spent the first twenty feet or so walking backward, MP5 raised at the alleys and streets behind them.

A patch of broken glass and a dried 'wet spot' on the pavement gave Tris the willies. She avoided it by a good fourteen feet, despite being moderately sure it had dried out. Virus supposedly persisted in the environment for at most seventy-two hours in that form before denaturing and becoming harmless. *Who knows what was a lie anymore?*

She got up to a rapid walk as the corner of the hotel approached. *So creepy being quiet.* The last time she'd been there, the downstairs had over fifty people in it. The racket lasted well into the night, making it hard to sleep even on the fancy pre-war beds. Across the street lay the large main office of the Roadhouse. Giant aluminum letters filled with threads of red neon hung over the awning; the place looked as though it might've been a restaurant before the nukes.

Armored barricades reinforced with sandbags braced the front door, allowing passage for a single person at a time. The single-story building had a roof full of similar barricades, but no fake soldiers. Seven months ago, that roof held at least twenty real soldiers. She eyed it as she approached, waiting, expecting someone to pop up and point a gun at her.

But no one did.

Twin wooden doors with shot-out windows offered no resistance to her tugging hand. She pulled the left one open and held it.

"That's not a good sign," said Zara. "If there was anyone making a last stand in there, the doors would be locked."

She moved inside, shifting the AK-47 back onto her shoulder and drawing the katana. To the left, a glass-enclosed refrigerated counter with ancient grease pencil writing announcing 'fresh cut steaks' held several handguns on display. Behind that, a kitchen of debatable usefulness stretched back to a far wall about forty yards away. It looked as though some kind of major gunfight happened in there since the last time Tris saw the place. Seven or eight bodies in green Kevlar lay sprawled about where they fell. The scent of death watered her eyes, but after the site inspector who liquefied when she tried to move him, nothing else would ever smell bad by comparison.

"That's unsettling. Most of them died to gunshots," said Zara. "At least their armor isn't made out of paper... not that it seemed to have mattered."

Tris headed to the right, past a counter where a host or hostess might have once stood, and gazed over the former seating area. A cube farm reminiscent of an office building had replaced it. Some of the workstations held multiple pre-war computers in various stages of assembly. Others had cameras, wiring, and a few other components she recognized as the inner guts of the power modules in the bases of the solar panels. A faint whirring piqued her ear, leading her around the host station toward the back hall. She passed between walls of dark wood decorated with plastic cacti the size of cantaloupes, advancing toward a 'restrooms' sign.

"They probably started shooting at each other after the first person succumbed and went feral."

Zara dodged a pushcart full of PC keyboards and whirled to the left with her MP5. "You sure there's anyone even here?"

Tris stopped and stared down. "No... but I can't leave until I find their last stand."

"What was that in the kitchen?" Zara relaxed, lowering her weapon. "I'm jumping at shadows here."

"Looks like people were shooting each other… before I spoke to Cassie." Tris pushed open a door labeled 'Manager' and swiveled around to put the katana between her and a dim office.

She almost wet herself as a pair of sentry guns on either side of a huge metal desk trained on her and emitted a rapid clicking sound. Her body refused to move for two seconds, until the paralytic terror fled her muscles.

Tris slumped back into Zara's arms, panting. "Shit… they're out of ammo."

Zara lifted her upright and indicated the wall with a nod. "Blood all over this little alcove here… too much for whoever bled to have walked away."

"Yeah… that means someone cleaned up the mess." She took a moment to recover her breath, and advanced.

Behind the desk, two folding tables held piles of computer equipment: PC cases, drives, wires, motherboards, memory chips, keyboards, and six flat-panel monitors. To the far right in the corner sat a tall safe, the type used for rifles. Near the safe, between a pair of bookshelves loaded with old software manuals, a plain grey metal door led deeper into the building. Next to a bathroom on the left, a steel-framed bed and dingy mattress oozed the stink of whiskey and sweat.

"Someone's been here recently." Tris eyed the table of tech; nothing was powered up, but a panel similar to the one used to charge cars hung on the wall nearby, rigged with standard 110-volt outlets instead of on/off switches or the 'Roadhouse-custom' plugs that everything else used these days. That someone had bothered rewiring the panel to pre-war outlets suggested it might've come first.

Zara moved left, sweeping the bathroom with the MP5. "Nothing."

Tris approached the gun safe, as tall as her eye level, and stared at a hockey-puck sized disc in the middle of the door, bearing a numeric keypad. *Hmm.* She thought back to the site inspector's jacket. *Naah… couldn't be that easy?* She tried 2061, which didn't work. 1602 didn't work either, but she noticed an unused space on the display. *Five-digit code.*

"What'cha doing?" asked Zara.

"Trying to open this. If there's weapons in here, the survivors are going to need them." She tried 2061 with 0 through 9 added at the end. When she keyed in 02061, the thing beeped. "Shit, it worked!"

She twisted the handle ninety degrees counterclockwise and pulled the door open. Rather than the weapons she expected, the safe was packed top to bottom with coins, many still in cardboard boxes. Her gaze settled on several pennies cartons she remembered helping carry into the building months ago.

Her mouth went dry; her heart pounded.

"Holy shit." Zara gawked. "That's like *all* the money."

"We could get the van in here…"

Zara chuckled. "Have we gone from rescue mission to looting?"

Tris opened her mouth to say something, but whirled at the squeak of a door moving. Not thinking about the weapon in her hand, she raised the katana like a pistol.

"Get yer asses away from that," yelled a rickety-looking old man with waist-length hair in pewter squiggles. A camouflage poncho obscured most of his body to the knees, but left his weathered AK-47 exposed. Strips of cloth tied around the weapon dangled at varying lengths, though whether they held it together or had been added to disguise it, she couldn't tell. "Easy now."

Tris felt like a fool holding a sword to a rifle. She lowered it slow and easy. Zara didn't move.

"You said somethin' bout a van?" asked the old man. He relaxed his rifle two or three inches.

"Is this where you tie her up and make me go get it?" asked Zara.

Tris bug-eyed at her. *What is she doing?*

"Uhh… not 'zactly." The elder coughed, launching a pea-sized glop of something white from his mouth that landed six inches down his beard. "Figgered on offerin' ta split the money with yas fer gettin' me outta here 'live. I cain't really drive no more, and I much prefer not havin' ta watch my back all the damn time. I force ya ta do shit and you'll stab me soon as ya can. Be better if'n I don't gotta hurt no pretty ones like you two."

"Do you know anyone named Cassie?" asked Tris.

"Yeah. She used ta work for me. Damn good with 'lectronics, that one."

Tris let her arms hang at her sides, sword pointed down. "I spoke to her two days ago over the radio. She said there were about twenty people left. Is she dead? You said 'used to.'"

The old man wagged his rifle to the left. "Look at this place. Shit's done. No one works fer me no more."

"So, she might not be dead?" Tris took a step closer. "We're more than willing to get you out of here, but I can't leave other survivors behind."

He twitched, left eye winking three times in an involuntary spastic motion. "T-they're all gone. The whole damn place is dead. Thousands. Ya gotta get me outta here!" Wide yellow eyes bored into her soul. "There ain't much time."

"I don't think you ever had thousands of people here," said Zara.

I know this voice... the old guy from the radio. "You're Amarillo... you were going to send..." *Oh, no.* "Did you send a site inspector to Gertrude's Roadhouse?"

"Whotrude?" The old man blinked. "The zombies are in the vents. I can hear them thinking about us."

Zara twirled a finger at the side of her head while eyeing Tris.

"Okay, whoever you are..." Tris raised her hands in a placating gesture. "You are obviously scared. We can get you out, but I need you to wait here until I find the others."

The elder's body trembled. Already-wild eyes grew more crazed. "No! Forget 'em. It's all a lie! We made it up. Never was any damn army. They're all gone. All two-hundred of 'em. They're gone."

"This guy's nuts," said Zara. "He's gonna—"

Blam!

The old man aimed and fired in a half-second. Zara let off a noise like a kicked chicken and crumpled in a ball. Tris leapt at him, raising the katana. The old man lunged back, getting his AK up in time to deflect the blade to the side. Before Tris could react, the butt stock caught her across the cheek.

Her vision filled with spots of dancing lights. Body followed head, and the next thing she knew, she lay atop a pile of pain on the table full of half-built computers. Circuit boards, aluminum cases, and other sharp corners jabbed into her everything. The old man had boosters... not quite as fast as Enclave tech, but he was almost as strong as an Infected, stronger than a normal human could be.

Pain faded in a wash of adrenaline. Tris flung herself into a roll that got her off the table a tenth of a second before the AK barked three rounds through the particleboard and one unhappy Dell computer. She landed flat on her back and spun into a floor-skimming kick that took the old man's legs out from under him.

He put two more bullets in the ceiling on the way down.

Zara struggled to push herself up and aim the MP5, but decided to dive behind the desk when he swiveled to aim at her. Tris hurled the katana at him as a distraction, which he fell for by blocking with the rifle again. Her jaw popped as nanites pulled it back into socket. Pins and needles swam over her face, riding the tail end of a wave of numbness.

She tore the Beretta from the holster, firing five times in the process of aiming. The first bullet shattered linoleum a hand's width from his leg. The second pierced his shin. Bullet three landed at the crown of his right hip, four and five hit with sharp *slaps* over his stomach. They holed the poncho, but within a quarter second, mushed bullets fell away from the Kevlar he had on underneath.

Tris raised her hand to go for his head, but the man's rifle came up too fast. She dove to the side, aborting her shot as he fired. One round skimmed past the Beretta, the second dug into her forearm, an inch below the wrist, and passed out clean. A burst of pain lancing from hand to elbow said the bullet had glanced off bone.

"Argh!" she screamed as her leap landed in a slide. The Beretta slid from her grip; her hand released without conscious control.

Three seconds later, the old man scrambled upright and rushed toward her for a kill shot. Zara popped up over the desk, waving the MP5 side to side. She found her target and fired three rounds into his back, which caused him to lurch to the side, firing past Tris' head by a few inches instead of into it. Shattered linoleum flecks stung her cheek.

Tris rolled forward into a punch with her left hand. He brought the AK up to defend; her edge in speed let her switch from punching to grabbing. Again, he tried to crack her in the face with the stock, but she ducked, expecting it. Fighting someone moving almost in real time reminded her of the simulation; it had been awhile since anyone but the trainer could keep up with her.

Zara angled for a clean shot, but didn't find one. She yelled something Tris' time-slowing combat booster dragged into an unintelligible demonic warble.

The old man lifted Tris off the ground by her grip on the rifle, twisted about, and slammed her down on her back atop the folding table full of computer junk while screaming, "Crazy! The lot of ya. You're after my money, but y'ain't gettin' it!"

Shit. This old fucker is strong. Ignoring whatever sharp mass of junk dug into her ribs, she raised her knee to her shoulder and stomped him in the chest. He went flying; wide, shocked eyes said he evidently never expected a girl her size to have that much power in her legs.

His shout of "Aiyeeeee!" ended with a wooden crunch. He hit the shelf to the left of the grey door and fell in a waterfall of books, figurines and DVD cases.

Zara fired somewhere between six and twelve shots, triggering one at a time but so fast it sounded like full auto. The old guy rocked and shuddered amid a spray of bloody paper bits. The AK fell from his grasp and clattered to the floor. He wheezed and slid down to his knees, teetered a second, and careened over sideways.

"Lieutenant," rasped the old man. "Takin' heavy fire. Got hostiles on three sides. Situation critical. Requesting immediate air support at my location." He gurgled. "Copy?"

Tris growled, left hand clamped around her forearm where the bullet had struck. She oozed down to her knees, gasping for breath. Her back felt like a knife-thrower's target board, her arm burned as though a red-hot rod remained jammed in it.

"Linda," wheezed the old man. "Captain, you gotta tell Linda I tried... Tell her I love her." He sucked in a short breath, then his voice rose to a shout. "Enemy sighted bearing zero-two-two degrees high. *Incoooooommmming*! Fire for effect!"

The man's body twitched and thrashed out of control. His right leg locked rigid, left undulating. Torso and arms jittered and bounced with the staccato motions of a dying android. Blood seeped down over his poncho at the base of the neck, and one bullet hole in his left cheek gushed crimson.

Zara strode past Tris, scooped up the katana, and speared the old man in the skull. His body went still and his eyes lifeless, though both arms kept twitching. "Son of a bitch."

"You okay?" asked Tris.

"Cracked my sternum I think." She rubbed her armored suit between her breasts. "Already knit, but it's still sore as hell." Zara made a sudden face as though she'd gone waist-deep in ice water.

Three seconds later, Tris' right forearm exploded with burning tingles so bad the idea of cutting it off seemed reasonable. Zara let out a strangled scream, which Tris soon joined in on.

A moment later, they stared at each other, out of breath and panting.

"Do you..." Zara shuddered, a tendril of drool hanging from her lip. "Have any idea what the fuck that was?"

Tris held up her healed arm. "Yeah. We haven't had enough food. Nanites are eating us to fix things."

"Great." Zara grumbled.

"That means we're close to the point where they'll stop doing anything." Tris stretched and clenched her arm, working out stiffness and a trace of burn. "We need meat soon or we're going to die to systemic shock if we get roughed up much more."

"Have we reached the 'fuck this' point yet?" Zara jerked the katana out of the old man's head, and chucked it to Tris.

"Almost." Tris caught the sword, eyeing the safe full of coins. "All ten grand of Kevin's money... plus everyone else who ever bought in. What was this guy planning to do with it all?"

"Fill a bathtub and smear it all over his wrinkly-ass nipples?" asked Zara.

Tris cringed. "Thanks for that mental picture."

"Hello?" crackled a female voice from near the floor.

Tris whirled to stare at a smashed radio unit, probably one of the uncomfortable things she'd landed on. She darted the two steps to it and swiped up the mic in her hand. "Hey. Cassie?"

"Yeah." The woman sounded even more like a little girl. Her voice quivered with fear and a trace of sniffles. "It's me. You... you're not coming, are you? You haven't even left yet."

Zara handed Tris her Beretta, then raided the old man's body for AK ammo.

"Cassie, listen to me. We're here. We're *in* Amarillo. We almost got killed by some crazy old man. Where are you and is there anyone else left alive?"

"Really? I... can't believe it." Cassie sniffled. "Yeah... there's fourteen of us now... but it's gonna be one less real soon."

Oh, shit. "Where are you?"

"We're under the United Market. You're at the HQ right?"

"Yeah."

"Go out the back door through the kitchen to the loading dock. Hop down and go right past the chain link fence to the alley. It's the sixth building on the left."

"We're coming. I've got a van. We can get everyone out. Don't do anything stupid."

"It's not me." Cassie sniffled again. "It's Warren."

"What's happening?"

"Uhh... He's gonna kill Abby." Cassie started crying. "He won't listen! She's only eleven."

Tris threw the mic aside and ran.

PLAYING RISK

With each mile closer to Pinos Altos, Kevin's confusion mounted. Dallas' characterization of the Redeemed didn't sit well with what he'd constructed in his mind about them. He wondered if perhaps Wayne had made enemies with some specific individual before he took on the mantle of Roadhouse proprietor, but dismissed it because the Redeemed trashed other 'houses. If there had been some specific problem with Wayne, why attack others? At least he'd gotten to watch that boy own Neeley at pool for a few hours.

Hell, Neels said they were pretty civil when he saw 'em, and they were the sons o' bitches who killed Wayne.

He slapped his hand on the wheel. "Shit, this doesn't make any god damned sense."

Light brown dirt studded with rocks zoomed by on both sides of NM-15. Wouldn't take too much longer to get there… question was, what waited for him in Pinos Altos?

A sudden change in light on the rear-view monitor drew his eye; reflexes not quite dulled by a mere six months off the road caused him to hit the master arm switch for his guns without thinking. Two ethanol-eating dirt bikes leapt up out of a culvert on the side of the road, shedding sand-brown tarps studded with scrub bush and sticks. He couldn't make too much detail out of the eruption of beige dust, though muzzle flare gave away their intentions before the second bike got all the way on the road.

Fitch swerved side-to-side, a spray of sparks dancing over the Behemoth. Black motorcycle helmets obscured the faces of both riders, though piecemeal leather riding gear, Kevlar kneepads, and emaciated bodies made him sure these two weren't Redeemed.

The slower bike steered for the Challenger while the first continued spraying the Behemoth from a submachinegun-sized weapon mounted on the handlebars. Kevin tilted the wheel a hair's breadth to the left and squeezed the button for the trunk guns. By some miracle, the rangefinder actually worked, and the two trunk guns converged on the same point.

A brief flash of orange fire came from the second bike's gun before its fuel tank ruptured, covering the man in a bath of ignited ethanol. The flailing, flaming, figure tumbled off the road in a heap.

Fitch slammed on his brakes, forcing the other dirt bike into a hard swerve that left him wobbling and more worried about not dumping than shooting anything as he zoomed past the truck. Neeley popped up out of the hatch in the roof with his Dragunov, but a tremendous *boom boom boom* shook the air as the cannon under Fitch's hood went off.

Four feet of muzzle flare looked more like a flamethrower from the center of the grille.

The biker exploded in a shower of arms, legs, and helmet, soon followed by bike parts going everywhere. Kevin blinked. That giant pipe was a gun! *What the fuck does he have in that thing?*

He slowed to a stop, relieved for only a few seconds before the sight of dark grey smoke peeling out from the Behemoth's left rear tire put a sick weight in his gut. The enormous black pickup truck stopped within two feet of his rear bumper. Fitch and Neeley got out. While the skinny man headed toward the tire, Fitch stomped down the road and paced about, crushing fragments of gore under his boot while cursing.

Kevin decided to let the man vent. He jogged over to Neeley.

Three small holes in the metal hubcap over the in-wheel motor made him cringe. Said smoke exuded from them.

"Damn, they's tiny." Neeley squatted and picked at one of the holes with his finger.

"Looks a bit like 5.56 to me." Kevin felt around the edges of the domed metal disc, locating the release catch in about eight seconds. The hatch opened, letting out a billow of darker smoke and the choking dry-sand flavor of burnt silicon. Fragments of circuit board rained onto the road. "Shit."

"Bad?" asked Neeley.

"Dunno yet. What kind of insanity are you mounting on this thing?"

"Huh?"

"That gun."

Neeley grinned. "Oh, that." His body shook with his donkey laugh again. "20mm machinegun."

"What?"

Neeley nodded like a cocaine-addled rabbit.

"Jebus able cripes. Do *not* point that at me. Findin' ammo for that's gotta be a joy." He sputtered.

"Tha's why Fitch so pissed off. Saw the motor indicator go red, so he got mad 'nuff ta use Mama. Then he get madder 'cause he spent three rounds. So's, it bad?"

"Dunno yet."

Kevin poked around inside the wheel. The stator looked okay, the wire coils hadn't been hit either. The hatch had to be almost a half-inch thick; the three holes resembled tiny volcanoes rising from the metal. One of the bullets went straight through the housing and out the back without hitting anything. The other two crushed a circuit board responsible for controlling the magnets' timing.

Neeley got up and wandered off. He returned before Kevin finished brushing circuit board bits out with his fingers. "Them bikes got space guns. Never seen bullets like 'at 'afore."

Kevin caught a small object, which turned out to be a bullet that resembled a 5.56 with a shorter, fatter case, necked-down to match the slug. "Five-seven. It's not from space, it's from Europe."

"Ain't that orbitin' Jupiter?" Neeley scratched his head.

"Might as well be. Almost ain't worth scavving that gun. You'd have an easier time finding 20mm shells."

"20mm bullets?" asked Neeley.

"Shells." Kevin pointed at him. "Anything big enough to fuckin' liquefy a man is a god damned cannon. Cannons take shells."

"Oh." Neeley bared his teeth while chuckling and scratching his head more. "Thems 'splosive rounds. Air force base had a bunch of 'em."

"So they're rare *and* old." Kevin cringed. "Be glad they actually fired and didn't just blow up like bombs."

Neeley blinked and went pale.

Out of breath, Fitch plodded over and leaned on the door.

"Feel better?" asked Kevin.

"Little." Fitch closed his eyes and appeared to be practicing meditation. "How bad is it?"

"Controller board's smashed. Best thing be to disconnect the power lead and run it as a dead wheel."

Fitch grumbled. "Nah, damn thing'll pull ta the side and I'll be stuck doing fifty. You're bitchin' enough how slow we are now. Pretty sure I got a spare board in the back." He walked around to the tailgate. "C'mon."

Kevin followed him up into the bed, where a housing built out of the back of the passenger cabin likely held the ass end of a single-barrel 20mm machinegun. He'd wondered what it contained before, but assumed extra battery like the other large boxes. Now it made more sense. A weapon like that had to be six feet long or more, and for it to be concealed under the hood, it'd have to pass straight through the passenger cabin and protrude into the bed.

Fitch unlocked a toolbox, stuffed the key back into his pocket, and rummaged. It didn't take him too long to find a spare board, and three more besides. "Here. Got 'em."

Kevin studied them: dusty, scuffed, one scratched. "Are you sure *any* of these work?"

"Pretty sure." Fitch smiled. "Got four chances, right?"

With Neeley perched sitting on the Behemoth's roof, Kevin and Fitch got to work disassembling the forward of the two rear wheels on the left side enough to replace the boards. The rearmost wheel ran off the 'spare' ethanol motor, but the Behemoth didn't carry enough fuel to use it for long… only enough for a boost. They found over a dozen copper dots in the tire band where five-seven slugs stopped in the solid rubber.

"Damned inconsiderate." Kevin worked a socket wrench on the wheel mounting at the same time Fitch worked a jack.

"What's that?"

Kevin smiled at Fitch. "Idiots who designed this wheel never took into account field repairs. Gotta take the whole damn thing apart to replace this board. Like they never expected anyone to shoot your ride out from under you."

Fitch laughed, continuing to pump the jack handle.

"Umm… weren't they designed a'fore the war?" asked Neeley, scratching his head. "They'd not be expectin' ta get shot at."

Fitch laughed harder.

Kevin didn't like the way everything *creaked* as the corner of the Behemoth left the road. Then again, with as much armor as they had on this thing...

"Never imagined I'd be back out here," said Kevin. "Once I signed on that dotted line... had my own 'house. Figured I'd grow old and happy. Thought I'd be done with this."

"I dunno." Fitch twisted the jack handle to lock it. He took a knee and another socket wrench and attacked the left side of the wheel. "Both got their ups and downs. Seems like the 'house is dangerous, too, these days."

"That guy in Silver City didn't care too much," said Kevin.

Fitch chuckled. "Maybe it's not roadside stops... maybe it's the Roadhouse?"

"There are no 'roadside stops.' Past ten years, anyone opens an independent, Amarillo shut them down."

"Except for that one." Fitch dropped a nut in a plastic cup. "How many more are out there?"

"I've been all over the damn west half of the continent, and I can't say I've ever seen one other independent. Couple 'houses mysteriously changed owners, but they was still official 'houses."

With all the bolts removed, Fitch grabbed the tire band. Kevin did the same on the other side.

Fitch nodded. "One... two..."

They yanked it off the axle, let it bounce once, and guided it to lay flat. Kevin took a screwdriver to the inside face, extracting ten-inch bolts that held the interior 'cage' together.

"You like it out here?" asked Kevin. "Most drivers I ran into, they all said the same thing. 'Can't wait to get a 'house. Tired of bein' shot at...' 'Course, they never saved their coin. Gambled it away, fucked it away, drank it away... all the while they're talkin' about how they're gonna buy in."

Fitch laughed. "Yeah. I embody that particular situation. That's too much damn money. With my luck, I figured I'd live like a goddamned monk for years, save up all this coin, and die within sight of it. So, I decided to drop all that damned stress and *live*. Earn enough ta keep the Behemoth runnin' and food in my gut. Ain't bad, though. Maybe someday, I'll get bored o' drivin' all over creation, and find some nice settlement or some shit."

Kevin set the screwdriver down and flipped the wheel over so the outside hatch faced up. Fitch helped, and they lifted half of a metal shroud out, which included the mounting point for the armored dome.

"Shee-it. All that just to change a board." Fitch grumbled.

"Oh, that's not the best part." Kevin winked. "If we put in a bad one, we won't know 'til the whole thing's back together and turned on... unless you got a component diagnostic in the back too."

Fitch held up his hands in surrender. "Nope."

"You think it's worth it?" asked Kevin.

"What's that?" Fitch raised a steel-wool eyebrow.

"Running a roadhouse or driving. People with vehicles that work are either driving something for someone, or trying to steal something from someone. Half the time, the lines ain't too clear. Figure one in three will turn around and try to take what's yours."

"That's a whole lot worse than yer average person." Fitch tapped his chin. "Maybe the freedom of havin' a workin' vehicle brings out the worst in people... or could be, just thems the sorta people who go outta their way to get a car."

"That's a fellatio," yelled Neeley. "You're mistakin' cause for kincidence."

"Fallacy," muttered Fitch. "Don't mind the boy; he whacked his head on the window too many times."

Kevin, hands on his hips, chuckled at the wheel. "Well, let's get this lump of shit back on and see if we gotta do this all over again."

Between Fitch and Kevin, they hoisted the ponderous truck tire back in place. The older man reached for the wrench, but Kevin waved him off.

"Hold off on that. All we gotta do is plug it in to see if it works. No sense puttin' all those bolts back on only to take them off again. In fact, bolting it down before testing it will guarantee it won't work."

Fitch nodded, dropped the socket wrench, and walked left to lean into the cab. A subtle change in the air hinted at the power running through the system, a sound too low for the human ear to register consciously. A pang of loss squeezed Kevin's throat at the memory of Wayne once comparing it to the way a person could stand in a room with an old TV set and 'sense' it was on, despite a blank screen. The only televisions Kevin had ever seen had been flat panels, which didn't do that.

"Flashing orange. Never saw that before," yelled Fitch.

Shit. "Board's blown. It'll run, but your batteries will go like an ethanol tank with six bullet holes."

The strange quality in the air ceased as the power cut off.

Fitch returned to the back end, grumbling. "Got three more tries."

They spent the next hour unscrewing, disassembling, and replacing. With sweat running down his face, and his armored jacket on the road beside him (against his better judgment), Kevin sat back on his boot heels and panted.

Neeley brought canteens over. After a short water break, they mounted the wheel again. Kevin swayed back and forth, waving his hands at the tire while chanting in his best approximation of a Native American… something. He wasn't sure what that old shaman had been asking his spirits for, but at this point, anything seemed worth trying.

"Ready?" yelled Fitch from the cab.

Neeley raced over and hopped around on one leg behind Kevin, who stopped chanting and gave him the finger.

"Here goes." Three seconds later, Fitch cheered. "We're back!"

"Woooo!" Neeley howled at the clouds.

"Well…" Kevin eyed the tire. "One thing about runnin' a 'house: won't leave ya stranded in the middle of nowhere."

Fitch twisted the jack handle; the Behemoth glided down, accompanied by soft hissing. "You so sure 'bout that?"

Neeley laughed for a few seconds before his face went serious. He shifted his gaze back and forth between the men. "Wait, what?"

"Nah." After replacing all the nuts to secure the tire, Kevin picked up his jacket and put it on. "I ain't sure about a lot of things these days."

"I hear that." Fitch patted him on the back.

Kevin trudged to the Challenger with the clatter of a hydraulic jack rolling over the road behind him. He considered pulling out in a 180 and going back to Rawlins. For the few minutes Neeley ran around like an over-caffeinated rat-dog picking up tools, Kevin looked back and forth along the road, debating if any of this trip had been worth it. He jammed his fingers into the handle and yanked the door open.

Aww hell. We're already here. Another couple miles won't kill me.

26

TAKE NO CHANCES

C assie's directions led Tris along a street lined with cars turned up on their sides, reinforced with sandbags and razor wire. All of it seemed as though it had been that way for years, making her wonder if its purpose had been defense or illusion. The old man's wounds continued closing after his death, though dense scar tissue formed around each bullet hole. Nanites, she assumed, though a version a few generations inferior to the ones she and Zara had crawling around their bloodstream.

She remembered enough of her historical documentaries to understand an Army Ranger had been some kind of major badass before the war. For him to be alive still, even as an old man, either put him at barely eighteen when the nukes fell or he'd lived a lot longer than people should. Tris examined her hands, wondering if Zara could've been right about her aging. She looked no different from when she posed for her high school graduation picture. *Still eighteen. Am I not getting older at a normal rate or was I in stasis?* Somewhere, that picture of her existed in a memory stick, a hard drive, or maybe even an optical disc. Did the people who claimed to be her parents keep it when she'd been arrested for sedition or, like her real father, had she simply ceased to exist because she stopped conforming?

Tris had never really loved them. Hell, she barely trusted them even though they'd been nothing but nice to her, if not creepy with their insistence that her Dad wasn't real. Why, then, did she feel hurt at the idea they could've so easily discarded her? Perhaps she *had* loved them in a way she'd never realized and had been lying to herself. What had Nathan told them of her? The sudden idea that these parents she'd always kept at arms' length might be devastated at the news of her death caught her off guard.

Zara squeezed her shoulder. "You okay?"

"It's too damn quiet." Tris sniffled and wiped at the corners of her eyes, tears that hadn't had the guts to fall. "My mind is wandering."

"Well, don't let it run away." Zara gestured. "Is that it? Looks like they're ready for a long siege."

Tris peeled her gaze up from the blacktop. A short distance ahead, a large building at the back end of an empty parking lot sat surrounded by walls of sandbags, corrugated metal, razor wire, and even some pallets. A hint of a 'United Market' sign peeked over the barricade around where the front doors would be.

"Yeah."

Zara glanced at the MP5. "Might wanna go loud. If we're going to try and extract people, the more Infected we kill now, the better."

Tris sheathed the katana and shrugged the AK-47 off her shoulder. "True, but I'd rather sneak them out. That old guy said two hundred. We don't have that much ammo."

The MP5 drooped a little. "Good point. Street looks clear."

"We've got about fifteen minutes before it's pitch dark."

Tris sped up to a jog across the parking lot. Whoever had barricaded this place appeared unconcerned with minor things like gates or doors. All the windows on the front had been blocked off, and even if there hadn't been razor wire, the gap at the top was too narrow to squeeze through. She diverted left, hurrying past a shopping cart holder and around the corner. The side street had plain brick walls, no windows. The alley beyond that led to a loading dock with five steel rolling doors big enough for semi-trailers to back up to, but none moved.

The person-sized door at the left end of the dock had been welded closed from the outside.

"Damn. Whatever's in here must be worth a shitload." Zara whistled between her teeth.

Tris jumped down to the pavement again and peered around the final wall of the building, a narrow channel between the United and what had once been a gun store. The thought of Kevin getting distracted by the hope of salable weapons (as futile as it was) made her smile. She stared at a mismatched assortment of dumpsters, some blue and some green with 'recycle' logos. Her brain juggled a quick game of Tetris.

"Zara..." She ran to the nearest dumpster and shouldered the AK again. "Help me."

Sometimes having strength around that of a large, athletic man came in handy for the shock factor in such a small package. Sometimes, like right at that moment, being strong came in handy for being strong. Tris and Zara, who had her by an inch or so and about twenty pounds, lifted and repositioned six dumpsters like building blocks. They arranged three end to end before hauling two more on top of those. The most grueling part entailed getting the sixth up to form the third tier of the stack. For that, they used one of the lighter plastic recycling bins.

Winded to the point of feeling dizzy, Tris forced herself to climb their improvised stairway and made the jump to grab the roof edge. Zara, equally as tired, shoved her by the feet before following. Tris rolled over onto her back atop the building, panting for two breaths before the fear in Cassie's voice got her moving again, despite the burn in her lungs. Some Warren asshole wanted to kill a little girl.

Fortunately, a way in took only a quick glance around to locate. A small outbuilding on the roof with a blue-painted door was free of barricades. Infected weren't known for their ability to climb. She'd even seen some trip over curbs.

Tris ran to it, finding the steel knob locked. She took a knee, opened the sole of her sneaker, and extracted her lock-picking tools. It had been quite some time since anything had entered that keyhole, requiring a little scraping before she perceived the tumblers. A short game of tap, bump, and wiggle later, she twisted the knob open.

After repacking her tools, she pulled the Beretta and crept down a switchback staircase that led to an employee-only section of the store. A dingy white-tiled corridor had doors to a manager's office, two bathrooms, a lounge area, and an alcove filled with lockers. No thoughts of salvage or looting delayed her. She gave each room only enough attention to determine if people were inside before moving on through a pair of red plastic flapping doors to the store proper.

The main area of the supermarket didn't look much different than it had prior to civilization coming to an abrupt halt, aside from having been looted to death. Row upon row of empty shelving stretched from wall to wall. Someone had (probably long ago) smashed out the glass in the deli counter. A few scraps of cold cuts remained, though they were quite far from the color she expected they should be, and looked rock hard.

It had been so long, they didn't even smell.

"Hello?" asked Tris at a normal volume.

"Why aren't you shouting?" whispered Zara.

"Same reason you're whispering. Infected have great ears, and I don't know if the twenty minutes it took us to get in here was twenty minutes too long." She found herself still breathing hard from moving dumpsters.

"I was whispering because I always like to have the element of surprise in an unknown situation. People do stupid things when they're desperate. If someone's going to get shot, I'd prefer it isn't me."

Tris held up her hand at a brief noise. It could've been a quick shout from a man or someone doing something unpleasant to a dog. She pointed ahead and left. Zara followed along as they crossed the bulk of the store, until Tris halted by another pair of flappy plastic doors between two cooler cases with price tags for milk, orange juice, tea, and other drinks. The white fiberglass bore liberal scuffmarks from pushcarts and boots.

The sight of it made her parched and in dire want of a drink.

"You can't!" yelled a man.

"Please don't make me!" shouted a young girl.

Tris shoved the door aside and ran down a plain grey cinder block corridor into a room full of warehouse shelves and pallet jacks. The din of people emanated from an alcove up ahead near what she assumed to be the outer wall of the store. Opposite a desk full of ancient clipboards, it held a stairway down into a basement level.

"Okay, okay!" wailed a childish voice. "Don't shoot me."

"Son of a bitch," yelled a man.

"Easy," shouted a different man.

Tris hurried down a set of stairs, paused at the corner of a landing, and aimed the Beretta down the next set. Shadows moved across the floor, but the people who made them stood too far away to be seen. She stalked the last six steps to the basement floor.

Beyond a series of hanging clear plastic 'walls' and shelves, a circle of people surrounded a skinny tween girl with straight, black hair down to her butt. She stood naked in the middle of them, arms raised, a wadded-up dress in her left hand. Clearly not yet twelve, she turned in a slow spin while shivering and crying, allowing the crowd to see every inch of her under pain of death. The only functioning light bulb in the entire basement hung directly above her, creating a cone of illumination in which her skin all but glowed.

A man with Hispanic features and a strong resemblance to the girl stood out due to the red in his cheeks, and sheer anger emanating from him. His rage appeared directed at a grey-haired pale man with a pistol leveled off somewhere between him and the child. When the girl had her back to the armed man, she looked up at the furious man, sniveling, trembling.

"Daddy... please don't let him shoot me. Please... I didn't do anything! I don't wanna die."

"Hold up your legs one at a time," said a black man in similar armor to what she'd seen on the mannequins—only his looked real. "Need ta see if you stepped on anything and got cut."

The girl, head down, face red, obliged.

A white haired, skinny man made an annoyed face and waved at the man with the gun. "I don't see no bite—"

"What the fuck is going on?!" yelled Tris. She stormed in, Beretta raised at the fortyish man pointing a gun at a little girl. "Kid, put your dress on. You. Explanation right now or your brains are getting air conditioning."

The man—Warren, she assumed—froze. He shifted his pale blue eyes toward her. The girl, sniffling, wasted no time wriggling into her dingy garment before clamping on to her father and sobbing into his chest. The tattered scrap of once-white cotton looked as though she'd been wearing it non-stop for a month.

"Easy, girlie," said Warren, his voice dusty and slow. "I'm just trying to protect us. The child's infected."

Tris' stomach gurgled. *Oh, no.*

"I'm not!" yelled the girl. She sniffled and coughed. "It's just a cold."

"It always looks like a cold at first." Warren glanced at Zara who'd moved around to flank him from behind. "Okay... okay." He let his pistol roll back on his trigger finger, barrel up and no longer aimed at anyone. "You're making a mistake."

Other children in the crowd stared on with mixed expressions of worry and terror. A scrawny six-ish girl with brown hair, barefoot in a child's tee shirt and jeans, hid half behind a boy of about seventeen, also in a white tee with blue jeans. Near the white-haired man, a maybe ten-year-old girl with deep brown skin and puffy hair held the hand of an equally dark boy a little older. Both of them stared at the possibly-infected girl with fear in their eyes.

A Hispanic boy, perhaps thirteen, with a dense mop of black hair, hung back and faced away as though he didn't want to watch. Tris' arrival had apparently gotten his attention; he shifted enough to stare at her. He didn't resemble anyone here enough to suggest family. Arms crossed, he glared at nothing in particular.

"You made it!" shouted a blonde blue-eyed woman in olive-drab fatigues and a camouflage shirt too big for her, who could've been anywhere between seventeen and twenty-five; Tris recognized the voice from the radio. Cassie, bedecked in a vest full of small tools and a liberal helping of dirt smeared everywhere, jogged over. "Warren... please calm down. Abby's only got a cold."

"Yeah..." Warren scowled. "And so did Jason, and Patrick, and Rachel and—"

"Enough," said the green-armored black man. He grumbled with a slight shake of the head. His tone carried enough military to quiet the room, even Abby who ceased sobbing into her father's shirt. "I don't know how you got in here, stranger, but I'd appreciate you standing down."

Tris lowered her Beretta a little. "I walk in on a scene like that, you're lucky I didn't shoot first. What the f—hell were you doing to that child?"

"These fools think she's bit." The girl's father glared at Warren as if trying to stop the man's heart with his eyes. "My daughter's got a cold. That's all."

Abby squirmed around behind her father, peering at Warren with huge brown eyes.

Warren's gun emitted a faint *snap* as he clicked the safety on and slipped it into a black nylon holster under his left arm. "This is stupid. She's going to kill us all. Is that how you want to die? Mindless?"

Abby whimpered something unintelligible into her father's back.

Tris approached the girl. As soon as she crossed into the light, most of the people gasped. She beckoned Abby out from behind her father. "Hi, sweetie."

"Hi." The girl sounded stuffy when not screaming. She coughed, but put a hand over her mouth.

"May I?" Tris reached toward her head.

Abby nodded.

Tris gingerly prodded the girl's eyes open a little wider one after the next. "Can I see your throat? Have you gotten any unknown blood on your skin?" She'd gotten a look at the child's soles during the 'exam,' and hadn't seen any wounds there.

"No." The girl obliged. Nothing looked overtly wrong, though she had a runny nose.

"I don't think this girl's got *the* Virus." Tris faced Warren. "Even if she did, and I think it's unlikely, the Virus is not an aerosolized contagion except the stage one solution released from the drone. Once it's in a person's system, it mutates. The form that attacks the central nervous system is only transmissible via bodily fluids."

"Are you a doctor, lady?" asked the tiny pale girl. She pulled a lock of brown hair out of her eyes, appearing a little less afraid of Abby.

"Isla, stay back." The teenaged boy she'd been clinging to tugged her close.

Tris advanced on Warren, winding up under the light again, which made her hair appear almost phosphorescent.

"You expect me ta believe all that?" Warren scowled. "It's a bad situation, but she's already dead. Only a fool lets sentiment kill people. How you know all 'bout this stuff anyway?"

"You're Enclave." Another man with a shock of grey in the front of a flattop afro emerged from a shadow between two shelves. While not elderly, he looked old enough to be Kevin's father. He also wore the green armor, but his bore the scars of combat. Though he had a pistol on his belt, he made no move to grab it.

"I was. It's a long story, but I'm not part of that anymore. I'm from a roadhouse by Rawlins, Wyoming. My name is Tris, and my friend is Zara."

"She came here to get us out!" yelled Cassie. "I *told* you I got someone on the radio. Please, can everyone relax?"

"Y-you've got a vehicle that works?" asked a woman in her early fifties with darkish skin and amber eyes. She couldn't look right at Abby, a hint of guilt on her face. "We should get out of here before they find a way in."

"We ain't going anywhere with a ticking god damned time bomb."

Warren gestured at Abby, who let off an *eep* and jumped behind her father.

Her father mumbled in Spanish; whatever he said got a wide-eyed look of 'oh, daaaamn' from the thirteen-year-old boy in the back. After spitting, the man thrust his finger at Warren like a dagger. "Anything happens to my daughter and you're gonna be wearin' your fuckin' testicles for a necktie."

"How long?" asked the older armored man, eyeing Tris. "Before she turns."

Tris stared into Abby's terrified eyes, thinking back to Sang's story of being unable to kill his son... and half a settlement getting wiped out because of it. *Sang's boy had bite marks... this kid doesn't.* She clenched her fists. *It's gotta be a cold.* "She doesn't have Virus, but if she did... a healthy adult man would last about two weeks before they lose all higher brain function. It varies on health, size, and degree of exposure." She sighed. "This girl is ten or eleven, underweight, barely clothed, and filthy. If she had Virus, she'd probably be gone in a week at most."

Warren's face scrunched up like he'd bitten a lemon. "Couple more days. No one's goin' anywhere 'til then."

The older woman, the white haired man, and the teenaged boy with the little sister started to raise their voices in protest, but the older of the two dark-skinned men with armor silenced them.

"We've been in here for twenty-six days. If the Infected haven't found a way in by now, they won't. There's enough rations to make it out to two months, so unless you all prefer we play it safe and shoot her right now, we wait."

"Sergeant Ellis is right," said the younger man in armor. "Right now, half of you wanna kill the girl out of fear; half of you are horrified at the thought. One thing we do *not* need is animosity brewing internally. That *will* get people killed if we try to make a run for it."

The young black girl and the boy holding her hand approached Zara, wide-eyed with curiosity. Her 'don't mess with me' glare softened, and she spoke with them in quiet tones, answering questions about her fancy armor and why she had black hair if she'd come from the Enclave too.

Warren got in Tris' face. "You ready to do what needs to be done if it comes to that?"

Tris cringed at a whimper from Abby. *I'm not sure I could...* "I..."

"If it comes down to that. I'll deal with it." Abby's father held up a hand grenade. "I ain't leavin' her. It'll be both of us going."

"It's too dangerous," said the thirteen-year-old boy. "Somebody gonna get sick from her and we all gonna die."

Somberness in his voice, quiet resignation of doom rather than hostility, kept the room in silence for a while. Awkward stares flew back and forth. A pale woman with black hair who'd been lurking among the shelves held a sour frown on Abby. She looked barely past twenty, with a physique almost as delicate as Tris'. Her black tank top, pants, and sneakers blended into the darkness, making her head and arms seem to float like a porcelain apparition.

The younger soldier made no secret of his distrust for Abby, while Sergeant Ellis betrayed nothing either way by his expression. Shuffling about, the man with wild white hair kept muttering "just a kid" and "not right" under his breath. He appeared to be the oldest person here. Tris put him in the 'we don't shoot her' camp.

Isla gripped and released the concrete floor with her toes while biting her lip. She appeared wary, but most of her fear had vanished. The teen Tris figured to be her brother also appeared none too fond of the idea of killing an eleven-year-old... at least not without concrete proof.

Cassie, as well as the older woman with amber eyes continued to glare at Warren.

The dark-skinned boy ran up to her. "Gramma, you gotta see this lady's armor. It's so thin!"

Sergeant Ellis held out a beckoning hand, and the ten-year-old girl walked to him. Army-style boots a few sizes too big for her galumphed over smooth concrete and throw rugs. After she put an arm around him, he cleared his throat. "Alright everyone. It's settled then. We'll spend a couple more days here until we know."

"What if the lady can't stay that long?" Isla looked up at Tris, worry radiating from bright green eyes. "Are we gonna die? Can you make ice with magic like the girl in the story?"

"Sorry, sweetie... no magic here." Tris shook her head. "I'm okay with waiting, but it's not necessary." She glared at Warren. "Abby's got a cold."

All the survivors except for Abby's father edged away when she coughed and spat up a glop of phlegm.

Warren twitched, close enough to pulling his gun that Tris leapt between them.

"No. I'll stay with her." She gestured at Zara. "We're vaccinated and can't get sick from the Virus."

The girl clinging to Sergeant Ellis mumbled something, only the word "Dad" clear enough to understand.

"My daughter's right," said Ellis. "Every minute we spend here is a roll of the dice."

The younger soldier raised a placating hand. "It's been three weeks, Mike. Another two or three days isn't the end of the world."

"We should go," said the willowy black-haired woman.

Warren glanced at the shadows. "Well. We either wait it out, leave her behind, or I deal with this right now."

"You wouldn't live long enough to get all six inches of gun out of the holster," said Zara. As if to prove her point, she pulled her scavenged Sig Sauer handgun so fast her arm seemed to disappear and reappear aimed at him.

Everyone gasped.

The dark skinned boy detached from his grandmother and ran back to Zara, adoration all over his face. "That's *so* cool! How did you do that?"

Warren's forehead reddened. He scowled at Tris.

"Don't give me that." She narrowed her eyes. "I drove across the god damned country to get you out of here. You're the one being unreasonable."

"I'm being cautious." He stared at Abby, vitriol melting to blank. "Too many already have died to soft hearts."

"People go crazy when they turn." The black-haired sprite strode out of the dark. "One minute she'll be all innocent and sniffling, next thing she's throwin' people around and gets six of us before we noticed she's turned in the middle of the night. Waiting is stupid."

The younger soldier pulled handcuffs off the back of his belt, and glanced at Tris. "You seem to know a lot about Infected. You reckon' one of 'em could break these?"

Abby recoiled from the sight of the restraints, whimpering a repeating loop of "please Daddy no" into her father's side.

Tris pondered shooting Warren for a second, but sighed. "Infected, an adult man could snap them like a toy. Probably a smaller woman too. I…" *Hope I never, ever, see a child Infected.* Knowing that it had to have happened somewhere already made her want to throw up, but she kept her face stoic. "Given her size, I'm tempted to say no… But even if she could, it wouldn't be easy and someone watching her would have plenty of time to react."

"All right." Ellis looked down for a moment. "Abby, I'm sorry, but it's better than letting him kill you. Emilio, please take her to the supervisor's office. We'll give it a couple days."

Abby, sniveling, offered little protest as her father led her by the hand to a small room built in the innermost corner of the basement. A large window next to a door looked in on a desk and a steel-framed bed. Zack, the younger soldier, fell in step behind them.

"I'm not gonna leave you," whispered Emilio.

Tris followed, taking Abby's other hand. "That goes for me, too."

27

JUST WALK IN

Kevin guided the Challenger along the narrow two-lane highway marked as NM-15 on his paper map. Ridges of varying height between a few inches and taller than the roof passed on either side beneath a sparsity of pine trees and scrub. Head-sized rocks scattered on the road forced him to swerve every now and then. He slowed as a rust-colored building came into view on the left. A four-columned porch fronted half of a building with two huge garage doors on the right side, giving it the look of an old west saloon married to an auto shop.

The dinky, bullet-riddled sign at the end of a gravel drive marked it as the Pinos Altos Volunteer Fire Department. He chuckled at the thought of other drivers who'd been confused, thinking 'fire departments' were pre-war services to start fires. Knowledge of what they'd really done led him back to the TV shows he'd watched on a battered laptop in his adoptive parents' trailer. Whenever he found a DVD as part of a scavenge, he'd take it back to Wayne's. *Hah. Guess the security computer was good for something after all. I'd find those historical documentaries all over.* He sighed. He'd meant to think 'old movies,' but the phrase leapt out. Those words put Tris at the forefront of his thoughts, and made him feel all the more an idiot.

"I should've gone with her."

A small farm property passed on the right, where a metal fence surrounded two horses on a field opposite a battered building with a slanted orange roof. On the left, a handful of long-dead cars rusted further into oblivion in a wide field of open dirt.

He drove past another house on the right and a huge barn-shaped building on the left with a piece of ancient sign advertising coffee. Nine e-bikes clustered out front, steel horses crowded up on a feeding post full of electrical outlets. It had a roof full of solar panels, and a room full of people. Down the curving road to the right, lay the spread of a normal-looking settlement. People, even a few children, walked and ran about. Their clothing provided the only indication war had ever happened here: all of it handmade from prewar scraps or animal hide. Few wore shoes, and the ones who did had moccasins or sandals. One boy about five even had on a pink dress. Scavengers couldn't be choosy.

The place struck him as a less-militarized version of Nederland. *Of course. I'm out in the middle of East Bumblefuck.* Two men, a woman, and four little kids stopped, staring at the two cars in the road. Grumbling, he pulled left into the gravel by the not-Roadhouse. A couple guys wearing Redeemed leather cuts gave him the eye from inside, though they radiated more of an air of curiosity than hostility.

Fitch and Neeley hopped out of the Behemoth and approached his door, boots crunching. Kevin shut down the car.

"Well, this just keeps getting weirder and weirder." He pushed the door open and got to his feet, gazing around. "It ain't what I was expectin'."

"Run o' the mill settlement." Fitch gathered a mass of saliva and spat it to the side. "Can't say I'd expected it either. Figured on a camp fulla bikers."

Kevin shut the door before wandering over to the others, still twisting left and right to take in the scenery.

Neeley craned his neck, peering at the cluster of dusty, barefoot children observing the newcomers from behind a small row of trees about thirty yards from the end of the building. "What them 'Deemed doin' here? Figger them raidin'?"

"Don't think so." Kevin sent a wary smile at the kids before looking at Neeley. "Locals don't seem scared of them." He sighed. "Something tells me this whole trip's been a giant bag of fuck."

Fitch chuckled.

Grumbling, Kevin headed inside. He didn't wait for the proverbial scratch of the record needle or much look around to see if anyone glared at him. A bit of chainsaw surgery on the back wall had expanded the pre-war building to a room big enough to hold a dozen or so tables and a bar counter.

Behind said bar stood an oddly proportioned man too wide at the shoulders, with a long face on a head two sizes too small for the body it sat on. Small, close eyes regarded Kevin from above a nose so large it verged on cartoonish, with a bulbous tip.

Kevin sidled up to the bar, discovering the man's head not to be unusually small, but normal upon a ridiculous body. Bicep-to-bicep, the bartender, who also wore a Redeemed cut, was almost as wide as two of him standing abreast. He cracked a wiseass grin. "Well, shit. I've heard rumors about radiation mutations, but I thought it was just too much moonshine."

"You're a funny man for such a little one."

The bartender not smashing his face in must have been a signal; most of the Redeemed in the place chuckled.

Kevin eyed the stitching on the man's cut, which read 'Praetor.' An appraising frown formed for a second. "So, Praetor, huh? That mean you're in charge?"

"Used ta be. Decided to retire. You got a lot o' questions."

"Yep. See, I tend to not take it all that well when someone I consider family gets shot to death inside his own roadhouse."

"Hey, bounty boy," yelled a weathered-looking man with a huge moustache connected to his sideburns by way of a goatee. "Your dick ain't big enough for this poon. Go find another tree to piss on."

"Best listen ta Anvil there, friend." Praetor leaned his weight into his knuckles on the bar, a gesture that gave him a simian presence. "Be a right shame ta get blood on my nice new floor."

Kevin glanced down between his boots. Dark blotches, petrified bubble gum, gouges, stepped-on shell casings... and bloodstains. "Hate to see the old shitty floor then."

Praetor growled, the corner of his lip curling up.

"Look." Kevin kept his disarming smile on, hands raised. He glanced at Neeley, who shook his head to the negative. "I don't got issues with anyone here. Nine men wearin' your colors walked into the Roadhouse in Hagerman and killed the proprietor. Five got out, two leaking. I ain't here to collect a bounty. I'm here ta have a few words with a couple of cowards who ambushed an old man in his home."

Redeemed around the tables muttered, stared, and fidgeted. The tone in the air changed from humor to mild hostility to overt anger. Eleven men and three women all gave him the 'go ahead, try something' stare.

"Oh." Kevin smiled. "And how much for a charge?"

WAITING, WATCHING

Aband of light swept over the darkness above Tris. She floated in endless nothingness, unable to perceive any sense of her body. No sound, no sight, no sense of anything reached her skin. Minutes later, another source of light passed from her head to her feet and disappeared. Another flash only a minute later, and another seconds after that. The pulsing light took on a reddish hue; she tried to peer out at the world through her eyelids.

Cloth scratched her skin and tightness manifested around her wrists and ankles. Her world wobbled and bounced with the clatter of gurney wheels. Bound hand and foot to a stretcher, she lost herself to a momentary panic. She screamed, but her voice projected only in her thoughts.

I can't move.

She tried to struggle against the straps, but her body didn't even twitch. Stony limbs refused to yield even a millimeter. She couldn't open her eyelids or even make her lip curl. Inertia leaned her to one side; a shift in the passing lights signaled a turn. For a terrifying eternity, Tris searched for any shred of willpower to let her overcome whatever force kept her as still as a corpse. *They gave me something to paralyze me... gave me what... who's they?*

Everything stopped moving. The light above remained steady. Male voices murmured in calm discussion before the sound of a metal door closing with a *thunk* echoed many times louder than it ought to have.

A hand pressed down on her chest, near her collarbone. She tried to gasp, twitch, react, or scream, but her body may as well have been made of stone.

"Hey, there, sweet little thing," whispered a voice close enough to puff her hair.

The sound infiltrated her skull, as sickening as a mucous covered tongue sliding into her ear.

Ripping Velcro. Cold air on her chest. A hand slid under the fabric of her Enclave jumpsuit and cradled her breast, squeezing and fondling. After a moment, he stopped. Tris tried to cry, but her body refused to obey.

Straps around her wrists released. The man she could not see pulled her by the arms into a seated position long enough to work the jumpsuit off her upper body before he let her flop down. Cloth slipped around her buttocks, down the backs of her legs. The restraints securing her ankles loosened one after the next.

Run. Get up. Move! Tris screamed again, but not one sign of life entered the waking world.

Small, metal, cold, slid up her chest. *Snip.* The icy tool glided down her stomach, under the waistband of her panties. *Snip.*

Naked.

Paralyzed.

Helpless.

"Oh, you are a lovely thing." A warm hand brushed down her stomach to the inside of her thigh. "It's just you and me now, baby." Fingertips teased at her womanhood while another hand slid up and down her thigh. "How 'bout we have a little fun before you go in?"

The slime of his whisper returned and slithered in deeper, winding about her brain. Tris wanted to convulse, bile already sliding up her throat. Dread that she'd drown in her own vomit because she couldn't move piled onto her fear of being assaulted, pushing her heart to near exploding.

"Yeah, I know what you mean." More Velcro ripped. "I can't wait either."

Clunk.

"Shit," whispered the man close to her. He fumbled amid the rustle of cloth.

A louder, but unintelligible male voice warbled in the distance. The gurney jostled. Her sense that a man hovered too close faded. The rush of the blood in her veins roared in her skull. At any minute, he could return... and her muscles still refused to even twitch.

Is... this real? Did this happen? Her mental voice gasped as if out of breath. *Nightmare... Memory?*

Hands tightened around her biceps, pulling her upright. An arm hooked under the backs of her knees. After an instant of floating, she plunged headfirst into frigid goop.

And woke up screaming.

Tris sat upright upon a foam mattress in an octagonal white room with a gloss black floor and ceiling. A bland grey blanket wrapped around her except for one bare foot poking out from the bottom. She reached down to discover her old Enclave jumpsuit, and doubled over with relief.

For a while, she sat in a shivering ball, staring at this eight-walled room with no visible door. She couldn't remember being molested except for a slice of what could've been a nightmare... but where could that possibly have come from? Never in her life had she ever imagined a man capable of doing something like that to a helpless woman until those bandits had captured her within days of 'escaping' the Enclave. If the attack had been real and not some wild nightmare, someone had interrupted him. The memory at once seemed genuine enough to leave her ready to throw up, yet at the same time so implausible it could've been imagined.

"The Wildlands..."

She stared at her wrist, somehow expecting to see rope burns. Pure white. Soft. Unharmed. Again, she sat in her Detention cell. Had it all been a dream? Kevin? The Roadhouse? Wayne? All of it? Were *any* of them real? Eyes closed, she pictured Kevin's face, imagined his scent. An argument in a dead airplane... him storming off, her breaking down in sobs. The pure elation when he came back for her.

"No... that wasn't a dream. This is."

Tris slipped out from under the blanket, finding the floor icy. Aside from a rippling sensation of stiffness crawling up her back, she didn't react to the cold. Past the little table with the e-learn terminal, she approached a small sink and stared at herself in the mirror. Snowy hair foofed about her head, her terrified, confused expression making her look like an overly tall ten-year-old.

The sapphire eyes in her reflection imploded to complete blackness, fragments of their surface shattering inward like the glass windows of a spacecraft drawn into infinity.

She recoiled with a startled yelp, staring at the wall. The floor. She turned. The other wall looked as plain as the last, only a faint high-tech pattern that repeated on each of the eight identical sections. The cell had no toilet.

Tris approached a clear patch of floor where instinct told her she would've gone to relieve herself, but emptiness offered no respite. She sank into a ball on the floor; leaning against the wall.

"No toilet."

She rocked back and forth hugging her legs.

"There's no toilet."

The third time she tried to speak, frigid liquid with the consistency of syrup came out of her mouth.

Tris shot upright, waking from the dream within a dream. She found herself sitting on the floor, a ratty sleeping bag between her ass and concrete. Bare cinder block walls surrounded a small office. A few feet away, a too-thin eleven-year-old girl lay on a bed, covered to the chin in an olive-drab army blanket. Her right arm extended over her head, linked to the metal frame by a pair of black handcuffs. Red marks on her skin showed her discontent at being tethered.

Abby... Amarillo. Oh, shit.

"Morning," said the man seated on a folding chair by the bed.

A weak memory of conversation with a furious father after the younger soldier handcuffed Abby returned. She pointed at him. "You're... Emilio."

"Yes. Guess everyone has demons."

She quirked an eyebrow at him.

"What you were muttering in your sleep." Emilio chuckled with a sad smile. "Hope it's bad dreams and not worse memories."

"Thanks," muttered Tris. "I'm not really sure."

Abby coughed. She tried to cover her mouth with her tethered hand before using her left. She sniffled, coughed again, and gave Tris the most heart-rending stare while trying to squirm her arm free. "Where is your friend?"

She's got one hell of a head cold... poor kid. The heaviness of interrupted rest seeped out of her brain like water from a sponge. Bits of the hour or so leading up to attempting a nap returned. "Zara's scouting the best way to get everyone back to the van, memorizing the shortest route and a couple backups. She's making sure the van's okay, too."

"Oh." Abby pushed the blanket down to her chest and fanned herself. "I'm hot now. Why are you talking about a toilet?"

Tris stretched, rubbed her face, and put her shoes back on. "I was having a nightmare. I had to go really bad and I was stuck in a room without a toilet."

"That's a bad nightmare." She turned to her left. "Dad, when I gotta go, are they gonna untie me? What did I do? Am I in trouble?"

Emilio's face darkened. "Bad shit's gonna happen if they don't. You gotta go, hon?"

"Not yet." She coughed again and struggled to get her face over the edge of the bed before spitting up another glob. "Eww."

"She needs to drink more water," said Tris. "All that sweating could lead to dehydration, plus water helps flush the toxins out."

"Is that…?" asked Emilio.

"No. That's phlegm." Tris walked over and sat next to Abby. "The bad virus doesn't produce such a heavy sinus and throat problem. It causes fatigue and lethargy in the early stages, often with headache and photophobia."

Abby scrunched up her face. "It makes you afraid of pictures?"

Tris laughed before she realized it. "No, sweetie. It makes people not want to be around bright light."

"I'm scared." Abby tugged at the cuffs. "If the sick people break in, I won't be able to get away."

Emilio looked about ready to kill someone, clenching his hands into fists atop his knees and releasing them in a repetitive cycle.

The girl's fearful breathing carried a mucous-laden wheeze. Tris put a hand on her forehead, finding her hot to the touch but not so much she got worried.

"Please tell Warren I'm not a zombie." Abby grabbed Tris' arm with her free hand. "It's just a cold, I swear. I didn't get bit. I didn't touch blood. We've been in this basement for weeks and it's cold down here."

Tris mentally wandered the kitchen in the Roadhouse HQ. Soldiers shooting each other before any had turned. She wondered if one of them had merely sneezed and set off a shitstorm. "I believe you." *Please.* She sighed in her head. *I gotta keep her mind off it.* "Can you tell me about the people here? I need to know what we're dealing with so we can get out safe."

Abby scooted back to sit up. Hours ago, she'd introduced herself as Abby Padilla. Sweat beaded on her forehead, and her large brown eyes radiated fear, making her seem even younger. The child's cream-colored dress had a myriad of stains, dirt, sauces, and dried snot all over it. Tris stared at the girl's spindly legs, feeling guilty for having had access to decent food.

Her father dabbed at her forehead with a rag, muttering in Spanish, probably cursing Warren.

"Do you want to check me for bites again?" Abby blushed. "Is that why you're looking at me like that?"

"No… I… You're so thin."

Abby stuck out her tongue. "Look who's talking. You barely have boobs."

"Abby!" said Emilio. "That's rude."

Tris smiled. "It wasn't right what they did to you. One of the women should've examined you in private, and it's just the way I'm slouching." She sat tall for a second to show off her 'peaches' as Kevin called them. The thought of the term sparked a twinge of worry. *Please don't be an idiot. He's going to walk into a damned room full of those primitives and say something stupid.*

"Warren." Emilio said the name like a curse. "My daughter's always been shy and quiet. He figured she'd refuse, and he'd have shot her while saying she wanted to hide a bite wound."

Abby shivered. "Warren was an asshole before the zombies came, too."

Technically they're not zom—whatever. She's eleven. "Why does he hate you so much?"

"I dunno." Abby turned away to sneeze four times. A gout of snot dangled from her nose. Again, she tried to wipe it with her right hand, which stopped short with a *clink* of handcuffs. Snarling, Abby yanked at the chain, muttering curses in Spanish.

Emilio wiped her face. She grabbed the cloth and blew her nose, which triggered more coughing. When she looked up again, her eyes were red and puffy. Tris hoped it a sign she had a run of the mill cold. The Virus didn't normally cause those symptoms, but that drone might've been testing something new.

The mere thought of it made her stomach feel like a lead weight.

Abby gazed down into her lap, murmuring in a soft voice. "A lot of people are dead. I guess he's just being real careful."

Emilio scowled. He had to be in his early thirties. Zara's comment about him being 'cute' set off a small argument about age. Of course, the woman threw in her face Kevin being three years shy of thirty and her claiming to be eighteen... then mocked her nutty conspiracy theory that time stopped passing while in Detention. Tris figured herself twenty. Seven years younger wasn't too bad. A twelve or thirteen year gap would've been creepier, though Emilio's devotion to his daughter and utter lack of ogling at either of the women inclined her to trust him.

"Isla and her brother Tom used to like me before I got sick." Abby dabbed at her nose with the rag. "She has real bad nightmares. Their parents died right away when the sickness started."

"They were some of the first to turn," whispered Emilio. He muttered something in Spanish and blessed himself. "It all happened so fast. Half of us ran straight from our beds in the middle of the night."

"I forgot my shoes." Abby flexed her toes under the blanket. "Daddy dragged me out the door before I even woke up all the way."

Emilio chuckled. "Couple of bullets came through the wall. We didn't have time for anything but haulin' ass."

"Zack and Mr. Ellis are from the army. They shot a bunch of people trying to keep us safe, but they weren't really people anymore, were they?" Abby leaned close to her chained wrist so she could get both hands over her mouth before she sneezed again. Clear snot oozed between her fingers.

"Yes. When the Virus gets to the point where it makes people violent, the person they were is gone forever." Tris sighed.

Emilio patted his daughter's back. With Abby looking down at the mattress, he gave Tris a pleading stare, as if she had the ability to grant his wish... that his girl wasn't going to die. "Is she?"

Tris tried to project confidence at him. "Everything I've seen says no..."

"But..." Emilio hung his head, staring at the grenade in his hand. "It's not your burden. If that's what's going to happen, I'll deal with it."

Abby sat up, strands of snot connecting her fingers to her nose, which Emilio spent a moment wiping. "Ugh. This sucks. I hate being sick, and can we please stop talking about killing me?"

"You should eat something," said Emilio.

"I'm not hungry." She squinted at Tris. "No comments from the peanut gallery, Miss Skinny."

Tris grinned. "That's good, actually." Her heart fluttered with hope. "Pre-Infected are ravenous."

Emilio sniffled, pocketed the grenade, and lapsed into Spanish muttering again.

Abby struggled to breathe for a moment before swallowing something and gasping for air. "Kristen's a whore."

"Abby!" yelled Emilio.

"What?" Abby blinked at him. "She was..." The girl looked toward Tris. "She used to work at the bar, sleeping with men who paid her. She's pretty, but she's not pretty inside. Selfish. She wants outta here, no matter what she has to do."

They sat in silence for a little while, Abby swishing her feet back and forth.

"Is this enough to convince them?" asked Emilio. "You said if she was... she'd be hungry?"

"I don't think that Warren guy is going to believe anything that doesn't conform to his preconceptions." *Probably going to wind up shooting him. I should just do it right now and save everyone the trouble of waiting.* She grumbled in her head. *I can't just kill a man in cold blood.*

Abby's teeth chattered. Her skin had dried off, and the little color she'd gotten back had faded again. Tris pulled the blanket up over her to the neck, and felt her temperature: clammy.

The girl drew her legs in close, shivering. "Cassie's pretty cool. She used to fix stuff and work on radios and crap in the panel house. Now she's bored. She kept sneaking out to the radio. Warren almost shot her too."

"He's an idiot," muttered Emilio.

"Cassie is why I'm here." Tris smiled. "I heard her on the radio."

"Lloyd... uhh, Mister Black is kinda strange, but he's funny. He said he used to teach at a college. He tells stories about talking rabbits sometimes, and a duck made of taffy." Abby tried to laugh, but it turned into a coughing fit that made her face red. When it subsided, she glared at the ceiling, exasperated. "Ugh, I hate this *so* much! Being sick sucks!" Her anger faded to worry. "I don't wanna get shot."

Tris held the girl's bound hand. "I'm not going to let anyone shoot you, Abby."

"Lauren's nice too," said Abby in a monotone, a phlegmatic wheeze in her voice. "She's the older lady. Micah's grandmom. She used to cook all sorts of stuff. When I first started sniffling, she's the only one other than Dad who told Warren to go screw himself."

The dark-skinned girl with frizzy hair peered in. She stared at Abby for about a minute before shuffling away without a sound.

"That's Trisha." Abby shivered. "She used to be my friend, but she's been... I dunno. Weird."

"Her mother became Infected. Luiz had to put a bullet in the woman right in front of her." Emilio grumbled. "Where did this come from? We had a wall. We had security."

Tris stared at Abby's hand, stroking her fingers over the back above the knuckle. The child smiled at the comforting touch. "I found an Enclave drone on the way in, crashed on a rooftop. *Why* is a harder question, other than them wanting to wipe everyone out because they think people who live out here are all savages with radiation-damaged DNA. Amarillo had a reputation for being powerful, with a great army that they might've considered a serious threat, but they're too cowardly to come out all this way to see. That... or Nathan was trying to get to me."

"This can't be *your* fault," said Abby. "You're nice."

"Thanks... but Nathan isn't. He's the reason I'm not in the Enclave anymore. I was arrested because I refused to marry this guy they chose for me." Abby gasped. "Nathan acted like a friend and helped me escape, but he really wanted me to take a bomb to kill some people." Tris patted her belly. "He put a bomb inside me. Tiny, but powerful enough to kill me and everyone within fifty yards. A friend..." She bit her lip. "The man I love..." Abby's eyes gleamed. "Cut me open and threw it. I got away alive and Nathan's the kind of bastard who can't let that go."

"So you think this guy attacked us somehow because of you?" Emilio raised an eyebrow.

"Kevin bought into the Roadhouse about seven months ago. Nathan probably found out... that's why I never used my name on the radio. If he thought he could get to me somehow by destroying Amarillo... I dunno. It's so crazy it's almost egotistical to think that he'd go to that much trouble for me."

"What kinda person could do this to us?" Abby gawked. "We didn't do anything to them!"

"Someone who isn't human." Tris scowled.

Abby broke out in a sudden sweat and shed the blanket. She flapped her dress against her chest to cool off. Micah, the twelve-ish boy, appeared in the doorway holding a tin can with steam wafting from it. Strong light in the outer area reduced him to a silhouette.

"Get outta there," yelled Warren, somewhere behind him. "You'll get your ass sick too."

The boy twisted, a sheen of deep brown appeared along the edge of his profile as the light wrapped around his face. "Sh'aint one 'o them things, Warren. She's got a damn cold like Gramma says. You's just bein' a shit to her."

"Dammit, boy," yelled Warren. A chair slid.

"One more step," yelled Lauren. "See what happens."

"You're all insane." Warren's grumbling faded into quiet.

Micah walked up to the foot end of the bed. He looked at Tris. "You said even if she got the bad sick, it ain't gonna breathe in, right?"

Tris nodded. The scent of baked beans reached her nose.

The boy offered Abby the can.

She jerked at her chained arm and scowled. "Please let me out."

Emilio took the can. He held it between his knees, staring down into it, muttering under his breath how everyone needed to feel safe she wouldn't hurt them. He seemed to be trying to convince himself not to go attack Warren more than comforting Abby. Micah hung his head and trudged back into the basement.

Abby showed little interest in the beans, but tolerated being fed like a baby by her father. Tris took the opportunity to hunt down a toilet. The survivors sat in clusters here and there around beds, sleeping bags, and shelves. Ellis and Zack wandered at the edges of the room where tiny rectangular windows sat at street level. Lauren sat on a folding chair facing a cot, upon which Isla, Micah, and Trisha sprawled, listening to a story. Jose kept to himself in the south end nearest the stairwell leading up. The thirteen-year-old had an M-16 as well as no apparent concern if he survived. He caught Tris looking at him and shot back a stare of 'whatever' before facing away.

She sighed.

Warren and Lloyd argued at the distant northeast corner, next to a pair of shelves loaded with toolboxes and unidentifiable mechanical parts. The old man tried to convince Warren that waiting was a horrible idea, and bringing Abby along in her current state was less of a risk than sitting around. A glint in the somewhat younger man's eyes gave away a hint of paranoia beyond reason. Tris tightened her jaw. *That guy is going to be a problem. Zara, where are you?*

To the left of the supervisor's office, a small, primitive bathroom looked (and smelled) as if it had been supporting twenty people for weeks. She gagged but did what she had to do before returning to the office.

Abby started cringing away and turning green about halfway through the portion of baked beans, at which point Emilio ate some. Tris caught a glimpse of a sliced sausage in the brown ooze as she took a seat on the edge of the bed. The girl held her gut with her left hand, looking like she'd throw up at any minute. She begged Tris to free her from the handcuffs with her eyes, before slumping, forlorn. Tris spent the next half hour or so staring at the floor, debating the ethics of shooting Warren in the head. She glanced at her shoe while considering picking the lock on the cuffs… but if these people panicked, multiple children could get hurt in the chaos.

"Shit, shit, shit!" yelled a woman's voice too far away to recognize. At the distance, it could've been Cassie or Kristen. "One got inside!"

Abby rolled onto her knees, thrashing at the cuffs while twisting her arm. "*¡No quiero morir!* Let me out! Please! *¡Dios mio!* I'm gonna die!" She burst into wailing tears, her right hand turning red. "Daddy, please!"

A gunshot echoed outside.

The child closed her eyes and screamed her lungs empty while trying unsuccessfully to pull her hand free. Terror got the better of her and she kept jerking at her arm as if one more tug might just break the chain if she pulled a little harder.

"Warren's a god damned dead man." Emilio leapt up, drew his gun, and stomped out. "Warren, *puta madre cabrón!* Key. Now!"

"Dad! No!" Abby tried to grab him, but the cuff jerked her to a halt before she could reach him. "Don't leave me!"

Tris got up and moved to follow, but the girl got her by the arm, clawing for a frantic grip on her shirt.

"Tris, please." Snot and tears gushed down her face, some running into her mouth. She coughed a little. "Please don't leave me alone. If they find me, I'm gonna die!"

"West side!" shouted Ellis. "Zack, Tom, get your asses over there."

A ripple of small arms fire preceded a *boom* that could only be a shotgun.

"Got one," yelled Lloyd.

Abby shrieked and threw her free arm around Tris, bawling.

"I won't leave you." Tris shoved Abby behind her and grabbed her AK-47 from the floor by where she'd napped. She one armed it, flicked the safety off, and aimed at the room's only entrance.

The cuffs kept clattering on the steel bedframe, mixed with Abby's determined grunts and panicked gasps. Pattering tiny footsteps approached; Isla appeared in the doorway. She stopped short and likely came close to wetting her pants, her already pale face blanching deathly white at the sight of Tris's rifle pointing at her head.

Tris lifted the weapon away from her. "Sorry, sweetie."

Isla darted in and crawled under the bed without making a sound.

Tris directed Abby's death grip to her belt and got both hands on the AK. She trained it at the door, her nerves fraying at random pops of gunfire and screaming outside. Emilio shouted somewhere in the din. *They're going to shoot each other instead of the Infected.* Tris took a step forward, but stopped at Abby desperately pulling at her while rattling the cuffs.

Micah ran into view some twenty feet away from the door, aiming a handgun in a two-fisted grip. The boy hesitated for a second before muzzle flare lit his face from a single shot. He grinned, yelled, "got one!", and darted out of sight.

"I don't wanna die," whined Abby. She tried to stand on the cot, stuck in a stoop with her right arm chained to the bedframe. "Please don't leave me like this."

The chaos outside was too loud and too frenetic to bother shouting over. Tris glanced out of the corner of her eye at the trembling girl behind her, and down at two pale feet sticking out from under the bed below a tangle of frayed blankets. For a second, she considered shooting the chain or going for her picks, but worried the instant the rifle stopped pointing at the door, the onrushing horde would arrive. With her AK, she literally held two children's lives in her hands.

"I got you, Abby. You too, Isla. I won't let anything get past me."

She squeezed the handle of the AK, glaring over the gunsights. *Come on you fuckers. I dare you to try and get in here.*

KOMODO

Praetor blinked his beady little too-close eyes at Kevin, twice. "Boy, you got some set of balls on you. I can respect that." He patted the counter twice. "Two coins, or an interesting trade if you got anything."

Kevin put four coins out. "Two cars."

"G'won and plug in then." Praetor chuckled. "F'you get your ass perforated, that car of yours is mine."

"Be a shame to waste it as a display piece." Kevin looked him up and down. "I don't think you'd be able to fit in it."

The room chuckled.

"Well now, we might as well hurry up and get your ass kicked." A woman with mocha skin and large almond shaped eyes emerged from the crowd, smiling at him. Hair sprayed wild from her head in an explosion of jet as wide as her shoulders. Her large tattered white shirt hung halfway down her thigh, leaving one shoulder exposed. "If you're plannin' on doing anything other than gettin' turned into road kill, follow me."

Fitch checked her out, smiling.

"Easy there old man. You're old 'nuff ta be my Pa." The woman winked. "Dip that thing in some cold water before you pass out."

Kevin couldn't help himself but stare at her tight leather leggings as she passed by on her way to the door. He paused outside only long enough to connect the charge cable to a post-mounted socket before following her down the street. The kids had run off out of sight, though the sounds of them playing still echoed in the trees. A few adults lingered in view, evidently curious at the outcome of what would happen inside Praetor's place.

"I'm Phoenix," said the woman without turning back to look.

Kevin glanced at three houses on the right that could've been lifted from any normal settlement, not one infested with a homicidal biker club that'd declared war on the Roadhouse. "That where you got conceived or do you have a habit of coming back from the dead?"

"Maybe a bit of both, smart man." She added a sashay to her stride that rattled the pistols on her hips. "Don't get the wrong idea here. I'm taken. This ain't no offer but trying to keep my favorite bar from getting shot up."

He debated saying he hadn't been interested, but that might piss her off. What was it about some women…? He considered mentioning he was taken too, but she didn't need to know that. In the end, he enjoyed the view of a fine, undulating, leather-wrapped ass for a little over two minutes as they walked into the heart of Pinos Altos. How utterly like a settlement this place looked confused him. Houses, families, farm animals… What on Earth was a biker gang doing here? Most bizarre of all, the people didn't have that air about them to suggest their town had been taken over against their will.

Phoenix headed for a large wooden building, more of a log cabin, which had likely been hand-built within the past ten years. At least twenty e-bikes of various size and condition lined up in front of it with a gap by a two-step stairway. A pair of black flags hung from the porch roof, bearing hand-painted renditions of the Redeemed logo—the white circle with the fist clamped around a sword by the blade.

To the left of the structure stood a lot with several tables full of parts and tools. Two had canvas canopies protecting electronic bits, motors and wiring systems. Around the workstations lay a sea of bike frames, tires, and a handful of almost-finished e-bikes that looked only a few screws short of being ready to drive.

Past the repair yard, a row of a ten or so small huts stood in a line with a number of Redeemed hanging out. Some drank, some slept in chairs, a few sucked face with women. *This* part of the city looked like what he'd expected. Had they rolled in on nothing but bikers, maybe he wouldn't have even gotten out of the car. Something like the scene where the Enclave man had been giving weapons to raiders played out in his head, with Redeemed falling under a hail of fire from the two M60 machineguns on his hood. He glanced back in the direction they'd come from. Speaking of which, he didn't feel comfortable leaving the car in the open.

"In here." Phoenix pushed open a plain wooden door covered in a haphazard layer of black paint that left smears of naked wood exposed near the edges.

He ducked the flags and followed the strange woman.

Dust flickered in trails of sunlight from small glassless windows around a single large room. The almost-warehouse had a second floor loft over the rightmost third, accessed by the bastard offspring of a staircase and a ladder. Seven or eight people up in the loft, at least three of them naked, lounged about on sofas and recliners.

Downstairs, a scattering of metal folding chairs in blue, beige and green surrounded a square dirt patch that reminded him of one old movie about kickboxing. Beyond that, twenty or so guys hovered at a pair of pool tables and a long folding table loaded with cases upon cases of prewar beer. The mere sight of fifty-year-old suds made him gag.

His gaze returned to Phoenix, but lingered on her ass for only a second before diverting to a large man in what he could only call a throne. While the man came nowhere near Praetor's degree of ridiculousness as size went, even sitting, his presence made Kevin feel small. Strong cheekbones, a patterned headband, dour expression, and a sharp nose conjured the image of an ancient Native American war chief about to pass judgment on an invader.

Phoenix draped herself on a fur-covered chair at his side, a simple C-shaped curve of wood covered in animal hides.

Kevin approached the man and nodded in greeting. He couldn't come up with a good reason to dislike him yet, and had about thirty or so good reasons not to start a gunfight arranged around the room, all watching him with intent curiosity. "Komodo."

The president of the Redeemed raised his eyebrows a notch at the sound of his name. "I am. Who are you that brings war to my doorstep?"

Here we go again. "I'd like to know why your people have declared war on the Roadhouse. I'm trying to understand why you think the Code doesn't apply to you, and I am here because some of your people killed a man I considered family."

Belt buckles and boots clattered on the loft, likely the overly casual getting dressed. A nude redhead woman grabbed pants from a man trying to put them on, grinning at him; they wrestled for a few seconds before he shoved her away, hard enough to send her over the edge, dangling by her grip on the loft. The others up top chuckled. She decided the two-foot drop easier than climbing, and walked as casually as if dressed back up the stairs to recline on a fur-covered couch next to a pile of clothes: judging by the size of the boots, hers.

Komodo regarded him for a painfully long moment, stroking a finger up and down over his lips. The man had to be into his mid-forties, nascent crow's feet and eye wrinkles marked his face, and he didn't show any of the rapid bloodlust he'd come to expect from bike marauders. "Your so-called Code is a sheep in the guise of the wolf. There is no stalking darkness pursing those who resist the thieves."

Kevin huffed, almost a chuckle. He brushed a thumb at the bottom of his nose. "Who told you that? Amarillo's got a standing army of almost two thousand. Someone breaks the Code, it's five thousand coins for a head. No one picks it up, they come looking themselves... and then it's painful."

The right corner of Komodo's mouth pulled up in a half grin. "So in the thrall of the Coyote are you that you cannot see the earth at your feet. Your Amarillo is gone."

Kevin stared at him. His mind raced over Tris' claim of Infected, no radio contact. No responses. *How could he possibly know...?*

"The truth of it shows in your eyes, boy." Komodo tapped his fingers on the armrests of his great chair. "Your thieves' dens have been cleansed, yet where are those who would chase the spoils of treachery? You are the only one to appear, and you walk a path of vengeance."

"I didn't come here about some bounty. Nine of your boys killed Wayne."

At the mention of the name, murmuring started among the Redeemed by the pool tables, and spread around the room.

Komodo offered a slight bow of the head. "All is not as we are led to believe. You are young, and so the world appears as it does to the young. The mists of time have not yet revealed the truth."

"What the shit did this guy smoke?" whispered Neeley from behind and left. "I want some."

"Wayne..." Komodo gazed up into the distance, as if seeing something only he could perceive. "The man you knew is not the man who was. A coyote becomes too old, and curls up beneath the protection of your code and its false shield."

"I'm serious," muttered Neeley. "I want some of that shit."

Kevin glared. "A guy could call Wayne a lot of things, but thief ain't one of them." His conviction faltered at the unwelcome memory of Tris telling him about the ledger. Could one of the Redeemed have been a former driver?

"When he was as young as you are, he made his company with a group who feed upon the efforts of others. Those who travel the land in great beasts of black, and prey upon any in their path. They raided settlements, including this one. Stealing, shooting, doing everything else men like that tend to do."

"Night Riders," said Phoenix, making finger guns with both hands.

Breath swelled up in Kevin's lungs, but he resisted the urge to yell 'bullshit.' He let anger simmer down to a low boil before letting words off his tongue. "There's no damned way in hell Wayne was ever part of that crew. For one thing, they're a bunch of psychopaths. Two, even if he had been... they don't let people leave."

Komodo raised an eyebrow. "And if two of their trucks depart on a mission of plunder, and one of the drivers betrays the other, how would the rest locate him before he has crawled deep within the smoke? You speak of unprovoked attacks. The Redeemed have avenged those who have been wronged. Your road houses, the ones we attacked, were all men like this who used the fear of Amarillo to hide from their sins. Now that we have learned the panther has no teeth, they must answer for what they have done."

"I don't know where you're gettin' this from, but it sounds like a load of manure." Kevin couldn't get the image of Wayne dead in his basement out of his mind. "They killed him like a dog. Your boys got into a beef over not wanting to pay for their food. *They* were the ones stealing. He had an android who saw the whole damn thing go down."

"This is beyond Wayne." Komodo raised his arm, turning his hand palm up. "Do you not see the harm they brought forth upon this land? *Ten thousand* coins to purchase their permission to operate. Their law permitted too few oases. How many innocent people who wanted nothing more than to make a living helping travelers were crushed by this Amarillo and their bounties?"

Kevin exhaled past gritted teeth. "That's got nothing to do with anything." Grief swirled around in his head; all the feelings of rage and loss he'd experienced at finding his mentor hit him at once.

"Oh, my friend." Komodo's voice, deep and silken, pervaded the room like it came from everywhere at once. He lowered his hand, grasping the armrest again. "Look at yourself. What trials did you endure to collect their money for them?"

Kevin looked up, his gut clenched. *This guy install speakers or something?*

"You think we don't know who you are?" Komodo smiled. "You slaved away for years, collecting coins for someone else. For what? To be allowed to operate a place where people eat and rest. You paid only to be free of your fear that those you so revered would kill you."

Kevin pointed at him, and thrice opened his mouth to shout back, but all three ideas jammed in his brain.

"It is my turn to be curious," said Komodo. "There is a proud wolf who hunts for himself, the strongest in the forest. Then, one day, Coyote tricks him… convinces him he can be lazy and have lesser wolves do the hunting for him." The man raised his head, eyes widening. "If you could have opened your road house at any time without the fear of retribution because you failed to pay tithe to the lazy wolf who no longer hunts, would you have continued to drive?"

Kevin closed his eyes. "Naw. But buying in was how it had to be. It kept everyone safe. Yeah, I would've set up a 'house sooner… but was I supposed to eat a bunch of sand and shit out solar panels?"

A few of the Redeemed chuckled in the wings.

Neeley slapped his shoulder as fast as a humping dust hopper. "Kev Kev Kev."

He glanced back.

"Loft. Far left." Neeley flicked his gaze up and to his right. "Sorry took so long. Big bastard."

Kevin followed the stare to a group of Redeemed watching from the loft edge. A tall man all the way to the left with ginger hair and massive arms wore Wayne's hat. Dried blood mottled his camo pants in a spray pattern suggesting he'd been standing next to someone else who'd been shot.

The man locked eyes with him, and kissed the air.

Kevin went for his gun, but Fitch grabbed his arm.

Komodo raised both eyebrows.

"Him. Right there. That's the fucker." Kevin pointed at the man.

Fitch blinked. "Hang on a minute. You said you found Wayne 'tween his sentry guns in the basement, and y'all had ta shoot them ta bits to get in. How'd that guy get Wayne's hat?"

The man on the loft laughed. "Fell right off the sumbitch when he ran."

His smile gave way to a deadly glare. "Them little fuckin' machines killed four o' my brothers. You're the one oughta be owin' us blood."

Komodo raised his arm, the back of his hand toward the man. "Vicar, this outsider merely patronized the Hagerman road house. The weapons which killed the others are not on him." He lowered his hand to grasp the arm of his chair once more. "The Redeemed have not been saints. We are far from it, but at one point or another in all our lives, we realized this wounded world is going to wither beyond hope if we continued to act the savage. Our goals are not as random nor as violent as you have been led to believe. Without Amarillo demanding an unimaginable tribute, more places will open. More opportunities for civilization to spread will appear. Can you not understand that this group you so admire has prevented the phoenix from rising?"

The woman at his right glanced to the side, muttering, "I prefer to sleep in."

Kevin stared daggers at Vicar. He couldn't tell who else among the group here had been with him; Neeley glanced over a few others with indecision across his face. The hat, however, proved at least one. He might be able to draw and fire before they put him down, but that whole 'putting down' part was all but guaranteed. Thirty-three on three and no cover in sight would've been shitty odds even if the three of them had Tris' boosts.

"You seem conflicted." Komodo gestured at him.

"Yeah. Conflicted. Sure." Kevin let his hand drift away from the .45. "Only thing I know for sure right now is I'd have to be a damn moron to piss in your beer." He pointed at Vicar. "But I'm not leaving without Wayne's hat."

Vicar thudded across the loft to the stairs, which didn't echo quite so loud under his boots. Kevin pivoted to face him, expecting an attack, but the man stopped at the edge of the square dirt patch. He winked, grinned, and removed his gun belt. "Come and get it then, pretty boy."

For no reason Kevin understood, he glanced at Komodo as if asking permission. The leader of the Redeemed remained impassive for a few seconds before nodding once. Other bikers gathered at the edges of the 'arena.'

"You got him," said Neeley. "He ain't that much bigger'n you. 'Sides, he's probably a pussy."

"How you figure that?" whispered Fitch.

Neeley shrugged with a grin. "He didn't die at Wayne's… Means he was the last one down the stairs."

Kevin didn't feel like losing his pants due to having no belt, so he cross-drew the .45 with the wrong hand, holding it upside down by the slide, and gave it to Fitch. No one so much as twitched. He removed the armored jacket after Vicar shed his leather one, exposing the Glock 17 under his left arm. That, too, he pulled in a telegraphed motion, and handed to Fitch.

His boots clunked over wooden floorboards until he stepped four inches down onto dirt. More Redeemed filled in the sides, creating a living wall around the ring. This didn't appear to be the kind of fight won or lost by ring-out, and getting too close to the edge would likely add a few extra fists. He eyed the crowd, wondering if they'd give Vicar a jab or two as well. He hoped they had some kind of honor thing and not a 'screw the outsider' rule.

Vicar leaned his head side to side, cracking his neck. He circled to his right, his expression said he'd been impressed that Kevin hadn't wimped out. The man had a two-inch and forty-pound advantage give or take five, though a good portion of the weight difference sat in his gut. A large knife perched in a sheath on the outside of his right boot, but Vicar didn't make a move for it.

Kevin expected a brawl, not a lethal fight, but tried to stay ready in case the situation escalated. When his opponent shifted, Kevin ducked, but the attack proved to be a feint. The crowd chuckled at his flinch. He grumbled and got in close again, the two of them still pacing about like a pair of dogs about to go at it. A quick jab landed on Vicar's cheek, the man having evidently expected a feint for a feint, though too much power traded for speed made it more insult contact than punch.

Vicar snarled and lunged in.

Arms up, Kevin blocked two high shots before he ducked and drove his fist into the man's gut. Vicar let out an *oof* and draped forward over him. Before Kevin could shrug him off, the man seized him by the shoulders and hurled him toward the floor. Kevin clamped on, legs airborne for a few seconds. The instant Vicar put him down on his feet, he fired an uppercut into the man's chest.

They popped apart, each taking a step or two back. Vicar appeared more angry than injured.

"Stop fuckin' dancing," yelled a man.

Figuring Vicar wouldn't expect it, Kevin charged. The man brushed his punch aside and rammed a forearm into Kevin's face, knocking him away in a stagger, seeing spots. A fist filled his vision for an instant before the ceiling did. Kevin snarled and rolled to his feet, the taste of blood on his lip.

Vicar, both hands raised in a crowd-goading triumphant gesture, turned back to face him as he ran in again. Kevin led with a lure of a fake left hook, switching to his right with a straight, hard punch. While Vicar grabbed his left wrist, Kevin's knuckles hit him in the pectoral with a meaty slap. He stared at Wayne's hat, no longer trying to hold back the mixture of rage and pain. Ever since he found his mentor dead, he'd wanted to end the life of the person responsible. That person stood in front of him, grinning, spinning round and round before a backdrop of bikers all cheering. Except for one or two voices yelling Vicar's name, the Redeemed appeared to adore the fight in general, the bloodletting, the contest.

Kevin roared and leapt in with a high shot, going for jaw. Vicar saw it coming and got under it. A right, left, right, left, right barrage to the chest blasted Kevin off his feet for the second time. He wheezed and gasped, trying to remember how to breathe. The biker took three steps back and came rushing at him like a field goal kicker with his eyes on Kevin's skull. Kevin rolled aside with barely a second to spare, ducking the boot and wrapping himself around Vicar's foundation leg. He took the man to the ground on his chest, giving him a mouthful of dirt, before pouncing on his back and pounding him in the head.

He managed to land four hits before Vicar's elbow knocked him away into a reverse somersault. Vicar shoved himself upright, dirt spraying from his mouth with an angry howl. The big man leapt on him, and they spent a moment or two wrestling and rolling on the floor before breaking apart again and clambering to stand.

Damn. Maybe I should learn some of that kicking shit Tris uses. He wobbled, wiping at his face during the short reprieve of two men staring, waiting for the other guy to move first. An empty beer can hit Kevin in the back; two more bounced away from Vicar's chest and shoulder. Neither man allowed the distraction to divert their attention.

A few tentative punches and blocks passed between them. Fire burned in Kevin's lungs; sweat covered him. The room spun worse than it had been before from the stifling heat. Vicar had lost some of his confidence as well, or at least the cockiness had gone away. *Good. He's getting tired.*

Kevin roared and feigned a charge. Vicar shifted to block the attack that wasn't, at which point Kevin lunged for real. The mistimed block allowed an uppercut to snake between the larger man's arms and find chin.

Vicar's head rocked back, sweat trails streaming from his hair. He flailed his arms, staggering. Kevin pressed, punching him again across the nose with two back-to-back rights, each with as much strength as he could wring out of his weary muscles.

Blood oozing from his mouth and nose, Vicar snapped his head up snarling, wild-eyed desperation on his face. He made no attempt to stop Kevin's third punch from landing in his cheek, but the attack cost Kevin a haymaker to the forehead. A pronounced *snap*—one of Vicar's finger bones breaking—reverberated in his skull.

Both men careened over sideways and hit the ground. The room swirled into a blur of color and shouting. After what felt like minutes of having his face in the dirt, Kevin pushed himself up a little. Vicar lay a few feet to his left, also blearily trying to stand again. Wayne's hat had fallen off a short distance behind his opponent.

Fitch's baritone yell lofted over the crowd's taunts and cheers. "Kev, get the fuck up! You got this!"

Anger filled his veins.

Kevin shifted to a three-point stance before letting off a wild battle cry and launching himself at the teetering Vicar. He tackled the biker over backward, kneeling on his chest, and punched him again and again in the face until his arm refused to move again.

Out of breath, he looked down. Red streams came from Vicar's nostrils, running down either side of his head to his ears. The man's nose looked broken, blood infused his teeth, and he moaned on and off, not quite unconscious, but far from lucid.

Kevin pulled himself off Vicar to the right and knelt in the dirt, gasping for breath. He stared at Wayne's hat, but lacked the energy or the inclination to stand. He met the stares of the Redeemed surrounding the fight pit, who regarded him with an almost malignant curiosity.

Well, shit. This just got complicated.

WASTING TIME

Holding an AK-47 in an unsupported firing position for ten minutes got Tris' arms aching. Abby alternated between clinging to her back and trying to squeeze her hand out of the cuffs securing her to the steel bedframe. An Infected moan pierced the web of shouting and gunfire outside. Isla, still under the bed, hadn't made the slightest sound.

Abby screamed.

In the subsequent silence that filled in after the girl's lungs emptied, a tiny whisper came from under the bed, eerie in its calmness. "Don't scream. That will only tell them where you are."

A single gunshot, sharp like a firecracker, rang out.

"Got him!" yelled Trisha.

Sergeant Ellis shouted, "Get your ass away from that thing!"

"You're bit," shouted Zack.

"No," said Ellis. "It got a mouthful of armor. I'm good."

"You gonna shoot Ellis now, Warren?" snapped Lauren.

Emilio stormed in, left arm extended with a handcuff key between his thumb and forefinger. He thrust it in Tris' face. "I'm too wired up and pissed off. It'll take me a damn hour to get it in the hole."

Tris tossed the AK on the bed and unlocked Abby, who clamped on to her father with both arms, trembling and sobbing in silence.

Zara marched in, MP5 held up in her right hand, aimed at the ceiling.

"We have to leave now. I think that old man was right about the two hundred thing, and they all know we're here. Wish the damn Infected gave me more than two minutes to rest my arms. That shit was heavy."

Tris tossed the key on the bed and recovered the rifle. "How'd they get in?"

Zara walked out of the office. "Smashed a ground-level window on the far end of the basement and dove into the boiler room. This building isn't secure."

Isla whined.

Tris squatted, beckoning. "Come on out. We're leaving."

The brown-haired girl squeezed herself deeper in the corner, feet sliding over the concrete as she tried to push herself into the cinder blocks. Tris took a knee and got a grip on one of the girl's ankles.

"You can't stay under there. It's not safe." She pulled the child out by one leg.

"Isla!" yelled Tom, sounding panicked. "Where are you? Has anyone seen her? Isla?"

"She's in here," shouted Tris. She shouldered the AK and picked the rigid, terrified seven-year-old up.

Tom Pines dodged around Emilio and Abby and hovered at the door. He and Isla both appeared to calm a little at the sight of each other. Tris handed the girl off to her older brother, and followed them out to the basement where the survivors congregated.

Warren had a blackening eye and a fat lip. Most of the venom in his stare flew at Emilio rather than Abby, which Tris counted as an improvement. Murmuring went around in circles.

"Let's go!" shouted Kristen. "It ain't like she's gonna go zombie in the next ten minutes. We gotta get the fuck out of here now... can deal with her once we're safe."

"We can hold the basement," said Zack. "They've only got one point of entry and it's a small window."

Sergeant Ellis seemed to consider.

"Fuck that," shouted Kristen.

"Ammo ain't gonna last for all of 'em," said Lauren. "Plus, I'm sick and tired of this damn store."

"It's *one* window. Easy to defend," said Zack. "Choke point. If we watch it, we can kill them as fast as they come in."

Trisha cradled a Beretta in both hands. "But we didn't. They got inside."

Isla whined into her brother's ear a bit above a whisper. "Do I have to have a gun too? I don't want one. I'm scared of them."

He rocked and comforted her.

Abby lapsed into a coughing fit, which silenced the room. All the survivors stared at her.

Tris raised both hands to the sides. "Everyone listen. Sitting around here is wasting time. We have a van stashed at Otto's, but the longer we wait, the more a chance someone might steal it. Abby is not a threat. She's not displaying any signs of cognitive degradation. *The* infection makes a person ravenous and she can barely look at food. An Infected at this stage would be eating everything they could get their hands on."

"Yeah, but you got kicked out of the Enclave." Warren dabbed blood from his lip. "How do you know they haven't changed it?"

"We are the best chance you have to get out of here alive." Zara stepped into the light, using a tone as though she addressed a platoon of Enclave soldiers. "We have neuronal amplifiers, reflex boosters, low-light vision, an immunity to the Virus, and a van." She looked at Abby. "And we are leaving now. *With everyone.* Anything happens to that kid, and I'll shoot anyone I even think might've done it."

Tris aimed a pointed stare at Warren. "If you're uncomfortable with that, you're welcome to stay here."

Zara waved at the stairs. "I'll take point. Zack, with me. Mike"—she looked at Sergeant Ellis—"you're the back door. Emilio, behind Zack. Warren ahead of Mike, second to last. Kristen in front of Warren. Tom behind Emilio. Tris, middle of the group with Lauren, Lloyd and the kids." She looked at Trisha and Micah. "You two don't worry about trying to shoot any infected unless you have no other choice. Uhh, Cassie... behind Lloyd."

Tom reluctantly handed Isla over to Lauren, tears in his eyes. "Dad never got around to makin' her any shoes. Please don't let her step in any blood."

Lauren cradled the girl. "I got her."

Trisha squatted and retied the laces on her oversized boots. Micah opened and reclosed the Velcro on a pair of well-worn orange sneakers.

Abby looked around at everyone shying away from her. She flexed her toes. "I'm okay. I guess I'll try not to step on anything bloody and sharp."

"Let Emilio carry her if he's so sure she's safe," muttered Warren.

"Kids in the middle. He's on point; too dangerous for her." Zara glared at him.

Tris glanced at her. "I'll carry you. I'm stronger than I look."

Abby smiled despite a coughing fit.

Zara led the way up the stairs to the ground floor. Not three steps into the store, she fired at something. A moan preceded a fleshy *thump*.

"Contact," yelled Zack. "Three."

A rifle went off, followed by two more pops from the MP5. A monstrous female groan lapsed into a gurgle.

"Clear," yelled Zack.

At the top of the stairs leading into the store, Abby climbed up on Tris' back, wedging the katana between them as she clung tight. The phlegmatic rattle in the girl's breath filled her left ear. Trisha and Micah walked an arm's length in front of Tris, occasionally looking back and up at her with wary expressions. Both held pistols, Trisha in two hands out in front, Micah more casual with his arm at his side.

Warren grumbled at Sergeant Ellis at the rear of their formation as they trailed through the store. Two large forklifts plugged the front door, their forks impaling a section of the massive barrier around the place. What had appeared from the outside as a solid wall was an improvised gate. Zack and Emilio hopped in and got them running after a few tries. They rolled forward with an ear-bleeding *shriek* of rusting steel, until enough of an opening existed for everyone to slip out. Emilio drove harder, skewing the gap wider on the right side.

A pudgy, shirtless man with blotches of exposed muscle on his arms and detached cheeks hanging down over his chest filled the new exit in a split second, pulling himself past the barrier.

Kristen and some of the kids screamed while Emilio yowled and dove to his left out of the forklift. Zara shot the fat man twice in the forehead before Emilio had even hit the floor. She rushed the gap to prevent the Infected from clogging it, firing seven more times on her way out. Zack hurried after her; Emilio scrambled to his feet and followed.

Tom hesitated, looking over his shoulder at Isla. When his face turned grim and he darted out, the girl wailed and begged him to come back.

Tris patted Micah on the shoulder. "You two stay behind me 'til we're clear, okay?"

He and Trisha obliged. Abby tensed up, emitting a nasal squeal of unease as Tris stepped around the dead Infected and the expanding pool of blood leaking from the back of his head. Jose stepped on the man's chest and hurried off to a position behind Tom.

Fortunately, the 9mm rounds from Zara's MP5 made small holes and no one put their foot in seep.

Lauren muttered 'grandmother curses' along the lines of "fiddlesticks," but the occasional "dammit" slipped in as she tried to carry Isla out the gap without touching any gore or corpse. The child hyperventilated, flapping her arms while caught between trying to scream and cry at the same time.

Tris squeezed her AK. *I am going to shoot Nathan in the balls and watch him bleed to death.*

Lloyd maneuvered around the body with little visible concern, as though he'd encountered an inconvenient duffle bag left on the sidewalk. Cassie hesitated for a few seconds, sucking in deep breaths, and jumped the dead man in one leap. Kristen navigated the obese Infected corpse like a teenager playing hopscotch on a lava flow while emitting little squeaking screams.

Warren and Sergeant Ellis stepped over the man in long, calm strides.

Tris turned away from looking behind her and zeroed in on Tom, who'd gotten almost a half block lead by now. She moved up to a light jog, Abby bouncing against her back. The girl squeezed her legs around her waist.

"You don't have hips. I'm slipping. You're too skinny."

Tris let the comment go as Abby trying to distract herself from the horror around them. "I eat a lot actually. The nanites burn it though. I'm not sure I *could* get fat even if I wanted to."

"What are nanites?"

At the front of the line, Zara, Zack, and Emilio opened fire on a pack of Infected racing from an alley. Tris raised the AK. Time slowed as her reflex boosters ramped up to full. She fired, blowing out the side of an Asian man's head and painting the two Infected behind him with brain. One of them jerked at a bullet stike, probably fired by Tom. Tris shifted her aim left and put two rounds one after the next into a dark-skinned woman with an exposed red skull for a face. The shots also struck a relatively normal looking Caucasian man behind her. If not for the thousand-mile stare, zombie-like gait, and utter lack of color in his skin, he'd have passed for healthy. A steady flow of more Infected came from both sides near the head of the line, keeping Zara, Zack, Emilio, and Tom scrambling to shoot them fast enough.

Jose stood casually in the street, aiming his M-16 and firing single shots as if on a range shooting at paper.

Trisha screamed.

Shit! I'm not paying attention. Tris whirled left at three Infected barreling out from behind a sandbag barrier, heading right for the middle of their formation, one already in a flying leap at Lauren. The grandmother tossed Isla at Lloyd as she fell back away from the diving man. Tris snapped off a hasty shot into the man's side before swiveling to her right and shooting the other two once each in their heads. Another leprotic woman dragged herself out from a rain gutter, eyeing Lauren from behind.

Isla hit Lloyd in the chest; her miniscule weight knocked the frail old man over. As if her bare foot touching pavement would mean instant death, blood or not, the girl stood on top of Lloyd's chest, shrieking and crying out for her Mommy or Daddy.

Lauren landed on her ass, the Infected on her legs, grabbing and pulling at her dress.

"Gramma!" Micah freaked; his eyes bugged almost out of their sockets as he fired six shots as fast as he could into the Infected's back.

Abby, hands clasped in front of Tris' chin, let go of her wrist to point at the other side. "Tris, more!"

"Get offa me you devil-sent thing!" Lauren stomped at the man's face.

Five fast-moving Infected raced past a tangle of razor wire, oblivious to it tearing up their clothes and skin. Two rushed for Isla, three went at the group of Tris, Abby, Micah, and Trisha. The one on Lauren's legs hadn't stopped moving yet either. Two on Lauren, five threatening children, Tris didn't have to think.

Reflex boosters were fast, but after shooting the five rushing at the kids in the heart one after the next in a barrage any normal person would've heard as a rip of automatic fire, she fully expected to find Lauren with an Infected chewing on her face. Instead, Sergeant Ellis had leapt across her, letting the crawling, one-legged fiend chomp on his armored side.

"Get off my Dad!" roared Trisha. She jumped forward, put the tip of her Beretta against the Infected woman's head, and fired. A glop of skull and brain splattered onto the street less than a foot away from Lloyd and Isla.

Isla's jeans darkened in the crotch. She leapt off Lloyd's chest, emitting a high-pitched, glass-shattering scream as she bee-lined for Tom thirty or so yards ahead.

The dead woman rocked back and up, a water-fountain arc of blood gushing from the back of her head. Sergeant Ellis rolled onto his side and kicked the body away before any got on him. Trisha froze for a second, gawking at the gore she caused.

Tris whirled to aim the AK in Isla's general direction; her instinct paid off, and she sniped two Infected who ran out of hiding amid dumpsters at the charging, panic-stricken seven-year-old. Tom turned toward the sound of his screaming sister, and scooped her up.

Cassie, gritting her teeth and emitting a growl like an angry hamster, spun around from a doorway that had been spewing Infected and fired her Uzi into the alley from which the Infected had charged Lauren. She mostly controlled the weapon on full auto, but it rattled her around.

Sergeant Ellis helped Lauren upright. After recovering her balance, the older woman casually raised her handgun and shot another Infected emerging from the same alley. Her bullet caught a man in priest's garb in the right cheek, making him spin.

"Damn." Lauren lowered her arm. "This town sure has gone to Hell."

Lloyd examined himself, shrugged, and stood. "Guess I get lucky again. I tell ya, they don't make zombies like they used to back in my day. Brittle old man like me should'a been dead days ago."

"Move!" shouted Zara from the head of the line.

Warren hurried over and studied Ellis' side. Apparently satisfied the armor absorbed any damage, he patted the man on the shoulder.

"Shit," said Micah. "Gramma's got blood on her dress."

"It's only dangerous if it gets in your eyes, nose, or mouth... or an open cut." Tris grimaced at the blood-soaked garment.

"Aww heck no." Lauren flung the dress off and used the clean part to wipe at her legs, though she only managed to smear blood around with the soaked thing.

Warren removed his blue windbreaker and wrapped it around Lauren. "What about that vest, Mike. Got some blood on you."

Sergeant Ellis lifted his arm to look. "Not that much and this is armor... I'll sterilize it later with fire."

"Come on," yelled Zara. "What's going on back there?"

Motion caught Tris' eye to the left. Two more Infected climbed up from inside a dumpster, knocking it on its side in their effort to get out. An echoing metallic *slam* reverberated down the street. She shot them both before they could stand.

Abby gurgled and coughed, stretching sideways to spit so it didn't get on Tris. "You're a good shot."

Cassie sprinted off after Zara and the front of the line. Lloyd followed with a blasé air, like he couldn't care less if he made it or not. Sergeant Ellis took his daughter by the hand and hurried along. Micah clung to his grandmother's arm. Kristen sprinted off as if she'd be left behind if she didn't get to the van first. Though she had a handgun, she hadn't fired a single bullet.

At the next corner, an Infected teenaged boy, faster than any of the others thus far, raced out straight at Kristen. The woman screamed and grabbed Lloyd, shoving him toward the charging teen. The scrawny, mindless boy mistimed a bite on a target flying *at* him and wound up head-butting Lloyd in the chest.

Zara skimmed a bullet across the back of the boy's head, tearing open the skull and doing enough damage to kill. Lloyd pushed him off and recovered his balance. The teen fell over backward, twitching. After finding his shirt free of bite marks or blood, Lloyd shrugged in disbelief.

Two blocks up, Zara stopped at the door to Otto's. The sight of the place made Tris' heart swell with relief; not a trace of her disgust at the former owner tainted her thoughts.

The group gathered at the doors. Cassie ran over and slammed Kristen against the wall by her tank top, slapped her, and screamed, "What's wrong with you?" over and over.

Kristen got her arms up to defend, muttering, "He's old!"

Lloyd hurried over and put a hand on Cassie's shoulder. "It's okay... Maybe she's rude and selfish, but she's a third my age. I'd have jumped in front of him anyway to protect her if my reflexes weren't shot."

Kristen fired a sour, guilty, stare at the road.

"Bitch," muttered Cassie.

Lauren glared at Kirsten disapprovingly.

When Zara pulled the door open, everyone piled in to Otto's. At the sight of the grey van, kids cheered, Tom wept, and Lauren yelled, "Hallelujah."

In a fleeting moment of total silence, Isla's tiny voice half-whispered, "I peed myself."

"I think we all did, kiddo," said Lauren.

"There's water in the van. You can wash her jeans if you want once we're moving. Side door's welded armor. Go to the back." Zara climbed up into the passenger seat and put the gun goggles on.

Tris set Abby down on her feet by the driver's side door. "Be right back."

While the others climbed in behind her, Tris worked the garage door chain hand over hand as fast as she could move her arms. The door clattered and banged, snagging halfway up. She screamed, "Fuck you!" at the top of her lungs and gave a yank that broke something at the side of the roll-top door's housing and sent bits of metal flying and clanging to the ground.

But the door opened.

As soon as she let go to run to the van, the door came crashing down.

Jose walked over and grabbed the chain. "I got this. Pull it out."

Tris darted to the van, shooing Abby from behind the wheel to the floor between the front seats, her back against the console.

Cassie stood into view in front of the van holding the charge cable. "Forgot to unplug it!"

The bright-eyed blonde let the wire retract and ran to the back doors. Tris hit the power switch and the console erupted with light. Whirring came from the gun turret within a half-second.

"Weapons hot," said Zara.

"Alright, we're in business," muttered Tris. "Who's ready to get the hell out of here?"

"God dammit; go already," yelled Warren.

Tris reversed out of the garage, stopping a few feet after the front bumper cleared the door. Jose pulled the chain with him out a step, then let go once he'd passed where the door would fall. He flipped the M-16 up in his arms and fired three shots off to the right. Zara swiveled her head that way, and the gun overhead followed suit.

Half the people in the back of the van screamed in surprise when the .50 cal burped, slamming the air with a heavy *thud*. Isla clamped her hands over her ears and wailed.

Jose popped off a few more shots as he fast-walked to the back end of the van. Mike, Warren, and Emilio hauled him in bodily while Cassie and Micah pulled the doors shut.

Tris laid on the accelerator, squealed into a sliding reverse K turn, slammed the shifter to drive, and stomped on the pedal. With fourteen extra bodies, the van had no pickup to speak of, but the wheel motors still generated enough torque to bash down one of the ramshackle barricades in the road. Sandbags exploded over the windshield; razor wire scraped down the side. Zara wagged her head back and forth somewhere between a seizure and heavy metal, accompanied by a labored whirring from the roof. After a faint metallic *plink* outside, she stopped.

"Gun caught on a strand of razor wire, but it's good." Zara shifted to kneel in her seat, facing rearward.

"Please hold together." Tris slalomed a series of barriers, driving a little faster than she liked. People grunted and groaned with the rocking. She jumped when the .50 went off a few more times.

"I love this thing," said Zara. "If I hit them just right, the rotten ones pop like melons."

Abby covered her mouth with both hands; some vomit leaked between her fingers.

As seconds ticked into minutes, the .50 cal went off less and less, and eventually fell silent.

A couple minutes later, Tris turned onto I-287 north out of Amarillo, and the ride became smooth. She glanced back over her shoulder and felt a wave of relief that no one bothered poking around the large mass of tarpaulin wadded up against the partition. Isla stood in the middle of the van, naked from the waist down, holding her jeans out to Tom as if he could magic them clean and dry.

"You gonna check her for bites too? Or is she too young for you?" asked Emilio while glaring at Warren.

Abby muttered something in Spanish that sounded none too friendly.

Warren returned a dirty look.

Zack found the canteens and handed them out. After a light rinse to clean herself, Isla sat down next to Tom, still bottomless. Her brother pulled her standing again before peeling off his tee shirt and pulling it over her head. It hung to her shins like a dress. Smiling, Isla cuddled up at his side once more. Lauren helped herself to the blanket in the back, eager to cover herself, and leaned against the wall mumbling something that sounded like prayer. When Amarillo became a mere speck in the rearview mirror, Zara turned about and sat facing forward.

Abby coughed into her hands and looked up at Tris. She appeared about to say something, but lowered her head.

Tris drove in silence for a few minutes before Sergeant Ellis' voice filled the van.

"Everyone check yourselves for blood spatter."

The rustle of motion ceased eventually, and the lack of anyone panicking allowed Tris to relax.

Abby sniffled mucus, wiped her nose, and coughed on and off for the next half hour or so. Eventually, she looked up again and put a hand on the seat by Tris' knee. Micah gurgled from how tight Lauren squeezed.

She held him like an oversized child clinging to a teddy bear for protection.

"I'm a'right, Gran'ma."

"I know, baby, I know." Lauren kissed the side of his head, tears gathering at the corners of her eyes. "I'm just glad you're okay."

Tris glanced down.

"What if it's not a cold?" whispered Abby.

"Are you hungry?"

"No."

"What's twenty-three plus thirty-four?"

"Fifty-seven."

"Feel like killing anyone?"

Abby shrugged and whispered, "Maybe Warren."

Tris chuckled, but couldn't deny a pang of worry. "Did anything happen to make you think it's not a cold?"

She fidgeted at her dress between her knees. "No. I just don't wanna die."

USED AND DISCARDED

Awkward silence pervaded the Redeemed clubhouse. Dust danced in thin streams of sunlight leaking from holes or cracks in the ceiling and walls. Kevin stood in a wide stance, swaying about, staring down at the man who killed Wayne. Well, one of them. Vicar's eyes rolled up in his head. If unconsciousness had a portrait, it would look like him. Kevin fixated on the man's throat, calculating how long it would take to get the knife from Vicar's boot and let Wayne rest.

Getting out of here afterward though...

He bowed his head. *They'll kill Fitch and Neeley too. Dammit!* Pain throbbed over his face. He cringed away from the mental image of Tris reacting to his death... or worse, her sitting in the roadhouse waiting for him to come back and never knowing what happened. "Fuck it."

Kevin stumbled over to the hat, swiped it up, and wandered to the edge of the pit. The bikers backed away to let him pass, but Komodo stepped in front of him.

"I did not expect you to win." The president looked him over. "Perhaps you did not."

"Yeah." Kevin glanced at the hat in his fist. "Guess some games, no one wins."

"The weak man is weak for he cannot unburden himself, and has no strength left for things that matter. A weaker man wishes to destroy what he cannot control."

Kevin tried to smile, but it hurt too much. "Now, you're just sayin' that so we don't kill everyone here."

Komodo tilted his head. No one made a noise for over a minute as the man stared at him with a measuring gaze tinged with incredulity. Seconds before the tension grew too thick for Kevin to continue standing still, the Redeemed leader leaned back and laughed. Other bikers joined in with varying degrees of sincerity; some sounded nervous, as if expecting the big man to kill him at any second. The redhead woman walked over, barefoot in jeans and a tight black tee shirt, and handed him a tin can of water.

"Not bad." She winked and padded over to the shelves behind the pool tables, where she rummaged a beer cooler.

"I like him." Komodo patted Kevin on the shoulder.

"Heh." Kevin suppressed a wince and took a long sip. "I was starting to wonder if my sarcasm was too dry."

"Your friend is dead." Komodo bowed his head and grasped Wayne's hat into Kevin's fist. "We lost five. Take this badge of honor and may the spirits accept your bravery."

Kevin stared at the hand engulfing his. He couldn't say if Wayne would accept a beatdown as revenge for them taking a giant shit on the Roadhouse, but at least four of them died. *Wait. Five?*" "Five?"

"Indeed." Komodo, and the rest of the Redeemed, offered a momentary reverent silence. "One of the men bled out."

Kevin grumbled, glanced back at Vicar, and grumbled again. *This is sending the wrong damn message, but... fuck it. I ain't dying for a message.* "How you fixin' ta handle it if someone comes after that bounty?"

Komodo smiled. "There is no bounty."

The bikers dispersed around the room, back to where they'd more or less been before the fight. Two carried Vicar out a back door, muttering about cold water. Fitch and Neeley approached, both with 'what now' looks.

"Not quite what you wanted?" asked Fitch.

Kevin shook his head.

"Big picture, man. Big picture." Fitch patted him on the arm. "Got that pretty little thing waitin' for you back home. I'd probably 'ave done the same."

"Well." Kevin looked up, a hint of a smile parted his lips enough for a trickle of blood to run over his chin. "Figured it be pretty rude of me to get you two killed as well."

"'Preciate that." Neeley touched his fingertips to his chest. "I'm delicate."

Fitch thumped him on the shoulder. Neeley overacted pain.

Kevin tromped outside, heading in the direction he figured the cars to be, grumbling the whole time he walked. Four dilapidated huts down on the left side, a flash of white caught his eye. His brain filled in Tris' hair, as it had done whenever he'd thought he'd seen random white patches appearing in his peripheral vision as of late. A few seconds after he focused on the porch of a tiny, brown shack, he realized Tris *was* standing there.

She had her back turned, and though her long pure white hair made it difficult to tell for sure, she appeared topless. Tattered shorts made from old camo pants rode so high into her butt her pubic hair would've shown if she had any. Heavy black boots most of the way up her shins looked like something straight out of the Enclave with graphite grey armor panels.

Seeing her here wasn't the worst part. Watching her suck face with two Redeemed men hit him like Praetor's fist in the belly.

Neeley and Fitch braced his arms to keep him upright

What the fuck? What the actual fuck? He blinked, trying not to believe his eyes. Tears gathered but retreated under a wave of rage. He tore his .45 out of its holster and stormed ahead, not quite able to walk in a straight line after the beating he took. Neeley and Fitch ran after him, again catching him by the arms.

"Get off."

Fitch pulled. "Wait, man. Don't do anything stupid."

"I already did," he grumbled. "Never should've given her a ride in the first place. This is god damned Morgan all over again..." *No, this is worse.* "Go on out of here. I'm gonna kill every last motherfucking one of them."

"Kev!" Neeley leapt in front of him, grasping both cheeks. "Re-freakin'-lax. Stop thinking with your bent dick and take a good look."

Kevin squeezed the handle of his pistol, pressing the patterned grip into his flesh. He stared at Tris. He stared at the woman he thought he'd loved. The woman who betrayed him, who may have set all this up. She had been so insistent on going off to Amarillo *alone*. "What?" Kevin shoved Neeley forward while yanking his face away from the man's squeezing hands.

"Look at her, mate." Neeley wrapped himself around Kevin from behind, pointing at her. "She don't look right. Bit thicker, bigger boobs."

Kevin's flood of anger tapered off to droplets. He walked forward at a pace confused rather than hostile, and slid the gun back into the holster.

She reacted to the scuff of his boots on the road and twisted around to look. The white-haired woman *did* seem to have more muscular arms, athletic not waifish. A black halter-top, the ties about her neck and ribs hidden by her hair, covered her chest. While he had no complaints about Tris' perfect round breasts as big as peaches, the woman before him had a larger pair. Of course, he couldn't get past her having a face like her twin sister who'd gone to boot camp rather than a detention cell. Then again, this woman appeared closer to middle-late twenties. Older, and more confident in the eyes.

"Well, hi there. You're kinda cute." She winked at him. "Sorry to disappoint, but I'm not for hire."

The two Redeemed pawing at her glared at him.

Kevin raised a hand. "Ain't gonna ask for that. You... look like someone I know."

The woman spun back to face her paramours, hair flowing as if underwater. "Gimme a minute. I gotta talk to this guy." When she moved to step down from the porch, the man on the left grabbed her arm. She whirled on him, hoisting him off his feet by a fistful of leather jacket at his chest, holding him aloft with no visible effort. "Did you just grab me? What? I'm your property or something like that now?"

"Uhh..." The man gawked.

She thrust her arm forward, tossing the man off the porch and through the wall of the next hut. He landed in a cloud of splinters. "Asshole."

The woman faced Kevin, a pleasant smile on her face as though nothing at all violent had happened two seconds before, and wandered about twenty paces from the building before spinning back to face him. This woman was *definitely* not Tris. She met him eye to eye at the same height.

"So you're the one."

"Which one?" Kevin walked up to her. "Why do you look like her?"

A long, low moan came from the hole in the hut.

The woman smiled. "Call me Snow... the guys around here started calling me that and, well, I kind of like it." Her lips morphed to a disapproving smirk. "Before that, I was 16-410. Tris is your girlfriend, right?"

Kevin glanced at the sleek, black handgun on the woman's right thigh—Enclave tech. "What are you doing here, and why do you look like her?"

Snow crossed her arms. "I can hear the anger in your voice. Before you do something stupid, you should know that I could kill the three of you faster than your brain could even think 'oh, shit.' I'm sure you've seen your girlfriend in action, yes?"

Shit. "Yeah." His muscles tensed, making all the bruises he'd have in the morning throb.

"Well. She's alive. Made out of meat. I don't have that drawback." Snow lowered her voice. "I am a Persephone series infiltration and combat android."

"Whoa." Neeley leaned in, face to tit. "She looks so real. I... don't believe it."

Fitch grasped Neeley by the head and made him look at the smashed hut with one Redeemed boot sticking out of the hole. "I'm inclined to trust what she said. Squeeze at thine own risk."

"So they *are* real." Kevin gnawed on the knuckle of his index finger, and spat when he tasted blood.

"Ya think?" asked Neeley with an eager expression.

Kevin hung his head. "I meant the Persephones, not her tits. I thought it was bullshit."

"I'm sorry." Snow looked down, her hair billowing to the side in the wind. "While I am perhaps as advanced as artificial intelligence managed to get prior to humanity deciding to blow itself back to medieval times, it is not impossible to fool me. Nathan sent me out here to find a large, organized group capable of mounting an effective offensive operation against the Amarillo military. While he'd presented enough of a claim to the command structure to permit the op, he failed to mention two critical things."

"Wait." Kevin pointed at her. "So *you're* the reason everything went to shit? *You* killed Wayne?"

"Not entirely. I never directed them at any specific target beyond Amarillo's interests in general."

"What did this Nathan dickhead leave out?" asked Fitch.

Snow sighed. "Well, for one thing, he didn't tell me this was all about your little girlfriend. He didn't care about Amarillo at all. It was merely a layer of armor he needed to peel away to expose her. The Enclave did not have accurate information about the true capabilities of Amarillo's

military or their numbers. Rumor was enough to make them hesitate...
you know how they oh so hate going outside."

"Yeah." Kevin glared at her. "The farther they go east, the more they
get their underpants in a knot."

"Well, these Redeemed thugs already had a thing against Amarillo for
making waystations rare and expensive. These fools really believe that it
retarded the spread of humanity."

"You don't?" Kevin cocked an eyebrow.

Snow pulled hair off her face, staring at the western horizon for a few
seconds. "It seems like it's already past the point of no return. Humanity
might die out no matter what anyone does. A couple extra power stations
along the road isn't going to make much of a difference... but I suppose
humans are nothing if not tenacious. Unless the Enclave changes its
stance and decides to provide technical knowledge and material, no
functioning vehicles will remain on the roads in twenty years, which of
course makes the number of rest stops a useless point to begin with.
Transportation will devolve back to horses until enough infrastructure
comes about to allow humanity to re-invent automobiles... if they
even do."

"And they're never going to open the doors." Kevin spat.

"Nope. So Nathan arranged for an Agent-94 drop right on Amarillo. I
was sent here to tell the Redeemed that the threat of retribution from the
fearsome army out of Texas was no more. They could do whatever they
wanted to the roadhouses and nothing would happen to them. Nathan
instructed me to feed them a bunch of misinformation about one place
though. Hagerman."

Kevin almost grabbed her by the throat, but somewhere between her
looking like Tris and being a killing machine, he held back. "What did
you do?"

"Just told them the man who operated that roadhouse was part of a
crew of Night Riders who raided this place on and off about twenty years
ago. I have no idea how Nathan knew that, but they ate it up. From what I
hear, it was a pretty bad raid. Lot of people were killed here. I guess
Nathan figured you and Tris would be there, so he wanted to make sure
they hit that one."

"Wayne had *nothing* to do with that!" Kevin yelled.

"In hindsight, I'm sure he didn't. Everything that comes out of
Nathan's mouth is a lie." She scowled. "Which brings me to the second

piece of critical information. He didn't bother to mention that he'd leave me stranded out here after my mission ended."

"You couldn't get yourself back?" asked Neeley. "C-can I touch your breast? Never saw no android lookin' so real."

Snow smiled and thrust her chest forward. "Go right ahead. But I touch back."

He recoiled.

Fitch snickered.

"I *could* go back," said Snow, "but Nathan gave me a surprise parting gift."

Kevin cringed. "Little bomb?"

"I-13-SEO. Subdermal explosive ordinance. That might've worked on Tris, but he forgot I've got a full spectrum wireless array. I jammed his detonation signal long enough to remove it. So, no. I'm not going back there. I'm a goddess out here. And don't worry, sweetie." She winked at Kevin. "I don't really have any desire to hurt you or your girlfriend. In fact, leaving you both alive is about the biggest middle finger I can send to Nathan."

Kevin blanched.

"Shit... Amarillo is... What is Agent-94?" Kevin tried to swallow saliva, but gulped down a mouthful of dust.

"The distribution phase of the pathogen that evolves into the bio weapon you people out here refer to as 'The Virus.' By now, everyone in that city is more than likely dead." Snow started to wander off back to the one man who surprisingly still waited for her. "Look, for what it's worth, I'm sorry. Most of the people in the Enclave have no idea what it's really like out here. They think it's all raiders, slaves, constant war, incest, murder, mutants, everything possible worst-case scenario. I've seen enough to reconfigure my outlook. Some of them don't believe ridding the world of everyone and starting over is a good idea, but people like Nathan are making the big decisions." She looked down at her boots, not moving for a minute or two. "I look like her because the man who designed us modeled our appearance over what he calculated she'd look like as an adult."

Kevin blinked. "Her father? What happened to him?"

"I don't have that data. During the design phase of the Persephone project, the girl was six years old."

"That's why she's not a perfect clone." Fitch snapped his fingers.

"Yah, well." Neeley bapped him in the stomach. "Tris also looks like the wind'd break her in half."

"Like I said." Snow lifted her gaze from the ground to the distance. "Our appearance was based on an estimation."

"So it's true. Amarillo's gone." Kevin sagged where he stood, feeling as defeated as he had after Wayne's death. Everything he'd ever wanted or counted on... gone. He pictured Tris in his mind, the way she smiled at him right after sex, the way she smiled at him while they ate, the way she smiled at him... in general. "Not everything I wanted."

"What?" asked Fitch. "Little louder."

"Take care of yourself, Kevin." Snow straightened her posture, the sense of projected guilt evaporating. "The least I can do is get Komodo to leave the remaining roadhouses alone. Those people are going to have enough problems."

"What if he says no?" asked Neeley.

Snow walked away. "Then I guess I could just kill them all."

Kevin closed his eyes and wished with everything he had that Tris was okay. "Fuck it. We're going home."

"Right on," said Fitch.

Neeley leaned to the side, peering around Fitch, staring at Snow's ass as she walked off.

Fitch grabbed him by the back of his vest and dragged him along after Kevin to where they'd parked. "Dammit man, that dick of yours is going to get you killed one of these days."

MATCHSTICKS

F our hours or so after the last bullet left the .50 cal overhead, Tris pulled the van into a parking spot by Mac's Roadhouse, a few miles over the Colorado/Oklahoma border, almost due north of Amarillo. According to the dash, they'd arrived at 3:04 in the afternoon. She shut down the van and leaned around to the right, peering into the back. Most of the survivors drifted in and out of sleep, save Kirsten, clearly out cold, and Warren who sat against the back doors staring at Abby. The only time he'd not drilled into her with his eyes had been a few minutes at a time during pee breaks on the side of the road.

The two faced each other, the girl still planted between the front seats, for the entire ride thus far. After only five minutes of the man's distrustful stare, Abby looked down and hadn't raised her head once.

"Hey," said Tris, almost yelling. "We're at a Roadhouse. The van needs to charge and you all need food, water, maybe a shower. Lauren, you can probably get something to wear here too." She looked at Isla, still wrapped in her brother's tee shirt. "Kid-sized clothes are pretty rare, but maybe. We're safe here, so I'd like to spend the night."

"I don't need new pants. They just need washed." Isla held the wad of denim up.

Tom mumbled something into her hair about it being perfectly okay for anyone to have an accident when Infected were running at them.

"I'm not sleeping around her." Warren pointed at Abby.

The eleven-year-old sniffled, more from sick than tears. "You can tie me to the bed. I don't want to hurt anyone." She coughed, her entire body shaking.

Emilio lunged at Warren, but Zack and Sergeant Ellis caught him. He pointed, fingertip inches from Warren's nose, and shouted something in Spanish.

"Dad..." Abby sneezed. "I don't wanna be shot... and if I *am* gonna turn into a zombie, I don't want anyone to die but me."

Emilio lost the will to fight and crawled into the front to embrace Abby, weeping on her shoulder. That, of course, got her crying, and made Tris ponder shooting Warren right in the van.

Sergeant Ellis cast an imperious eye down on Warren. "Not ta wish it on 'er, but you better hope that girl turns. If that's just a cold, I'm gonna beat seven shades of shit outta you."

Zara exited the van and headed around front to connect the charge plug. The others climbed out the back doors, Tom carrying Isla who held her jeans out at arm's length. Tris remained in the driver's seat despite really needing to pee. Not until Emilio regained his composure some minutes later did she move.

"You okay?"

He put a hand on her thigh, then his forehead against his knuckles. "You gotta tell me she's gonna be okay."

"I'm not a doctor, but she looks too sick to be affected by *that* virus. The symptoms don't fit." *I hope.*

Abby smiled. Emilio helped her up and they walked around the van to the roadhouse door. Tris climbed into the back once no one could see her, and tugged at the tarp over the pile of cardboard boxes and metal tins. *Thank you, Zara.* She pulled two of the boxes out of the pile of fourteen or so, and covered the stash once more. After wrapping them in a blanket, she hefted the bundle in her arms, grunting a little with the weight, and exited the van via the back doors. After using her foot to nudge them closed, she met Zara by the front bumper.

"Gee, you think that'll be enough?" Zara smirked.

Tris chuckled. "It's only fair."

"You're a sucker for kids. Mac's daughter's sweet." Zara looked down.

"I dunno." Tris walked to the roadhouse entrance, Zara at her side. "Maybe because I didn't really have a childhood, I feel bad. I'm really having to work hard *not* to shoot Warren in the head."

"What? Don't tell me you're a Persephone..."

"No. Look at these spindly little arms." Tris gave her a raspberry. "I mean… the replacement parents weren't bad to me, but I always felt like I was 'in custody' more than 'at home.' You know?"

"Can't say I do." Zara opened the door for her. "My parents are pretty cool. They're probably all kinds of upset now. I wonder what kind of bullshit Nathan fed them about why I'm missing."

Inside, the survivors had dispersed among tables, with Abby and her dad way off in the corner by themselves. Tris lugged the boxes over to the counter, where Mac stood, flashing his huge grin at the crowd.

"Hey Mac."

Denise glided out from the back, took one look at all the people, and started to go right back in. Mac grabbed her wrist.

"Come on sweetie, I need your help."

"Aww but Dad, the book was just getting to the good part." Denise grumbled.

"Book ain't gonna grow legs. Save it for when there's nothin' goin' on… otherwise you'll be bored when nothin' goin' on."

"Okay." She started to turn to the room, but stopped facing Tris. "Hi, again." After a smile, she headed to the nearest table.

"Hey Mac." Tris nodded at the curtain. "Can I talk to you in back for a few minutes?"

"Yeah sure." He held the curtain aside for Tris.

"Guess I'll take the counter." Zara winked.

Mac gave her an 'I'm watching you' point, then chuckled.

Tris headed down the hallway and took a left into the office. She stood there until Mac walked in.

"What's up?"

"Here." Tris held up the bundle.

He got his arms under it. When Tris stopped supporting them, the boxes almost took him to the floor. Wide-eyed, he rushed to the desk to put it down. "Jesus F… little warning." He blinked at her. "How you lift this? What the fuck is it?"

Tris sighed. "I've got some good news and some—"

"Bad news. Yeah. Okay, hit me."

"Those people out front are all that's left of Amarillo. By the way, the whole thing was bullshit. They never had an army. Chances are, they couldn't have done a damn thing other than throw money at bounties."

Mac gave her a look as though she'd told him he had five seconds to live. "That bad?"

"Yeah. At most, they had about 250 people. All the soldiers on the rooftops? Mannequins and rudimentary androids with fake weapons. The old guy running the show was lying to everyone."

"So what's the good news?"

Tris grinned, gesturing at the boxes. "Well, since Amarillo was phony, I figured you deserved your money back."

He swooned into the chair.

"Should be ten thousand in there."

Mac pawed at the blanket, exposing the cardboard coin boxes holding dimes and pennies still in their pre-war bank wrappers. "Fuck!"

"Sorry, Mac. I've got a boyfriend." She winked. "There's no security blanket anymore. Eventually, the bad element will figure that out. You'll probably want to hire some muscle to help keep things safe here. Think you can feed these people, let us crash the night, and maybe spare some clothes for those who need it. Hope ten grand is enough."

"Shit, yeah!" He leaned toward the door. "Liv, get in here."

"Mind if I use the radio?" asked Tris.

Mac waved her at the table full of electronics with a 'be my guest' gesture and turned his attention to the older version of Denise who walked in. "Sweetie, baby… you ain't gonna believe this."

Olivia yelled out in surprise and lost all strength in her legs at the sight of the coins. Mac guided his fainting wife into the chair.

Tris took a seat by the console and squeezed the mic button. "Hey, uhh, breaker or whatever… Sang? Come back." She listened to the radio hiss for about a minute while Mac tried to calm Olivia down from her exuberance. "Sang? Okay, if you can hear me, pick up the little back thing on the squiggly cord and push the button on the side before you talk into it."

Silence.

"Shit. Maybe he's out front." Tris set the mic on the table and stood. "I really need to piss."

PERHAPS AN HOUR LATER, AFTER FOOD AND A TRIP TO THE BATHROOM, TRIS followed Emilio and Abby into one of the tiny bedrooms upstairs. Warren and Zack hovered in the doorway like prison guards. The tween gave them a pouty look, but said nothing as she crawled into the bed and held her wrists up to the bedposts on either side of the headboard.

Emilio hesitated a long time before winding cord around her right wrist and tying a knot. "There."

"That won't hold her if she turns," said Warren. "Both hands."

Tris glared. "Infected can't even figure out ladders. She'd try to get up and just keep tugging at her arm, not knowing why she was stuck."

"I won't be able to wipe my nose," said Abby, sniffling.

"This is suicidal. Forget it." Warren reached for his gun. "You're being too sentimental. She's going to kill us all."

Tris had the Beretta at his temple in an eye blink. Warren froze. Emilio paused as well, his gun half-drawn.

"Please don't kill me!" yelled Abby. "It's okay. Just... stay with me, please." She sniffled, trying to breathe through her nose, coughed a little, and moaned.

Muttering a continuous stream of apologies, Emilio tied her other wrist to the headboard. Warren scoffed.

Abby, glaring daggers at him, struggled as if to prove she couldn't get loose.

"You're right," said Tris. "I think a bullet in the head *is* the solution to our problem, but it's not going into Abby."

"Whoa." Zack held his hand up at Tris. "Everyone needs to calm down."

"They're sneaky." Warren forced his voice past clenched teeth. "One second, they look innocent, then before you can react, they're chewing on you. You think I like this?" He huffed. "I don't want her to be sick at all, but I'm also not going to let emotion kill everyone who managed to get out of there."

An animalistic growl, like nothing that could ever come from a human throat filled the air out in the hallway. Abby screamed, struggling against the ropes and kicking at the air while shrieking. A lone gunshot rang out, followed by the heavy *thud* of a body hitting floorboards and another shot. Warren and Zack pointed pistol and rifle down the hall at the foreboding silence.

Emilio tried to comfort Abby as best he could; wild with panic, the girl thrashed and tried to break free.

Tris stopped pointing her gun at Warren's head and aimed down the corridor.

A doorknob twisted. The men tensed as if ready to shoot whatever came out.

"It's me," said Micah. "Don't shoot."

He stepped into the hallway, his face a mask of total blankness, a Glock dangling from the fingers of his right hand. Blood smeared his shirt and jeans. He let the gun fall to the thin carpet before peeling his clothes off and walking up to the three of them stark naked.

"Gran'ma got scratched." His lip quivered. Giant tears streaked his dark brown face. "She tried to bite me, but it wad'nt her. She gone already." He turned in a slow circle and held his arms out. "Am I bit or scratched?"

"Jesus." Warren lowered his gun and gave the boy a quick look-over before patting him on the head and moving past him to the open door. "Nah, son. You're good."

Mac bounded up the stairs at the end of the hallway, submachineguns drawn. "Hell was that?"

Tris holstered her Beretta and waved him over.

Abby stopped fighting the rope, apparently having heard enough to understand Lauren had been shot... by her grandson. She sniffled and coughed in gasping sobs. After two seconds of watching his daughter struggle to hug him, Emilio pulled a knife and cut her loose. She leapt into an embrace, shivering and crying.

Zack examined the boy. "Don't see any broken skin. This blood's all spatter. What happened?"

Micah looked downcast. "Gran'ma must'a got scratched when that man jumped on 'er. She'd been sleepy the whole ride. She ate up a bunch and wanted ta go ta bed. I was tryin' ta read and she's mutterin' 'sorry' in her sleep. Then she sat up lookin' all confused. She tell me ta run, so's I ask what's wrong. Then she made that noise. Grabbed me. Her eyes were yellow... an' I... an' I—" He collapsed to his knees, sobbing into his hands.

Mac relaxed. "Shit..."

Tris bit her lip. "He's smeared in blood..."

"I'ma goin' to Hell now, ain't I. For killin' mah own gran'ma." Micah stared down.

"That wasn't your grandmother anymore, boy." Warren pulled the door closed. "The Virus killed her. You helped her find peace."

Mac looked torn between being upset he had an Infected in his place to clean up and feeling bad for Micah. "C'mon, kid. I got a water well out back we can rinse you off. Think I got some clothes'd fit ya too."

Micah shuffled off after Mac.

"Hey, Mac, you got any real strong moonshine?" asked Tris. "That should disinfect. I'll clean up in there so no one gets sick."

He looked at her with two raised eyebrows.

"Vaccinated... I can't get it." Tris sighed down at her clothes. "Can you send up a cheap long shirt or something? I'd rather not run around naked or have to burn what I'm wearing."

"Yeah," said Mac. "I'll ask 'Liv to bring you something. Might have some holes but if you're gonna burn it anyway..."

"That's fine. Beats tits-out."

Warren walked back down the hallway, pausing to shoot a smirk at Abby. "She's loose."

"Yes. She is." Tris scowled. "You're going to tell me you'd have left a terrified eleven-year-old tied to the bed when she's desperate to hold on to her father?"

Warren sighed. "No, perhaps not, but... before we all sleep."

"Lauren. It's only been a few hours and she turned. Abby's got a damn cold." Tris glared.

Zack exited the room. "Got her on the thigh, deep gouge."

"Abby hasn't turned because she doesn't have a massive wound down the inside of her leg." Warren glanced sideways at Tris, most of his attention still locked on the girl. "You did say the level of exposure mattered, didn't you?"

Tris wanted to shout him down, but enough doubt lingered that she couldn't quite do it.

"You're an asshole," said Abby. She coughed. Her glower faltered at a dire look from Warren, and she slipped away from her father to lie down again, extending her arms up to the headboard. Her expression looked calm, but the rest of her body trembled. "Fine. Whatever."

Emilio shook his head in disbelief. "I'm gonna be right behind Mike. When she kicks this cold, and you all see it's nothing, I'm going to break my boot off in your ass."

Olivia appeared at the top of the stairs with a faded, coral colored knee-length tee shirt. Mac was right about the holes. At least one promised to give a nipple a great view of the world.

I can put it on backwards. Tris took it. "Thanks."

She ducked into her rented room, stripped, and put on the tee, which had evidently been dinner for an army of bugs. It smelled like it had spent the past half-century in a wooden box as well. Emilio and Warren's argument seeped through the wall in low murmurs.

After putting her shoes back on, she crossed the hall to enlist Zara's help.

TRIS WOKE FEELING SORE EVERYWHERE. THE WINDOW REMAINED BLACK, leaving her confused as to why sleep had abandoned her. A faint wail hinted that there'd likely been a not-so-faint wail before it. Tris rolled to her feet, grateful to be rid of that awful tee shirt and in her own clothes, and headed out into the hall.

The air still reeked, thick with the vaporous horror of moonshine capable of peeling varnish. She advanced to the door from which the noise emanated. From the sound of it, Isla had a nightmare. The girl's quiet crying continued under a constant mutter of reassurances from her brother. Tris relaxed and trudged back toward her room, pausing to listen at Abby's door.

A man's snoring accompanied a child's wheezy, labored breaths. She took a knee and peered into the keyhole. Emilio lay on his side on the floor by the bed. Abby had managed to pass out despite having her arms tied out to the headboard; she looked far from comfortable, but also far from being an Infected.

Tris grabbed her heel, ready to twist open the lockpick case in her sole. Sang couldn't shoot his son even when it had become obvious the young man had become Infected. As horrible as Tris felt... if the girl *did* turn in the middle of the night, unlikely as she hoped that to be, anyone she killed would be Tris' fault.

Grumbling, she tromped downstairs to the bathroom before returning to bed. Guilt and worry over Abby did their best to fight off exhaustion, but after all that had happened that day, plus cleaning up Lauren, fatigue won.

TRIS DIDN'T SLEEP WELL FOR THE NEXT FEW HOURS. AT THE FIRST TRACE OF sunlight, she got up, geared up, and raced to Abby's room. The door was unlocked when she tried it. Abby looked like death warmed over. She lay with her arms at her sides under the blanket, shivering, lips blue. Emilio paced.

The girl brightened a little at the sight of Tris, and rasped, "Morning."

"What's wrong?" Emilio sounded choked up.

"I think the fever's breaking... she should be getting better soon. She needs fluids. Maybe Mac has some soup?"

"I'm not hungry."

Emilio peeled the blanket off and picked her up. "You need to get some food in you."

Abby whined, but appeared to lack the strength to protest.

Soon, Tris sat at a table picking at eggs Denise brought over. Zara pushed food around her plate, evidently also uninterested in eating. After carrying Lauren outside hours ago, they'd doused the body in moonshine a safe distance away from the building and sent her into the next world with a match. Micah, in a dust-hopper leather tunic and sweat pants, held Olivia's hand while he watched his grandmother 'go to Heaven.' Tris hadn't quite grasped the concept, but didn't dare breach the somberness by asking what that meant.

Even Kirsten appeared morose upon learning about Lauren. Everyone, Warren included, knew and respected her. Isla hadn't stopped crying since she'd heard forty minutes ago. Lloyd showed the least reaction of anyone. If Tris had to hang any mood on him, she figured guilt at it not being him that had died, but he kept quiet and didn't give off any indication he planned to do anything crazy. The man didn't strike her as suicidal, more like he'd calculated himself as the most expendable.

Warren stared at Abby the whole time everyone ate. He had that paranoid glint in his eyes as if any second he expected the girl to go insane and throw her father across the room—and he wanted to be ready to put a bullet in her.

Micah walked out of the back, still with a shell-shocked expression, and went over to where Trisha sat with her father. He stood at the edge of their table, murmuring with them. Trisha's eyes lit up and she looked at her father as if begging for a puppy. Micah sat beside Trisha while Sergeant Ellis went to join Warren and Zack at their table.

Some minutes later, Ellis and Zack stood and shook hands like a pair of old friends about to part ways. Ellis returned to the table where Micah and Trisha waited. The kids got up, and he brought them over to the counter, starting a conversation with Mac.

Snippets of words filtered through the fog in Tris' mind. Micah had apparently gotten under Olivia's skin. Mac's wife had offered to take him in since he'd wound up an orphan. He hesitated, not wanting to lose his best friend Trisha. This led to the boy suggesting Trisha and her father stay with Mac as well since they really didn't have anywhere specific to go.

Once everyone finished off breakfast, the group of survivors met in a cluster at the center of the room.

"Well everyone, I don't have to say that the past month has been some of the hardest times any of us are ever likely to see." Sergeant Ellis stood behind Trisha, a hand squeezing each of her shoulders. "By now, you all know that our dear Lauren is no longer with us." A momentary silence lingered, during which Micah sniffled and wiped his nose. "Olivia and Mac have offered to take Micah in. Since my daughter likes the little bastard, I've wound up getting talked into sticking around here too."

Murmurs and nods went around the room, as well as many sympathetic looks to Micah. Kristen stared at the floor. Cassie came out of nowhere, clinging to Tris from behind and bawling like a little girl. Tris put an arm around her.

The woman kept muttering, "I can't believe she's gone," over and over.

"So you're just going to stay here?" asked Warren.

Sergeant Ellis shrugged. "Not like any of us are in a real hurry to be somewhere... other than *not* in Amarillo."

Zack looked at Tris. "Where were you planning on taking us anyway?"

"Well, I was driving back to the roadhouse I run with Kevin... but there's a well-defended settlement on the way that we sometimes visit. I could drop you at Nederland. They've got a militia, gates made out of old dump trucks, a large farm... it's nice. Highly organized. About four hundred people." She looked off, thinking back to Ann and Bill's house. She missed having Zoe around, and it sure had been easier to fall asleep there... even before the Code proved to be smoke and mirrors.

"Settlement sounds like a good idea." Kristen looked up finally. "I'll go there. I mean... Even if I gotta like be someone's wife or something. It's safe there, right?"

"Safe as I suppose anything can get anymore," said Zara. "I decided to stay there awhile back and I don't regret it." She rambled on about the militia organization, the farms, even some holiday festivals they'd started to bring back.

Isla wandered around, uninterested in the conversation. Her brother had his tee shirt back now that her jeans had been washed, and he kept a close eye on her as she weaved among people. Mac's shop didn't have any shoes small enough for her, but she didn't care. She even hovered by Abby for some time while Zara talked about Nederland.

Eventually, those who weren't staying filtered outside to the van. Tris went to shake Mac's hand, and got a hug instead.

Micah walked up to her, speaking to his toes. "Thanks. It ain't your fault what happen' ta my gran'ma. F'you didn't come for us, we'd all be dead."

I was slow... I... She sighed in her head. *I chose to protect the kids.*

Tris hugged him, and a flood of apologies spilled out of her. It took some time to pry herself away from him. "You be good, okay?"

He nodded. "'Kay."

She trudged outside, disconnected the power lead, and climbed in behind the wheel. Abby had resumed her perch between the front seats, only with Isla kneeling in front of her playing with a bunch of plastic dolls that hadn't been there before. Tris assumed they came from the shop, or perhaps Denise donated them, and didn't bother to question it. Abby humored the smaller girl while she explained all about how scared the plastic people were and that she would protect them from the 'bad monsters.' Abby kept glancing over the child into the rear of the van, fear plain in her stare. She too played with the dolls, but seemed to do it more out of wanting to humor Isla than amusement.

Warren muttered in the back, trying to convince Tom to pull his sister away from 'that girl,' but the seventeen-year-old told him to relax. Kristen whispered to herself, begging no one in particular to protect her. Cassie sat with her arms wrapped around her legs, knees to her chest, looking terrified and in desperate need of comforting. She caught Tris making eye contact, and offered a grateful smile before her fear returned.

Tris checked her map, planning to take 287 up to Route 70, and probably follow 25 around Denver before cutting west on 52. Once she got there, she felt pretty confident she'd remember the way to skirt Boulder and get into Ned. If not, she had Zara to help navigate.

<hr />

An hour and forty-four minutes later, Tris found it next to impossible to resist the urge to whirl around and scream at Warren to shut up. He'd been chattering incessantly, muttering about Abby looking worse and worse, and how she'd turn at any second.

"Argh!" yelled Tris, startling everyone. "I need some air. Anyone else need to water the bushes?"

A few affirmative responses came, so she pulled over on the side of a dusty road. The area offered nothing but flatness and scrub brush, so men and women split up on different sides, using the van for cover. Jose didn't care who saw what and let fly on the road a few steps behind the door.

Emilio carried Abby back from where they'd wandered off to pee and eased her to sit by the side of the road in the shade of the van, then forced her to drink some water. She choked and gagged on it, but swallowed some. Snot continued to stream out of her nose.

People gathered around in a semicircle, attracted by the heavy wheezing in her breath. Abby tried to put on an energetic smile, but her eyes appeared dull. Emilio ran his hand through her hair, long and straight to his curly. Tris wondered what had become of the girl's mother, but didn't want to ask. Looking at their faces left no doubt of the relation.

Abby trembled, though whether from fear or illness Tris couldn't tell.

Amid the huddle, Kristen sniffled, covered her mouth, and looked away. Cassie glanced back and forth between Kristen and Abby, confused for a second before her blue eyes went wide.

"No… no no no no," said Cassie. "You can't. You just can't!"

Zara's expression hardened.

"I'm sorry, Emilio. It's time." Warren put a hand on his pistol.

"Don't," said Tris. "It's a god damned cold, you paranoid fuck."

Emilio lunged up from his knees, whirling on Warren.

Warren went to pull his gun; Abby tried to scream, but sounded like a dying frog. Emilio drew faster, and shot Warren twice. The grey-haired man careened over backward, firing three times on his way to the ground. Emilio grunted and collapsed at Abby's feet.

Isla shrieked and leapt flat to the ground.

Zara whipped her MP5 up, aimed at the survivors. "Nobody move."

Warren growled, cradling his lower left gut. He wheezed and gasped. Emilio moaned, nearly face down on the dirt, bent legs keeping his butt in the air.

"Daddy." Abby draped herself over him, sobbing. "Daddy, no!"

"What if he's right?" asked Zack. "Look at her? She's practically a damn zombie now. What if she snaps?"

"No one even suspected Lauren," muttered Cassie. "She didn't even look sick at all. That only took hours."

"She," wheezed Warren, trying to crawl backward on one elbow. "Had a large wound. A lot of it hit her system at once. The girl got a smaller dose."

"You're so convinced she got a dose?" asked Zara.

Cassie rushed to Emilio, rolled him on his back, and pulled at his shirt.

The young blonde woman's hands shook, but she pressed them down on a bullet wound near the center of his chest.

"Abby," yelled Tris. "Her *name* is Abby. Don't call her 'the girl.' You're trying to make her seem like a thing you can kill and not a person!"

"Please stop yelling," said Isla, cowering on the ground. "You're scaring me."

Jose flicked his thumb at the safety on his M-16. "She would've turned by now if she was gonna. Mom and Dad didn't take this long."

"I dunno." Lloyd looked down. "Maybe, maybe not. Feels wrong ta just shoot her 'til she's all the way gone."

"Abby," said Tris. "Are you hungry?"

"No!" she wailed.

"What's nine times nine?"

"That asshole shot my father and you're asking me math questions?" Abby glared for a second before doubling over with a wheezing cough. She threw up while sobbing, and nearly choked on it.

Tris ran to Abby's side, sliding to a stop on her knees. She patted the girl on the back while glaring at Warren. "She's not losing her mental faculties. She's got a flu or something!"

"That's what the Virus was designed to do," said Zara, a hitch of guilt in her voice. "Exactly what you're doing to each other right now. Paranoia, fear, turning on yourselves. They projected seventeen percent of the casualties would be caused by 'fallout events' like this."

"She's... infected." Warren gave up trying to crawl and lay there breathing while clamping his hand over his gut.

Abby sat back on her heels, one arm clinging to Tris, the other reaching for her father.

Emilio raised his hand at her, unable to lift his head. "Abby... I'm... sor—"

His arm fell flat.

Abby burst into a screaming, sobbing missile launched from Tris' shoulder. She fell on her father, pounding a fist into his chest while screaming, "Daddy, no!" over and over.

Rage boiled over in Tris' heart. She leapt to her feet and put three rounds from the Beretta into Warren's face in one second.

Zack swiveled; his M4 barked, and a lance of fire ripped through her chest. Tris stumbled backward, an inferno flooding her lungs. Zara's MP5 lit up with muzzle flare, though the sound of the gunshots seemed miles away.

Both of Zack's eyes exploded in spouts of blood, a pair of matching crimson spigots poured from the back of his head. He crumpled in place. Tris staggered two paces left and collapsed half-seated on the edge of the paving. The Beretta hit the dirt, and she held both hands over a bullet hole near her breast while rationing her breaths so it didn't burn so damned much.

I'll be okay... She grunted as gravity pulled her toward the road. *Hurt more when Zara shot me.* Tris clutched her chest, gasping for air. She tried to lift her head to examine her wound, but couldn't move it. *This is gonna itch.* The world spun around and around, and drowned in black.

33

HAUNTED

K evin leaned his arm out the window and gave Fitch a thumbs up. This stretch of I-80 lay about forty minutes from home and he'd had enough of trundling along. He leaned on the accelerator and the Challenger pinned him to the seat. In four seconds, the speedometer hit 194 and strained to go up one more tick. The car rattled and wobbled at the limits of the frame's aerodynamic capabilities. The Behemoth shrank into a speck and vanished.

With any luck, Tris will have been home already as Amarillo presented a there-and-back route as opposed to his 'running around all over the place pointless waste of time.' He pounded the center of the steering wheel.

"Dumbass." He made a grand gesture with his right hand. "Yes. That's me. John Q. Dumbass." Fingers drummed on the wheel. "Why do those names always have a Q for a middle initial?"

The need to grab the real Tris and hold her drew forth a howl of anticipation. He bounced in his seat like a child before a birthday party. It didn't take long at that speed for his roadhouse to come up... and shoot right by. He slowed, cursing his excessive enthusiasm, and pulled a U-turn across the middle of the interstate. A moment later, he skidded down the approach ramp to the rest stop he called home.

Kevin rolled to a halt in one of the front parking spaces; driving around to the garage where the Challenger belonged would add two minutes. He swiped his finger across the rocker switches to shut down; bright azure went dark with each click.

He leapt out and ran to the door, flinging it open.

Three men and two women, all in their mid-to-late-twenties sat around as if they owned the place. Bee, or at least an inert chassis that used to be her, draped over the counter with several new bullet holes in her back.

"'Sup," said a bald pudgy guy with a curly black goatee that resembled pubic hair.

He blinked at Bee before glancing at the people off to the right. "Who shot my android?"

"*Your* android?" asked a skinny, tanned, shirtless woman in a denim skirt and pink flip-flops.

"Yeah." Kevin hardened his stare. "*My* android. This is my roadhouse."

"Ain't no one here when we found the place," said Pube.

The other woman, clad in a patchwork of leather armor that covered everything but her head, glanced at Pube. "Yo, you sure? Shit's gonna come down if this guy's legit."

"I said, Place was fuckin *empty*." Pube stood and spat a half-eaten fried potato disc to the side.

She backed away, avoiding eye contact with Pube.

Kevin glanced at the floor, tapping his boot. Anger flew straight past the point where any showed on the outside. As soon as the rumble of the Behemoth approached outside, he yanked the 1911 from its holster and drilled Pube twice in the chest. The heavyset man managed to pull his gun before his life fled, but couldn't raise it high enough to fire.

The topless woman drew a pair of thick, squat swords with spike-studded guards over the handles. A small man in one of the booths let out a shriek of terror and slithered under the table. The other male squatter made the mistake of going for a shotgun, which took too long to come around.

Kevin rushed against a low tile-covered wall while firing two more rounds. One struck shotgun-boy in the teeth on pure luck, the other caught him high and right on the chest; the corpse fell backward over a bench seat and landed with legs up.

Swordswoman stared for a split second before deciding it stupid to risk a twenty-foot sprint at a man with a gun, and dove out of sight under a table. Leather girl had frozen where she sat, hand under her coat, eyes on the window.

Kevin glanced to his right; Neeley had popped up out of the Behemoth's roof and had his Dragunov aimed at her. Fitch rushed the door with his shotgun at the ready. The cowering man let out a shriek when the doors slammed open.

"What the fuck is this?" bellowed Fitch.

Kevin stood from behind his cover, keeping the gun trained on the woman in the leather jacket. "Pull your hand out real slow. I don't need to say what'll happen if it ain't empty. And you with the knives, come on out."

Leather woman complied. Once her hands rose over her head, Neeley ducked into the enormous black pickup truck, emerging from the door a few seconds later. The woman with the swords crawled out and stood, her bare chest smudged with dirt from the floor.

Kevin eyed the back hallway. *Where the hell is she?* "Answer this question real careful. Did you see a woman with white hair?"

Fitch stifled a laugh.

"No," said the woman in leather.

"What did you do to Sang?"

Sword-woman showed a little guilt. "He tried to pull a gun on Bob. They beat him up pretty bad, but I don't think he's dead."

Kevin pointed at the still-hiding man. "You. Out."

The guy dragged himself into the open and stood. He reminded Kevin of one of those 'computer geeks' from some of the old movies. Despite having a pistol on his belt, he'd made no move for it or even seemed to remember he had it.

"Now what?" asked sword woman.

"Your group killed Bee, invaded my roadhouse, helped yourself no doubt to whatever you wanted... I could, probably should, just shoot you and be the fuck done with it, but, I'm one of those morons that has a problem hurting girls." Kevin narrowed his eyes. "Not so much when they try to kill me. Since I don't want to kill you, I'm going to confiscate everything you have and hope it equals out the damage you caused."

The woman in leather shivered. "E-everything?"

"Yep." Kevin nodded. "It's naked time."

"Walk of shame," said Neeley.

"Shit," muttered the remaining man.

"The usual?" asked Fitch. "I'll get some rope. Hands behind their backs and let 'em walk off?"

"Please don't." The woman in armor trembled. "I..." She looked down. "Escaped from raiders only a couple months ago..."

Fitch rolled his eyes. "Oh sure. You went and told 'em you got a soft spot and she's playin' it."

The woman, hands raised, approached Kevin. "Look for yourself." She tugged down a neck guard made of supple dust hopper hide, exposing circular scars around her neck. "Steel collar from when I was thirteen 'til a year ago. I'm probably like twenty-one now. I'll do anything you want, but don't send me out there helpless."

Neeley looked forlorn.

"Your choice," said Fitch. "Thieves get the walk of shame or a bunch of pellets." He patted the shotgun.

A far-off look took over her eyes for a moment. "If those are my choices... shoot me."

Kevin put a hand on Fitch's gun, pushing it down farther. "Watch them. They twitch, do as she asks. If Sang's dead. We'll be digging five graves."

He stormed down the back hall, yelling Sang's name a few times. The man moaned from the kitchen. Kevin found him on the cot, bruised and roughed up, with a nasty cut over his right eye that resembled the handgrip of a pistol. Out front, the thin man stuttered while trying his best to convince Fitch that the entire idea to take the place over came from Bob and they were all too afraid of him to do anything else.

"Kevin... Good to see you back." Sang forced a weak smile. "I okay. They didn't do any permanent damage."

"You sure you're okay? You look like you got run over." Kevin checked him out, as much as the old man would tolerate. "Where's Athena?"

"Gave her stuff for pain, think she still sleeping." Sang swatted at his hands. "Is good. Let me rest. You find the man you wanted to kill?"

"It's complicated. I'll tell you the story when you're not tenderized. What happened to Nevada?"

"She run to Cahvah's place. These bandits didn't go into the rooms yet. Only been here 'bout an hour."

"You sure you're okay?" Kevin patted him on the shoulder.

"Yes. Good. Sleeping." Sang rolled on his side and pulled a blanket up.

Kevin peeked at the office, finding it rifled through, but more or less as he'd left it. When he returned to the main room, he collected the weapons from the two dead men and left them in a pile on the counter after unloading them. "Okay. You three are gonna take pube-face here and that other guy out back, collect everything off their bodies, then bury them. Play it cool and I'll skip takin' your stuff that ain't a weapon, and maybe Fitch here will change his mind about the rope."

Fitch wagged the shotgun. "Alright, you heard the man. Hop to it."

"Tut tut." Neeley relieved the leather-clad woman of two handguns.

Kevin walked off as the trio grunted and groaned trying to carry two dead men outside, heading back down the hall to the storage room for the 'store.' They'd made a go at picking the lock, but only managed to get a thin metal rod wedged in the doorknob. *That's going to be a pain in the ass to open, but at least they didn't get in.* He grumbled across the hall to the office and grabbed the mic. That 'Snow' was aware of him having a roadhouse made him grateful for Tris' instinct not to talk about herself too clearly over the radio.

"Breaker. This is Kevin. Has anyone seen my other half?"

"*Nein*," said Gertrude after a moment. "Ve have been vaiting for her to tell us vhat has happened in Amarillo. Ze damned site inspector has still not shown up."

"Haven't seen her," said Mirabel.

"Yo, Kevin!" yelled Mac. The excitement in his voice made the entire table vibrate. "Your lady left here a little while ago. She tried to get you on the box before, but no dice."

"Yeah. I just got home. Had a roach problem." Kevin grumbled.

"Sure, sure," said Mac. "I think they's gonna stop by some place... Ned? Drop off a bunch o' people. Amarillo is gone. Infected wiped it out. Nothing left."

Harold, Clive, Mirabel, Gertrude, Jenny, and Enrico all tried to talk at the same time, likely yells of "What?" or "Shit."

"Whazzat?"

Kevin laughed himself to tears.

"Whazzat? Not hearin' yas!" yelled the old man.

"Yeah all," said Mac. "We're on our own now. No more Amarillo, but there's a shitpile of solar panels there if anyone's got the balls to go after them. Couple hundred Infected around too. Anyway, your lady should be gettin' on back to you real soon."

Kevin leaned back in the chair, feeling a wave of relief. "Thanks, Mac. Owe ya one."

"Nah, we good." Mac's smile all but formed on the front of the radio. "You guys don't owe me a damn thing. You did right by me already. More than."

He sat for a while not really listening to the radio chatter, which consisted mostly of 'now what the fuck are we supposed to do,' and stared at the wall. All he wanted was Tris to come walking in that door, and couldn't care less about anything else that had happened. For so long, all he'd ever wanted was a roadhouse to call his own, but for her, he'd give it away without a second thought.

The chatter died down after an hour, and he made his way to the front room. He couldn't explain it, but standing behind the counter didn't feel like what he ought to be doing anymore. The whole room had changed somehow, less of a shield and more like a little hill in the middle of a battlefield that made a guy an easy target. He brushed Bee's hair about, staring at her, it, or whatever. How could a damned machine make him feel sad? Well, he'd been pretty worked up over the Marauder when that red-haired she-devil Morgan took it... He brushed his fingers over the B-10-C printed on the back of Bee's neck. Comparing her to Snow was like comparing a golf cart to the space shuttle, but... he'd miss her like a person. Kevin hoisted Bee off the counter and propped her up in the chair Tris usually sat in. The plastic and aluminum head lolled back and to the right. Two of the bullets went all the way through her, leaving finger-sized holes in her chest.

"I suppose I should thank you for trying to protect the place. Bet they came in acting like customers, didn't they. Got you in the back when you weren't looking." The scene played out in his head, and perhaps because of what the brown-haired woman said, he imagined pube-face doing it all before the others could stop him. *Meh, those women would'a sided with whoever won.* The way the leather-armored one had cringed away from Pube convinced him she hadn't quite gotten over being ordered around like a slave. *From thirteen... dammit. Is that something anyone really can get over?* Dad reared his head, and Kevin felt like an asshole all over again for threatening her.

He leaned one elbow on the counter, staring at Bee, trying to make up his mind if he should bury her or leave her there like some kind of strange statue as a tribute. It felt sacrilegious almost that people died in the 'house, and Bee wasn't running around collecting their shit.

Not too much later, the three squatters came in. The topless woman carried a bundle of all the dead men's gear; the other two had their hands up. Fitch and Neeley walked in behind them, rifles still trained. The trio looked as though they'd gone for a roll in the dirt, which had become mud due to the amount of sweat they'd worked up.

Kevin looked up. The former slave appeared exhausted and vulnerable, mousy brown hair loose over her face, puffing out with each breath. Wayne for sure would've made the three of them strip, tied them together, and left them to walk the road until justice found them. Sure made it a hell of a lot less likely they'd come back in the middle of the night and shoot him in his sleep. Course a man did tend to make enemies that way. Send a person off bound and naked into the desert, if they don't die, they tend to remember that shit for the rest of their life—and payback is a bitch at that time of the month.

"Okay, fine. You three can take off. Keep your clothes."

"Rope?" Fitch's eyebrow wiggle suggested he teased.

"Nah. Caught me at a weak moment."

"Uhh." The woman in the denim skirt and flip-flops sidled up to the counter. "Any chance I can get my swords back? Those things weren't easy to find. I don't mind fuckin' all three of you if I have to."

Neeley cheered, then looked self-conscious and folded his hands behind his back while coughing.

"Apologies for any misunderstandings," said the man. "Our... associates were a rather violent sort, and they had a rather loose grasp of the concept of personal property. I assure you, we'll be no further trouble."

Kevin eyed the woman. Her armor was half motorcycle Kevlar and half dust hopper. "You were serious about tellin' Fitch to shoot you."

She stared into his eyes. "Yes."

"Not sure if this guy's useful at all"—Kevin gestured at the man—"but if you got nerve like that, and your friend here was *this* close to running at me with goddamned swords when I had gun on her."

"That could'a been dumbassery." Fitch chuckled.

"She did duck." Kevin smiled. "Things aren't quite as they used to be. Place like this could use some more hands around. Hands who ain't afraid to get bloody if we get another influx of idiot."

The women exchanged glances.

Topless tilted her head. "So you went from kill us to send us on a death march to offering us a job-slash-home?"

"It's been a crazy few days... but yeah. More or less." Kevin leaned on the bar, trying to do his best Wayne.

"I... could probably help out with the computers in the other room or the solar panels on the roof." The man smiled. "I'm Neal. That's Lissa"—he pointed at Topless—"and that's—"

"Jenny..." The other woman looked into nowhere. "No one's called me that since I was little." She made eye contact again. "Alright. I accept."

Lissa shrugged. "That works. Uhh, can I get a shirt or something though?"

"Aww," muttered Neeley.

Neal offered a cheesy smile.

Kevin glanced at Fitch who tried not to laugh. "Well, Neal... I'll give you a shot see if you're useful enough to pay."

"Very good, sir." Neal bowed.

"You three look worn out." Kevin handed them each water in a jar. "I dunno about you two"—he smiled at Neeley and Fitch—"but I'm damned hungry."

They nodded.

Sang moaned.

"I got it." Kevin headed into the kitchen. "You rest."

A short time later, Kevin carried a plate of steaks (animal questionable) into the room and joined everyone at a table formed by two smaller ones pushed together. "Some asshole got a shiv stuck in the storeroom knob. I'll see about a shirt as soon as I can get it open."

Lissa whistled innocently.

He laughed. "Well, at least you're a bad thief. Hope you're better with your swords."

"Yeah, that I've done before. Pickin' locks is kind of—was kind of a new hobby."

Nevada walked in with a large crate, gave Kevin a 'welcome back' nod, and disappeared into the kitchen. "Oh, shit. What happened?"

"You, bad timing," said Sang, his voice laden with moan.

Later, after showing the three new 'employees' to their rooms, Kevin leaned against a column, once again staring at Bee. Nevada resumed her 'guard' station at a table after agreeing to take that seed run despite the relatively low pay for such a long drive as a make-up for her lousy timing... not that he blamed her at all.

Fitch and Neeley walked over. Fitch gestured at the liquor, which had taken a visible hit from the two dead morons. Kevin nodded. *Sure, why not. Feels like I'm going down with the ship already.*

"You okay, man?" asked Neeley.

"Yeah. Fine. Gotta thank you guys for helping out, even if that was a colossal goat fuck of a waste of time."

"All good," said Fitch. "Was worth it for the variety, even if I did haveta waste three damn rounds outta Mama."

"Cool." Neeley stood. "I, uhh, gotta check on something." He headed off to the corridor full of rooms.

"Hope she's not a screamer." Fitch downed a shot of something. "So, what's with the haunted look? You ain't seemin' too happy to be back."

Athena wobbled in from the hallway, looking a far cry from a badass driver in a pink nightie and bright red pajama pants covered in white stars. She braced her right arm across her chest, clutching her ribs, and dark circles lined her eyes. "Hey... Is Sang okay? He didn't check on me."

"Had a little issue..." Kevin got up and helped her to a seat. "Hungry?"

"Yeah." Athena nodded, cringing. "Feeling a little better actually. Not thinking about shooting myself so it stops hurting anymore. Sang gave me some shit... I don't think I've *ever* slept that hard in my life. I still kinda feel like my head's going to float off into the sky."

Kevin gave her right shoulder a gentle squeeze, and headed to the kitchen. After cooking up a burger for her, he carried it back out and explained the little drama she'd missed. "Tris ought to be back soon."

Fitch and Neeley raised their water in toast.

Where is she? He glanced out the window. Clouds of dust swirled in small cyclones that danced among the scrub. After a moment, he swallowed an odd sense of worry something had happened to her. All the years he'd busted his ass for a roadhouse, and it struck him how little he'd hesitate to give it up for Tris. *I never should've gone off without her.* "Yanno, I think I've just figured out the worst part about chasing a dream."

Fitch refilled his shot glass and gave him an expectant look.

Kevin stared at the empty road, fidgeting from a sudden sense of worry. "Catching it."

34

CONTAGIOUS

Jerky rocking invaded the nothingness in which Tris floated. She tried to scream, but couldn't figure out how. Rocking became up and down shaking.

"Tris," yelled a distant, echoing voice. Female, it had an odd sense of familiarity. "Tris!"

The sound and light of the world exploded into being; Tris shot upright, sucking in a great breath of air. Pain like a red-hot metal spear lanced through her chest paralyzed her. Mouth agape, she could only sit on the dirt and stare at a length of road leading off into heat blur.

A cute blonde about her age with grime smeared on her face—the kind of woman who gets thought of as 'the kid sister' but never called 'hot'—held her by both shoulders. "She's alive!"

"C-Cassie?" Tris coughed; her mouth filled with a pungent metallic flavor that tingled like soda. *Ugh, I hate the taste of nanite blood.*

Dazed and disoriented, Tris squinted at the blinding glare of the sun and the indistinct people-shaped blobs nearby. A childlike voice cheered while another sobbed. She focused on the direction from which the crying emanated. A blur moved, and a thin body plowed into her, knocking her flat on her back. Gasping sobs, laced with a wheezing cough filled her right ear.

Abby... Emilio... Warren. "Oh, shit."

Tris let out that scream she'd been thinking of as the army of pins and needles outlined her ribs around her left lung. She shuddered through it while Abby coughed and gagged. Once the concept of moving became something her brain didn't crawl into a deep, dark place to avoid, Tris sat up and patted Abby on the back.

"He killed him… Warren killed my Dad." Abby burst into tears again.

To the right, Zara kept watch over the others. Jose appeared calm. Kristen oscillated between looking ready to cry and giggling to herself out of neurotic fear. Tom stood a few feet away, holding Isla back. The little one appeared to have been crying too, but aside from wet lines down her dusty cheeks, her face radiated joy at Tris. Lloyd stood off by himself, muttering about idiots.

"We're good," said Zara. "No one else wants to shoot anyone."

"What are we gonna do with them?" asked Tris.

Zara looked at her like she'd been shot dumb. "Drive them to Ned."

"No, I mean the dead."

Abby tried to squeeze the air out of her.

"Hey, hey… I'm okay. Just… wow. Hungry. Someone please grab me one of those meat strips?"

Tom nodded and headed to the van.

Isla ran over, gawking at Tris. "You're shot and you didn't die."

Tris patted her on the head. "Told you we're tough."

"Did it hurt?" asked Isla.

"Oh, yeah." Tris prodded her side, wincing. "It hurt a lot."

Zara sighed. "We don't have the tools to dig in this kind of ground. We don't have anything to start a fire with."

Tris glanced at the bodies, noting Warren and Zack lay arranged in parallel, cleaned of useful items. No doubt, Zack's armor sat in the van. Abby leaned back as if to speak, but as soon as she looked at Tris' face, tears overwhelmed her again and she bawled. Tom handed her a large strip of jerked dust hopper, likely an entire rear leg.

She devoured it, hardly leaving room for air between bites, terrified the nanites would start breaking down her internal organs in fatal ways without protein to work with. It made her think of when Kevin first fed her. *He's gotta be okay. He's gotta be okay.* She stood, holding Abby. "We gotta get going." Tris raised her voice. "Does anyone have a problem with us taking Emilio back to Nederland for a proper burial? I have no issues leaving that other jackass out here. Anyone particularly fond of Zack?"

"S'pose'n you ain't, seen as how he shot you," said Lloyd. "I don't think it personal. Just reacting to you firing on Warren."

"Warren killed an innocent man because he was a paranoid bastard."
Zara glowered.

"Not sayin' that was right." Lloyd looked around and grumbled. "We shouldn't leave Zack out here for the buzzards."

No one raised a serious objection.

TRIS RUBBED HER CHEST WHERE A BULLET HOLE AND DRIED BLOOD MARRED her shirt. The skin beneath remained tender, probably would for a few days. Dull pain in the lower part of her chest worsening in time with each breath made her think some blood settled in her lung that the nanites hadn't quite reabsorbed yet. She held the wheel steady, pushing the van a little hard at 72 MPH.

Abby sat again on the floor between the front seats, leaning toward Tris with her arm and head resting on the cushion. The smell of *sick* hung in the air, and sweat covered her. Isla huddled in the well by Zara's legs, having wanted nothing to do with the dead bodies in back. At least she'd stopped asking if they were going to get up.

Tris focused on the road, arguing in her head over Abby's condition. Most of what she observed implied the girl had a simple (though severe) cold or perhaps flu. The tiniest sliver of doubt remained, replaying in her thoughts with Sang's voice. This girl wasn't related to her at all, but the idea of having to kill an eleven-year-old made her heartsick. Sang's son had been nineteen. Awful, but less so than the idea of having to shoot a child. Jae-Yong had gone off scavenging and gotten himself in trouble. Abby had trouble dropped on her quite literally from overhead.

Despite how much of a shit the man had been to her, she didn't truly hate Warren, or blame him for Emilio's death. That, she reserved for Nathan. None of this had to happen. Tris wrung her hands on the wheel. The Council of Four wouldn't have bothered with Amarillo so far east. And if they *did* worry about them as a threat, it would've been a recon drone first and they would have noticed the fake soldiers. Some new recruit at a desk with a joystick would've had a good laugh, and they wouldn't have wasted a Virus drone on such a small number of people. What they dropped on Amarillo would've been enough for a city with hundreds of thousands.

Lack of planning, massive overkill; that had Nathan written all over it.

Her internal debate about *if* she'd be able to pull the trigger on Abby should the girl turn got her crying in silence. She tried to think about it in terms that the girl would already be technically dead, even if her biological processes continued. All a bullet would do is protect others and put a tainted body stolen from its rightful owner to rest.

Abby looked up, mucous draining from her nostrils. A cry sniffle collided with a sick sniffle, making her choke and exude more snot. A small rag flew in from the back of the van and draped over her head. She pulled it down and blew her nose before sending a pleading stare up at Tris.

Guilt crushed Tris into the seat. At least she hadn't been right next to him when her father died... Abby came within inches of being hit by the bullet after it passed through him. Tris grumbled as she took a turnoff onto Route 52 west and dodged a scattering of long-dead cars melding into the earth. She couldn't bear to look at Abby's mournful expression.

A bearded idiot wearing a bright blue tarp for a poncho and a Viking helmet leapt out from between two of the hulks and chased the van on foot with a hatchet waving over his head. He gave up before Zara rotated the .50 cal all the way around to the rear. For a while, they drove in total silence, no one talking. The constant thrum of tires on paving filled the air, along with the occasional congested sniffle.

"I'm sorry." Abby curled into a ball, toes gripping the carpeted floor.

"For what?" Tris didn't look down.

"Getting snoz all over you."

Tris cried and laughed at the same time.

"I think I'm getting better." Abby emitted a heavy, wet snorting noise. "I can almost breathe with my nose again."

Isla screamed and burst into tears.

The shrill noise came so unexpected and loud that Tris swerved half out of the lane. Zara banged her head on the door and grabbed the smaller girl.

"What?" Zara shook Isla. "What's wrong?"

"My node ith stuffy!" Isla wailed. "I dode wanna get shot!"

Tris' heart pounded in her chest. She about slammed on the brakes but remembered they had two dead men in the back and decided against inviting them up front. She stomped on the pedal hard, but not enough to screech the tires. As the van slowed, she pulled to the side of the road, too excited to drive. "That's great!"

Isla stopped crying, staring up with a face of total confusion. "Wub?"

"You caught her cold!" Tris pointed. "That means she is... or was contagious."

"How ib thaf a goob thing?" asked Isla.

Abby sniveled, shaking.

"Agent-94 isn't transmissible in the air." Zara glanced down. "You just *proved* that Abby is not going to die."

Kristen heaved, but stopped short of throwing up.

Lloyd sighed. "Warren..."

"That man don't wanna listen to no one. Now he listenin' ta Tris' bullets," said Jose. "I told him it ain't the same as Mom and Dad. He seein' them things everywhere."

"Psychological warfare," muttered Zara.

Isla crossed her arms and glowered.

"What's wrong?" asked Tris.

"I'm thick and everyoneth happy!" Isla fumed. "Ith not fair!"

"I will shoot the first person who suggests my sister be tied to a bed," said Tom.

"That's not funny," said Kristen.

"Wasn't trying to be funny. If I was Emilio, I would've shot him as soon as he told her to take her dress off in a room full of people. Don't know how y'all stood there and watched that."

Abby grabbed at Tris' arm. "I'm not gonna die."

"No, Abby... not yet, anyway."

The girl looked up, wide-eyed.

Tris ruffled her hair. "Everyone dies eventually."

"That wasn't funny." Abby punched her in the leg.

"Sorry." Tris pulled back onto the road, grinning ear to ear as she sped up.

TRIS HOPPED DOWN OUT OF THE VAN IN THE MIDDLE OF NEDERLAND, staring at the orange building from which the militia operated. Bill emerged and trotted over as the survivors exited the van and filed around into a small crowd.

"There's a story here." Bill smiled. "Marty said something about a trip into an Infected zone? Are all these people clean?"

"Yes," said Tris and Zara at the same time.

"Two have colds." Tris nodded toward Abby and Isla. "It's just a normal cold. We confirmed aerosol contagion. Plus, Abby, the older girl, has been sick far too long for it to be *the* Virus. All these people are from Amarillo. They are interested in joining the settlement here."

Tris introduced Kristen, Lloyd, Tom and Isla, Cassie, Jose, and Abby.

"Wow." Bill stared down, hands on his hips. "These are all the survivors from that whole city?"

"There were a few more, but they decided to stay at a 'house near Oklahoma. With Amarillo dead, the roadhouses are going to have to worry about their own security now. The whole thing was a lie. Just one old man and a couple of mercs. Wasn't thousands of soldiers, more like a hundred with about a hundred and fifty settlers." Tris bit her lip. "Speaking of which, I… really need to get back home."

"You don't live here?" Abby looked up at her.

Tris squeezed her shoulder. "No, I live at another roadhouse with someone very special to me."

The girl looked about ready to burst into tears again. "Can I stay with you? Please!" She grabbed Tris' hand in both of hers. "You stopped them from killing me… You cared about me. I don't have anyone left anymore… Please. I wanna stay with you. I can wait tables or sweep or tend a garden or whatever."

"That's… You…"

Abby jumped into her, arms wrapped around. "Please…" She clamped on to Tris.

"It might not be safe there anymore. I'm not even sure *I* could protect you at a 'house now."

Mouth to Tris' ear, Abby whispered, "I don't like them. They were gonna kill me. Please, you're the only one I trust."

Tris wrapped her arms around the girl. "Okay… okay."

"Triiiiiis!" Zoe came running down the street in a woman's denim skirt turned into a spaghetti strap dress, blonde hair trailing after her. She added herself to the group hug, bouncing up and down.

"I can't stay too long, Zoe. I'll try to get Kevin to come back as soon as we can and stay for a couple days, okay?"

Zoe pouted. "Okay. I got a new doll. She wants to meet you."

Tris smiled.

"She can nail a bandit in the kneecap at a hundred yards with iron sights." Zoe beamed.

Cassie, Tom, Lloyd, and Kristen gawked at the little blonde.

Tris kept an arm around Abby while the town militia brought the new arrivals over to the clinic to get checked out. Zara tapped her on the shoulder.

"Hey."

Tris faced her. "Hey, yourself. Thanks. I owe you one."

"Call it even. I feel a little less guilty about that whole trying to lop your head off thing." Zara started a handshake, which turned into a hug and a back pat. "If Kevin gives you any shit about keeping Abby around, let me know. I'll help you change his mind."

Tris laughed. "I'll do that. I meant what I told Zoe. We'll be around to visit soon. Did you leave anything in the room?"

"Nah, I got everything that wasn't in the truck. I'm gonna go let Marty know I didn't get killed."

"Thanks again." Tris patted the back of Zara's hand twice before letting go of the handshake. "Oh... uhh... Bill?"

Bill looked over.

Tris pulled Zoe into Zara's grip. "Hold her a sec." She trotted over to Bill. "I need to ask a big favor... There's two dead men in the back of the van. One is Abby's father, one... an Amarillo soldier who died on the way back. We didn't have the tools to bury or burn them, and it didn't seem right to just leave them out in the open."

Bill nodded. "No problem. If you don't mind, pull the van down to the clinic. We'll make arrangements; probably do the burial in a day or two. You gonna stay for the, uhh, ceremony?"

Abby's arms threaded around her from behind. *Kevin... I can't stay here for two days; he'd go out of his mind with worry.* "We'll definitely be back, but Kevin's going to go crazy if I keep him waiting much longer. I bet he's pacing around about ready to drive circles across the wildlands until he finds me." *If he's not dead.* She covered her mouth, sniffling.

Bill grasped her shoulders and looked her in the eyes. "I'm sure he's okay. The man's pretty resourceful. You get on back to him then. We got some cold basements. We'll take care of her dad 'til you're here to see him off proper."

Abby sniffled.

"Thank you." Tris walked back to Zara and ducked eye to eye with Zoe. "I'll be back in a couple days, okay? And Kevin will be here too."

"Yay!" Zoe bounced.

Tris walked to the van, Abby in tow. The girl climbed in the driver's side door and hopped into the passenger seat. They sat in silence for a while until Tris reached over and took her hand.

"I'm so sorry about your father."

Abby scooted her feet back and forth on the floor mat. "Thanks. It's not your fault. Warren was nuts."

I wanted to shoot Warren in Amarillo. I should have. Guilt settled like a lead weight in her stomach. She hit the switch and the van console lit up. *Nathan... please just stop. I'm no threat to you.*

"Thank you for letting me stay. I never met my Mom. I don't know what happened to her, but Dad said she was gone before I was old enough to remember. He never really talked about her. I guess she died, or left him for another guy, or something he didn't wanna talk about."

"I'm not old enough to be your mother. I'd have gotten pregnant when I was seven." Tris smirked. "Unless I'm wrong about the whole freeze thing and then I'd have been an old lady of nine."

"So?" Abby squeezed her hand. "You care. You didn't even know me, and you cared. That's enough."

Tris teared up. "I'm sorry, Abby. I should've shot Warren before we left Amarillo. It's my—"

"Stop." Abby sighed. "If you did that, everyone would'a thought you were crazy too. Then we'd still be stuck there."

"Maybe." Tris wiped her eyes. "I..."

"I promise I won't be too much of a pain in your ass." Abby smiled for two seconds before a cough made her turn away. "Ugh, I hate being sick."

Tris chuckled with tears in her eyes.

⸻

SIX HOURS AND FOURTEEN MINUTES LATER, TRIS STOPPED THE VAN NEXT TO a gargantuan black pickup truck outside the Rawlins Roadhouse. A woman with dark frizzy hair and no top on appeared in the window, watching until the door opened and Tris jumped down to the dirt.

Tris stared at her. "Well, *someone's* been having fun..."

Abby climbed over the driver's seat and slid down to sit on the floor before lowering her bare feet to the blacktop. She drew in a sharp breath and kept hopping from one leg to the other while hovering at her side. Tris shoved the van door closed and walked across the lot toward the sidewalk leading to the front entrance.

Abby gasped and muttered, "Hot, hot, hot," as she scurried after.

Kevin came flying out of the doors when she reached the top of the steps in the sidewalk. She ran into his arms, clinging as he swung her around and around in an almost painfully tight embrace. He held her motionless for some time before pushing her away enough to look into her eyes. Redness tinged his eyelids, but he looked as happy as he'd ever been.

He peered past her. "Zara looks a little smaller."

Tris laughed, and held out an arm. "This is Abby."

"Hi." The girl crept closer.

Tris put a hand on her back. "She asked to stay with us. Her father was killed on the way out. I, uhh, warned her you're a professional asshole, so we should be okay."

Kevin glanced between them, and chuckled. "I am *so* glad you're okay. I was getting worried." He hugged her for another few minutes before letting go and raising an eyebrow. "If you think we can handle a kid... I suppose we can give it a shot. At least we skip the sleepless nights and diapers part."

Tris leaned into him until the door forced them to single-file it. She stopped as soon as she caught sight of Bee behind the counter. "What happened to Bee? Oh, shit, is she *off?*"

"Some shithead shot her. I returned the favor." Kevin scowled. "I couldn't bring myself to toss her... wasn't sure if I should bury her..."

"Oh..." Tris pulled Kevin close with one arm, Abby with the other, and sniffled. "Wow... I'm getting misty over an android. What's wrong with me?"

"Don't feel bad. I miss her too." Kevin grasped her chin and kissed her deep.

Tris *mmm*ed into his mouth.

He let go in a moment. "Holy shit, I missed you. Promise me we never do this again?"

"What? Split up?"

"Yeah. I had the damndest feeling something happened to you." He squeezed her hand.

Tris stared down. "Okay. I promise."

"You got shot." His finger touched her chest through the hole in her shirt.

"Yeah. Wasn't as bad as when Zara shot me."

"Wait," said Abby. "Your friend Zara shot you?"

Kevin laughed. "Yep. Zara shot Tris, I shot Zara about ten times, she shoved these electric spider things up my ass. We had a grand old time."

Abby stared. "Uhh."

"Well, not literally in my ass..." He tapped his chest. "She covered me with these little stinging zappy darts."

"Oh." Abby coughed and sniffled.

Kevin gave her the raised eyebrow.

"Just a cold." Tris shot a deadly stare at him. "It's fine. Let me get her situated."

Tris led Abby upstairs to the room with the bathtub. A few trips up and down the stairs to the kitchen with buckets of hot water resulted in a warm bath. While Abby soaked, Tris took her dress to a shop sink in the office and washed it. She went to the store to grab something dry for her to wear and stopped at the spur in the keyhole.

"Kevin?" she yelled. "What's with the store lock?"

"Long story," he shouted back from the bar room. "Can you clear it?"

She walked to the end of the corridor and poked her head into the main room, giving him the 'you're an idiot' stare. Leaning on the wall behind the counter, he cocked an eyebrow at her.

"What?"

"You've got pliers in the office."

He laughed.

She glided over and hugged him. "You really were worried about me. Your brain shut down."

"Like nothing I've ever been afraid of before." He kissed her.

"Hey. You back." Sang limped into the room.

She blinked at all the bruises on him. "What happened to you?"

"We have a lot to catch up on." Kevin shook his head. "Right now, I don't want to think about anything but you and a soft bed. I want to hold you and stare into your eyes and stay up all night."

She melted against him. "Me too... Can you whip something up for Abby to eat and I'll be right up? Soup maybe? She's getting over a hell of a cold."

"I got it." Sang smiled, winced, and ambled off to the kitchen.

"Oh..." Tris narrowed her eyes at him. "What's up with that girl all tits out?"

Kevin pinched the bridge of his nose. "Couple of jackasses decided to take the place over not realizing this was our 'house. They gave up without a fight, kinda a bad situation for them. The two dead men with 'em... not so much."

"Do you trust them?" She glanced across the room at the bare-chested woman.

"I don't trust anyone… 'cept you." He kissed her. "An' maybe Fitch, Neels, and Sang. But, I don't think they'll be a problem. Just a couple of lost souls looking for some kinda protection in numbers and windin' up with an asshole."

"Okay." She patted him on the ass. "Need to get Abby something to wear."

He answered her butt-pat with a squeeze. She winked and jogged to the office to find the pliers, then hurried across the hall to yank the metal wire out of the storeroom knob. In the storeroom, she found a lavender sweatshirt big enough to fit Abby like a short dress. Perhaps a bit awkward to go outside with, but she could sleep in it.

She returned to the bathroom with a towel as well, and stuck them through a gap in the door.

"Come in. It's okay," said Abby part way between whisper and speaking. "You're like my mom now."

Tris walked in and set the sweatshirt on a shelf near the tub. "I washed your dress. It's still wet, but you can wear this for now."

"Thanks." Abby stood and reached for a towel.

A few minutes later, Tris led her downstairs to one of the large bedrooms.

"This is temporary until we can fix up another room upstairs for you."

"Okay." Abby hopped on the bed, lay back, and held her wrists to the bedframe.

Tris took a knee, stroking her hair. "You're not going to turn."

Abby looked worried. "I'm hungry. That's not good."

"Do you feel like you want to eat enough food for five people?"

"No."

Tris guided the girl's arms back to her sides. "That's normal. You're getting better. It's over, Abby. No more Infected."

She sat up and clamped on, sniffling.

A knock came from the door. Sang peeked in. "I have soup for girl."

Tris sat with her while she ate, then tucked her in. "I'm exhausted, too. We'll be upstairs. Remember where you had the bath? Right across the hallway is our room. You'll get your own bedroom up there as soon as we can clean a space."

"Okay. Goodnight, uhh, Mom."

Tris gave her a raspberry, which Abby promptly returned.

35

SOMEONE ELSE'S LIE

Kevin scraped a fork over his plate, chasing down the last of the eggs Sang cooked. Tris sat at his right, with the forlorn waif of a girl at her right. The way Tris had acted around Zoe, he figured she'd have brought up kids by now. *Maybe she's afraid she can't...* She'd told him the Enclave harvested her eggs, but even she didn't know if that meant 'some' or 'all.'

The girl behaved fearful of everything except Tris, though it did keep her quiet and well-mannered... for however long that lasted. *Yep. I'm an asshole. That kid's seen some awful shit. Poor thing.* Pre-breakfast conversation had more or less caught Tris up on his ill-conceived quest for revenge and ripped the foundation of his life out from under him. No Amarillo. He wasn't sure exactly what that meant for him, but it sounded likely to involve bullets in some form. It also struck him as an exceedingly bad idea to have a child around in such an environment. All it would take is for someone to grab her as leverage, and that part of him he got from his father would make things complicated.

He thought of Zoe kneecapping bandits with her M-16 and chuckled to himself. *Okay, perhaps it depends on the particular child.*

Sang had expressed some worry about keeping Lissa, Jenny, and Neal around, but he did confirm only pube-face and the other guy had hit him. He remembered the topless one (Lissa) at least whining at them to stop 'because he's just an old man.'

Kevin closed his eyes, stared at the ceiling, and decided to seek relief by burying his face in the crook of Tris' neck.

"What are you doing?" Tris giggled.

"I'm glad to have you back." He held her in silence for a moment. "Trying to get my head to stop spinning."

"Kevin…" Tris stared into her lap. "Nathan sent Virus to Amarillo."

"Yeah. I got the story from Snow, remember?"

Abby pulled her right leg up, toes curled over the edge of her chair, and rested her chin on her knee. She had a far-away look in her eyes, though her gaze didn't appear to focus at anything or anyone in particular. A hint of snot swelled a bubble from her nostril, expanding and shrinking as she breathed. Back in the beat-up white dress she'd—according to Tris—spent the past year and change wearing, she looked every bit the foundling she'd become. He wondered if the dark red dots along the lower part of the garment came from her father's blood. Nothing they had in the store would fit her except for a pair of tee shirts, but one smelled like hog piss and the other had a pair of silkscreened tits on it. Intact or not, letting a girl her age wear that crossed some line of *wrong* he couldn't handle.

I should make a trip to Ned… they make their own clothing. Someone'll be willing to trade a dress or something.

"They need to be stopped."

His eyebrow shot up. "Oh, sure. I agree. As soon as we figure out how to stop a technological giant with hovercrafts and missiles and nanobot weapons and armor that my bullets can't scratch, I'll get right on that."

She poked him in the side. "Don't be an ass. I'm serious. They're going to keep doing that. I… there's nothing more evil than that Virus. I… *have* to stop it. I know I was somehow meant for…"

"Tris… I love you more than I've ever loved anything in my life. I know you don't want to hear this, but Nathan used you. There was no cure. You didn't fail. You didn't fall short. If we put Abby in the middle of the road and told her to stop Fitch's truck with her bare hands, and he runs her over, is that her fault in any way?"

"Uhh…" Abby snapped out of her distant stare and looked at him. "What?"

"Just a meteor," said Kevin.

"Metaphor." Tris rolled her eyes. "I know. I know."

"I don't wanna get run over," said Abby.

Kevin lifted Tris' arm by a gentle grasp on the wrist. He traced a finger over the veins on the back of her hand. "How would you feel about going to Ned?"

Abby dropped her fork.

Tris took the girl's hand in a comforting grasp. "We have to go back in a day or two... her father's going to be buried there."

"I mean going to Ned for a little longer than a visit."

She looked up at him. "You want to stash me somewhere safe? You're forgetting I'm not a helpless little woman."

He eyed the room, Fitch at the counter, Neeley sitting with Lissa on the far right in what had been shaping up to be a sort of 'lounge' area, the hallway to the kitchen, the 'Bee-statue,' still in the chair. The mental ghosts of pube-face and his buddy appeared with a distant echo of remembered gunfire. "It's all bullshit." He sighed. "I spent my whole life chasing someone else's lie. Komodo was right. We're out here on the side of the highway, exposed... alone. Next time, what if it's ten bandits instead of two idiots and some tagalongs? What if the Night Riders show up? This isn't a place to settle down. This is a place for a single guy with nothin' to lose and a small personal army."

Tris bit her lip. She gave him a mournful, yet adoring look. "Y-you'd give up your roadhouse for... me? Your dream? I never asked..." She grabbed her throat, swallowing, sniffling.

"My dream was to stop getting shot at for a living, and be safe. I thought the Code would do that." He gestured at the room. "This ain't much safer than driving now. Worse even. On the road, at least I *expected* shitheads to take pot shots at me all the time so I kept my guard up. Here... you think someone's gonna say hello but they say *bang*, your shit is mine." Kevin leaned close to her, almost nose to nose, and lowered his voice to almost a whisper. "I've spent enough of my life scraping up coins, so many years running after something because I didn't know anything better existed. I'm done chasing my tail. I want to *live*." He kissed her gently on the nose. "And I want to live with you."

Tris flashed a wicked grin. "If it's what you want to do. I think we'd be happy there, but not if you're going to feel like you're settling for a lesser dream."

He kissed her. "I can't settle for lesser. You've spoiled me."

"Oh!" She blinked, and jumped to her feet. "I forgot. I have to show you something."

Confused, Kevin got up and let her pull him by the hand outside, down the sidewalk, to the van. Abby made a whiny sort of grunt suggesting she didn't really want to go outside, but hurried after them anyway. Kevin waited, holding the door as Tris jogged down the sidewalk to the grey van. Abby paused next to him, still with the wary look in her eye. After a second of staring at him, she managed a weak smile and took his hand.

"Tris says you don't think I'm a zombie."

Kevin walked out to the parking lot; the girl's skin felt a little hot, but not alarmingly so. He glanced at the small fingers wrapped around his. He'd gotten too close to Infected when he'd been her age. *Poor kid. Did I look that lost, too?* "Nope. Not as long as you've been coughing like that. Someone should'a slapped some sense into that idiot."

Abby stared downcast as they crossed from sidewalk to dirt to blacktop parking lot by the van. "He scared me... I thought I was gonna die."

Tris ceased waiting for them, opened the door, and jumped in. Abby pulled back, uninterested in being anywhere near that vehicle. Kevin gave her a 'just a sec' look, and climbed up, following Tris past the driver's seat into the back. It smelled like a small army had lived in it for days.

"Damn. We need to air this thing out."

Tris knelt and sat back on her heels. "Remember what I said about the old man in Amarillo?"

"Yeah. Crazy old bastard was like that wizard behind the curtain in the... you know Oz was made up, right? That wasn't historical."

"I know some of them are for entertainment." She pointed at a pile of blue tarpaulin and blankets. "I didn't tell you everything about him. I wanted to surprise you... then I got sidetracked and I was so tired. You said chasing... and... well."

Tris pulled the covering away, exposing cardboard boxes labeled 'Pennies,' 'Dimes,' 'Quarters,' and 'Nickels.' He stared straight at the boxes he'd gotten from Bill at Nederland, and handed over to that woman at Amarillo behind the clerk desk. Poor thing was probably dead now... or worse, running around a moaning, mindless, wretch.

"That's..."

She nodded. "All the money he had in his safe... less what I gave to Mac."

"You gave him money?"

"Yeah. Ten thousand. Amarillo felt bad for conning him, so they gave him a refund." She looked up at him like a child who'd done something well meaning, but still expected to be yelled at for. "He had kids."

Kevin fell to his knees, staring at the pile of coins, at least ninety thousand at a quick eyeball. Enough money to grow old with several times over... assuming money continued to mean anything if the Roadhouse network disintegrated. Still, sometimes settlements traded between themselves with coins out of expedience.

"So what'll we do with this place?"

He put an arm around her, still too numb to think about much. "Money."

"Yes, a lot of it." She poked him in the side.

"What about this 'house?"

Kevin looked at her. He brushed a strand of hair off her face. It fell back over her eye, and he moved it again. "Fitch and Neeley are going to run it for a while. Course, the old bastard said he'll still consider it mine, and he's running it 'for me'... but I don't expect to be back. Probably just him being polite."

"Should we give them some of this? What about Sang?"

"We've got about 5850 or so in the lockbox. That's still a lot of money. I was going to tell them to keep it but..." He grabbed a $50 Pennies box. "Guess I'll round them up to ten and call it a night."

THE QUIET LIFE

K evin slowed the Challenger to a stop at the pair of massive overturned dump trucks forming the main gate into Nederland. Emma, the thirteen-year-old AK-47 toting sentry, waved and hopped down out of sight. Socrates gave him a welcoming nod from the left side truck. The sight of a grey-silver haired old man in a cowboy's hat and coat triggered a pang of sorrow over Wayne, even if Socrates came up about forty pounds shy.

Abby leaned forward from the back seat. Her sniffling had lessened, though her voice still sounded a bit funny whenever she talked. A bag of clothes occupied the seat next to her, a bundle of things she'd liked that Kevin found in the storeroom. Course she wouldn't fit into most of it for a couple years. She'd kept her plain dress on for now, having become agitated at the suggestion of wearing something else. Tris told him to give her time; she'd been through a lot. Perhaps the sameness helped in some way make her feel secure.

Maybe that blood's like keepin' her dad around. He cringed.

The dump trailer on the right scratched the road as it 'lowered' against the bed of the flipped truck. Emma darted across to the other side, and the second diesel grumbled to life, spraying an odd cooking-oil-and-burned food smell into the air. Abby clamped her hands on her ears as the giant metal box scraped pavement. Once the gap grew big enough, he pulled in, waving to Emma and Socrates on the way. Kevin drove past a few buildings, red and brown wood reinforced with corrugated metal and stacked bricks. He skirted around the laughably small traffic circle in the middle of town, glided by the 'mining museum' on the left, and headed down the larger road that looped around up ahead toward Nederland's deep interior. Bill's red house came up on the left, set a few feet off the road. He turned onto the gravel-dirt driveway and brought the car to a stop in front of the garage door that probably hadn't opened since the place's pre-war owners had been here.

A few stalwart blades of green grass sprouted from the dirt in front of the porch. Ann appeared at the left corner, between the house and a row of pine trees, laundry in her hands. Whenever the woman wore a tee shirt and jeans, it had to be laundry day, as she loathed pants. Zoe followed right after in a blue denim dress. As soon as she spotted them, the little one sprinted right out of her too-big moccasins and came flying over. She started climbing him before he'd even gotten to his feet out of the car.

Tris smiled at him over the roof.

He spent a few minutes whirling Zoe around, tossing and catching her, before setting her back on her feet.

Ann walked over to Kevin. "Wish it was under better circumstances to see you back." She bowed her head at Abby, who half-hid behind Tris. "Is this her?"

"Yes," said Tris. "We've taken her in. As far as anything counts for anything, she's ours."

Ann beamed. "It's sad what happened, but she's lucky to have found you."

Bill thumped out onto the porch, chewing. Sandwich crumbs dangled off a few weeks' worth of black beard with a few strands of premature white. "That was fast." He strode into a handshake.

"Bill..." Kevin hooked his thumbs in his pockets. "What you said a while back... 'bout there bein' room here. That still stand?"

"You're serious?" Bill glanced between him and Tris.

"Yeah. I'm serious."

Bill backed up to the porch. "Come on inside."

For the next hour and change, Kevin sat with Tris, Abby, Bill, and Ann at the kitchen table. Abby amused herself by tracing her fingers along the grooves of the aluminum edging. Bill made more sandwiches for them while Kevin went over everything that had happened with Amarillo. Zoe's dad Paul, and Cody, her older brother, had moved in to fill out the spare space in Bill's house, since Zoe considered Bill and Ann her grandparents.

It didn't much matter to the nine-year-old that her 'grandmother,' at thirty-three, only had two years on her father.

"That's the long and short of it, Bill." Kevin drained the last of his water glass. "The whole Roadhouse Code thing, don't dare mess with it or you'll regret it? All a load of shit. Isn't gonna be long before that gets out. No place for a family on the side of the road."

"I'm sure you could make it work if you wanted. Just takes a bunch of reliable hired guns." Bill chuckled.

"And a lot more to worry about than I'm interested in worrying about." Kevin put his arm around Tris' shoulders.

"Nederland is a veritable fortress thanks to you donating those rifles, an' that armor we took from the Enclave bastards. And that Zara... wow. She's worth ten or fifteen soldiers."

Tris waved at him while flashing a cheesy smile. "Hi."

"Oh, I know you're just as tweaked up as she is." Bill chuckled. "Shouldn't be an issue. I'm sure they'll be fine with it."

"They're *staying!*" Zoe squealed with delight and ran in circles around the kitchen, cheering.

Abby stood and grabbed the hem of her dress. "I don't have any zombie bites."

Tris pounced on her before she could pull it up and flash everyone. "It's fine. You don't have to show them."

Bill eyed his water. "For what it's worth, I'm glad you shot that bastard."

Abby trembled. Tris took a few minutes to calm her down and reassure her that they wouldn't lock her up or kick her out. Conversation filtered out to more routine topics after a little while, and Zoe dragged Abby upstairs to her room to play.

"There's a nice little open place down the road about a quarter mile." Bill stood. "Wanna see it?"

Kevin waited for Tris to smile before he got up. "Sounds good."

The dirt road that passed Bill's house curved around a sharp bend that basically doubled back in the direction they'd come in from, only veering uphill a bit more and left. Bill walked with them to a little house in the narrow strip of earth inside the hairpin, perhaps sixty yards away. It had a basic brick shape with no porch, and a half-built deck in the back.

Bill strode up to the front door, produced a key, and walked in.

It smelled like forest inside, likely due to having been empty for some time. They stepped through the front door into the living room, which connected by way of a small kitchen to a medium-sized empty room. A patio door in the kitchen opened to a narrow strip of decking that wrapped around to the hairpin side of the house where the yard nestled between roads.

Stairs along the far right wall in the living room led to an upstairs with two bedrooms, a tiny third room with nothing in it, and a bath, though he doubted any of the plumbing worked. *I'll probably have to get into a shootout with whatever's living in the pipes.* The house *looked* pre-war, but the town didn't have much in the way of infrastructure beyond electricity yet.

After wandering for a bit, they all met in the living room. Abby hadn't left it, still mystified by the feel of mushing her toes into pile carpeting.

"Got a septic tank, no idea what kind of shape it's in though. Not much of an issue 'til we get the well pump working again." Bill gestured at the north wall. "We're still in the process of wiring up all the houses to the panel array."

"There's a lot of panels in Amarillo just sitting there." Tris fidgeted. "If you think it's worth the risk, a large enough force could hit it. There's a flatbed right in the warehouse, but I don't know if it works."

Kevin shook his head, sighing. "If you're going to make a run like that, you'll need to do it soonish before someone else gets there."

"Most people expect Amarillo to have thousands of people infected, but it's not that bad. Hundred maybe." Tris fidgeted. "They had a whole warehouse full of never-used solar panels sitting there. Even a giant flatbed truck to carry them."

"Something to float at the next meeting." Bill scratched his chin. "This is the nicest place we got left. All the other empty houses we built ourselves, and they tend to rattle in the wind."

Kevin gave him a conspiratorial squint. "You were saving this one for us, weren't you?"

Bill shrugged. "Not supposed to do that sort of thing, but I had been hoping you'd come around."

Tris stared at Kevin, a small bite of her lower lip the only break to the calm on her face.

"Sounds good. So how's this work? Do we buy it from the town or what?"

"There's a fee, but we usually waive it as we tend to take in people who don't have much but the clothes on their backs."

"How much?"

Bill cringed. "Oh, this place? About 3500 coins."

"What's the town use money for anyway?" Tris blinked.

"Mostly trading with outsiders. Buying ammunition from Ween too." Bill scratched his head. "Couple times we buy and trade with other settlements."

She nodded.

Kevin faked a wince. "It'll be tough, but I think we can swing that."

Tris rolled her eyes out of Bill's sight, and shot him a playful smirk.

REBOOT

Tris leaned up and away from Bee's chassis, coughing from the foul-smelling smoke that peeled up from hot wires. Someone worked at a machine on the other end of the workshop that kept making this high-pitched screeching while throwing plumes of orange sparks. Each time it went off, the noise crawled deeper and deeper into her skull. Being that the Nederland workshop occupied a giant metal-walled warehouse building, sound traveled.

"Ugh." She rubbed her forehead, trying command the nanites to eat her headache. Not that they'd ever been able to do so, or even listened to her conscious control. "Come on, Bee."

She'd been tinkering with the android for most of the morning after her meeting with a rather fastidious fifty-ish woman named Crystal who was apparently in charge of managing Nederland's 'technical people.' Since the basic education Tris had received far outstripped what most in the Wildlands could even comprehend, the town council asked her to help out there. Which, of course, was fine with her. On some level, she missed her old roof full of solar panels, but Kevin did have a point. That place sat out in the middle of nowhere, and if anything bad came calling, they'd be on their own.

Thoughts like that didn't make for restful sleep.

After a bathroom break and a refill of water, she returned to the workbench and dove into Bee's innards again. To get her up and mobile again would require parts they didn't have here, parts she'd only seen in one place... the airport outside Omaha. Kevin felt about Bee much the same as she did, so he'd probably be willing to take the ride if it offered a chance at salvaging the android. The bigger question being whether or not her memory core/personality matrix survived. Her efforts thus far focused on repairing the link between the power cell, which still appeared to be good, and the logic boards in her head.

"Good thing that idiot didn't shoot you in the face."

She soldered two more connections in the chest cavity and leapt back from a spark that hit her fingertip like a wasp sting. Something whirred to life deep inside Bee's chest, and a *bee-oop* sound played from the speaker inside her mouth, reminiscent of an old PC hard-boot beep.

"Yes. I am glad," said Bee. "My AI unit does not have a backup module installed. A projectile entering my head would have erased me."

"Bee!" Tris squealed. "You're okay!"

"I am not detecting a connection to arms, legs, or hip actuators. I am unable to move. Tris, I do not consider my current status to be... 'okay.'" Bee blinked with a *click*.

"Sorry. Your capacitor blew out. I spent most of the morning cleaning lithium cobalt oxide off your guts. I'm completely stunned you didn't explode or catch fire."

"I am grateful you are repairing me. Most would not have bothered."

"You're like family. I'm sorry, but I can't fix you all the way without parts that'll take a long drive to get." She leaned closer and whispered, "Don't tell him I told you, but Kevin was pretty upset finding you injured."

"I understand. It is good to be awake again. How much time. What day is it?"

Tris thought. "Uhm. 2073..." She faced the warehouse floor. "Hey, anyone know what day it is?"

Two men yelled "Thursday."

"June, right?"

One of them nodded. "Twenty-second."

"Tris." Bee rotated her head to stare upward.

"Hmm?"

"Now that my operating system has completely loaded, I have performed a memory sweep and found orphaned sectors. Reallocating those sectors has allowed me to reclaim an event I was previously unable to."

"I think I follow you..." Tris smiled.

356 | THE REDEEMED

"I forgot to tell you something. I just remembered." Bee blinked with a *click*. Her voice shifted pitch at random with each word, making her sound more robotic than usual. "While you and Kevin were away, a transmission came in via the radio. A man who indicated his name as Terminal9 wished me to tell you the following:"—from the android's mouth played a familiar nasal male voice framed in static crackles, as though she'd recorded the radio output—"Tris. There's more to The Cure than I thought. We need to talk."

Holy shit. Tris bent forward, hugging the prone Bee. "You're amazing!"

"I am paralyzed."

Tris looked left and right like a lost cat. "I... need to find Kevin."

Unable to do any more for Bee without parts, Tris scooped her up and ran out, earning several odd looks at the sight of her carrying such a load with ease.

AND MILES TO GO

The idea that he'd be kneeling in mossy mud while working on water pumps feeding an enormous network of pipes going into a greenhouse would never have come up in Kevin's imagination at any point over the last ten years. It didn't involve cars, bullets, high speed, explosions, armor, or earning coins. Yet, as he knelt in the squidgy bog fighting with an old diesel engine, he smiled.

This isn't so bad.

Two hours in, the problem became apparent: too much gunk. They'd been feeding it biodiesel, and from the looks of things, a crappy mixture that gummed everything up to heck and back. Of all the things that could've been wrong with it, breaking it down to clean it was low on the list of bad, but high on the list of tedious. A few hours after he'd started, he'd gotten it mostly back together when Tris came running around the corner of the greenhouse. She looked excited rather than angry or scared, so he kept on reassembling the engine as she zoomed up beside him.

"Kevin…" She gasped for breath. "I…"

"Slow down. Breathe." He set a series of bolts in place to hold down the cylinder head, and got to work ratcheting them down one after the next.

"Bee's awake."

"Awesome. Kinda feels like someone killed my favorite dog and you brought her back to life." He grinned. *Damn that stupid machine...* "How's she feel—uhh, doing?"

"I don't know if she'd think of being compared to a dog as good or bad."

He looked up at her. "If I had a dog, I'd be pretty damn upset if someone killed it."

Her face brightened. "She had a message! She's awake, but she can't move. I can't fix her without parts... remember that guy on the airplane?"

"Terminator or whatever?"

"Terminal9." Tris nodded. "He sent us a message over the Roadhouse radio."

"How the hell would he do that?" Kevin glared at the engine in front of him.

She swatted him on the head. "He's a hacker... he hacks. He said 'There's more to the Cure than he thought,' and he wants to talk to us."

"Maybe he found a bonus track."

"What?"

"You know, an extra song on the disc that's not on the label."

She growled. "Stop making jokes. This is serious! What if it *is* the cure?"

"It *was* The Cure. A band." He stopped ratcheting the socket and gave her that same patronizing/sympathetic stare that usually got her ready to either cry or hit him.

"I know that." She crossed her arms. "There's a hidden message. He didn't want to say anything in case they're monitoring the radio channel."

"I doubt it. Nathan wouldn't let anything useful out."

She put a hand on his shoulder. "What if Nathan didn't know?"

"How could he not?"

Tris stared into his eyes. "You said that Snow told you not everyone in the Enclave is a monster. What if there is some resistance left? All I'm asking is for a trip to the airport. Besides, I need parts for Bee anyway. It's not like we need to run right out now... but..."

"Tell me you're not happy here. This is safe."

She stared at the engine for a while, long enough for him to resume tightening bolts. "You want to get revenge for Wayne's death? Blame the Enclave. It's all Nathan's doing."

The socket wrench stopped. "That's a little below the belt. I've come to terms with it."

Tris squatted at his side and put her arm around him. "I *am* happy here. I *am* happy with you… but they're going to keep poisoning people and… Okay, I won't get ahead of myself. It could be something stupid. It could be nothing at all but another slap in the face from Nathan, but I don't think Terminal9 would've told me I had to see it if that was true. Even if it's nothing, we still need to get parts for Bee."

Kevin tossed the wrench and caught it twice. He glanced up at her, past her wavering snow-white hair to the vast sky spotted with puffs of cotton, and back into her gem-blue eyes. *Behind every dead man is a woman with an irresistible stare and a good cause.* "Yeah… I suppose someone really ought'a try and doing something about that damn virus."

fin

ACKNOWLEDGMENTS

Thank you for reading The Redeemed – Book Two of the Roadhouse Chronicles!

I'd also like to thank Will Stanton (author of *The Artful* and *Gears of Fate*) for suggesting I write this series after reading the original short story version of the first book.

Special thanks to Mark Woodring for editing this book (and the whole series). It's always a pleasure to work with him, even if he does loathe my puns.

ABOUT THE AUTHOR

Originally from South Amboy NJ, Matthew has been creating science fiction and fantasy worlds for most of his reasoning life. Since 1996, he has developed the "Divergent Fates" world, in which *Division Zero, Virtual Immortality, The Awakened Series, The Harmony Paradox, and the Daughter of Mars series* take place. Along with being an editor at Curiosity Quills press, he has worked in IT and technical support.

Matthew is an avid gamer, a recovered WoW addict, Gamemaster for two custom RPG systems, and a fan of anime, British humour, and intellectual science fiction that questions the nature of reality, life, and what happens after it.

He is also fond of cats.

Visit me online at:
Facebook: https://www.facebook.com/MatthewSCoxAuthor
Amazon: https://www.amazon.com/author/mscox
Pinterest: https://www.pinterest.com/matthewcox10420/
Goodreads: https://www.goodreads.com/author/show/7712730.Matthew_S_Cox
Email: mcox2112@gmail.com

OTHER BOOKS BY MATTHEW S. COX

Divergent Fates Universe Novels

Division Zero series

- Division Zero
- Lex De Mortuis
- Thrall
- Guardian

The Awakened series

- Prophet of the Badlands
- Archon's Queen
- Grey Ronin
- Daughter of Ash
- Zero Rogue
- Angel Descended

Daughter of Mars series

- The Hand of Raziel
- Araphel
- Ghost Black

Virtual Immortality series

- Virtual Immortality
- The Harmony Paradox

Divergent Fates Anthology

(Fiction Novels - Adult)

The Roadhouse Chronicles Series

- One More Run
- The Redeemed
- Dead Man's Number

Faded Skies series

- Heir Ascendant
- Ascendant Unrest
- Ascendant Revolution

Temporal Armistice Series

- Nascent Shadow
- The Shadow Collector

Vampire Innocent series

- A Nighttime of Forever
- A Beginner's Guide to Fangs
- The Artist of Ruin
- The Last Family Road Trip

Standalones

- Wayfarer: AV494
- Axillon99
- Chiaroscuro: The Mouse and the Candle
- The Far Side of Promise anthology
- Operation: Chimera (with Tony Healey)
- The Dysfunctional Conspiracy (with Christopher Veltmann)

Winter Solstice series (with J.R. Rain)

- Convergence
- Containment

Alexis Silver series (with J.R. Rain)

- Silver Light
- Deep Silver

Samantha Moon Origins series (with J.R. Rain)

- New Moon Rising
- Moon Mourning

Maddy Wimsey series (with J.R. Rain)

- The Devil's Eye
- The Drifting Gloom

Samantha Moon Case Files series (with J.R. Rain)

- Blood Moon
- Dead Moon

Young Adult Novels

- Caller 107
- The Summer the World Ended
- Nine Candles of Deepest Black
- The Eldritch Heart
- The Forest Beyond the Earth
- Out of Sight

Middle Grade Novels

Tales of Widowswood series

- Emma and the Banderwigh
- Emma and the Silk Thieves
- Emma and the Silverbell Faeries
- Emma and the Elixir of Madness
- Emma and the Weeping Spirit

Standalones

- Citadel: The Concordant Sequence
- The Cursed Codex
- The Menagerie of Jenkins Bailey
- Sophie's Light

www.ingramcontent.com/pod-product-compliance
Lightning Source LLC
Chambersburg PA
CBHW051942240626
47153CB00005B/1590